FROM BAD

to cursed

FROM BAD
to cursed

A BAD GIRLS
DON'T DIE NOVEL

·····················

katie alender

HYPERION
NEW YORK

For Juli, George, and Alexandra

Text copyright © 2011 by Katie Alender

All rights reserved. Published by Hyperion, an imprint of Disney Book Group. No part of this book may be reproduced or transmitted in any form or by any means, electronic or mechanical, including photocopying, recording, or by any information storage and retrieval system, without written permission from the publisher. For information address Hyperion, 114 Fifth Avenue, New York, New York 10011-5690.

First Edition
10 9 8 7 6 5 4 3 2
V567-9638-5-11258
This book is set in 12-point Garamond 3.
Printed in the United States of America

Library of Congress Cataloging-in-Publication Data
Alender, Katie.
From bad to cursed : a Bad girls don't die novel / Katie Alender.
p. cm. — (Bad girls don't die ; bk. 2)
Summary: After taking an oath to a seemingly benevolent spirit, a high school girl finds herself changing in frightening ways.
ISBN-13: 978-1-4231-3471-8
ISBN-10: 1-4231-3471-0
[1. Supernatural—Fiction. 2. Ghosts—Fiction. 3. High schools—Fiction. 4. Schools—Fiction. 5. Sisters—Fiction. 6. Horror stories.] I. Title.
PZ7.A3747Fr 2011
[Fic]—dc22

2010036297

Reinforced binding
Visit www.hyperionteens.com

SUSTAINABLE FORESTRY INITIATIVE
Certified Fiber Sourcing
www.sfiprogram.org

THIS LABEL APPLIES TO TEXT STOCK

Acknowledgments

My sincerest thanks to the many people who have made it possible for this book to exist, either by direct assistance, encouragement, or just putting up with me in general (which, I begin to suspect, is actually quite a lot of work).

Agent/therapist/cheerleader/friend Matthew Elblonk, and the entire crew at DeFiore and Company;

The one and only Arianne Lewin;

Abby Ranger, Stephanie Owens Lurie, Hallie Patterson, Laura Schreiber, Marci Senders, Ann Dye, and all of the wonderful people at Disney-Hyperion, whose dedication, insight, and hard work I witness with awe and gratitude;

My family, most especially my husband, but also the many parents, siblings, cousins, aunts, uncles, and sundry other relations who are so supportive;

My dear friends, who happily for me are too numerous to name;

My dog show cronies and everyone at Soapbox;

The author friends, book bloggers, blog readers, Twitter followers, Facebook fans, sister Debutantes, and Backspace folks who have made this journey so much fun and have occasionally been credited with saving my sanity (and by "occasionally" I mean "on a weekly basis");

Librarians, teachers, booksellers, and all of the people who make it their business to champion a love of books and reading;

And, finally, to all of the amazing readers who make me laugh and think, and whose sweetness and intelligence never fail to make my job easier and my days brighter.

I'm absolutely humbled by your generosity and kindness. Group hug!

1

AT FIRST GLANCE, the town houses in Silver Sage Acres are as white and identical as an endless row of bared teeth. Looking down the single road that winds through the community is like holding a mirror up to another mirror and watching the world curve away into infinity.

If you search hard enough, you can find landmarks, even though the place is engineered not to have any. The ficus tree with the one branch that sticks out sideways. A thick splotch of paint (white, of course) on the asphalt from the can that rolled off the back of a contractor's truck. Each discrepancy is a little scar on the landscape, in constant danger of being buffed away by the all-powerful homeowners' association.

Every few hundred feet is a turnout with a colony of mailboxes and a row of guest parking spaces, because heaven forbid your guests should park in your drive-way, much less on the street. And that's just one of the billion rules: No dogs bigger than twenty-five pounds.

No decorative items in the windows. And trash cans are like Cinderella—only allowed out for a few hours at a time. After that, the citations start piling up.

But for all its artificial cosmetic appeal, the development feels like it was built to last only until somebody came along with a better idea. When it's rainy, the gutters get so full of water that you have to take a four-foot leap to keep from getting your shoes soaked. When it's breezy, the street becomes one big wind tunnel, freezing you to the bone and pelting your eyes with an asteroid belt of grit and crushed leaves.

We've lived in #29 for a year and only know one other family, the Munyons in #27, who pay me five dollars a day to feed their cat when they go on vacation.

Really, though, it could be worse.

One thing about a place this locked down—there are no surprises.

Twenty-nine Silver Sage Acres Road is everything our old house wasn't:

Modern. Sterile. Generic. Efficient. Compact. Controlled.

Most importantly, it's completely devoid of murderous ghosts.

And that suits my family fine.

2

GRIMY PATCHES OF MUD, drops of dried blood, a sprinkling of gravel, and a full-body sheen of sweat that plastered his long-sleeved tee to his back . . . and I was still tempted to fling myself into Carter Blume's arms and declare my undying devotion.

Not that I ever would. In my opinion, the L-word deserves better than to be tossed out on a sweaty August Saturday afternoon like some sort of emotional -Frisbee.

Furthermore, I'm not the flinging type. And even freshly laundered and not bloody, Carter wasn't the sort of guy to invite girlfriend-flingage.

I *did* fling the car door open, but that's different. He stepped out, wincing as he put weight on his left leg. As we walked to my front door, pebbles skittered to the ground, dislodged from his knee or his thigh or wherever they'd ended up when he ate it on our hike.

"It's your own fault," I teased, pulling out my key

chain. "Holding back your fellow racers and then running off ahead is very bad karma."

"Is it?" he asked. "I almost forgot, in the thirty-five seconds since you last brought it up."

I opened the door, and Carter hesitated at the welcome mat like a well-trained dog. "I don't want to get the floors dirty."

"Don't worry," I said. "I mop on Sundays anyway."

He cocked his head. "I thought you mopped on Wednesdays."

The main part of the town house was basically one big, echoing room that held the kitchen, dinner table, and family room. A hallway extended to the left, bending around a corner to conceal the bedrooms.

"Come on," I said, heading for the pantry, where the first-aid kit lived.

Carter trailed behind me into the kitchen and stood still, afraid to touch anything. I wet a washrag and wiped the dirt and blood from the palms of his hands, which he'd used (semi-unsuccessfully) to keep himself from skidding down the mountain.

"You didn't answer me," he said, voice low. "You mop *twice* a week, don't you?"

"This is going to sting," I said, plying his hands with a layer of antiseptic spray.

He flinched and then held his palms steady. "Don't

4

distract me when I'm making fun of your OCD."

"It's not OCD," I said. "I just like things clean."

"I'm not clean."

"No," I said. "But for you . . . I'll make an exception."

He leaned down, using his wrists to pull me close. I pressed up on my toes to meet him halfway, then we kissed.

The only way to describe kissing Carter is this: it's like being on a roller coaster in a pitch-black room, and you're going downhill, and for a few moments you're weightless, and you want to throw your hands in the air and scream.

After a minute, a thought popped into my head, and I pulled away. "You'll need to pretreat those bloodstains and wash everything in *cold* water."

Carter gazed into my eyes and brushed a strand of my pink hair away from my face. "You're insane."

"You might need to use a toothbrush to get the mud out. I keep extra old ones around, if you don't have any."

He gave me a crooked smile. "All I want in the world is to be close to you, and all you want is to clean my dirty clothes."

"It's the twenty-first century," I said, pulling his face down toward mine. "I want it all."

And we were kissing again, the edge of the tile

5

countertop pressing a cold line into my back. Carter rested his hand against my shoulder.

"Oh, no!" he said, jerking away. "I'm sorry."

"No big deal," I said, glancing down to see two tiny spots of blood on my Surrey Eagles T-shirt. "Not like it's an heirloom or anything."

He leaned down so his mouth was deliciously close to my ear. "You're going to want to pretreat that," he whispered. His breath sent a ripple of chills down my spine. "And wash it in warm water."

"*Cold* water! You're not even listening!" I slipped out of his grip, as much as I would have enjoyed prolonging the moment. My parents didn't mind him being at the house when they weren't there, but only because they trusted us not to spend hours in the kitchen making out.

"I can only learn so much in one day," he said. "Such as, cheaters never win."

"Cheaters go flying face-first down a hill," I said. "And end up with gravel stuck in all sorts of exotic places."

I took in the whole picture of him, new tennis shoes scratched, knees mottled, shorts muddy, shirt stained and stretched.

"I know what you're thinking," he said. "How can a man with pebbles embedded in his butt be so irresistible?"

Sun shone through the kitchen window, casting a glow on his summer-tanned skin and making the curls in his blond hair look like strands of gold.

I smiled at him, not wanting to interrupt this perfect moment.

"It's going to be a good year," he said.

"The best year," I said. And I believed it. I had a boyfriend who was going to be Student Council president, the perfect best friend, and I even got along with my parents. In that moment, it seemed like nothing could possibly go wrong.

He reached a hand out to me, and I took it. As we melted closer, something caught my eye, a change in the light somewhere in the room.

I glanced up and then slammed back against the refrigerator, like I'd seen a ghost.

It wasn't a ghost—but it was close enough.

My little sister, Kasey, stood at the end of the hall in a baggy black T-shirt and sweatpants, her hair in a long braid. Her once-round baby face was thin, and sharp shadows underlined her cheekbones. Her eyes were rimmed by faint gray half-moons.

In half a heartbeat, I was across the room, crashing into her. We tumbled to the floor, our limbs tangled underneath us.

"Lexi!" she sputtered. "Wait!"

"*Don't move*," I said, grabbing both of her wrists in my hands.

"Be careful!" Carter said, rushing over to us. "I'll call the police!"

"*LEXI, STOP!*" Kasey's screech cut a hole in the chaos. In the sudden silence, I realized she wasn't struggling.

"What are you doing here?" I demanded. "Did you run away?"

"Run away? No, Lexi," she said. "I'm home. I'm just home."

3

NINE MISSED CALLS.

I lobbed my useless cell phone at the couch. "It was on vibrate."

Mom's hands were pressed against her forehead like she was fending off a headache. "Your father and I were gone for twenty minutes, max. We had to sign some papers at the school."

About thirty seconds after I self-defensed my sister into submission, my parents came tra-la-laing through the front door to find me still sitting on her. High jinks ensued.

I tried to apologize to Kasey, but she slunk off into her room.

"But *honestly*," I said. "She's at Harmony Valley for ten months and you had *no clue* she'd be coming home three weeks early?"

Mom did a palms-up shrug. "Honey, we didn't know for sure. I didn't want to get your hopes up."

"Hopes," I repeated.

The flatness of my voice made my mother cringe. "Alexis . . . you're happy about this, right? Not the—the tackling part, but—Kasey coming home?"

We both caught the pause before my answer. "Of course," I said. "Mom, I was *surprised*. I get back from hiking with Carter, thinking the house is empty, and Kasey comes trotting out, all, 'Oh, hey, remember me, your sister from the mental hospital?' I thought she *escaped*."

Mom shuffled through the stack of papers in her hand, her faux-casual attitude giving away how upset she really was. "I just really want this to work for her. I want her to make friends, and find her way around school, and—what if she doesn't?"

"Don't worry," I said. "She will."

Kasey being home meant she was going to Surrey High, where I'd spent two years building up and then dissolving a variety of enemies and alliances.

She wasn't just a freshman; she was Alexis Warren's little sister.

And that meant it was my job to make sure she didn't crash and burn.

Even though Mom didn't mean to make me feel responsible for Kasey, we all knew that *my* reputation preceded her. I'd mellowed way out, but there were still a lot of people who would never see me as more than the rebellious punk I'd once been.

Cyrus Davenport was one of them.

"Oh"—he sneered at me over the cheese tray on the snack table—"Alexis. I didn't know Cecilia invited *you*."

"Hey, Cyrus," I said. "How's UCLA?"

"I assumed you'd be in juvie by now," he said, pursing his lips and turning away.

"Okay . . . good to see you, too," I said to the air where he'd been standing. The low buzz of the Davenports' first-week-of-school party closed in around me.

"So Cyrus is still a drama queen," Megan said, appearing at my side. "Nice to see college doesn't always change people."

Kasey stood a few feet away, clutching a bottle of water in her hands like a security blanket. She was wearing stiff, brand-new jeans and a shirt she'd borrowed from our mother, this gold silky blouse that made her look about forty. "Why does that boy hate you?"

Carter slipped his arm around my waist. "I'm a little curious, myself."

"It's one of Alexis's bad girl moments," Megan said. "I'm sure you guys wouldn't be interested."

Carter lowered his chin. A smile played on his lips. "What did you do, you monster?"

I glanced at my sister, whose eyes were as round as quarters, not sure if I wanted her to hear this story. "Well . . . two years ago—you were still at All Saints, Carter—I was going through one of my . . . phases. I hacked into the drama club website and switched some casting decisions for *The Sound of Music.* I mean, their password was *password.* They were asking for it."

"And Cyrus got the part of . . ."

"Fräulein Maria," Megan said.

"Turns out it was the one role he always wanted," I said. "He's hated me ever since."

Carter pulled me closer. "Know what I always wanted? A girlfriend who was a junior."

"Aww," I said. "I always wanted a seventy- to three-hundred-millimeter zoom lens. With macro."

He gazed into my eyes.

Even though we'd been a couple for almost five months—since the April prom night when we officially admitted our feelings for each other—a battalion of happy butterflies still launched in my stomach when he looked at me like that. He wrapped his hands around mine, and it was like we were in our own little world, not a single angry thespian in sight.

"You two are gross. I'm going to mingle." Megan gave her dark shoulder-length hair a shake and scanned the crowd. "Want to come with me, Kasey?"

"What?" Kasey asked, choking on a mouthful of water. "No, thank you."

"Yes you do," Megan said, herding her away. "Because the alternative is staying here with Edward and Bella."

When we were alone, Carter's expression darkened with concern. "Everything okay with her?"

I nodded. "She still flinches whenever I walk into a room, but she accepted my apology."

His hand rested lightly against my lower back, almost like he was trying to prop me up. "I'm surprised she came."

"Me too." In fact, I'd only asked her because I was sure she'd say no.

But then she said yes, and the night became less about having a good time and more about making sure nothing disastrous happened to her.

I began to get the feeling that having a good time in general was about to get a lot more complicated.

As things began to wind down, Carter got stuck in a conversation about Student Council elections and I got up to find Megan. I found her in the kitchen—alone.

I tapped her on the shoulder. "Where's my sister?"

"Oh, I'm not sure," Megan said, like it was no big deal.

I looked around, panic rising inside me.

"Lex," Megan said, putting a hand on my arm, "she's not a two-year-old lost at Disneyland."

"But she's never been to a party like this before." I knew most of the kids there, but not *all* of them. A couple were even in college. What if somebody spiked my sister's drink? Lured her away from the crowd?

Seeing my face, Megan relented. "All right," she said. "Commence Operation Find Kasey."

We wove through the house, finally ending up in the hallway in front of a closed bedroom door. Sloppily taped on it was a handwritten sign that said, BAGS IN HERE.

"You check that room," Megan said. "I think there are some people in the garage. I'll go look out there."

I opened the door.

"Kasey?"

No answer.

The room was dark, but it wasn't empty. Three kids—none of them my sister with her golden ponytail—sat on the floor, with flickering candles scattered around. My pulse perked up at the sight—we Warrens weren't big decorative flame (or any kind of flame) folks anymore. Watching your house burn to ashes sort of reduces the appeal.

On the floor between them was a Ouija board.

14

"You know, those aren't toys," I said, trying to keep my voice as light as possible.

"Oh, really?" replied a voice I knew. "Because I bought it at a toy store."

As my eyes adjusted to the light, I saw Lydia Small in the central position. Her long dyed-black hair was in a deliberately messy updo, and her brand-new eyebrow ring glinted in the candlelight. Her fingertips rested lightly on the planchette, a little wooden piece that moved around the board, and the other two girls had their fingers on either side of hers.

Lydia and I were friends for freshman and part of sophomore years. But lately things were pretty strained. She couldn't get over the fact that I could possibly prefer to hang with anyone besides her and the rest of the pretentious, black-clad Doom Squad. And I couldn't get over the fact that she was insufferably annoying.

"Hurry, ghost of the Ouija board," she said in an oogie-boogie voice, "tell us something interesting before scaredy-cat Alexis runs away."

The other two giggled. I stood with my back to the wall.

"What was that?" Lydia said, lowering her ear to the board. "What did you say?" Then she looked up. "The ghost wants to know if you've always been boring, or if

15

it's something that happened when you started hanging out with clones—hold on, I'll answer."

I sighed. "Grow up, Lydia."

She leaned down to talk to the board. "The answer is B," she said. "Clones."

"Oh, yeah," I said. "I should try harder to be unique . . . like you and the other fifty people at school exactly like you."

The door opened, letting a slope of light fall across the room.

"Lexi?" my sister's voice asked. Her hand groped the wall and flipped the light switch, blinding us all and bringing forth groans of protest from the girls on the floor.

The light popped off again. Kasey stepped in, with Megan behind her.

"What is this, a Losers Anonymous meeting? You guys are totally killing the mood," Lydia said, getting to her feet. "I'm going to get something to eat." Her minions followed her out.

Kasey stood motionless, staring down at the Ouija board. After a second, her body gave a little jolt and she looked up. "Megan said you were looking for me?"

"Yeah," I said. "I wanted to make sure you were okay."

"I am," she said. "Just tired."

I knelt, grabbed a candle, and blew it out, then reached for another. "I can't believe they would leave these burning."

"Um . . . Lexi? You should maybe . . . see this. . . ."

While I'd been focused on the candles, Kasey's eyes were locked on the board itself.

I looked down and froze.

The planchette was moving.

It glided from letter to letter, making a light scratching sound against the board.

Megan breathlessly rested her hands on my shoulders, bending down to watch.

"It already said B-E," Kasey whispered.

The movements seemed feeble, but it was perfectly confident about where it was headed.

C-A-R-E-F-U-L

"Will do," I said, trying to figure out how to get the three of us as far from this situation as possible in the smallest amount of time. "Let's go, you guys."

"No, Lex, wait," Megan said, grabbing on to the leg of my jeans. She knelt on the floor.

Kasey was standing with her palms flat against the floral wallpaper. "It's not my fault," she whispered. "I didn't do it."

"I know, Kase. It's all right—we're leaving. *Megan,*" I said, looking pointedly at my sister. "Come on."

"Shh," Megan said, not moving her eyes from the board. "Be careful? Why? Who are you?"

The pointer wobbled and began to move again. Megan grabbed the pad of paper and little wooden pencil from the open box and wrote down each letter.

In spite of my eagerness to go, I found myself watching its progress.

E-L-S-P-E-T-H

Enough. I tried to tug Megan toward the door, but she leaned forward, her eyes blazing. The bow from the front of her shirt dangled almost to the board. I had a horrible vision of something reaching up and grabbing on to it.

"Elspeth," she asked, "why do we need to be careful?"

E-X-A-N-I-M-U

I yanked my arm free and slapped my hand on the planchette, holding it still. Under my palm, it pulled insistently, trying to get away. I turned to look into Megan's indignant eyes.

"We talked about stuff like this," I said. "About *not doing it*, remember?"

"This could be important, Lex," Megan said. "She's trying to tell us something."

"We don't even know who she is!" I protested. But before we could get into a debate, the door opened with a crash.

Lydia and her followers came back in, smelling vaguely of cigarettes. "Oh, whoa," one of them said. "It's dark."

But my darkness-adjusted eyes could see fine.

And what I saw was: the pointer turning around and around, faster and faster, until it spun in place like a top.

Just as Lydia turned on the light, I backhanded the spinning planchette across the room. It hit the wall with a clatter.

"What are you doing?" Lydia demanded. "That's not yours!"

"Relax," I said, relieved that no one else had noticed the spinning.

"They blew out all the candles!" one of the girls whined. "That sucks."

"Alexis sucks in general," Lydia said. She looked at Megan, who was still clutching the paper and pencil. "And *that's* mine too!"

"Let's go," I said, my hand on Kasey's arm.

We were on our way out when Lydia called to me.

"Hey!" She stared at the pad of paper, which Megan had handed back to her. She looked at us, half-questioning and half-accusatory. "Elspeth? Why did you write that down?"

"Nothing," I said. "It's nothing."

"What's the matter, Lydia, are you *scaaaaared*?" one of the girls asked.

Lydia scowled. "Shut up! I'm returning this stupid game. I'm going to get my money back."

"No you're not," the second girl said, laughing. "Look, this piece fell in a candle and melted."

"Sorry, Elspeth!" the first girl cackled, and they dissolved into a fit of giggling.

I could feel the heat of Lydia's glare on my back as we closed the door behind us.

Megan checked her phone. "My curfew's ten thirty. Are you guys staying, or do you want a ride?"

Staying was the last thing I felt like doing. I found Carter at the end of the hall, still surrounded by preps. I heard the words "outreach" and "social consciousness," but he abandoned the conversation to draw me close to him.

"What's going on?" he asked.

"Megan's taking us home," I said. "Kasey's worn out."

His brow furrowed. "I can leave now if you need me to."

"No, don't worry," I said. "You stay. Schmooze up some votes."

Megan stared at the road and tilted her head thoughtfully. "Do you think Elspeth—"

"Megan, *no*," I said, trying to use the tightness of my voice to remind her that Kasey was in the backseat. "Seriously."

"What?" she said, pausing at a stop sign. "There are ghosts everywhere. You know it as well as I do. And so does Kasey."

"But we don't have to be their friends!" I said. "*Rule one:* Don't be friends with ghosts."

"She was *nice*, though."

"That's what I thought." Kasey's weary voice came from the backseat. "About Sarah."

Megan was stunned into silence, and I was, too. I'd never heard Kasey mention Sarah—the evil ghost who'd possessed her the previous October, thirteen years after murdering Megan's mother.

"Thank you, Kasey. See?" I said. "Kasey thought Sarah was nice. And look where it landed her. You want to spend a year in a mental institution?"

4

I TURNED AWAY FROM the brightness of the muted television and rested my eyes on the ceiling. The glow from the screen made the whole room flicker like a rainbow campfire.

And then I heard it—

A footstep in the hall.

I froze. All my concentration shifted to listening for another sound. The flashing TV hovered on the outer fringes of my awareness. I felt like I was seeing, hearing, breathing out of my ears.

Another step.

I was on my feet and standing at the entrance to the hallway so quickly I felt a little light-headed. I balled my empty hand into a fist.

Kasey stood perfectly still in the middle of the hall, her body angled toward our parents' bedroom door. Her long, old-fashioned Christmas nightgown hung to her ankles, still creased from being folded in its gift box for eight months.

I'd seen her like this once before—silent. Waiting. Plotting.

Against our parents, against me.

Slowly, hesitantly, she raised her hand.

"Kasey!" I said.

She jumped about a foot in the air and landed hunched over, clutching her chest.

"*God,* Alexis!" she hissed. "You scared the crap out of me!"

I didn't move any closer. "What are you doing out of bed?"

"Going to the bathroom," she said. "What are *you* doing out of bed? It's one o'clock."

I shrugged. "Couldn't sleep."

"So you're playing security guard? You think I'm going to try to kill everyone?"

"No, of course not." Although . . . hmm. Maybe that *was* what I was doing.

Kasey reached for our parents' doorknob.

"Wait," I said.

"I need to *pee*, Lexi," she said. "Do you have to analyze every detail of everything I do?"

"I'm not trying to analyze you," I said. "I'm trying to keep you from peeing on Mom and Dad's carpet." I pointed to the door on my right. "Bathroom."

Her shoulders slumped. "Everything looks the same in this place."

"You'll get used to it."

I went back to the couch, feeling virtuous for not pointing out that it was, after all, *her* fault that we'd had to move to Silver Sage Acres.

A minute later, Kasey drifted into the room and sat on the loveseat, her arms crossed in front of her. "Why's the sound off?"

I shrugged. We stared at the silent infomercial.

As I started to nod off, Kasey spoke. "How about we skip school tomorrow?"

"I don't really do that anymore," I said. "Besides, everybody knows you never skip your first day."

She curled her knees under herself. "Maybe I can catch chicken pox between now and eight o'clock."

"It'll be fine," I said, trying not to think of the bazillion things that could make it not fine. "I'll help you."

"I wish I hadn't missed the first week. Everybody else knows each other, and I don't even have my schedule yet." She went pale—or maybe it was the blue light from the TV. "I don't know where anything is."

"Mom can take you a little early," I said. "They'll have somebody show you around, point out where all your classes are."

24

Kasey clamped her mouth shut and gazed at me through her wide blue eyes. She seemed to be a tiny ball of a person—even her toes curled inward. "Lexi? Is there any way I could ride with . . . you?"

All weekend I'd been waiting for some bit of my little sister's personality to work its way out from under her odd, fragile shell. And now, with that one question, she was being herself for the first time—her old, wheedling self. Mom and Dad used to call her "Slick," and Dad always said Kasey could sell a broom to a vacuum salesman.

Even if it was her needy side that came back first, it was a glimpse of Kasey.

The *real* Kasey.

The first glimpse I'd seen in a really, really long time.

Megan didn't even blink when she saw my sister standing beside me in the foyer the next morning. "Hi, guys. Ready to go?"

By the time we were all buckled up, Kasey looked liked a prisoner about to walk the green mile.

"There's nothing wrong with being nervous," Megan said, looking at her in the rearview. "You'll be all right."

"I'm *not* nervous," Kasey said, but her voice wobbled, betraying her.

We had to maneuver a little to get her out of the

backseat with her shortish, tightish denim skirt on. When she was safely on solid ground, no risk of flashing her underwear to the entire parking lot, I started walking toward the double doors with Megan.

After going about thirty feet, I got the distinct feeling that we *weren't* being followed. Sure enough, Kasey was rooted in place by the car, gazing back out at the road like she might make a break for it.

"Um," I said to Megan, "I think I'd better go with my sister."

She shaded her eyes to look back. "Seems like it," she said. "See you in Chem."

I walked over to Kasey, who held her backpack in front of herself like a shield.

"Kasey," I said, "you have to go *inside*. Otherwise it doesn't count as going to school."

"I changed my mind," she said, her voice an octave higher than normal. "I don't want to be here."

"The good news is, nobody asked." I gave her a gentle push.

As we walked toward the front office, I saw a bunch of people I knew. But Kasey didn't seem to recognize any-one—not even the kids she'd gone to school with for years. Nobody acted like they knew her, either. Maybe her generation had shorter memories than mine. I blamed texting.

Kasey couldn't stop gaping at the kids in their

happy, animated groups. She gradually slowed to a stop in the middle of the corridor.

I raised my eyebrows and waited.

She took a breath and held it, her chest rising without a fall. "I don't have a locker."

"They'll assign you one," I said. "They'll even give you a lock."

"Near yours?"

"No. Near your classes."

Kasey started gnawing on her fingernails. Why did she look so childish? She was fourteen—only two years younger than me.

"Listen." I pulled her fingers out of her mouth. "It's going to be fine. I'll help you. I can show you where—"

"Stop acting like I'm a baby!" she said, yanking away from me.

People peered at us curiously. Kasey was pretty, maybe even beautiful, even with her hair in a hurried ponytail, and her denim skirt, Minnie Mouse T-shirt, and Converse tennis shoes.

I lowered my voice. "Kasey, it's only high school. If I did it, you can do it."

As if her shoes were made of lead, she pushed one forward, then the other, and we were walking again. When we got to the front office, I pointed at the registrar and leaned in to hug her.

She jerked back.

"Okay," I said, stepping away. "Have a good day, then."

"No, wait, I didn't mean . . ." She flapped her arms helplessly. "At Harmony Valley, we weren't allowed to touch each other."

"Well, news flash, Toto," I said, stinging from her rejection. "You're not in Kansas anymore."

"Nice camera," the girl said. "How many megapixels? Mine's twelve-point-one."

"Oh, it's not digital," I said. "I shoot film."

She blinked. "But how many megapixels?" She pressed a button and the flash shot open, startling her. The dozen-megapixel beast took a hard landing in the grass.

I watched her wipe blades of damp grass from every part of the camera except the lens. When she was finished, she looked up, still waiting for an answer.

"Um . . . nine-point-seven?" I said.

"Cool." She smiled. "Let's go to the library. I really like the bricks there."

I followed without protest.

During one of their many Kasey-themed phone calls with the Surrey High guidance counselor over the summer, my parents had slipped up and mentioned my photography hobby. This prompted said guidance counselor to mention the school's photography class, which prompted said parents to bug me endlessly about enrolling in it.

I'd given in partly to make them happy and partly out of curiosity.

But it was a massive mistake.

That day, I'd been paired with a senior named Daffodil or Delilah or something, and sent out to take some exploratory photos. Never mind that there was nothing worth exploring at Surrey High, but Daffodil/Delilah insisted we hike all over the campus, examining tree bark, sidewalk cracks, and now the bricks in the library wall.

I'd taken four photos. Film is expensive.

But digital is free, and Daffodil couldn't get enough. She had me scroll through eighteen identical images of a pinecone so I could tell her which one was the best. I chose one at random.

"That's my favorite, too!" she said.

I wished I could be charmed by her enthusiasm, but the words that kept creeping to the edge of my tongue were dangerously noncharming. So I opted for silence, under cover of which I plotted out the main points of the argument I'd use to get unenrolled from the class.

As we changed course to head for the bricks,

something across the courtyard caught my eye—a late-arriving student and her mother. The mother was young and pretty, sitting in a wheelchair. The daughter was a study in awkwardness. She wore denim overalls over a shiny, cheap-looking pink shirt, like a dance recital left-over. Her stringy hair hung loose around her face, with an enormous fake sunflower pinned above one ear.

I thought there was something odd and stilted about the way she moved until I noticed that she walked with a cane—like, an actual old-people cane.

I snapped a couple pictures of them and then noticed that the girl was looking right at me. I blushed and turned away, the camera still hiding my face.

5

LUCKILY, THIRD PERIOD WAS English with Mr. O'Brien, who knew me from sophomore year. He saw my pink hair and occasionally prickly attitude as evidence that I was one of those temperamental creative types. In other words, I got away with a lot in his class.

I asked if I could go to the office about a personal issue. He said he hoped everything was okay and wrote me a hall pass.

When I told the office secretary I needed to talk to Mrs. Ames about my schedule, she sat back in her chair and gazed at me through her reading glasses, which magnified her no-nonsense glare.

"It's the sixth day of school," she said. "You think the principal has nothing better to do than listen to you complain?"

"That's all right, Ivy." There was no mistaking Mrs. Ames's voice, deep and resonant in the way only school principals' voices are. She appeared at her doorway.

"I can spare five minutes. Come in, Alexis."

During my more, shall we say, "impetuous" period, I'd sat on her scratchy old couch about once a week. Now I got upgraded to the guest chair. Looking around, I saw an unfamiliar, possibly fake, plant in the corner, and a new diploma on the wall—a master's degree.

"When did you get that?" I asked.

"Just this past June," she said, putting her reading glasses on. "Thanks for noticing."

"You're welcome," I said, and we sat and stared at each other. Apparently, apart from my misbehavior and its consequences, we didn't actually have much to talk about.

Then we both spoke at once.

"You've been on my mind this morning," she said, just as I said, "I have to get out of Photography."

She sat back. "And why is that?"

As calmly as I could, I gave her a rundown of how thoroughly I detested the class. I led with the fact that we never actually spent any time in the darkroom because everyone else shot digital, and ended with an impassioned visual critique of the brick wall. Mrs. Ames nodded from time to time, seemingly content to listen to as many complaints as I could dredge up.

"If there was moss growing on it or something, that would be one thing," I said. "But seriously. They're *bricks*."

Finally, out of ammunition, I gripped the armrests of my chair and waited.

She folded her hands and sighed. Then she tilted her head to the left and the right, stealing glances of something on her desk. "School district policy," she said, "does not allow transfer out of an enrolled class without pressing circumstances. Which don't traditionally include students' opinions on the aesthetic merits of building materials."

I started talking as soon as I could get another lungful of air. "But Mrs. Ames—this class is incompatible with my skill level. I truly believe that I will become a *worse* photographer every day I'm forced to participate."

She held up a hand. "All right, Alexis. Calm down."

"Please," I said. "I didn't even want it on my schedule. My father found out about it and wouldn't leave me alone until—"

"*Stop.*" She gave me a sharp look. "While you're ahead. I liked your arguments better when you weren't blaming other people."

I shut my mouth. But not for long. "There's no chance, then?"

She was still studying whatever was on her desk. "It's so serendipitous that you came in here this morning," she said, as if we'd finished the discussion and were moving on.

"Why?" I asked, suddenly suspicious.

She handed me a sheet of paper.

LOOKING FOR THE NEXT GENERATION OF SUPER-STAR PHOTOGRAPHERS, read the heading at the top. ANNOUNCING THE FIRST ANNUAL "YOUNG VISIONARIES" CONTEST.

"It's a photography competition," she said. "The grand prize is a scholarship and a paid summer internship."

"Ah." I tried to hand the flyer back. "Thanks for thinking of me."

She wouldn't take it. "You're not even going to consider it?"

I shrugged. "Not like I could possibly win."

"Why not?"

Because I'm not going to enter. Because I have better things to do with my time than compete in some cheesy contest, surrounded by overachieving college-application padders.

Mrs. Ames turned her attention to rearranging the pens in a mug by her phone. "You don't just send your work in and either win or lose. It's more of a process than that. There are interviews, social functions . . . but the deadline for applications is tomorrow."

"Contests aren't really my thing," I said, reaching for my bag.

"That sounds like a groundless line of reasoning to

34

me." Her chair let out a loud creak as she swiveled toward her computer. "But I know you, Alexis. And I imagine no amount of money could entice you to do something you don't want to do."

"Wait," I said. "How much money?"

She smirked but tried to wipe it off her face before she turned around. "I believe the scholarship is five thousand dollars, and the internship is paid—probably minimum wage."

"Oh," I said, and then, "Oh."

So, okay, before you call me a sellout, here's the thing:

My parents have decent jobs, but even with our health insurance, I suspected they'd had to lay out a bundle of money to keep Kasey at Harmony Valley instead of the county facility. College didn't worry me—I figured I'd get a summer job and save up enough money to go to a state university, hopefully with some kind of "Hey, at least you tried" academic scholarship.

But there was just one little variable:

I wanted a car.

I mean, I really, really wanted a car. Bad.

And if I got a scholarship, maybe Mom and Dad would shave a few dollars out of my college fund and apply it to something pretty with four wheels and a gas tank.

Mrs. Ames was watching me.

I examined my fingernails. "The only thing is . . . I'm

not sure I would have time for all that," I said, "what with all the extra time I'm spending on photography class."

I folded the paper in half and set it on her desk, trying to look both angelic and apologetic.

"That's a shame," she said softly.

I raised my eyes to meet hers.

"I would just *hate* for an elective class to get in the way of your ambitions."

"I totally agree," I said, my voice almost disappearing.

"Do we understand each other?" she asked.

Afraid to drop my gaze, I nodded.

She smiled but tried to hide it. "Better head back to class."

I stood up, reaching hesitantly for the flyer and tucking it into the pocket of my bag.

Before third period ended, an office runner came into the classroom with a slip of paper. He handed it to Mr. O'Brien, who said, "Warren," flapping it at me. I yanked it from his hand and read it right there, at his desk. It was a memo from the guidance office: *Class substitution: Alexis Warren, Period 2, report to Library Study Hall, Miss Nagesh.*

Mr. O'Brien looked up. "Good news?"

I pressed the slip to my chest like it was a telegram bearing news of a soldier's homecoming. "You have no idea."

hips. Mimi turned around, blushing furiously; for all her beauty rituals, she wasn't what you'd call a petite girl.

Lydia was six inches shorter than Mimi and probably forty pounds lighter, but she waltzed right up to her.

"Could you please keep your mooing at a more appropriate volume?" she asked sweetly. "People are trying to eat."

Mimi let out a squeak of rage as the tables around them tittered.

Lydia feigned alarm. "Why would you even do this now?" she asked. "Do you realize you're missing out on valuable cud-chewing time?"

"Go away!" Mimi countered feebly.

Lydia put her hand on the table and tipped her head to one shoulder in an over-practiced pose. "I'm not going anywhere," she said slowly. "*You* go away."

At this point, one of Mimi's friends swooped in and dragged her back to their table.

I went over to my sister. "Kasey," I said. "Are you all right? Come sit with me."

Kasey looked intently at her brown lunch bag. "I'm okay, Lexi."

Lydia smiled brightly. "Oh, hi, Lexi! You're *so* welcome for saving your sister from Moomoo. She could have been eaten, you know. High school is a very dangerous place."

"What are you doing here?" I asked.

Lydia's eyes widened. "Talking to a new student. Making friends. Welcome-wagon stuff."

"Well, leave my sister alone. Come on, Kase," I said. All poor Kasey needed was to be endlessly ridiculed by a revolving door of jerks.

"*Or,* Kasey," Lydia said, "you could come hang with me and my friends."

Kasey's mouth did its open-and-shut thing. She didn't know what to say.

Lydia changed tactics, looking at my table by the window. "Did it really take you this long to find her?" she asked me. "Or did you wait until Mimi attacked to take pity and *condescend* to let her sit with you?"

Kasey's cheeks were fiery red. After a long pause, her chin lifted in slow motion. "I might go with Lydia."

"You don't have to do that," I said.

Lydia's head jerked up like I'd hit her. "Oh, please. We're not good enough for your sister? We were good enough for *you* once upon a time, Alexis."

"Thanks anyway, Lexi," Kasey mumbled, slipping her lunch sack back into her book bag.

I watched in silence. Lydia gave her a glittery grin, the kind the wolf wore when he opened the door for Little Red Riding Hood.

"Excuse me." The voice behind me was soft and hesitant. "Is this table available?"

I looked up to see the awkward girl with the cane standing near us, holding her tray crookedly in one hand.

"Yeah," Kasey said. "I'm leaving."

Lydia put on her best poison-strawberry smile and, keeping one eye on me, said, "You know what? Don't eat alone. Come sit with my friends. What's your name?"

The girl looked up disbelievingly from under a curtain of slightly greasy bangs. "Adrienne?"

Lydia gave a brisk head-bob. "Come with us, Adrienne. Need help with your stuff?" She lifted the tray from the girl's hands and headed for the double doors, towing Kasey and Adrienne in her wake like some emo Pied Piper.

I stood watching them until they disappeared into the sunlight. Then I made my way back to my table, feeling stiff and self-conscious.

I'd failed at something, but I couldn't pinpoint what it was.

"Is Kasey all right?" Carter asked.

"Mm-hm," I chirped, opening my plastic pudding container. I started shoving food in my mouth so I wouldn't have to speak.

Inside my head, the thoughts were buzzing fast and furious. And the loudest of them was—when did I turn

43

into *that* girl? The girl who's too busy with her pack of friends and boyfriend to be nice to unpopular kids? The girl who treats Lydia and her group like they're a bunch of freaks-by-default?

In other words . . . when did I turn into the kind of person I claimed to hate?

After the final bell, I texted Kasey: MEET @ MEGAN'S CAR.

Megan was at her locker, next to mine. "Hey," she said.

Then Pepper showed up, red hair on skin so pale it was almost blue. At some point she'd been wise enough to give up the idea of ever getting a smidge of a tan. She looked at me and sighed. "So, Alexis," she said. "I hear my sister lost it during lunch."

"Yeah," I said, making a very concerted effort to keep my feelings about Mimi separate from my feelings about Pepper, which had been carefully cultivated over a year of mutually wary good behavior.

Pepper managed to look apologetic. "The timing's just bad. She had her first drill team practice this morning, and apparently the team's a joke this year."

Megan closed her locker. "I'm surprised she even signed up."

Pepper shrugged. "Well, she couldn't get a doctor's

note for cheerleading. Because of her arm." What she didn't say was: *Because of Kasey.*

Megan nodded. She understood. She'd been co-captain of the cheerleading squad before she'd been tossed into a wall (also *Because of Kasey*). Doctors had told her grandmother that so much as landing a cartwheel wrong would cause Megan's left knee to explode like a fireworks display. Now she was called a student coach, and she helped with choreography and scheduling. But I knew she missed being part of the action.

"Drill team, cheerleading," I said, stacking my books. "Same difference, right?"

Silence.

"Um, no, Lex," Megan said, eyebrow raised. "I mean, maybe at some schools, but here . . . ? Not even close."

I shut my locker. "I get why she's upset. Just ask her to leave Kasey alone, okay?"

"Yeah, I'll talk to her," Pepper said.

"Speaking of Kasey," I said, "I wonder where her locker is? I'm not even sure if she can find her way out to the parking lot."

My phone vibrated, and a text message popped onscreen.

WALKG HOME W ADRIEOMF

"Oh, never mind," I said. "She's walking home with Adrieomf."

6

LIKE CLOCKWORK, when Dad got home from work, he parked in the garage, hung his keys on the hook by the door, put away his jacket in the coat closet, and changed into his favorite sweats, which were still an offensively bright shade of orange even after a year of being washed twice a week.

Mom, on the other hand, never changed out of her work clothes before 10 p.m. It was a habit leftover from the time when she ran back to the office at all hours of the night. Since her promotion to VP, she left the running back to her underlings, but the suits stayed on until bedtime. She'd even curl up on the couch to watch a movie in a skirt and panty hose.

Her, dressed for the boardroom. Him, dressed like a highlighter. It gave our daily family dinners a lopsided feel. But I was used to it.

"How was school?" Dad asked. The question was addressed to both of us, but everyone looked at Kasey.

"Okay," I said, taking a bite of lasagna.

"Fine," Kasey said. Mom and Dad were still staring at her, so she froze, fork in the air. "What am I *supposed* to say?"

I could practically hear the gears turning in Mom's head, trying to figure out how to coax some information out of her. I would never have said anything about Mimi, or even Lydia. But Adrienne was fair game.

"Kasey made a friend," I said. "They walked home together."

My sister shot me a stormy look, but Mom's eyes lit up.

"Sweetie, that's great!" Mom said. "What's her name?"

Kasey looked at me sideways and breathed in loudly through her nose. "Adrienne."

"She's a freshman, right?" I asked.

My sister gritted her teeth. *"Yes."*

"Did you know her at your old school?" Mom asked.

"What is this, an interrogation?" Kasey asked, dumping the food off her fork and setting the fork on the edge of her plate. "She's normal. She has a dog named Barney and two brothers in college. Her parents are divorced. She and her mom moved here from Phoenix in June. What else do you want to know? Her blood type?"

Dad chewed tranquilly, then swallowed and picked

up his water glass. "Well, she sounds great."

"Alexis, how's photography class?" Mom asked. I could imagine the line in the Harmony Valley discharge brochure: *Ensure that the patient's siblings don't feel overlooked. Try to distribute your attention equally, when possible.*

"Oh!" I said. *"Outstanding."*

Her forehead crinkled happily. "Really?"

"Yes, because I'm transferring out."

"After a week?" Dad asked. "You have to give it a chance."

"First of all," I said, "I did. Second of all, it's not a film class. Ninety percent of the kids are shooting digital. And I don't have a digital camera."

"Maybe you should ask Santa," Dad said.

"I'm sure Santa won't have room for a camera in his bag," I said, spearing a bite of cauliflower. "Since it's going to be filled with a car."

Dad smirked. "Or maybe eight tiny reindeer."

I twirled my fork. "Or maybe eight tiny cylinders?"

"Or maybe a bicycle," he said.

"Great idea," I said. "Then you could bike to work, and I can drive *your* car."

Dad laughed, his head tipping forward so the overhead light reflected off his bald spot.

"Any more back-to-school parties?" Mom asked.

Oh, Mom. You give her an inch, she'll take a road

trip. She'd been so astonished by my friendship with Megan and my coupleship with Carter that she expected me to vault to the top of the social standings any day.

"Yeah," I said. "Megan's having one Friday."

Then Mom drew up all of her Mom energy and achieved a perfect Awkward Mom Moment. "And Kasey's invited?"

Dead silence spread over the table.

Kasey kept a very close eye on her food.

"I'm sure she . . . must be," I said.

"Thanks, but I have plans," Kasey said, her nostrils flaring. "With Adrienne."

"That's wonderful," Mom said, beaming. Dad nodded along. It was a little pitiful, to be honest. "Is it a sleepover or a regular party?"

"I don't want to talk about it right now," Kasey said. "I don't want to talk about anything. I just want to eat. Can you pretend I'm not here?"

Mom's chest pulled back into her body, as if she'd been punched.

"No problem," I said. "We survived without you for ten months. I'm sure we can make it through dinner."

When second period arrived Tuesday, I reported to the library, where I found I was the *only* student enrolled in second-period study hall—and that "study hall" was a euphemism for "help the new librarian organize the whole entire library."

Arranging thousands of books in numerical and alphabetical order might not seem like a good time, but compared to wandering around campus with Daffodil/Delilah, it sounded like heaven.

And Miss Nagesh, the new librarian, was practically drooling about having someone to help her. Though, from the way she kept talking about how desperately she'd begged for help, and how great and generous it was of Mrs. Ames to send me, I started to get the feeling I'd been played. Still, I was too relieved to care.

I promised I'd start organizing the next day if she'd let me work on my Young Visionaries contest application that day. Miss Nagesh was all for it.

And as soon as Mom got home from work, I borrowed her car and hit the road.

It was 5:17. The deadline for entries was 6 p.m., and the address was about twenty miles away. Even if I ignored Mom's "the speed limit is the *limit*, not the starting point" rule, I would be cutting it a little close.

A surge of adrenaline and apprehension buzzed through my body as I glanced at the bag containing my application and portfolio. I wasn't even sure if you were *allowed* to drop your stuff off in person. The application said, "SEND MATERIALS TO . . ."

The freeway was busy with commuters—impatient, cranky drivers headed for home. When I noticed that it was 5:47 and the exit was still two miles off, I started to worry. I didn't think I'd win; photography-wise I might hold my own, but get me in an interview and I was sure to destroy my own chances—but I was doing something real with my pictures, for the first time ever. I really wanted to enter, and not just for the money.

I pulled into the parking lot of a sleek glass and steel building at 5:54. I grabbed my bag and headed for the giant metal entry door. Inside, the lobby was cavernous and dimly lit. I approached the receptionist at her huge semicircular desk in the center of the room.

"Hi, I'm dropping off my application for the Young Visionaries contest?"

She spared me less than half a glance. "You were supposed to mail it."

My breath stuck in my throat.

She pointed toward the endless white hallway to my left. "Down the hall. Suite six."

I was glad I'd worn a black sundress and blue cardigan instead of just jeans and a T-shirt. Even my shoes were decent—a pair of Megan's grandmother's hand-me-down gray suede ankle boots.

The door to suite six was closed, and there was no doorbell or sign, apart from the metal number six.

I knocked a few times, but nobody answered.

Finally, I pushed the door open a couple of inches, revealing a miniature version of the main lobby with a partition dividing it from the rest of the office.

"Hello?" I called. No answer.

Off to the side was a table covered in stacks and stacks of envelopes, even a few small boxes. I wandered closer, checking the TO on one of the address labels: "Young Visionaries Contest." I did a quick sweep and guessed there were seventy, maybe eighty entries. Way more than I'd imagined.

I almost turned around and walked out, taking my portfolio with me, but I stopped before reaching the door. I'd already gone to the trouble of filling out the application. Even if they hated my work, even if I was ranked seventy-nine out of eighty, it wasn't like they'd be rejecting me in person.

I could handle long-distance rejection. I grabbed the padded envelope from my bag and looked at it.

Unopened, it was a pretty good-looking entry, top ten at least. Mom works for an office supply company, so she gets all the freebies she can handle. I'd printed up a nice quarter-page address label with the TO address on it and stuck it on a pale blue mailing envelope. And mine hadn't been knocked around by the postal service.

So I had that much of an edge.

Before I lost my nerve, I dumped my envelope on top of the stack and hurried out to the hall. In the ladies' room I used a handful of toilet paper to dab the beads of sweat from my forehead and tried to imagine what the judges would think when they looked at my pictures.

I'd lost almost everything in the fire the previous October—not only my camera, but years of negatives and prints. Portfolio-wise, I'd started in November with a blank slate. And now I began to worry that none of it was particularly interesting. It was just stuff I'd found around town, some pictures of my family, and—

That "and" threw my world off balance. The floor seemed to slide out from underneath me.

I shut the water off and raced out of the bathroom, back to suite six.

The door was locked. I pounded on it. "Hello?" I called. "Hello?"

Mid-knock, a woman pulled the door open. She was in her fifties, about my height, and beautiful, with thick, wavy black hair that rested on her shoulders. "Can I help you?"

I glanced past her toward the table where I'd left my envelope.

"I dropped off my stuff a few minutes ago," I said, "but it was a mistake. I need it back."

She didn't move. "Are you Alexis Warren?"

I nodded and stood there panting until she took a step back.

"Come in," she said, with a sweep of her arm.

I went straight for the table, but the blue envelope was gone.

"It's over here," she said, walking to a worktable with a daylight lamp shining down on my portfolio. "It's the first one I opened."

"Oh, no," I said.

The woman gave me a pointed look. "Generally, if you want your work lost in the crowd, you don't submit it in an eye-catching envelope."

The book was open to the very last picture, a close-up of the grille of a rusted old car. I'd cleaned the hood ornament and grille until they were as brilliant as the day the car was made, but left the rest of the rust, grime, and cobwebs.

"That's nice," she mused. Never before had the word "nice" stung so sharply. What she meant was: *Nice—but forgettable.*

But that was the least of my worries. If she'd seen that photo, that meant she'd seen the others. The ones I'd never meant to show anyone—much less a judging panel full of strangers.

I grabbed the book and pushed it back in my tote bag. "I'm sorry," I said. "There's been a mistake. I withdraw."

The woman gazed down at the table where my pictures had been, almost like she was still looking at them. "What a shame," she said. "All right, then. Good night."

If she'd pressed for details, I wouldn't have given them to her. But her easy dismissal bugged me. "It's just that there are pictures in here I didn't mean to include."

She glanced at me sideways. "Which ones?"

"Some that are . . . personal."

"All of your photographs should be personal," she said.

"I guess I could take them out," I said, "and leave the rest of the book."

"You'd lose."

I'm pretty sure my mouth fell open right about then.

"Bring it here," she said, motioning me over. Something in her manner made me obey. She flipped directly to the first of the photos I would have removed. "Do you mean these?"

"Yes," I said.

"This is you?"

Yes. It was a self-portrait, taken in a mirror: me sitting next to my new camera as warily as the bride and groom in an arranged marriage. It had taken forever to set up that picture, because my collarbone and wrist were broken. I was all bandaged up; there was a cut on my cheek, and some of my hair had been singed off, but I hadn't been to the salon to get it trimmed yet. I'd spent a frustrating hour trying to understand all of the camera's fancy automatic settings, and I still wasn't sure if I'd gotten it right.

I looked wild, battered, exhausted—but it was a good picture.

She flipped the page.

The two facing pages had pictures of my parents. I'd based them on that old painting, *American Gothic,* of two farmers just standing there. For the first one, I'd made them stand in front of the town house, dressed in their work clothes. It was about forty degrees out, and neither of them had a jacket. Mom is trying to smile through the cold. Dad is stoic, favoring his right leg the way he does when his leg injuries bother him (yet another *Because of Kasey).* They look miserable but determined.

The second one is the same pose, but they're standing in front of the burned out shell of our old house. The pillars that once held up the roof of the porch jut out of the ground, looking like they fought their way to the surface, zebra-streaked with ash and scorch marks. Beyond lies all that remained of the grand front hallway—the first couple of stairs, the frame of the basement door, the fireplace against the back wall.

I waited for a reaction, but she wordlessly turned the page.

The next photo was a close-up of two naked wrists, lit sharply from one side, causing the crisscrossed scar tissue to stand out in vivid relief. I had to fight the urge to hold my hands over the image, to hide it.

They were Carter's wrists. His wounds, from when he tried to kill himself during his freshman year at All Saints. I remembered the day we shot that picture, how Carter's arms shook as he held them under the lights. And how I wondered why he was okay with my taking a picture when he never showed his scars to anyone but me and his parents. He'd worn nothing but long-sleeved shirts since the day I met him.

The one after that was Megan, sitting on her mother's grave, the first time she was ever allowed to visit it. She slumped against the tombstone, her eyes closed, her face turned toward the sun. She'd forgotten about me, about everything except her grief.

And the last one was my sister in her Harmony Valley loungewear, smiling wanly over her fourteenth birthday cake in the visitors' lounge. Except we weren't allowed to light the candles, and we weren't allowed to have knives, so the cake was an uneven grid of presliced pieces with unlit candles sticking out at crooked angles. The scene was drab, joyless. The bite came when you looked into Kasey's eyes—which were like the eyes of a caged animal.

I'd betrayed myself and the people I loved most, letting those photographs be seen. It was almost as if I'd posted their naked pictures on the Internet or something—only this was worse, because these moments were more private and painful than being caught naked.

"I'm sorry," I said, picking the book up—more gently this time. "I can't."

"If you take those pictures out, you won't win," the woman said. "If you leave them in, you have a chance. They're excellent. You're very talented."

I turned to look at her. "Excuse me—who *are* you?"

She switched off the work light. "I'm Farrin McAllister. This is my studio."

I took an involuntary step backward.

Farrin McAllister?

The Farrin McAllister? The photographer who'd shot every major celebrity and half the rest of the important people and events in the world? Who had thirteen *Vogue* covers and who knows how many Pulitzers?

And she'd said my photos were . . . excellent.

I felt a little queasy.

"I'm closing up for the night," she said. "You'd better make your decision."

I hugged the portfolio to my chest. "But . . . if I enter, who will see these pictures?"

"Quite a few people."

"But I don't know if it's okay with my"—I gestured at the book—"for other people to see them."

"Nonsense," she said. "What did they think you were doing—bird-watching?"

I swallowed hard.

"Am I even still eligible?" My last escape hatch. I wasn't sure which answer I wanted. "Since we've talked?"

"This is a competition based on talent," she said, grabbing her purse from the counter. "Not a bingo game. You have until I reach the door to decide whether you're in or out."

But she was walking so fast!

Without thinking, I stuffed the book into the blue envelope and set it on the table.

Farrin—*Farrin McAllister*—held the door open for me and gave me a little wave as she stayed behind to lock up.

I'm not sure I exhaled once, the entire drive home.

7

THE WEEK WORE ON. Miss Nagesh and I cleared the 000s and were most of the way through the 100s—philosophy and psychology. She was young and cool, and while we worked, she told me all about the novel she was writing. I told her about the photography contest, even though I hadn't mentioned it to anyone else. Not my parents—not even Megan or Carter.

Kasey and Adrienne continued to eat with the Doom Squad, but Lydia didn't seem to be outright mocking them, so I didn't interfere.

Friday night, Mom and Dad were going to dinner with Mom's regional managers. Mom put on her swishiest dress, with her blond hair in a low bun; Dad wore his only suit and gelled his hair back. Mom kept calling him her trophy husband. I thought it was sweet, but Kasey huffed back to her room, muttering about having embarrassing parents.

I wiped down the kitchen while I waited for her to

finish packing her overnight bag. Finally she came out and sank onto a barstool.

"Almost ready?" I asked.

"I think I'm going to tell Adrienne I can't come," she said, dragging her fingertip along the countertop.

"But you said you'd go."

Her shoulders slumped. "Yeah, but . . . I don't *feel* like it."

"Kasey, you can't do that to people—back out when you say you're going to do something." I wrung out the sponge and set it on the edge of the sink. "This probably means so much to Adrienne. If you had a party, how would you feel if everybody canceled?"

"Ugh, fine! Quit nagging!" She heaved an enormous, woe-is-me sigh and went back to her room.

To be perfectly honest, my reaction was probably as much about me as it was about Adrienne. If Kasey didn't go to the sleepover, I'd have to figure out what to do with her. Leaving her home alone wasn't an option, and—selfishly, I'll admit—I didn't want her at Megan's house. I just wanted to relax with my friends, and having my sister around virtually guaranteed that wouldn't happen.

A few minutes later, she came silently back to the great room, dragging her duffel across the floor by its strap.

I made a mental note to remind her of that next time she made fun of me for sweeping every two days.

Adrienne lived a couple of miles away in a neighborhood called Lakewood, which was built in the 1970s and filled with bizarre, asymmetrical wooden tract houses. Near the entrance was a small man-made lake and a few acres of woods.

As we pulled into the driveway, my phone rang. It was Megan.

"Hey," I said. "I'm ten minutes away."

"Don't bother." She sounded drained. "The party's canceled."

"What? Why? Is everything okay?"

A huge sigh. "No."

Kasey was poised, her fingers on the door handle. I gave her a little wave, but she stayed put.

"Hang on, Megan." I covered the mouthpiece and turned to Kasey. "Bye. Have fun. *Hint hint.*"

Kasey's frightened expression made her look about ten years old. "But—I don't know—what am I supposed to do? What if I don't like the games?"

"Games? You're not in sixth grade anymore. It's a slumber party," I said. "Just don't fall asleep first, and you'll be fine."

She shook her head, faster and faster, working herself

up into a panic. "No, no, I changed my mind. Take me home."

"Kasey, go inside. You'll have fun. I'll pick you up tomorrow."

She gave me a desperate look.

"See you at noon," I said.

She took her time getting out of the car and walked up the driveway at quarter-speed.

I went back to my phone. "Megan?"

There was a pause, and for a second I thought she'd hung up. Then she spoke. "At cheer practice today, I demonstrated a back handspring."

"Are you hurt?"

"No," she said. "Not at *all*. But Coach Neidorf called my grandmother. Apparently they had some secret agreement to keep an eye on me." She was quiet for a long few seconds. "Grandma was *spying* on me, Lex."

"Only because she cares about you," I said, but I knew it was a weak excuse.

"So I'm grounded for a week, and the party's canceled. Can you call a few people? I'm phone-grounded, too." Then there was a muffled voice in the background and bumping and shuffling. "*I'm almost done!*"

"Sure," I said. "Text me the names."

"Lex?" she asked, her voice suddenly small. "Don't have a party without me, okay?"

I imagined Megan sitting in a jail cell, her grandmother—the warden—pacing outside. "Never," I said. "I swear."

Carter and I ended up back at my house, watching a *Twilight Zone* marathon on TV. We were halfway through the one where Captain Kirk finds a magic fortune-telling machine when Carter jostled me. "My foot's buzzing," he said.

My purse was under the blanket. He tossed it to me, and I pulled out my phone. Kasey's name popped up on-screen.

"Kase?" I asked.

"Lexi?"

She sounded upset. I sat up. "What's wrong?"

She sniffled. "Barney ran away."

"Who's Barney?" I asked, mentally running through the roster of Adrienne's siblings. Weren't her brothers in college?

"The dog," she said, and I exhaled a giant breath. "Can you come help us find him?"

"Can't Mrs. Streeter help you?"

"No. We think he's in the woods, and she can't go there in her chair," my sister said. "Please? Adrienne's about to lose it."

"All right," I said. "I'll be right over."

"For real?"

I was taken aback. "Of course, Kasey."

"Oh," she said. "Thank you so much."

I hung up the phone, wondering why she found it so shocking that I was willing to help her. Wasn't I *always* the one who helped her?

As we pulled into the Streeters' driveway, the girls converged on us. Adrienne was in tears. Kasey hugged herself tightly and looked warily around the dark neighborhood.

"Thanks for coming," she said.

"No problem," I said. There were four girls there: Kasey, Adrienne, a pretty girl I didn't know, and Lydia, who saw me looking at her and turned away to kick at the loose gravel in the driveway.

What was *Lydia* doing at a lame slumber party?

To my surprise, my sister had a plan. "I'll go into the woods with Lexi. Adrienne, go in the car with Carter," Kasey said. "Tashi and Lydia, go on foot. Call everybody if you see him."

We all fanned out, carrying flashlights and bags of dog treats. Kasey and I started down the street, shining the flashlight between houses and shrubs.

"What kind of dog is it?"

"A Westie," she said. "He's white, luckily."

Or not-so-luckily. Sure, a white dog was easier for us

to see, but that also meant he was easier for coyotes and other predators to see, too. I quickened my pace.

"How'd he get out?" I asked.

"I'm not sure." Kasey exhaled. "Something scared him."

"Mrs. Streeter must be going crazy," I said. "Not being able to help."

"Yeah." Kasey shined the light under a car.

"Why is she in a wheelchair?"

"It's a degenerating disease," Kasey said. "Adrienne has it, too."

"Degenerative?" I caught a glimpse of something white, but it was a trash bag by someone's side door.

Kasey fidgeted with the treats. "Alexis, if we find Barney, you should probably get him."

"Why?" As far as I could recall, the lengthy list of things that scared my sister didn't include dogs.

She turned the light over in her hands, trying to decide what to say next. "I don't know if he likes me very much."

"What we should probably do, if we see him, is call Adrienne and let *her* come call him."

"No," Kasey said. "He won't go to her, either."

"But she's his *owner*."

She sighed. "It's a long story."

We came to the parking lot by the lake. There was a small log cabin with padlocked bathrooms and a

66

water fountain. We stepped off the paved surface onto the clumpy grass of the picnic area, which led to a small stretch of beach dotted with dilapidated picnic tables and a barbecue grill covered in caution tape.

I scanned the lake. The fountain in the center sputtered irregular streams of water, illuminated by the few floodlights that hadn't yet burned out.

"There he is! I see him!" Kasey said, pointing down toward the water's edge.

The beam of the flashlight bounced off a small white dog trotting along the shoreline.

"Here," Kasey said, handing me the bag of treats. "Call him. Make sure he sees that you have food. He'll do anything for food."

"What do I do if he comes to me?" I asked. "Do you have a leash?"

Her face fell.

"I'll grab his collar," I said. "Go back to the Streeters' house and get his leash."

"Okay," she said. "And I'll call Adrienne."

There wasn't time to say more. I started slowly toward the shore.

The dog heard me approach and looked up, his ears pricked at attention.

"Baaaaaaarney," I called, keeping my voice as smooth as possible, "here, boy."

He glanced at me through suspicious eyes and began to amble away, checking back over his shoulder.

I didn't want to get too close, for fear that he'd run. So I stopped moving. The dog stood still and watched me.

"Hey, boy," I said, dropping to my knees and landing in a puddle of wet dirt. *Great.*

I reached into the bag for a treat.

Barney cocked his head.

"Yummy!" I said, holding it out. "Who wants one?"

I tossed it so it landed a couple of feet in front of him, and he pounced on it, tail wagging.

I tossed another one, and he came closer. Now we were only separated by a few yards. A third treat, and then a fourth, and I decided to go for it—instead of tossing the next one, I held it on the flat of my palm. "Come see what I have. Come on."

Barney, by now pretty psyched about the goodie-throwing stranger, wagged his tail once and took a curious step toward me, his eyes trained on the bit of food in my hand. I raised it to my nose and took a sniff. It smelled pretty good, actually.

"Mmmm . . . maybe *I'll* eat it," I said. "Better hurry."

He came closer, his gaze never leaving the food. I shifted my body so he'd have to come within grabbing distance of my left hand to reach the treat.

Almost there—

There was a loud clattering sound from behind the maintenance building on the far side of the picnic area. Barney's ears shot straight up.

"No! Stay!" I said, making a grab for his collar. But he scrambled away from my grasp and stopped at the very edge of the tree line.

A second noise—this one louder.

Barney flattened his ears and took off, straight into the thick woods.

I ran after him, but was forced to slow down once I got past the outer layer of trees. There were low, scrubby plants and exposed roots everywhere, and the last thing I wanted was to face-plant in the middle of a forest.

"Hey!" I yelled. "Here, boy! Come back!"

I kept going until I saw a flash of white.

"Barney!" I called. "Who wants a cookie?"

I'd stumbled on the magic word. Twigs snapped furiously as the dog tumbled back through the trees and stopped directly in front of me, his stumpy tail wiggling madly.

"Okay," I said. "We're doing this my way." I leaned over and grabbed his collar. He was too transfixed by the bag of treats sticking out of my pocket to notice.

"Cookie?" I offered him one. He gobbled it down and looked back up at me, hoping for more.

Since I didn't have a leash, I reached down and scooped him up. For such a little dog, he was solid. He settled contentedly into my arms, licking my face and snuffling the air, evidently enjoying the ride.

I looked around for a way out, but there was no discernible path. I tried listening for the lapping of the water on the shore, but I couldn't hear anything over Barney's excited panting and the chirping of the crickets.

And of course my cell phone was in Carter's car. Perfect.

"It's a good thing your food smells so good," I said to Barney. "We might be sharing it."

He glanced at me, then went back to the business of sniffing, his nose quivering.

"Which way is home?" I asked. He probably knew—superior sense of smell and all that—but I couldn't set him down and take the chance that he'd run off again. So I turned in what I figured was the approximate direction of the parking lot.

Then we reached a spot where the brush grew too thick to pass. Barney looked at it, twitched his ears, and yawned. I shifted him in my arms. He was getting heavy, fast.

I knelt down to study a bit of grass, wishing I'd lasted past the friendship-bracelet-making stage of Girl Scouts.

Suddenly, the dog tensed. He scrooched deeper into my arms, ears back, and showed his teeth for a moment. A low, menacing growl rumbled in his throat.

Then, through the brush:

Snap.

Barney snarled and whined, straining toward the sound. I had to wrap both of my arms around him to keep him from jumping to the ground. His dirty paws left black streaks all over my clothes.

"Are you crazy?" I hissed. "Stop that!"

What if it was a coyote? Or what if it's not a coyote? I suddenly thought. What if it's a mountain lion—or a bear? Did we even have bears in Surrey?

I started walking. Any movement *away* from a scary sound was better than standing like a lump. Even if we walked so far we came out on the other side, the woods had to end eventually.

As we went farther, Barney calmed down. But then, after about a hundred feet or so, he tensed and growled again.

From behind us: a scratching noise, and a scrambling, and the *thud* and *whoosh* of something falling and running away.

I looked around for a large branch to use as a club, if it came to that—but the one decent-sized stick I found disintegrated in my hand.

Barney whined miserably, panting and trying half-heartedly to get away.

"It's okay, boy," I said.

Snap-snap-snap-CRASH!

The dog yelped and vaulted out of my arms, already poised to run by the time his paws touched the ground.

I launched myself at him, belly-flopping on the pine needle floor, barely managing to hook my fingers around the edge of his collar. When he realized he was caught and couldn't escape, he changed tactics and went on the offensive, rolling off a series of vicious-sounding barks and frantically hopping around.

"Cut it out! Get back here!" I said, tugging him toward me. I'd gone through way too much trouble finding the dumb dog to let him get eaten by a bear now. "Barney, *stay!*"

His barking became one extended growl, and he was pulling so hard his front legs were off the ground. My fingers felt like they were about to pop off.

Whatever was back there, he wanted to kill it.

After managing to get a better grip on his collar, I got to my feet and picked him up, pressing my cheek against the back of his head as I looked around.

"Now what?" I asked him.

"Woof!" he answered, looking over my shoulder.

I swung around to see Carter appear between two

trees, looking ridiculously out of place in his starched oxford shirt and spotless brown shoes.

"Alexis? Are you okay?" He came over and scratched the dog's neck.

"Relatively," I said. "I have no idea how to get out of here. I hope you dropped some bread crumbs."

"Right back this way," Carter said. "Want me to carry Barney?"

"He's filthy," I said, but Carter reached out anyway, and my aching arms were dying for a break. So I gladly handed him over, and we started back through the brush.

"Kasey went back to get a leash," I said. "I hope she stays back in the parking lot. I think there's some sort of wild animal out here."

Carter squinted. "I doubt it. We're still in the suburbs."

"Suburbs or not, I heard something," I said. "Something big. Barney heard it, too."

"Maybe a raccoon?"

"Bigger than that. Forget it. I don't know."

And then, another *snap*.

"Did you hear that?" I asked.

"It's probably a bird, Lex," he said. "Wait, where are you going?"

His dismissal annoyed me.

"Just to take a peek," I said, walking away. "I'll be right back."

"But what if it's dangerous?" He looked around, suddenly seeing the forest for what it was: Big. Dark. Spooky.

"Like a raccoon?" I asked. "Or a baby bird?"

He waited, one hand idly rubbing the dog's belly, while I went deeper into the forest. The farther I went, the more opaque the canopy grew overhead, branches and leaves weaving into a dense cover that blocked out what little starlight there was. The trees were crowded here, the brush thicker.

More scratching . . . but as I got closer, it didn't sound like scratching, exactly. It was more like . . . I looked down at the bed of pine needles on the floor of the woods.

Like *moving*. Like something was being dragged through the pine needles.

And whatever it was, it was getting closer.

Fear sent roots down through my feet, locking me in place. I gulped in half-breaths of chilled night air, waiting for an outraged, wounded mountain lion to pop out at me.

Then I saw it—between the tree trunks, which were almost as close as crayons in a box.

A shadow.

This was no wounded mountain lion. It was no

wounded anything. It moved too fast. And in the deep darkness, I couldn't tell whether it was coming closer or getting farther away.

How could I be so stupid? I'd basically lived through a horror movie and *still* hadn't learned my lesson.

At some point, my eyes had squeezed shut and I'd lost the ability to breathe.

Snap out of it. Get control of yourself. And then get out of here.

I forced my eyelids open, positive that some beast would be standing right there, drooling blood and exhaling the smell of death.

But the woods were empty. And the only sound was a *snap*—

Right behind me.

A hand snaked around to cover my mouth, but my self-defense training kicked in. I bent my knees, reached back to grab the attacker's arm, and delivered a swift kick as high as I could, dropping my attacker to the ground. Then I turned around to get a good look at it—him—

Her. It was my sister.

"Seriously, Kasey?"

She whipped a finger to her lips, librarian-style. *"SHUT UP!"* she hissed. Her eyes were wild, frantic, as she jumped to her feet and grabbed my arm, scanning the woods behind us.

"What are you doing out here?" I whispered.

She said, *"Shhh,"* and pulled me along, treading as lightly as she could.

The scraping grew louder as Kasey looked around. She dragged me behind a bush next to a thick pine tree and crouched down, hauling me with her.

I shot her a questioning look. But she was staring back at the clearing.

The animal, the beast, whatever it was, stepped into a small patch of light. There was a peculiar lightness in its step. It raised and lowered its head in a subtle bobbing motion as it moved.

I shivered. It was primitive, feral . . . inhuman.

In the darkness, I still couldn't get a good enough look to tell what it was. It didn't move like a person, or a bear, or even a werewolf.

I thought of Barney wandering these woods alone and shivered, glad we'd found him and that he was safely with Carter.

But were they *really* safe? Carter was alone, unsuspecting. I had to get back to him.

And we all had to get out of the woods.

But the creature was too close; we didn't dare move a muscle until it disappeared. It was traveling again, that quick movement that sounded like a bundle of branches being dragged along the ground.

And it was coming closer. Much closer.

Kasey and I were pressed together, holding our breaths, as the thing came within ten feet of us. Maddeningly—or maybe it was for the best—you still couldn't make out anything about it. It seemed to be made of shadows.

It paused briefly at a tree near us, sniffing the air like Barney had done.

And then there was an explosion of outraged barking, the release of an hour's worth of pent-up fear and anger, and Barney came crashing through the woods.

"No, Barney!" I called. I tried to grab for his collar, to keep him away from the creature, but right behind was Carter, using his belt as a leash, holding on to the leather strap.

"What are you guys doing?" Carter demanded. "Lex, you said you'd be right back!"

"Nothing," I panted, looking around. The shadow-creature had vanished. "Nothing, we're fine."

"I thought I heard something," he said, his lip curling in irritation. "I was *worried*."

"I'm sorry," I said. "But we're totally okay."

I glanced back into the darkness. Carter looked around, too.

"Let's get out of here," he said. "If you don't mind."

Kasey clipped the leash to the dog's collar, and

Carter put his belt back on. We made slow progress through the forest and emerged right where Carter had left the car.

"Where's Adrienne?" I asked.

"She wanted to walk," Carter said. "Said she'd go home if the car wasn't here when she got back."

"Maybe we should look for her," I said, thinking of that thing in the woods.

"I called her," Kasey said. "To tell her we found Barney. She could see Lydia from where she was, so they're probably at the house by now."

We drove to the Streeters' house, and Kasey rang the doorbell. We heard shuffling inside, and finally, Mrs. Streeter pulled the door open. Her hair was pulled back, and she gave off an air of stylishness that clearly wasn't hereditary. Her eyes were ringed with worry lines.

"My Barney!" she cried, wheeling her chair around the door. The dog flew into her lap. "Thank you guys *so much*."

"No problem," Carter said.

"You sweet, dirty little dog!" she said, letting Barney lick her nose. "I was so worried about you!"

It was cute. I smiled at Kasey, but she frowned.

Mrs. Streeter turned her attention to us. "Hello!" she said. "You must be Alexis. I've heard a lot about you."

"Yes," I said. "Hi. And this is Carter."

"You guys really saved the day. Can I get you something? Water? Soda?"

"No, thanks," I said. "We should probably get going."

"Please, just stay till Ay gets back. She'll want to thank you." She wheeled backward and closed the door behind me. "How'd your pictures turn out?"

I froze.

"That was you, right?" she asked. "I recognize the hair."

"Yeah," I said. "Um . . . Actually, they're good."

And they were. Mother and daughter, hopeful companions. A little optimistic for my taste, but not bad.

"I'd love to see them," she said.

I nodded, too fast, too apologetic. "I'll send a print home with Adrienne."

She shook her head, her earrings swinging gently from side to side. "Don't do that," she said. "I'll never see it. She hides from cameras these days."

"Oh, okay," I said.

"Forgive me!" she said. "I didn't even introduce myself. I'm Courtney."

Just as she said it, the front door opened and Adrienne came in.

"Barney's home! Now, tell me what happened." Courtney gave Adrienne a knowing look. "You left the gate open, didn't you?"

"I don't know." Adrienne sighed. "Not like he ever goes anywhere."

"But I keep telling you, dogs don't think the way we do. If something scared him, he could take off." She gave the dog a kiss on the head. "He *did* take off. Poor old stinky guy."

"We'd better get going," I said. "I need to change out of these wet clothes."

The front door opened again, and Lydia and the other girl came inside. They hovered behind Adrienne.

"I—I might go home with my sister. I don't feel very well," Kasey said. In the light of the hall, you could see pine needles in her hair and my well-defined shoe print on her shirt.

The girls tried to cluster around her, but she ducked away and disappeared down the hall.

I took the bag of cookies from my pocket, and Barney hopped off Mrs. Streeter's lap and zipped over to me. "You've probably had enough for one night," I told him.

"I'll take them." Adrienne came up to me. As she approached, Barney backed away.

There was silence.

"He's *scared* of you, Ay," Courtney said. "Did something happen during your meeting?"

Adrienne blinked. "No," she said. "Nothing happened."

Meeting?

The voice came from behind me.

"Alexis, right?" I turned to see the fourth girl standing with her hand extended. She had beautiful light bronze skin and a mess of golden brown curls. "I'm Tashi."

I shook her hand and gave her a quick smile before turning toward the front door. Kasey was coming down the hall, and I was ready to get home.

In the car, Kasey stared out the window.

"What's wrong?" I asked.

She was quiet for so long I thought she was ignoring me. But finally, she spoke.

"Mrs. Streeter really loves that dog," she said.

Carter seemed all right on the drive, but when we got to Silver Sage Acres, he pulled past the guest lot and idled in the driveway, keeping his seat belt fastened.

Kasey went inside, but I lingered in the front seat.

"Want to come in?"

Carter traced the underline of his jaw with his thumb. "I . . . I don't think I should. I mean, you need a shower, and it's getting pretty late."

"I can shower in three minutes," I said. "I'll put on a pot of coffee. We can watch a movie."

"Lex." Carter turned to me and grabbed my hand. "I don't want to lie to you. I really am tired, but . . . even if I weren't, I've had enough for the night."

"What does that mean? Enough of me?" I pulled my hand away as a thought occurred to me. "Or enough of Kasey?"

He sat back. "Out in the woods . . . did you see what was making that sound?"

I counted three heartbeats before I could answer. "No," I said. Technically it wasn't a lie. I *didn't* see what it was, after all.

He rubbed his eyes. "I know this sounds mental, but I think I kind of did see . . . something. I heard more noises, and I thought I saw a shadow go by. The dog went nuts and I got really worried, but by the time I reached you, there was nothing around."

"Right," I said. "Nothing."

He grabbed the steering wheel. "Except your sister."

"So, okay, if the noises were Kasey," I said, "which maybe they *were* . . . then what's the big deal?"

"The big deal is . . ." He shook his head. "I think I saw her try to kill a squirrel."

I was pretty shocked that Carter thought my sister would be capable of attempted squirrel murder. But what could I say? *No, it wasn't Kasey, it was just the shadowy beast lurking in the trees.*

"No way," I said. "There's no chance of that. I know my sister."

His head jerked up. "Do you?"

"Yes! Of *course*."

"I saw something out there," he said. "I know I did."

"It was probably a raccoon," I said archly.

"Don't get mad at me, Lex." He raised his hands helplessly. "It's not an accusation. I just thought it was weird. The whole thing was really . . . weird."

"Maybe it's a full moon," I said.

"There's no moon tonight," he said.

I sighed and leaned on my door; Carter leaned on his—and we were as far apart as we could be while still sitting in the same car. A shadow came to the front window of the town house and paused for a moment before disappearing.

"Parents are stalking," I said. "Better get inside. Thanks for driving."

He turned and looked at me, and his jaw finally relaxed. He reached for my hand and ran his thumb across my palm. "Of course," he said. "I'm glad we found the dog."

"Yeah, me too."

"Oh," he said. "That girl left her cane in the back-seat. Can you give it to Kasey?"

We smiled at each other shyly, like a pair of seventh

graders parting after a school dance. I gave him a quick kiss and walked up to the front door, the cane hooked over my arm, thinking that this would all blow over soon. Maybe it already had.

The next morning, I awoke to the sound of the gardeners mowing the grass in the median. The buzz of the leaf blowers and the sun streaming through my window made it impossible to get back to sleep, so I went to the living room. But Kasey was already sprawled out on the couch, watching TV. She moved over to make room for me, but I shook my head and went to the fridge instead, making a mental note to be the first one out to the living room on Saturdays.

Kasey and I hadn't talked at all about what had happened in the woods.

It wasn't a conversation I was dying to have, to be honest.

Best-case scenario, Kasey thought what we saw was an animal, and she wanted to hide me from it. Worst-case scenario . . . I don't know. I'm sure there was a whole range of mid-grade scenarios, too. But where my sister was concerned, I'd gotten pretty used to the worst.

Finally, after sitting through two hours of cartoons, I gave her a soft kick. "So . . ."

She stood up. "I need to take a shower." And then

she trudged off down the hall to the bathroom.

After her shower, she locked herself in her room for another hour. I finally gave up and took a shower myself, only to find her door wide open and bedroom deserted when I emerged.

In the kitchen, Mom was shuffling through the mail. "Morning, hon," she said.

"It's afternoon," I said. "Where's Kasey?"

Mom glanced up at me. "Dad drove her to a friend's house. The girl you used to hang out with—Lydia?"

"Oh," I said.

"Didn't she used to live in Riverbridge? In that big house with the little stream in the front yard?"

"Yeah," I said. All the yards in Riverbridge had bridges. Imagine that.

"They live over west of Crawford now," Mom said, making a sympathetic face. "It's not a very good neighborhood. I'm surprised she's still in the same school district."

Lydia's parents had been serious go-getters. Her dad drove a sports car, and her mom owned a high-end salon, which made Lydia's sloppy home hair-dye jobs all the more offensive. It was hard to imagine them in a dumpy house on the outskirts of town.

I was about to turn and leave when Mom tossed an envelope to me. "Young Visionaries?" she asked. I took it back to the sofa, deliberately ignoring her curiosity.

So this was it. My form rejection, with a request to come collect my portfolio. I slid my finger under the corner of the flap. All week, the contest had been bugging me—the thought of being ranked somewhere in the middle of that giant stack of entrants.

CONGRATULATIONS! was the first word I saw, and I felt the oddest combination of emotions—happiness and apprehension at the same time. Like my heart inflated and then ran away and hid under the bed.

The letter went on to say that I'd survived the first cut and was now one of twelve semifinalists. At the bottom was a scrawl in a thick, black permanent marker: *Your work stands up well against the competition.—FM*

And there was a note about an interview session being conducted the following week.

"What is it?" Mom asked.

"Nothing." I shoved the letter back inside its envelope. At some point I'd be forced to tell my parents. But for that moment, I wanted it all to myself.

Dad and I arranged the Chinese take-out containers on the counter while Mom got plates and silverware.

"So . . ." I said. "I have some news."

In about four milliseconds, bustle turned to dead silence. Dad froze and looked up at me, and Mom came around the counter.

Wow, that worked.

"I'm not pregnant or anything," I said, and Dad exhaled. "Seriously, Dad? You think that's how I would tell you?"

"What is it, honey?" Mom asked, setting down the plates.

"That letter I got today," I said. "It's for this photography thing. Like a contest. With a scholarship."

Her eyes lit up. "You're going to enter?"

"No," I said. "Well, yeah. I did enter . . . and I made the semifinals."

I couldn't decipher their expressions. Mom looked pensive. Dad looked blank.

"That's the news," I said, pulling out a bar stool and reaching for a fried wonton.

I would have given my parents credit for having more self-control, but they immediately started carrying on, Mom hugging me and saying, "I'm so proud of you! I'm so proud of you!" and Dad cuffing me on the arm like an old college buddy.

"All right, that's enough," I said, peeling away. "It's not that big of a deal. There are twelve semifinalists."

"But Alexis, this is wonderful!" Mom said. "It *is* a big deal. Wait until Kasey hears!"

I looked around. "What time is she coming home, anyway?"

"Not until tomorrow," Mom said. "She's sleeping over. I guess they all are. Since she had to miss the party last night, I thought it would be all right. I actually have to take her some clothes."

"I'll take them," I said.

"Really?" Mom asked.

"Yeah," I said, forcing a smile. A chance to drop in on Kasey and her friends, possibly learn more about these "meetings" they were holding? I couldn't pass it up. "I can tell her about the contest."

Right on Crawford, left on Morrison, right on Baker.

This was an older section of the city, a grid of tiny houses packed together like eggs in a carton, not a fancy subdivision in sight. Lydia's house must have been cute once, but its glory days were long gone. The siding peeled like a bad sunburn, showing multiple layers of old paint, and the upstairs window was blacked out with aluminum foil. In the driveway was her father's red sports car, his baby. But the whole length of the driver's side was dented, and the bumper seemed to be hanging on for dear life.

I grabbed Kasey's overnight bag and Adrienne's cane from the passenger seat and made my way up the weed-covered sidewalk. The doorbell was broken, so I knocked.

A few seconds later, Adrienne opened the door. "Oh, hi!" she said. "Come on in!"

"Here," I said, holding out the cane. She took it and bounced through the house, without even using it. She was as hippity-hoppy as a toddler.

As we entered the kitchen, all activity stopped. The four of them were sitting around a small breakfast table with arts and crafts supplies strewn everywhere. Each girl worked on her own poster board. To my left was a stack of yellow flyers.

I reached for one.

WANT TO DEVELOP YOUR CHARM AND INNER BEAUTY?

JOIN THE SUNSHINE CLUB!

There was a big cartoonish drawing of a grinning sun with flirty eyelashes, and underneath that was a phone number—not ours, thank goodness—and an e-mail address, info@jointhesunshineclub.com.

"What's this?" I asked.

"The Sunshine Club," Adrienne began, like she'd rehearsed it a billion times, "is a self-improvement club for young women who—"

"Why just women?" I asked, ignoring my sister's warning glower.

"Because it's only for girls!" Adrienne chirped, as if that answered my question. "For young women who want to nurture their inner beauty as well as their outer beauty.

You should join, Alexis. You'd have so much fun."

"Well, thanks," I said. "But I'm kind of busy this year."

"We're going to do really cool stuff!" she said. "Like study groups. And makeovers."

I basically had to bite a hole in my tongue to keep from reacting. If Adrienne thought making people over in her image was a good idea, she was highly misguided.

But then I looked at her, and noticed that her outfit wasn't as wacky as usual. She wore a pair of jeans and a nice shirt. Nothing fancy, but a huge improvement over her typical ensemble.

I mean, look. I'm not going to win any awards for personal style. Some people, like Megan, could look at a closet full of clothes and put together a great outfit without even trying. Even Kasey was pretty good at it—she'd only been home a week, but she was already the more stylish sister.

I admired Adrienne for the fearless way she put herself out there. But she was more like me. Her pants were always too long or too short; her shirts were too baggy or just a little too tight. Any time I ever went out of my way to try to look cool, I ended up feeling like some celebrity's dressed-up Chihuahua.

While Adrienne chattered on about all of the wonderful things the Sunshine Club would learn and experience together, I glanced at the other girls. Kasey glared at me while Tashi glued glitter to her poster. And Lydia—well, let's just say that cheerful self-improvement definitely wasn't on Lydia's to-do list. I expected her to be rolling her eyes or snickering. So it was a pleasant surprise—heavy on the surprise—to see her politely following along.

When the pitch was finished, they all looked at me.

"Um, great," I said.

"We're going to put flyers up at school on Monday," Adrienne said. "And Tashi goes to All Saints, so she's going to put them up there. New members, here we come!"

Surrey High didn't have metal detectors or anything, but it wasn't really the type of place where kids are on the lookout for the next wholesome activity to devote their afternoons to. I felt bad, thinking how disappointing it would be when nobody joined.

"Good luck," I said. "It sounds really fun." *And really pathetic*, I didn't say.

But you can probably imagine how much I was thinking it.

The next Friday night, we celebrated Megan's ungrounding with a much smaller version of the party she'd planned the previous week—just her, me and Carter,

91

Pepper Laird, and a couple of other cheerleaders. We sprawled out on the leather sectional in the family room.

Megan's house was like a cross between a hunting lodge and a corporate boardroom. Heavy wood furniture held cutting-edge electronics. An iron candelabra kept watch over Mrs. Wiley's three cell phones at their charging station.

Megan's grandmother was the CFO of an investment brokerage. She was queen of all she surveyed, and she demanded perfection and faultless obedience—from her interior decor, her two secretaries, and her granddaughter.

Mrs. Wiley adopted Megan after her mom died. And she was among the scariest people I'd ever met in my life. You just didn't mess with the woman. And everyone—Megan included—knew it.

Our conversation had been doddering along when Pepper turned to me. "I forgot to tell you," she said. "Did you know our sisters are totally friends again?"

"Really?" I waited for a sarcastic smile or something, some signal that she was joking.

"Yeah," she said. "Weird, right?"

Forgetting even the broken arm and the cafeteria incident on Kasey's first day, Kasey and Pepper's sister were as incompatible as . . . well, as a drill team dancer and a person who ate lunch with Lydia.

I turned away, studying the seam of the armrest.

Carter took my hand and bent my fingers like they were poseable toys.

I mean, yes. Kasey having friends was a good thing. A couple of weeks ago, if you'd told me the most popular girl in ninth grade wanted to hang out with her, I would have been thrilled.

But my sister, goofy Adrienne, beautiful Tashi, hostile Lydia, and now Mimi Laird? It didn't add up. I mean, sure, life isn't like an 80s movie where everyone's locked inside their perfectly defined boxes, but our school wasn't quite progressive enough for a mix that diverse.

Or maybe it was. What did I know? I was a former Doom Squad member with a prep boyfriend and a cheerleader best friend.

I felt a tapping on my leg. "Oh! I forgot to tell you!" Megan said, her eyes wide. "Earlier, when I said I thought Emily had a doctor's appointment? She didn't. She ate lunch with your sister and Lydia."

"With the *Sunshine Club*," Pepper said.

"That's your sister?" Carter asked, his nostrils flaring like he'd smelled something bad. "I've seen their posters . . . I thought it was a campaign stunt."

"Emily likes everybody," Pepper said, waving it off. "She gets around."

"Not at lunch," I said, feeling oddly territorial. "Is she with them tonight?"

"Maybe," Megan said. "She never texted me back."

There was an unsettled silence. For Pepper and the other girls, it was probably more about the unexpected mixing of the social groups than anything else.

Carter's chest heaved with a sigh, and he let go of my hand. Megan was staring at the ceiling fan, chewing her tongue like it was a piece of gum. Her fingers lightly drummed on the coffee table.

As for me, I was trying to scold myself back into a rational line of thinking.

So my sister was making friends across the established boundaries. That wasn't cause for alarm. All it said about her was that she was open-minded, friendly. What did it say about *me* that I instantly jumped to the conclusion that she was mixed up in something bad?

But the more I tried to talk myself out of it, the more convinced I was that there must be something going on under the surface. To make a single friend in eighth grade, Kasey had to befriend a horrific vengeful spirit. Then she hits high school and immediately rounds up a posse of BFFs—by poaching *my* friends?

Look on the bright side, I told myself. It might not be ghosts. Maybe it was just drugs. Or blackmail.

But ghosts? It couldn't be.

Because Kasey knew better than to go flirting with the dark side again.

Immediately, a pair of twin headaches blossomed at the back corners of my jaw.

After last year's episode, we'd been visited by a woman in a nondescript gray suit driving a nondescript car (the woman, not the suit) and looking like she worked for a nondescript insurance company. But her name was Agent Hasan, and I don't mean "insurance agent" Hasan. I still have no idea who she works for, because her business card only lists her name and a single phone number. But she took care of talking to the police, getting Kasey booked into Harmony Valley, and getting us moved out of the old house. She combed through the rubble and left with a thin, sealed envelope.

And she gave us her card with a "strong suggestion" to call if there were any other incidents "of interest." That was how she talked—using words that seemed harmless but were actually bursting with ominous meaning.

Before she left, I cornered her and asked what would happen if it wasn't over—if Kasey wasn't cured.

She didn't want to answer me, I could tell. But finally, she said, "Whatever arises, we'll contain it."

Their kind of containing was what kept my sister at Harmony Valley for ten months, even though, technically, there was nothing wrong with her. Calling the number on that card might get my sister locked up for a lot longer than ten months.

Or worse than locked up.

"I'm sure it'll be over soon. Mimi'll get sick of them and move on to something better—" Pepper cut herself off and blushed. "You know what I mean."

There was a time when I would have been insulted, but I nodded and gave her a distracted half-smile.

The thing is, I wasn't offended.

I actually hoped she was right.

After lunch on Saturday, I went out to the great room to find Mom sitting at the island, looking over some work stuff. And—as always—Kasey had claimed the sofa, even though she was barely paying attention to the TV.

I leaned on the bar next to Mom. "Can I use the car later?"

She looked up. "Sorry, what?"

"I need to go take some pictures. For the contest."

"Oh." Mom hardly glanced away from her computer. "Sure, honey."

I chose my words carefully. "I really want them to be good, you know? To make up for all of the old ones I don't have anymore."

Mom minimized her spreadsheet window, which meant she was really paying attention. Maybe using her sympathy to get what I wanted makes me a bad person. But I couldn't worry about that. I had to figure out what was going on with my sister.

"Where will you go?" she asked.

"I don't know," I said. "Out. I might call around and see if anybody can help me."

Studying the back of my hand, I took a half step to the left—revealing to my mother's eager eyes the sight of Kasey flopped on the couch.

"I know someone who can help you," Mom said.

"How much farther?" Kasey asked.

"I don't know," I said. "It depends on the light."

We were trooping through the forest at Lakewood. The guest lot and picnic area were deserted—big surprise—and we slipped into the woods, ignoring the rusted NO TRESPASSING sign. I carried my camera and a couple of pieces of white poster board to bounce light off of. Kasey was lugging a pile of costumes and props. She kept falling behind and having to trot to catch up.

She let herself be talked into helping with minimal groanage, which surprised me. Only when I said we were going to Lakewood did she try to back out. But by then, Mom had latched on to the idea of us taking pictures together—just like old times—and ordered her to help.

I was kind of excited about the shoot, but my real motivation was to get my sister alone. I kept trying to think of ways to introduce the topic of Mimi, but I couldn't come up with anything besides *Why on earth would Mimi Laird lower her exalted self to hang out with you?*

"Here," I said, as we reached a clearing. It looked similar to the one where we'd seen the creature the week before. My skin prickled with goose bumps, and I waited to see how Kasey would react. But she just seemed relieved to be able to drop the pile of clothes.

"What's our theme?" she asked.

"Um . . ." I looked around. "Why don't you grab the violin?"

She made a dissatisfied face. "It doesn't have any strings."

"Fine," I said. "How about the wedding gown?"

Kasey looked horrified. "It's ninety-five degrees!"

"Yes," I said. "Definitely the wedding gown."

I'd picked up the dress at the thrift store for ten dollars. It had a plain top with spaghetti straps and a full tulle skirt, like a tutu. Kasey pulled it over her head, and then I turned away so she could finish changing. I zipped it up and she looked around.

"You know," I said, "that looks kind of like Pepper's prom dress from last year."

It was weak, but I was dying to start interrogating.

Kasey shot me a sideways look, which I ignored.

"Speaking of Pepper . . . what brought on this whole Mimi reunion? I didn't think you guys got along."

"We used to be best friends," she said coolly. "What's so weird about us talking?"

"I didn't say it was weird," I said. "But since you brought it up, what's weird is that you broke her arm."

"Are we going to actually take any pictures?" Kasey asked.

I raised the camera and checked the settings. "What's weird is that you broke her arm *on purpose*," I said. "As I recall."

I braced myself for an explosion.

I got an unruffled gaze. "Well, I apologized," Kasey said. "And she understood. So."

Hey, sorry I broke your arm? That was all it took to get back on Mimi's good side?

Suddenly, Kasey started spinning, her arms outstretched, her face turned toward the sky. The skirt bloomed out like a flower. I quit talking and started taking pictures.

A minute later, she stopped to rest. It wasn't a cool day, and the edges of her hairline glistened with sweat. She raised her arm and wiped her forehead. Without warning her, I took a picture, and she gave me a dirty look.

I looked back at the pile of props. "Just *try* the violin."

She picked it up, her eyes still veiled with hurt.

"You really think it's that strange?" she asked. "That someone wants to be my friend?"

Okay, no. That's not how I meant it. "No . . . I only think it's strange that *Mimi Laird* wants to be friends with you."

"Everyone seems to want me to get on with my life. To be happy." Kasey's voice was thoughtful, and she gently tucked the violin under her arm. "Everyone but you, Alexis. Even Pepper is nicer to me than you are. And she's a senior. And popular."

Unsure if that was supposed to be a jibe about my own unpopularity, I let it go.

I snapped a couple of pictures, which made Kasey turn away again.

"I do want you to be happy," I said. "But not if . . ." *If it means you're doing something bad. Something wrong. Something that would ruin everything for all of us.*

She stood up straight—she was almost as tall as me now—and looked me right in the eye. "Not if it means hanging out with people you don't like?" she asked. "Like Lydia?"

"Yes, in fact," I said. "Like Lydia. You don't know her, Kase."

"No, Lexi, *you* don't know her. She's had a terrible year. Give her a break."

"Excuse me!" I said. "What about *my* year?"

Kasey's mouth fell open.

My mouth fell open, too. At first I couldn't figure out where that had come from. But then it was like a door had been opened. "You think it was easy?" I asked. "Being home with Mom and Dad? Trying to pretend things were normal? Losing everything we owned? You got to move into a furnished town house, Kase. We had nothing. No clothes, no dishes—my camera, all my pictures—everything was *gone*."

Kasey's jaw relaxed, and she looked at me with—was it compassion?

Nope. Totally not compassion. Her face transformed. "Are you kidding me?" she hissed. "Excuse me, I was in a *mental institution*. I couldn't wear clothes with *buttons*, Lexi, because they thought I might *choke* somebody!"

Then, in a burst of anger, she took the old violin ($4 at the thrift store) and swung it. I managed to snap a picture just as the brittle wood hit a tree trunk and cracked.

Kasey stared at it, shocked at what she'd done. Then she smashed it again, and again, until all that was left was the neck. I took almost a whole roll of film.

Panting, she dropped the violin and turned to me. "I'm sorry if you had a hard year," she said. "But don't I deserve a chance to be happy? Why can't I have friends of my own?"

"Go ahead," I said. "Find out for yourself that Lydia's

a backstabbing, conniving gossip. But if she ever finds out what really happened to you, you'd better be ready to deal with the Lydia I know. Because not everyone is as forgiving and accepting as I am."

Kasey sank down to the ground, the wedding dress puddled around her. She closed her eyes and shook her head.

I lifted my camera, but for once I couldn't find a shot.

All I could see was a fourteen-year-old girl in pain.

Pain caused by me.

She'd lost everything, and now as fast as she could piece together a new life for herself, I was chipping away at it. She was my *sister*—why couldn't I be supportive?

Was it really because I was afraid Lydia would hurt her? Or did it go deeper than that? Had I grown so smug in my new life that I wasn't willing to let go of any of it to make room for Kasey? I couldn't even share the stupid *sofa*.

"Kasey . . . I'm sorry," I said.

So we'd seen something in the woods. So Lydia was reaching out to lonely freshmen. So (against all odds) Mimi had found forgiveness. What did that have to do with Kasey?

"I'm really, really sorry," I said again, feeling the sting of tears in my eyes. "I made a stupid assumption. I got suspicious, and I thought—" Might as well confess, even if it made me sound evil. "I thought there might be something going on. Something like—like Sarah."

Her shocked eyes darted up to meet mine, and she recoiled.

"But that was wrong," I continued. "I know you wouldn't get involved with that stuff again. You're smarter than that."

I hoped she'd stand up, forgive me. We could cry and hug and get the heck out of the woods before we both ended up covered in ticks.

I'd have settled for her storming away.

Worst case, she'd sit there and cry, too hurt to respond.

She didn't do any of those things. She stared up at me, as surprised as a little fish, her eyebrows perfect arcs.

And when she spoke, her voice was a rush of confession and release.

"But what if I'm *not*, Lexi?" she asked. "What if I'm *not* smarter than that?"

8

I PUT MY HAND OUT and plunked to the ground.

They'd lock her up for years—maybe forever.

It would break our mother's heart, clean down the center.

Kasey grabbed my hands and held on to them like we were in danger of being swept away. "It's not like last time," she said. "It's not, I swear."

Weighed down by the props, we went back toward the parking lot, leaning on each other like shipwrecked survivors. Kasey's gown kept getting caught on sticks and roots, and by the time we made it back to the pavement, the bottom layer of tulle was a shredded mess.

We spent the next few minutes sitting in the motionless car, staring out the windshield at the decaying fountain in the middle of the lake. Finally I put my seat belt on and started the engine.

"Did you do anything to the car? Brakes, fuel line?" My voice was flat, heavy.

She scowled. "No."

"Tires, power steering, axles?"

"No, Lexi!" she said, folding her arms across her chest and sinking into a deep pout.

As if she had *any* right. As if she hadn't, eleven short months earlier, messed with the brakes in the car our dad was driving and sent him careening into a tree. As if it weren't her fault that he has metal plates in his leg and will never again get through an airport security line without being patted down.

We came to the old LAKEWOOD sign at the entrance to the community.

I hit the brakes so hard that the tires squealed and the car filled with the unmistakable odor of burning rubber.

Kasey shrieked and slammed into her seat belt. "What are you doing?!?"

"Did that thing in the woods last week have something to do with this?"

She was as wide-eyed as a kitten. "What thing?"

"Come on. The *thing* in the *woods*!"

"Oh, that." She sighed. "I don't know."

Un-freaking-real. I sat back against my seat.

"Lexi, there's a car coming behind us."

"He'll go around," I said.

"There's not room to pass."

"Fine!" I pulled onto the main road without even looking for traffic. Kasey squealed and bashed against the passenger seat. The other car passed us anyway.

There was no sound except the rumble of the engine and the tires on the road. Halfway home, it started to drizzle. Kasey leaned forward and looked up, as if she could see into the clouds. Miraculously, I made it all the way into the garage without losing my temper again.

"What now?" Kasey asked.

Our parents were out at Dad's coworker's wedding; they'd be gone for a few hours, at least. I unbuckled my seat belt and turned to face her. "We're going to have a talk."

"Where?"

"The kitchen."

"Fine," Kasey said, unbuckling and opening her car door. "But I have to change first."

"Go ahead of me," I said. "Keep your hands where I can see them."

"Alexis, if I wanted to hurt you," she said, stepping out into the garage, "I'd whack you with a shovel." To prove it, she reached out toward the rack and poked one of the shovels with a single finger, setting it bobbing on its hooks. Then she opened the door to the house and disappeared down the hall.

She was right; if she meant to harm me, she'd had

the chance. I went into my bedroom and put on a pair of pajama pants.

Kasey met me in the kitchen. We sat on opposite sides of the island. Outside, the wind howled resentfully down the narrow street, thrashing the poor saplings in the median.

"Now," I said. "Get to the point."

"I was at Adrienne's last Friday," she said. "Remember?"

Like that was a night that would just slip your mind. And then suddenly, horribly, I remembered how she'd tried to back out but I'd made her go.

She either didn't think about that or was too polite to rub it in. "We were playing 'truth or dare' and I said *dare*, but they wanted me to do *truth*. And they asked me why I had to go to Harmony Valley."

"So you told them," I said, like a prosecutor on a TV show, "what we all, as a family, agreed to tell people. That you have a mild form of schizophrenia."

"Yes, Lexi, I *did*." Her eyes flashed. "But Lydia did a research paper on schizophrenia last year, and she asked me a bunch of questions that I couldn't answer."

"She accused you of lying? Typical Lydia."

"No, she didn't say it like that," Kasey said. "She thought maybe I'd been misdiagnosed and I should get a second opinion. She wanted to help. But then . . .

I messed up. She asked what medication I took, and I couldn't remember what I was supposed to say . . . so I said none."

I knew it without even having to think. I'd know it in my sleep. Haldol. If anyone asked, Kasey was on Haldol.

"Then Adrienne said she was going to call her big brother, who's in medical school, and she wouldn't let me talk her out of it." Kasey's hands fluttered in the air in front of her. "So I had to tell her . . . tell them the truth."

"No, you didn't *have to*," I said. "You could have told her to mind her own business, Kase. You could have said you wanted to go home. You could have called me. You could have left the room."

Her face fell. "But Lexi," she said. "They were *nice* to me."

She hung her head and studied the countertop.

I sighed. "Then what?"

"Lydia didn't really believe it at first."

"You had a chance to take it back?" I asked, but I'd lost the will to play the angry lawyer.

"Not really. Tashi believes in ghosts, and they all talked about it for a while, and then we talked about how depressing it was to be—to be social rejects." She took a shaky breath. "And then Adrienne said she'd found this book that promised to make you prettier and more popular."

"Found it where?"

Kasey shrugged. "I thought it was like a party game. I tried to talk them out of it, but they didn't listen. I wasn't going to do it—but they said we should all—"

"You weren't going to do what?" I asked.

She was on the verge of tears. "Did you know people put notes in my locker? They called me *psycho*. Once, when I went to the bathroom, someone put a—a dead cockroach in my purse. And Mimi got everyone to throw the ball at me in dodgeball—even people on my own team."

"Just finish your sentence," I said. "You should all . . ."

"They said we should start a club," she said. "Based on the book. Really, it was Adrienne's idea."

"What's the book about?"

She looked stricken. "I'm not sure," she said. "It's not in English. Adrienne thinks it's Norwegian."

"Oh, *Kase*, seriously?"

"Then the pizzas got there, and we ate, and Barney ran away. And then . . . well, you know that part. The next day, we started the Sunshine Club to try to improve ourselves."

"Wait, wait, wait," I said. "So it's just a book?"

I was on the edge of being massively relieved. A book of advice didn't seem so bad. In fact, if Kasey was that hypersensitive—that just playing around with antiques made her nervous—I could rest a little easier at night.

"Well, yeah." She traced the grout in the tile countertop with her pinkie finger. "I mean, it's actually more of a . . ."

"What was that? You're mumbling."

Her eyes flashed up defiantly. "It's a *dwelling*."

My neck muscles seemed to go slack, and I found myself staring up at the recessed lights in the ceiling. A dwelling. As in, someone—or some*thing*—lived inside of it.

"Right," I said. Because nothing that has anything to do with Kasey can ever be easy. "And whose dwelling is it?"

She turned to gaze out the window. "I'm not supposed to say."

"Kasey," I said. But she wouldn't look at me. I reached over the countertop and shook her shoulder roughly. "Hey."

She peeked over at me, biting her lip. "His name is Aralt."

I made a little pocket with my hands and breathed into it, trying to clear my thoughts.

"His name is Aralt," I repeated.

Her reply was practically a squeak. "Yes."

"Unreal." I sighed and turned away.

"Not all ghosts are bad, Lexi—Megan's mom was good." She bit her knuckle.

I didn't even acknowledge that. "So the book is written in Norwegian, but somehow you guys convinced Aralt to come out and give you makeovers." And when I thought about it, Kasey had been getting steadily prettier as the days went on. Doing her hair, wearing makeup, accessorizing.

She nodded. "But it's more than that. I mean, Adrienne doesn't even need her cane anymore!"

"Yeah," I said. "I noticed."

"And at school, people want to be around us. We got four new members this week."

"But *how*, Kasey? What did you do to get Aralt to help you? If you don't speak the same language—"

"Oh, I'm pretty sure he understands English," she said. "He seems really smart."

Like he was some dreamy foreign exchange student.

This situation was quickly spiraling beyond my ability to control myself. I reached for the phone.

"What are you doing?"

The sound of Kasey's voice caught me. It wasn't a lack of fear—she sounded plenty scared. But there was a note of something else. Like she was issuing a challenge.

I faced her. "You mean, am I calling Agent Hasan?"

She blinked.

"No," I said. "I'm calling Megan."

Five minutes later, there was a loud knock at the door. Kasey jumped back in her seat. Then the doorbell rang about ten times in a row.

"Alexis! Are you there? Open up!"

I pulled open the door. "Hey."

Megan came in, pushing up the sleeves of her jacket. She was out of breath. "I had to totally lie to Grandma. Are you serious about this? We have to call Agent Hasan. Where's your sister?" Her face tensed as she caught sight of Kasey.

"We're talking," I said.

Megan glanced from me to my sister and back.

"I don't think we need to call. Yet." That earned me a *you've got to be kidding* look, but I pointed toward the kitchen. "Come sit down."

Megan didn't make a move. She beckoned me closer. "Alexis, what are you doing?"

"Gathering information," I said.

She spoke like a kindergarten teacher. "And are you a hundred-percent sure information-gathering is the best thing to do right now?"

"No. I'm zero-percent sure," I said. "But if we tell on her, they'll be here tonight. And we might never see her again."

112

"You don't know that that's how they work." She cast another glance over my shoulder.

"No, I don't know anything about how they work," I said. "That's what scares me."

Megan sighed and looked at my sister, who was resting her head on her folded arms.

"Please," I said. "A little more time. What happened to 'There are ghosts everywhere'?"

"Lex, don't *even*." Megan narrowed her eyes and reached into her pocket for her phone. "The number's loaded in here. All I have to do is hit 'send.'"

"If it comes to that," I said, "fine."

Megan walked past me and took a seat across from Kasey, leaving the phone on the counter, fingers poised over it.

We went through the story again. Megan grilled where I'd merely skimmed.

"Have you ever *seen* Aralt?"

Kasey shook her head. "No. I don't think you see him."

Megan leaned forward. "How do you know it's a him?"

She shrugged. "We just know he is."

"But who *is* he?"

Kasey blinked. "He's Aralt."

Megan rolled her eyes. "But where's he from? How old is he? Is he a ghost?"

"He's from the book," Kasey said. "That's all I know."

"Does he talk to you? What does he say? How do you know what to do, if it's not in English?"

"It's not like he talks out loud." Kasey bit down on her lip. "I guess it's more like . . . a feeling."

Megan leaned forward, the tips of her fingers pressing into the countertop. "What does he make you feel?"

"I don't know." My sister leaned back. "I guess, like, you feel what *he* feels. If you try hard to look pretty or do something good, he likes it."

"And what if he doesn't like something?"

Kasey scrunched her nose. Somehow it hadn't occurred to her that having a supernatural boyfriend might not always be sunshine and puppy dogs. "Um . . . I guess he'd be sad?"

"Not angry?"

"Not like Sarah?" I interjected.

"Uh-uh," Kasey said. "No. Not at all like Sarah."

Megan gave her a cool look. "So what's he after?"

"Nothing," Kasey said.

"Ohhh, cool, so you guys get to be beautiful and smart and popular, and that's all he needs to be happy?"

"I guess so."

"*Wrong*," Megan said. "That's not how it works. And when does it end?"

"At graduation," Kasey said.

"And when is that? Next week, next year, never?"

My sister blinked at her hands, clueless.

"Do you remember any of the words from the book?" I asked.

Kasey shook her head.

"And that thing in the woods?" I asked. "Was that him?"

Megan raised an eyebrow. "What thing in the woods?"

"No," Kasey said. "He's made of spirit energy. He doesn't come out of the book. I don't know what that was."

"I refuse to believe that a giant mysterious animal just *happened* to visit Lakewood the same night you started messing with a new ghost."

"Wait," Megan said, her brown eyes accusing me. "I never heard anything about this."

I sighed. "I'll explain later."

Megan sat back. She slid her phone back and forth across the counter from hand to hand.

"If the book is a dwelling, it has to be the power center," I said. "The ghost's energy is tied to it. So we need to destroy the book."

The color drained from my sister's face. "Adrienne hides it somewhere. I don't know where. She would *never* let anything happen to it."

"But she brings it to meetings, right?"

"Yeah . . . but it's not like she just passes it around." Kasey sighed. "Listen, you guys. I know it sounds bad, but please . . . I can handle it."

She must have seen the skeptical expressions on our faces, but she pressed on.

"If I talk to them, and tell them it's not a good idea, they'll listen to me." She glanced pleadingly from me to Megan. "They're my friends!"

"Not very good friends," Megan said. "If they got you wrapped up in this mess."

Kasey stared up at us, her eyes wide. *"Please."*

"You know what?" I said. "Fine, Kasey. You want to fix it yourself? Go ahead."

My sister hesitated. Across the table, Megan was watching me.

"She's right," I said to Megan, shrugging. "They're her friends. Go ahead, Kasey. Get them out of it."

Kasey swallowed hard. Her fists were tight balls pressing into the counter. "I will."

"Fine," I said. "Then it's handled."

"Whatever," Megan said, giving me a wary glance. "I'd better get going."

"I'll walk you out," I said.

Once we got outside the front door, she stopped and looked at me.

"You aren't serious," she said.

"No, of course not," I said. "But there's no point in arguing with her."

Megan sighed. "Okay, thank God," she said. "Because for a minute I thought you'd lost your mind. Now, could you please explain to me what this thing is that you keep talking about? A mystery animal? When were you in the woods? And why didn't you tell me about it before tonight?"

"It's not important," I lied. The last thing I wanted was Megan suggesting a late-night trip to Lakewood. "It was a coyote or something."

I'd hurt her feelings. Her eyes were too bright, and she looked like she had something to say. But she didn't say it. "Fine. So what's the plan?"

"We're going to go to their next meeting," I said. "And we're going to get the book and destroy it. And no one is going to get hurt."

"Right." Megan glanced at the time on her phone. "Except me, if I don't make it home by ten thirty."

9

MONDAY MORNING, I found Carter sitting on a low brick wall in the courtyard, bent over a copy of *Moby Dick*. When I stepped into the sun, casting a shadow over the pages, he marked his place with the dust jacket and set the book down.

"Good morning," he said, squinting up at me.

"Hi," I said. "Sorry I missed your calls yesterday. I was doing a photo shoot with my sister and things got . . . hectic."

"No worries."

"But I missed you," I said, scooting next to him. As soon as I said it, I meant it. I closed my eyes and pressed my forehead against his sleeve.

"You're coming this afternoon, right?" he asked.

"What?"

"To my poster party?"

"Refresh me on what a poster party is again?"

"A campaign thing. Zoe Perry arranged it. She's

the girl I was talking to at the party for like a half hour. Keaton Perry's little sister."

I tried to remember her, but I couldn't recall her face, just a voice and a bunch of political buzzwords: alignment, empowerment, proactivity. "The boring one?"

He laughed. "I hope not. What would that say about me?"

"That you're good at humoring boring people?"

"Anyway, I need you there. I can't be alone with her and her friends. They seem to be confusing high school politics with real politics."

I put my hand on his shoulder. "I can't come."

"Seriously? Why not?"

Honesty is the best policy, right? "I'm hanging out with my sister and her friends."

The corner of his mouth went up in confusion. "The Sunshine Club?"

I shrugged. "You don't have to call them that."

"Why not? Everyone does. They're like a cult." His shoulders pressed back. "And when did you decide this? Because I asked you about the party last week and you said yes."

"I'm sorry," I said. "I forgot. Any other day except today. I need to do this for Kasey. She's having some problems fitting in."

"Are you joking?" he asked. "Does *that* look like someone having problems fitting in?"

I followed his gaze to the picnic tables, where the Sunshine Club had claimed a spot under the mottled shade of the school's big oak tree. They sat close together, like sisters, talking and laughing among themselves. And Kasey was right smack in the center.

"You don't understand," I said. And he couldn't. Because if he knew the truth, he'd flip out.

"Maybe I don't," he said. "You're one of the people who really wanted me to run for president this year, and now you're disappearing when my campaign needs you."

"I'm not disappearing," I said. "I'm missing one little arts and crafts party thrown by a bunch of boring preps."

His laugh had no humor behind it. "Thanks, Lex. I love being called names."

Just like I love being expected to make campaign appearances like some lame wifey with no life of her own. "That's not what I meant!"

"Okay, well, I wish you could stop saying things you don't mean. Like that I'm one of a million boring preps—or that you'll spend time with me."

"Where's all this coming from?" I asked.

"I guess I don't like being lied to," he said.

"Who's lying?"

He enumerated on his fingers. "You said you'd come today. You're not going to. You say it's because Kasey is having problems. She's clearly not. If you're somehow suddenly too cool to help with my campaign, I wish you'd just say it."

"I've never been too cool for anything in my entire life," I said, bristling at the accusation of lying. "I *forgot* about the stupid party, Carter. Sue me!"

"All right," he said. "When you can clear some time between cult meetings, let me know." He checked his watch. "I have to go find Zoe and tell her we'll need extra help."

"Stop. Please. I hate this," I said, reaching out to him. "Can't we just not be angry?"

"I'm not angry, Lex . . . I'm sad." And he walked away.

We spent the morning exchanging terse text messages.

First, I apologized, and he said he accepted it.

The rational, grown-up thing to do would be to let it go. But I could feel the tension behind his words. So I texted him back that he didn't *have* to accept my apology, and he replied that I was the one who couldn't accept that *he* could accept it perfectly well . . . and then my fourth-period teacher made me put my phone away.

We managed about twenty words between us

during lunch. Nobody noticed. Emily would have, but now she sat with the Sunshine Club. They'd moved inside to a table in the center of the cafeteria—not the prime real estate by the window, but creeping closer.

Certainly not the Janitor's Table or the Doom Squad's courtyard exile anymore.

So we sat like a pair of cordial strangers. We'd never had a disagreement this serious before. Some small part of me kept trying to suggest that maybe he'd overreacted and it wasn't my fault. But it was shouted down by the rest of me, the part of me that wanted things to go back to normal as soon as possible, even if that meant taking all the blame.

Because without Carter, I didn't even have a normal to get back to.

10

WE WERE EARLY, so Megan parked a few doors down from the enormous, well-manicured Laird house, and we sat in the car with the windows down, listening to the contented sighs of the engine.

After about fifteen minutes, a group of happy-go-lucky girls, including Kasey, turned the corner, coming from the direction of the school. We watched from the safety of the car, like tourists on safari.

"Look," Megan said. "They're all wearing skirts."

"Kasey told my mom they're more flattering than pants," I said.

"Only if it's the *right* skirt," Megan snorted, staring out the window. "But they all do seem to be wearing the right skirts."

"They do everything right. Haven't you noticed?"

Adrienne, Kasey, and Emily went up the front walk together, all shiny hair and teeth, and disappeared through the door.

Another girl crossed the street in front of the car. She looked familiar, but it took me a moment to place her.

"Megan!" I gasped. "Is that *Lydia?*"

For three years, Lydia Small had prided herself on being the gothiest goth ever to stomp through Surrey in her giant steel-toed boots. But this . . . this was . . .

"Impossible," I whispered.

She was dressed like Jackie O., and her stringy black hair had been cut and blow-dried in a perfectly turned-under bob. She glanced at us, and I saw that she was fully made up, her eyebrow ring gone, her lips a demure pink.

"She wasn't at school today," Megan said. "I guess we know what she was doing."

Lydia flounced over to the car and leaned on the window ledge.

"Alexis! Megan! Hi!" She ducked down to glance into the backseat. "Where's Miss Kasey?"

"Hi," I said. "Uh . . . she's already inside. How's it going?"

"Perfectly!" Lydia beamed, peppy as a 1960s soda-pop commercial. "How are you girls?"

"Super-duper," I said.

"No kidding?" Lydia asked. "So. When are you two going to join the Sunshine Club? I'm telling you, you won't regret it." She assumed the saintly expression of a beauty pageant contestant talking about world peace. "It has totally *changed* my life."

"Actually . . . today," Megan replied. I was looking down at Lydia's hand. Gone were her many skulls and plastic spiders and other assorted jewelry (a lot of which, I'm sort of embarrassed to say, were purchased on shopping trips with yours truly, back in the day). The only thing on any of her fingers was a single, gleaming gold ring.

"Lovely!" she cried.

"Yes," I said. "Lovely."

"Do us a favor?" Megan said. "Don't tell Kasey you saw us. We want to surprise her."

Lydia's face lit up. "No way! So fun. Of course."

She mimicked zipping her lips shut.

If only that could be a permanent setting.

Lydia flashed us another smile and bounded away, up the rose-bordered sidewalk toward the house.

"What . . . on earth . . . was that?" I asked.

"That," Megan said, "is what the Sunshine Club is all about."

We were the last ones inside. Pepper sat in the kitchen, eating a banana and keeping a suspicious eye on the front door. When she saw Megan and me, her jaw dropped. "What are you guys doing here?"

I shrugged. "We're going to the meeting."

Pepper dropped her peel in the trash. "Megan? Explain?"

Megan smiled, like the whole thing was a lark.

"Whatever." Pepper grabbed her car keys. "I'm going to Kira's."

Megan knocked lightly on Mimi's bedroom door, and Adrienne pulled it open.

"Oh my God!" she squealed. "Hi!"

Behind her, I saw my sister's face turn white. But Megan and I pushed our way in, and there was nothing Kasey could say in front of the other girls.

The ten of us fit in Mimi's bedroom with room to spare. It was pristine, like an ad in a decorating magazine—the perfect backdrop for the array of immaculately dressed girls, wearing blissful, self-satisfied smiles, legs crossed at the ankle, posture perfect.

The whole room fell silent when Adrienne went to her bag and lifted out a large object wrapped in midnight-blue velvet. She set it on the dresser and unwrapped it, then held it in front of herself while everyone in the room sat perfectly still.

You had to admit—it was quite a book.

Ten inches wide, sixteen inches tall. The cover was leather, densely embossed with runes and symbols—stars, moons, vines, Celtic knots.

For a moment, I considered just grabbing it and taking off, but then Adrienne spoke.

"We protect your dwelling with our blood and our lives," she said, in the vague drone of a pod person.

"We protect your dwelling with our blood and our lives," everyone repeated.

Megan and I glanced at each other. They did *not* sound like they were kidding.

Even if I did manage to wrench the book out of her hands, there were five girls between me and the door. Self-defense training or no, odds were I'd never make it.

Adrienne broke into a smile. "I'm *thrilled* to announce that Alexis and Megan are joining us today! Alexis was one of the first upperclasswomen I met at Surrey, and she was so nice to me, even though she's popular and has a boyfriend and I was a gross loser. And of course, Megan is well-known for her leadership."

The way Adrienne talked about herself, you'd think she was dishing on some sad reject—not the sweet, well-meaning girl she'd been a few short weeks before.

"Megan and Alexis." Adrienne could hardly speak through her giant smile. "Please stand."

Stand? I glanced at Kasey, whose face was buried in her hands.

Suddenly I felt like maybe we should have thought this whole thing through a little more.

I got to my feet, my heart beating as if I'd climbed ten flights of stairs. Megan stood next to me.

"Please put these on your ring fingers." She passed each of us a thin gold ring. I slipped it over my finger. Adrienne looked into my eyes, her gaze as smooth as a polished stone. "Place your right hand on the book, and repeat after me."

Megan blinked with alarm and obeyed. Angling my body, I lifted my *left* hand and set it against the underside of the open book, hoping Adrienne wouldn't notice. And if she did, I could just pretend I was confused.

But she didn't notice.

"Geallaim dílseachta . . ."

"Geallaim dílseachta . . ."

She went through a whole long spiel of words that were nothing but nonsense—to us and to her, I could tell. I repeated as well as I could.

"A tu, Aralt," Adrienne said with finality.

"A tu, Aralt," we repeated.

My nerves felt like a writhing bundle of live wires.

Adrienne gently closed the book and leaned in to give us a kiss on each cheek.

"Our sisters," she said.

Everyone clapped politely. A path cleared back to my seat on the bed, and I sank down, trying to figure out if I felt different. I felt on edge, somehow, but that was probably adrenaline. After all, I'd taken an oath in a language I didn't understand to a supernatural being I knew nothing about.

An oath. Why hadn't Kasey said anything about an oath?

It occurred to me that maybe she'd planned this all along. She had to know that Megan and I wouldn't just leave the subject alone . . . just because we'd said we would.

No. She'd been shocked to see us. And she didn't look happy. She really believed she could fix this herself.

But an *oath* . . .

I caught sight of myself in the mirror over Mimi's vanity and was struck by how dumpy and unkempt I looked, especially in contrast to the perfection surrounding me. My forehead and nose gleamed with oil. I raised my sleeve to try to wipe my face.

Someone gave my arm a gentle pat, and I looked up to find myself staring into Lydia's untroubled eyes. She smiled reassuringly.

"What a joy," Adrienne said. "Now, sisters, let's get down to business. Does anyone feel called to start off Betterment?"

Betterment?

For a moment, no one said anything, and then a hand rose. "Monika?" Adrienne said.

The girl she'd called on, a tall brunette, stood up. "Everyone looks wonderful today," she said, her glance traveling quickly past me. "But I noticed at lunch that some girls were eating very large portions. *Small* meals in public, and then eat in the bathroom if you're still hungry. You know we want to appear our best, inside and out." She sighed and continued with a mournful *it has to be said* air. "I'm talking about Emily and Paige."

For a few long, uncomfortable seconds, everyone stared at Emily and Paige, who ducked their heads and gazed at the carpet.

It went on for another ten minutes, girls being called out for infractions of an extremely strict and meticulous behavior and dress code. Even Adrienne was chastised for the length of her skirt—more than three finger-widths higher than her kneecaps.

Megan looked at me, her eyes asking when we were going to make our move. Then I watched as her gaze traveled to the mirror, and her eyes narrowed in distaste.

I didn't understand—she looked fine. Just as good as any of the other girls, maybe better. *I* was the ugly one.

After bettering each other through the magic of nitpickery, we listened to Adrienne give a pep talk about the qualities of a successful young woman.

It was fine, I guess, if you wanted to spend every waking hour at constant attention, never relaxing, never letting down your guard. But how could a group of teenage girls keep it up? By the end of the hour, I felt like we'd been through a self-help seminar at a religious cult.

The thing was, for the time being, Aralt only seemed to want his Sunshine Club girls to be pretty, fashionable, thoughtful, and well-spoken.

It was kind of twisted—but was it evil?

"All right, everybody, that's it," Adrienne said, closing the book and setting it on the dresser. "Stay sunny!"

With the meeting over, all of the girls wanted to welcome Megan and me personally. There would have been no way for us to grab the book without being noticed. They held our hands and looked into our eyes and said sweet and encouraging things, like something out of a sorority in the 1950s.

"I can't wait to see you . . . *after*," Emily said, giving my hands a squeeze.

"After what?" I asked.

Her smile faltered. "Well . . . after . . ."

"Remember: the only people we're called to judge are ourselves," Lydia said. "Except during Betterment, obviously."

Emily hurried away, leaving me alone with Lydia.

"Welcome, Alexis," she said, touching my shoulder.

"Thanks." I tried to act like the other girls were acting, a peculiar blend of eyes-down modesty and utter self-consciousness about the way they held themselves and moved.

"I know you don't totally get it yet," she said. "But it's only your first meeting. Let me tell you—I didn't even really want to join." She lowered her voice to a stage whisper. "*I thought the whole thing was a joke.*"

"No kidding."

"Then I took the oath, and suddenly it all made sense."

I was starting to feel like I'd had enough of this for one day. "I'm so glad for you."

"Anyway, you have to let me do your hair."

I'd been drifting, but that snapped me back to attention. "Do *what* to it?"

She laughed. "*Fix* it. You can't leave it all . . . pink and . . . unfinished. A real lady doesn't need flashy clothes or dyed hair."

"Or eyebrow rings?" I asked.

"Exactly!" Lydia grinned like I'd finally gotten it. "She has poise, charm, and intelligence."

"I think . . . I'll just wait a few days," I said.

Lydia's joy evaporated. "Why would you do that?"

Obviously I couldn't tell her that I intended to destroy the book that night, thereby removing any need to try to impress Aralt.

"You represent *us* now, Alexis," Lydia said. "You're

not a single person anymore. You're one of many."

"Good point," I said. "I just can't tonight. I have a huge project to finish." I smiled apologetically. "Gotta keep those grades up!"

"I guess." She tried to hide her displeasure but did a pretty bad job. "Well, I'm around, as soon as you're ready."

Over by the bed, Megan and Kasey were busily talking to Adrienne. I edged closer to listen to them.

"And I'm excited about all the meetings and the improving and the—Alexis!" Megan said, turning to me. "I'm telling Adrienne and Kasey how much I look forward to growing and improving!"

It was totally obvious to me that she was acting. And Kasey was just as manic. But Adrienne was so delighted by their gushing enthusiasm that she just looked from one to the other while they fluttered around her like a couple of hyperactive fruit flies.

Then I saw what Megan and Kasey were doing as they talked: packing up their book bags.

Megan kept pushing. "I'm just so elated! Aren't you, Alexis? I'm, like, beyond . . ."

Beyond sanity, I thought. But I had to pull my own weight. "Yeah," I said. "Totally. I'm totally, I mean . . . I can imagine that this is going to be a great opportunity to . . . uh . . . grow. And, like, improve."

"Yes!" Adrienne said, practically glowing. "*Totally*!"

"Okay, that's everything!" Kasey said. "Let's go."

"Oh—" Adrienne said, looking around. "My bag."

"I packed it for you," Megan said. "I wanted to help! I love helping! I love being part of a sisterhood!"

Adrienne blinked a couple of times. There might have been a tear glinting in her eye. "Wow . . . thanks, Megan."

"Yay!" Megan said, giving Adrienne a hug. I thought she was kind of laying it on a little thick, but Adrienne was loving it. She "yayed" back and stared dazedly at Megan, like a little kid presented with the most magnificent birthday cake in the world.

"We should drive Adrienne home," Kasey said. "It's a long walk."

Adrienne blushed and self-consciously adjusted the hem of her pink blouse. "You don't have to do that."

"Oh my gosh, of course we do!" Megan squealed. "We're *sisters!*"

As soon as Adrienne disappeared inside her house, Megan flopped back against her seat.

"Holy buckets," she said. "I feel like my eyes are about to pop out of my skull."

"'*I love helping?*'" I asked, raising my eyebrows.

Megan shot me an annoyed glance. "We got the book, didn't we?"

I turned to see Kasey sitting in the backseat, staring out the window. "Thanks a lot, by the way," I said. "Love the thing with the oath. Really appreciate you mentioning *that*. It was great. Just marvelous."

Her face contorted with indignance. "You said you'd let me take care of it!"

"*You* should have told us the whole truth!"

She sat up. "You didn't even tell *part* of the truth, Lexi!"

"Well, it's a good thing I didn't," I said. "If you didn't know enough to know that the oath was, like, the most important detail of the whole thing, you could never have figured it out on your own anyway."

"It doesn't matter," Megan said. "We're going to trash the book, and it'll be a nonissue."

My sister leaned forward, her face between the two front seats. "Maybe I didn't bring it up because I knew you guys would butt in if I did!"

"Hey!" Megan snapped. "Stay sunny!"

Kasey folded her arms and slumped back.

I distracted myself by switching on the radio and searching for something good. Or at least loud.

I briefly considered telling them about how I'd

foiled the oath with my left-hand switcheroo, but what would be the point?

A wave of foreboding passed through me, almost like a premonition of danger.

But danger was what we were avoiding, by destroying Aralt's power center. We'd be getting rid of him before he could come collecting on whatever promises the Sunshine Club had made.

"So let's make an actual plan for destroying the book," I said, as Megan made the turn into Silver Sage Acres.

"If it's not waterproof ink," Kasey said, "we could dump it in the hot tub by the community pool."

"That would ruin the hot tub." Frankly, I was more afraid of the homeowners' association than of Aralt. "We need an incinerator."

"A grill?" Megan asked.

"Yeah, that would work," I said. "We can use the one near the playground."

We sent Kasey inside to make a snack tray—really, we just needed her out of the way—while Megan and I looked for grilling supplies in the garage.

I hoisted the bag of briquettes over my shoulder and turned to go. "I'll carry the charcoal and the book," I said. "Can you bring the lighter fluid and ask Kasey for matches?"

I walked across the street to the tiny park and spread the charcoal out in the grill. Then I delicately set the book, velvet wrapper and all, on the metal surface.

Staring at it, a beautiful piece of handcrafted artistry, I felt a sudden twinge at the thought of dousing it in lighter fluid and setting it on fire.

But then I remembered the way, the previous year, Kasey's evil doll almost convinced me to hide it and kill my family to keep it safe.

"Sorry, Aralt," I said. No question—the book had to burn.

I did let my fingers trace its intricate leatherwork. You didn't often see craftsmanship like this—like our old house, stunning and ornate just for the sake of itself. Not a generic, mass-produced box, like the town house.

I gently lifted the front cover and looked at the title page.

In impossibly elaborate script, it read: LIBRIS EXANIMUS.

Exanimus . . . ? I felt like I'd heard the word, but I couldn't recall where.

What could be keeping Megan? I turned to look for her.

She was four feet away, standing perfectly still.

"Oh!" I said. "You startled me."

Her eyes were wide and curious. In one hand, she

held a book of matches. In the other, a bottle of lighter fluid.

"We protect your dwelling with our blood and our lives," she droned.

Then she lifted the bottle of lighter fluid and doused me with it.

Time seemed to stand still, and I saw the moment suspended before me like I was watching it happen to someone else. Me, dripping noxious fluids; Megan, impassive as a statue.

"What—?" After a few blinking milliseconds, my brain caught up with reality. "Megan, stop!"

She stopped. Her blank eyes fixed on me. Then she raised the bottle again.

I didn't try to talk anymore. I just ran.

She chased after me, flinging lighter fluid as she went. I felt the liquid in my hair, on my clothes. My shirt was soaked in it. The fumes rose up and stung my nostrils.

She cornered me against the wrought-iron fence and sprayed me with the last of it.

"Megan, this is insane!" I said. "Think about what you're doing."

She looked down at the bottle and dropped it into the soft grass, wiping her hands on her jeans. For a second, I thought I'd gotten through to her. She didn't look homicidal; she looked perfectly normal.

Then she opened the book of matches and pulled one out.

Before she could light it, I plunged forward, dodging her, and raced across the street, down the sidewalk toward our town house. I could tell she was behind me, not only keeping up but gaining.

"Kasey!" I yelled, taking the front steps in one leap. "*Kasey!*"

She pulled open the door. "Alexis? What's wrong? Why are you wet?"

"Megan's trying to kill me!"

Megan came tearing up the front walk, trying to light a match as she ran.

I stopped and looked around the house for something we could use to defend ourselves.

But my sister had it covered. As Megan flew into the house, Kasey stuck her leg out, sending Megan sailing through the air and landing hard on her stomach. The matchbook skidded harmlessly across the tiles.

"What is going *on*?" Kasey asked.

I started tearing my clothes off. "Megan tried to kill me," I said. "She was going to set me on fire."

"What are you talking about?" Megan sat up, looking like she'd woken from a heavy sleep.

"You? Me? Matches?" I said. "Ring a bell?"

Megan looked up at me, wincing and pressing her fingertips to her eyes, as if to wipe away tears. "What? No . . . I just felt really peaceful all of a sudden."

I knew it wasn't her fault, but I was shaking with anger and residual fear. "Well, I'm glad you find tranquility in attempted murder."

My sister's face was gray. "Where's the book? Did you burn it?"

"No." I pulled off my pants and dropped the matches in the kitchen sink. "Megan had better things to burn. It's still outside."

"I'll go get it," Kasey said, backing toward the foyer. "Are you sure you're okay?"

"Do you mean, am I going to try to kill Alexis again?" Megan brushed her hands off. Her knees were hot pink, and a small bruise was forming on her chin. She touched it and sucked air sharply through her teeth. "I doubt it. I don't even think I can stand up."

Kasey skittered out the door and I stood at the kitchen sink in my bra and underwear, splashing water on my face, for once not caring if the floor and counters got sloshed. I could still smell the lighter fluid all over me, still recall the vacant look in Megan's eyes. If I tried hard enough, I could imagine the brutal heat of flames coating my body like a second skin.

As I patted my face down, I heard Megan make a

sound that was a cross between a grunt and a squeak.

"Want ice?" I asked. Not waiting for an answer, I got two bags of frozen peas out of the freezer and tossed them to her. She draped one over each knee.

"Sorry, Lex," she said. "I swear, I didn't mean it."

My laugh came out like a huff. "Well, yeah, I hope not."

"I don't understand what happened."

"We were threatening the power center," I said. "It reacted, that's all."

"I guess," she said.

The front door opened and Kasey came in, the rectangle of blue velvet tucked under her arm. Now her colorless face was punctuated by two pink cheeks from the effort of running back to the park. "You guys, look," she said, her voice hoarse.

She set the book on the countertop and flipped the cover open to reveal the title page.

LIBRIS EXANIMUS.

I was about to say I'd heard the phrase before when Megan made a fist in front of her mouth. "The Ouija board!"

I felt supremely stupid for not making the connection myself.

Kasey was already headed back to our parents' bedroom, where Mom's laptop was. It was the only computer in the house. The fact that it lived in our parents' domain meant our research options would be severely limited once the workday was over.

Megan held on to my arm and limped along beside me down the hall. Not wanting to drip lighter fluid on my parents' carpet, I stayed in the tiled hallway with a towel wrapped around me, while Megan hovered over Kasey's shoulder as she typed.

"'*Libris*,'" Megan read. "'Book or volume. *Exanimus*' . . ."

Kasey sighed and sat back.

"'Lifeless,'" Megan said. "'Dead.'"

"So we have a dead book," I said. "Or a live book with somebody dead living in it. Somebody who doesn't want anything happening to his 'dwelling.'"

Megan turned back to Kasey. "So what was the oath for? What did we promise?"

"Hold on," Kasey said, running back to the kitchen. She returned with the book and opened it next to Megan on the bed. "Can you read to me?"

"I'm going to take a shower," I said. "If I got a static shock right now, I'd go up in a fireball."

I shampooed my hair three times and loofahed my body to a bright shade of coral before I was satisfied that I was really noncombustible. By the time I put on a new shirt and a clean pair of jeans and set my other clothes to soak in a cold tubful of water, twenty minutes had passed. I went to my parents' room and plunked down on the bed next to Megan.

"Any progress?" I asked.

Kasey was too busy studying the screen to look up. Megan shot me a heavy glance and handed me her notebook, where she'd been jotting notes as they worked.

I PROMISE LOYALTY TO HE WHO GIVES ABUNDANT (JEWEL/ COSTLY GIFT/TREASURE?) AND (GRACE/FAVOR?).

I INVITE HIM TO A (UNION/ CONNECTION?) AND SWEAR THAT UPON HIS CALL I WILL RETURN A (JEWEL/COSTLY GIFT/TREASURE?).

TOGETHER WE WILL (GROW/ PRODUCE?) AND BESTOW HONOR TO HE WHO IS _____ IN THIS SACRED VESSEL.

THIS I SWEAR TO THEE, ARALT.

"It's Gaelic," Megan said. "Irish."

"What's the missing word?" I asked.

Suddenly, Kasey raised her head slowly and turned

to look at us, her lips open. She licked her dry lips and shook her head.

"Kasey, spit it out," I said.

"Noble," Kasey whispered. Just as I was thinking, Well, that's not so bad, she went on. "Vigorous . . . lusty."

"Lusty," I repeated.

Megan sat back. "*Ew.*"

Kasey was starting to look like this was all too much for her. I was about to suggest we take a break, when the doorbell rang.

We broke into action all at once. Kasey scrambled with her notes at the computer, Megan wrapped the book up and limped back toward her book bag, and I ran to Kasey's room to peer through the blinds.

Tashi stood on our front porch, looking radiantly serene in the way only a Sunshine Club girl could. Her dress, a dark sky blue, was cinched to show off her tiny waist, and her curly hair gleamed in the sun like something out of a Renaissance painting.

The three of us met at the door at the same time. Megan smoothed her hair, and Kasey straightened the sleeves she'd pushed up over her elbows.

Tashi didn't ring again. When I opened the door, she wasn't even looking at me. She gazed out at the sky, which was streaked with the first pink clouds of sunset.

"Hi, guys," she said, turning around.

"Hi," we all said at once.

She looked slightly embarrassed. "So . . . Adrienne just called me in a panic. She can't find the book, and she thinks you might have it, but none of you are answering your phones. She asked me to walk over and check, because I live right down the road."

"Oh, you do?" I asked. "Which unit?"

"One thirty-three," she said. She peered inside my house and gave a short laugh. "It looks . . . the same as this one, actually."

"Big surprise," I said.

That was when I noticed her eyes on my wet hair. I froze.

But she didn't ask about it. "So . . . my mom's holding dinner for me," Tashi said. "I kind of have to go. Do you guys have it?"

"The book?" I asked, glancing behind me into the house. "I don't *think* so . . ."

Tashi raised a finger and pointed. "Could that be it? In that purple backpack?"

We all three spun in place to see a tiny piece of blue velvet sticking out of Megan's bag.

"Oh, my gosh!" Megan exclaimed, walking over to it. "*Wow*, how weird is that? Yeah, look. Somehow it ended up in my bag. I'll drive it back over to her house right now."

"I can take it," Tashi said. "I'm going over there later to study." She had a slow, easy energy about her—like a cowboy. You got the idea that nothing ruffled her. But then I noticed how her left hand was gripping her skirt so tightly that the fabric was wrinkled and sweaty when she let it go.

"But if Adrienne wants it now—" Megan said.

Tashi rolled her eyes, which seemed to me to be pushing the outer edge of Sunshine Club decorum. "Adrienne needs to learn to relax," she said. "She's *way* too obsessed with that book. It'll be good for her to see that she can take her eyes off it for twenty minutes."

There was a pause.

"Are you sure?" Megan asked.

"Honestly?" Tashi said, "*I* don't care. But there's no reason for you to drive all the way out to Lakewood when I'm going over after dinner. If I tell her I have it, she'll be fine."

Megan hesitated.

"Do whatever you want," Tashi said, starting to turn around. "At least call her."

"No," Megan said. "Here, you can have it."

She stepped out into the golden evening light, holding the book like an offering.

Tashi laughed again as she took it. "Adrienne would die if she knew you were just carrying it around. She thinks if somebody sees it, they'll automatically guess it's a sacred vessel and want to steal it or something."

As the door started to close, she reached out and stopped it.

The energy in the room seemed to crackle.

Tashi squinted. "Megan, what happened to your knees?"

"I tripped," Megan said. "Getting out of the—on the—tile. I should probably wear a long skirt tomorrow, or I'll get massacred in Betterment. Bruises are totally un-sunshiny." Then she faked a laugh. *Ho ho ho, massacres are hilarious.*

"I wouldn't worry," Tashi said. "But your shirt is stained."

We all looked at Megan's light green shirt. On each side, near the hem, were a pair of grayish smudges.

"You're right," Megan said.

"That might not come out," Tashi said, turning to leave.

I took that as a personal challenge.

"Stay sunny," I said. She gave me a wry smile and started for the sidewalk. We watched her go all the way past the park before breaking formation.

"She knows we took the book," Megan said. "She totally knows."

"I'm sure she thinks it was an accident," Kasey said,

still gazing out the window. "She's very trusting."

"Here's what we know," Megan said. "Until we can figure out how to safely destroy the book, we're somehow connected with Aralt. We swore that in exchange for all the fun stuff, we would give him some gift. And . . ." She made a disgusted face. "He's lusty."

Fun stuff? I gazed at Megan for maybe a millisecond too long before I started talking. "We can keep researching *libris exanimus*," I said. "But maybe we need to face the fact that we can't fix this tonight. And we definitely can't destroy the book."

"Because it's gone," Megan said.

"Even if it were here," I said. "It's too risky."

The thought popped into my head like a hunch: *But we'll be fine.*

"But we'll be fine," I said.

Megan and Kasey shrugged.

"I guess," Kasey said, not totally convinced.

For the next hour we searched for more information. Kasey manned the computer while I worked on Megan's shirt.

There wasn't much to be learned about a *libris exanimus*. All we'd been able to look up were the definitions of the two words and a paragraph at an occult website making them sound like some urban legend of the dark side: *If any went undiscovered long enough to escape the most common form of destruction (burning by pious locals or clergy), they were generally believed to have been so well-hidden as to have almost certainly decayed completely.*

"Well, ours isn't decayed," Megan said, a hint of defiance in her voice.

But if something was dead, how would you keep it from decaying?

By connecting it to something that was alive?

I sat straight up.

Maybe the oath allowed Aralt to feed off the girls, sort of the way they were feeding off of him. They tapped into whatever it was that made you popular, pretty, and smart, while he got to suck on their life energy. Symbiosis. Like hippos and those little birds that eat their fleas.

"Hey, guys. Listen," I said, picking up the notepad where Megan had written down the translation. "'I invite him to a *union.*' '*Together,* we will grow.'"

Kasey's lips turned down in dread.

I was breathless. "The power center," I said. "It's not the book. It's the girls who took the oath. The Sunshine Club."

"All of us," Megan said slowly.

Not *all* of us. I avoided meeting her glance.

"So what does that mean? What do I look for?" Kasey asked.

"It means there's no point in burning the book. It's just a glorified instruction manual. Maybe it's where he lives when he doesn't have a Sunshine Club to leech off of." Energized by my own insight, I took Kasey's chair at the computer. "Here, let me try."

I typed *Aralt.* But that produced too many results. So we added various words, from *oath* to *ghost.* Nothing worked, until I typed in *Aralt + Ireland + book.*

There was a single result: THE FAMILY HISTORY OF THE O'DOYLES OF COUNTY KILDARE.

I clicked the link and got an error message saying, *Page not found.*

"Dead end," Megan said. She sighed and turned toward the mirror over the dresser, combing through her hair with her fingers.

"Not necessarily," I said, going back to the search engine. I clicked on the link that said CACHED, which pulled up an archived version of the page. That brought up the image of a single paragraph of all-caps red writing on a black background.

I AM REMOVING ALL CONTENT DUE TO EXTREME PRIVACY VIOLATIONS WHICH I FEEL HAVE GONE ABOVE AND BEYOND WHAT I WOULD OF CONSIDERED POLITE OR MAYBE EVEN LEGAL!!! BUT I DON'T FEEL LIKE FIGHTING U FASCISTS ANYMORE ITS JUST A STUPID WEBPAGE!

"Um . . . interesting guy," Kasey said. "But it still doesn't tell us anything."

Searching the phone directory for "O'Doyle" produced thousands of listings.

"Hold on," I said, directing the browser to another website. I typed in the domain name where the error message had been posted, and the registry information popped up.

ADMINISTRATIVE CONTACT: 233Я9Ω/V^73Я
123 N0NE 0F YOUR BUS1NESS STREET
N0WHERE, USA

. . . And a fake phone number.

"Oh, *now* we have all the answers," Kasey sighed, flopping onto the bed.

I stared at the administrative contact name. It was just a bunch of letters, numbers, and symbols, but something about it was familiar. All of the 0s were zeroes. And the *i* in *business* was a one.

"It's leet." I wrote *1337* on Kasey's notebook. "L-e-e-t. One of the guys in the Doom Squad thought he was some mastermind hacker. He wrote everything that way."

I went back to the search engine and typed in ZEERGONATER.

A list of results popped up—Zeergonater's postings

on various Internet forums, mostly about urban legends and conspiracies, with a good dose of video game chat thrown in besides.

"This doesn't help us," Kasey said. "It's not like he posted his real name anywhere."

"Yeah, but . . . he had to slip up sometime," I said. I read through some of the postings. Zeergonater had a chip on his shoulder the size of San Francisco, and he seemed hyperaware of covering his tracks, staying anonymous.

Finally, we found a clue. On a post he made about why he chose to live where he lived, Zeergonater wrote that in the span of three hours he could be skiing, surfing, or camping—plus, there was no sales tax.

"Oregon," Kasey said.

"What makes you think that?" I asked.

"No sales tax," she said. "Mountains. Ocean. Forests."

Searching for O'Doyles in Oregon still left us with hundreds of results.

"Go back to the thing about skiing," Kasey said.

I clicked back through the history and scrolled down to Zeergonater's second entry in the thread, where he'd posted a picture of his prized snow skis.

"Look," Kasey said, pointing at the screen. Lightly etched in the red paint of each ski were three letters: LBO.

I scrolled down the phone directory listings.

Lance B. O'Doyle. And a phone number. I grabbed my cell phone and dialed.

"Hello?"

"Hello, is this Lance?"

A pause. "Maybe."

"I have a question for you. About a person named Aralt."

"I told you people to leave me alone!" he snapped. "I took down the stupid webpage. It was just a genealogy thing I did for my grandmother!"

"I don't know what you mean," I said. "I don't care about the page or why you took it down."

He paused. "Then . . . how do you know about Aralt?"

"I just heard about him somewhere. I'm curious."

"Ha," he said. "Haven't you ever heard that curiosity killed the cat? Listen, little girl. You don't want to get messed up with Aralt. There are people out there who can—and *will*—wipe the floor with you."

I'm going to be honest. It sounded a little melodramatic to me. "Please," I said. "I'll never bother you again. Just tell me what you know about Aralt."

"Oh, I *know* you'll never bother me again," he said. "You'll never *find* me again."

But he hadn't refused to answer my questions.

"Your website said something about County Kildare?" I said. "Ireland, right? Is that where he's from?"

He sighed. "The O'Doyles—my ancestors—were one of the best families in the county, even though they weren't titled. Titles aren't everything."

There was a defensive edge to his voice that told me I'd better turn on the flattery. "No, of course not."

"Aralt Edmund Faulkner was the Duke of Weymouth. He lucked into the title after his uncle died at sea. He was a playboy—he'd make women fall in love with him, then break their hearts and leave them ruined. And it was a bad thing to be a ruined woman back then. A few of them killed themselves. So his family basically shipped him off to Ireland to keep him out of trouble."

"Sounds like a jerk," I dared to say.

"Yeah, well, when he messed with the O'Doyles, he went too far," Lance said, and I heard a note of pride in his voice. "My great-great-great-great-great-grandfather was Captain Desmond O'Doyle, an officer in the Royal Navy. He came home after a long campaign to find his wife five months pregnant with another man's child."

"Aralt's?" I asked.

"Bingo," Lance said. "She was so overcome with shame that she threw herself off a bridge."

"That's terrible."

"So Desmond challenged Aralt to a duel, which of

course Aralt lost, because he was a lazy playboy. And even as he lay on his deathbed, another young woman he'd seduced was with him, weeping and professing her love."

"Who was that?"

"Some peasant. Maybe a traveler—like a gypsy? She disappeared after he died, but legend says she took his heart with her so he would always be hers."

Um, ew. "And what about the book?" I asked. "The *libris exanimus*?"

"The what?"

I decided to change the subject. "Who made you take down your website?"

"I don't know who they are," he said. "They're cowards. They hid behind a pair of lawyers who did everything but break my kneecaps."

"But why?" I asked.

"Who knows? They aren't descendants—the line died with the Duke, I'm happy to say. I mean, out of twenty pages of history, I had *one* that mentioned Aralt Faulkner, and they sicced their lawyers on me like a couple of junkyard dogs." He paused. "Now. How did you find me?"

As I answered his question, I heard clicking keys in the background. By the time we were off the phone, the Internet postings and picture of the skis would be long gone.

"Now, listen," he said. "I'm not kidding, little

girl. You don't want to mess with these people."

Kasey tugged on my sleeve. She flipped back through her notebook to the page marked OUIJA BOARD. Under EXANIM was written ELSPETH.

"Um, one more question—was Desmond's wife's name Elspeth, by any chance?" I asked.

"No," he said. "It was Radha."

I shook my head at my sister.

"Was *anybody* named that?" Kasey whispered.

"What was that? Who's there?" Lance asked. "Who's listening?"

"Nobody," I said. "Just my little sister."

"Okay," Lance said. "Now listen up, Dora the Explorer. If you dig any deeper on Aralt, you're going to get in way over your head. Why don't you and your little sister go find some dolls to play with?"

The line went dead.

"Dolls," I said. "Right."

"He's a little uptight," Kasey said.

"We know who Aralt was," Megan said. "That's pretty good for one day."

It didn't seem all that good to me. "Knowing he was a womanizer doesn't help us. It just reinforces the whole 'lusty' thing."

"And the gypsy—that's something." Megan went to my mother's dresser and stared dreamily at herself

156

in the mirror. "It's kind of romantic, don't you think?"

"Which part?" I asked. "That he left a trail of ruined women, or that they killed themselves to erase the shame of falling for the wrong guy?"

She drew back, looking offended. "I'm not saying I want it to happen to me. I'm just saying, to love someone so much you'd give up everything for them is . . ."

"It's sick," Kasey said. "Sorry."

Megan lifted her nose snootily. "We'll have to agree to disagree."

It wasn't that I approved of the way Megan was defending Aralt. But when you loved someone—really loved them—was it really so wrong to want to give up everything for their sake?

You know, objectively speaking.

I'd never thought about it before. I studied the computer screen.

Kasey closed out of the browser. "I'm with Megan," she said. "I think that might be enough for today."

I was about to reply when we heard the rumbling of the garage door.

"Mom's home!" I said. "Clear the history!"

I handed Megan her shirt, and she ran to the bathroom to change. Tashi had been right. None of my usual stain-removal methods had even come close to working.

Kasey's fingers dashed around the keyboard. "I'm

going to say I've been working on an English essay," she said. "You go!"

I hurried to the living room and plunked down on the sofa seconds before Mom came in from the garage.

She reached the end of the hall and looked me up and down. "Honey, you're not ready!"

"For what?" I asked.

"Are you kidding?" she asked. "Your interview! We really should have left already."

Oh, right. Young Visionaries.

Megan waved good-bye and left, and I went back to my room and stared into my closet, at a total loss.

Finally, I dug out a ruffly red blouse Mom had given me for Christmas and a slim-fitting gray skirt one of her coworkers gave me (people who lose everything in a fire get a lot of hand-me-downs). I tucked the shirt in and, on impulse, wove a thin yellow belt of Megan's through the belt loops. And I found another pair of Mrs. Wiley's cast-off shoes from the pile in the corner—dark brown leather pumps with little cutouts around the edges. I caught sight of myself in the mirror and decided the outfit was all right—but I couldn't suppress the unease I felt about the greasy, awkward girl who was wearing it.

Did I really go around looking like this all the time? Had I only realized it by being surrounded by a mob of beautiful girls?

I went to the bathroom and brushed my hair back into a ponytail. Then I started experimenting with Kasey's makeup. I was unfamiliar with the brushes and powders and bottles and palettes, but I bumbled my way through, trying to recall what I'd seen Megan do.

To my relief, with each stroke of the makeup brushes, my reflection became less offensive.

Mom came to the door of the bathroom and glanced at her watch in a very obvious way.

"Almost done," I said.

"We're already behind," Mom said. "I'm very disappointed about this. You know how important punctuality is."

"Can I borrow your dangly earrings with the roses?"

That caught her off-guard. "Yes—but I wish you'd hurry. Do you *really* need to wear three shades of eye shadow?"

"Mom," I said, turning toward her. "You standing there nagging doesn't help. Go get the earrings!"

She returned a second later and dropped them on the counter. "I'll be in the kitchen whenever Your Highness is ready," she said, walking away. "Something's really gotten into you tonight, Alexis."

You don't know how right you are, I thought, leaning in to blend my eye shadow.

11

"WARREN? ALEXIS WARREN?"

The receptionist directed me to a conference room with a long table in the center. On the far side were the five judges, including Farrin McAllister. On the near side was a single chair.

It looked like a firing squad.

I wondered if I was supposed to say hi to Farrin, or pretend we'd never met, or what. But as soon as I sat down, she spoke.

"I talked to Alexis when she dropped off her application," she said, not looking up at me. "I was quite impressed with her work."

I could tell that Farrin's word carried weight among her fellow judges. A couple of them sat up straighter and looked at me almost like *I* was the one who needed to be impressed. The guy on the end even straightened his bow tie.

"So . . . tell us what photography means to you," the woman in the middle said.

"What it means to me?" I repeated. Under the table, my hands fidgeted.

They waited.

What came to mind first were a bunch of bland platitudes: It means sharing my ideas with the world. It means creating a beautiful and exciting image. "I . . . don't think it means anything."

Good-bye, car, good-bye.

"I mean," I said, and suddenly the answer sort of cobbled itself together in my head, "it's not something I think about. I don't do it to mean something. I just do it. It's part of me."

Farrin leaned closer. "What's your favorite photograph?"

Now that I could answer without thinking. "'Can of Peas,' by Oscar Toller."

"Tell us why," she said.

"Oscar Toller was a photographer who found out he was going blind. So every day, he took a picture of something he wanted to remember. And one of his pictures was a can of peas on the kitchen counter. And the way the light hits it, it's almost like there's this halo."

They were all watching me, and I wondered if I'd made a huge tactical error. "Can of Peas" wasn't one of Oscar Toller's more famous images.

Nobody said anything, so I faltered on. "And even though it's just an ordinary tin can sitting on a kitchen counter, it makes me think that the real power of photography isn't finding a new way to look at stuff, but like . . . showing other people how *I* see things."

"You think the way you see the world is special?" the man in the bow tie asked.

"I don't know," I said. "Probably not. But even if it's not . . . being able to share it with someone—that's what's special."

I noticed that my portfolio was being passed down the line, and my heart fluttered. But the words kept coming, so I kept saying them. "I mean, a tin can is just a tin can to most people. But if it were the last one you'd ever see . . . it might be beautiful. Or sad. And you feel that when you look at that photo."

There was a long silence. Suddenly I felt a layer of nervousness melt away. I wasn't sorry for anything I thought about photography. I was just going to answer.

"At least, I do," I said.

"You don't work with digital?" one of the women asked. "Or color?"

"I had some color pictures," I said. "But they were lost."

She looked up, alarmed. "Losing stuff" probably wasn't high on the list of intern qualifications.

"In a fire," I added.

A few of the judges made sympathetic noises, and I realized that, if they were photographers, they understood what it would mean to lose everything.

"I might get a digital camera for Christmas," I said. "Until then, I just work in the darkroom."

"At home?" someone asked.

"No, at Surrey Community College." I shrugged. "I had one at home, but I lost it."

A couple of them looked up at me and smiled, getting the joke.

"Have you taken classes?" the bow-tie man asked.

Surely one disastrous week didn't count. "No."

"Good for you," one of the women muttered, and they all laughed.

"Do you think you could survive a summer making coffee and photocopies and answering phones?" someone else asked.

I looked straight into her eyes. "I've survived worse."

They were quiet.

Then Farrin spoke. "One last thing."

I looked up at her.

"Describe your work in one word," she said.

The word slipped out of my mouth before I could stop myself: "Mine."

* * *

As Mom and I snaked through the crowd of my competitors, I was glad I'd worn something unique—there was a punk boy with a Mohawk, a boy wearing a purple suit with a skinny tie, and a super-preppy girl who reminded me of Carter. Everybody else was dressed like they were going to a fancy dinner with their great aunts. They dissolved into the background.

Behind me, I heard the sound of the doors opening, and several sets of footsteps.

"We'll be resuming after a five-minute break," said the man with the bow tie, and the judges came filing out.

We'd made it out to the car when Mom remembered she'd left her book on the bench inside. She went back to get it. I stood, looking down at the recent calls list on my phone to see if Carter had tried to reach me. So I didn't see Farrin approach.

"'Can of Peas,'" she said. "Really?"

I nearly dropped my phone.

"You don't like it?" I managed to ask.

"It doesn't matter what I think," she said, smiling like the Mona Lisa. "We asked *you* the question."

"I love it," I said. "I don't know how to put it into words."

"That's not your job," she said. "You're a photographer. But yes, I love it too."

I tried to smile back, but I'm pretty sure it came out as a lopsided smirk.

"You should wear your hair back more often," Farrin said. "You have good facial planes."

"Thank you," I said, trying not to blush.

It didn't matter, though—Farrin wasn't looking at my face anymore.

"Let me see your hand," she said, her voice hushed.

I lifted my right hand for inspection, thinking maybe there was some sort of ideal camera-holding bone structure.

Farrin touched my wrist and looked at me.

"I knew there was something about you," she said. "But I would never have guessed . . ."

She let go of my hand, and I stuck it in my pocket.

"You don't have a darkroom at home?" she asked.

I shook my head.

Mom was on her way back, close enough to be watching with intense curiosity.

"Please," Farrin said. "Feel free to come here and use mine. Anytime."

She took off, as excited as a kid getting saddled up for a pony ride, and all I could do was stand there and try to keep my jaw off the ground.

"What on earth was that all about?" Mom asked.

"I have no idea," I said.

Either I had the best camera hands west of the Mississippi, or Farrin had been waiting a long time to find someone who liked "Can of Peas" as much as she did.

THE NEXT MORNING my skin looked as splotchy as a mud-spattered car, and I could see dark circles under my eyes, no matter how much concealer I used. My face seemed wider and my features seemed flat and some-how . . . swinelike.

Kasey stopped at the bathroom door and watched me studying myself. "Lexi," she said, her voice cautious, "what are you doing?"

I leaned in to look closer, and immediately regretted it. My pores looked as big as craters. "Did it suddenly get more humid this week?" I asked. "Do I look bloated to you?"

"No." She stood next to me. "You look perfectly fine. Same as usual."

"So I'm usually a troll?" I asked. "Good to know."

Megan picked us up, as petite and perfect as ever, making me feel even worse about myself. But after we parked, she flipped her visor down and began frantically primping.

"Megan, please," I said. She looked a million times better than I did. For her to pretend she didn't was actually a little insulting.

"I'm a gorgon," she answered, using her pinkie finger to touch up the gloss at the corners of her lips.

If she was a gorgon—*note to self, look up "gorgon"*—what did that make me?

When she finally felt presentable, we went inside. Walking through the halls of the school was like torture, with the sheen of the fluorescent hall lights reflecting off my bulbous nose.

I sat down next to Carter on the courtyard wall.

"I'm really sorry about yesterday," he said. "I overreacted."

God, that was only yesterday? I felt like I'd lived a month since then. I could hardly even remember why we'd fought. "Me too."

"We should go out to dinner tomorrow," he said. "I'd say tonight, but I have therapy."

"Okay," I said, but then I remembered—there was a club meeting every Monday, Wednesday, and Friday. "Actually, I don't think I can. I have a . . . thing."

He looked up. "What kind of a thing?"

I didn't want to say it was the Sunshine Club and ruin our delicate peace.

"A dentist appointment," I said. "Maybe Thursday?"

"Yeah," he said. "That should be fine."

"How was your party?" I asked, eager to change the subject.

"Oh my God," he said, reflexively reaching up and covering his ears. "*Shrill*. Those girls are nice, but when they get excited, they do this screaming thing."

"I'm sorry I missed it," I said, leaning my head on his shoulder.

He laughed. "I'll bet you are."

And I knew we were good again.

For the rest of the day, I was so overwhelmed with relief that I couldn't even get upset about my greasy face or my disproportionate feet or the scaly skin on the back of my hands. I sat next to Carter at lunch and focused on how good it felt to be forgiven, and how great he was for caring about me despite all of my very obvious shortcomings.

Kasey stood in my doorway, a strange look on her face. "Want to do some research?"

I sighed and sat up. "What hopeless cause are we Googling today?"

She didn't answer. And instead of turning down the

168

hall to our parents' room, she went back to hers. I followed her.

"Kasey?" I asked. "What are you doing? Did you bring Mom's computer in here?"

Kasey sat on the floor. "No," she said. "We're not using the computer."

She reached under the dust ruffle and pulled out a Ouija board.

"We're asking Elspeth."

"What?" I asked. "No way! Where did you even get that thing?"

"Lexi, she knew about the *libris exanimus*. She might know more. She tried to warn us—she wants to help."

"But she could be lying, for all we know!"

"We're just looking for information," Kasey said. "We don't have to do what she says." She pointed to a spot on the carpet. "Sit."

Despite my reservations, the idea of maybe getting some real answers was tempting. So I sat and let my fingers rest on the planchette next to Kasey's.

She looked at me. "What do we say? I've never done this before."

I leaned over. "Um . . . hello? We're looking for Elspeth?" I looked up at Kasey, who shrugged. "It's Alexis and Kasey Warren from Surrey, California?"

Kasey sighed. "Somehow I don't think that's going to work."

"Maybe there are multiple Elspeths," I said. "Maybe one lives in Lydia's board and one lives in this one."

Kasey shook her head. "Don't make jokes."

My fingers lurched.

Kasey and I looked at each other as the pointer began to move across the board.

"For the record, I really don't like doing this," I said. "And I don't like you doing it. I think we should find another way."

"Stay," Kasey said, her voice shaking.

"What?"

"That's what she just spelled—*stay*."

My stomach churned. We already had one supernatural problem. Wouldn't inviting Elspeth back potentially make things twice as bad?

We still had two options: stay, or leave. I was leaning heavily toward *leave*, but Kasey swallowed hard and charged ahead.

"Elspeth, we need your help," she said. "Can you tell us about Aralt?"

For a long, tense minute, there was no response.

This is useless.

But then the pointer began to move. We awkwardly tried to keep our fingers steady.

Utterly pointless. A waste of time.

I looked up at Kasey, her eyes wide and afraid, stretching her upper body to allow the planchette to travel across the board.

What kind of fool would think you could solve a ghost problem with another ghost?

T-R-Y

The movement was agonizingly slow, like watching a little old lady cross the street on the "Don't Walk" signal. My frustration grew until I was on the verge of pulling my fingers away and telling Kasey I was done.

Without warning, the pointer jerked out from under our hands.

It moved fine—better, actually—without our help. I huddled close to my sister, gripping her elbow.

A-G-A-N

"Try what again?" I said, slumping back. I didn't *want* to try again. I wanted to stop this, opening doors we didn't know how to shut. Inviting trouble for ourselves.

She could be dangerous. We have no reason to trust her.

N-O-J-U-S-T-T-E-A-S-I-N-G

"See?" I said aloud, even though I hadn't actually voiced any of my doubts.

"No, just teasing," Kasey read. She sat back on her heels. "So . . . *don't* try again?"

"Wow, Elspeth, how incredibly helpful," I said, patting the pointer as if it were a dog.

Kasey slapped my hand. "Be nice!"

"I don't want to be nice," I said, feeling my face begin to flush. "She's messing with us, Kasey!"

"I'm sure she can explain," Kasey said, shifting her body slightly away from me. "Elspeth, please tell us something so we'll know you're on our side."

"Like she couldn't just lie," I sniffed, crossing my arms and turning away.

But as she began spelling again, I turned back.

A–B–A–N

Staring down at it, I realized that I was holding my breath, bracing for some sort of impact. And then, before I could stop myself, all of that energy focused into a little bomb of anger, and I brought my fist down on top of the pointer.

Kasey gasped. "Why'd you do that, Lexi?"

Her eyes were wide, wary.

"I don't know," I said. Another flush was spreading through my cheeks, but this one was embarrassment. Avoiding my sister's eyes, I focused on collecting dust bunnies from the edge of her bed skirt. "I guess I'm tired of being yanked around."

"She wasn't yanking us around—she was giving us answers! To questions we asked! And now she's gone."

Kasey flopped sideways onto the carpet. I turned away, just in time to hear her inhale sharply. *"Lexi,* what's going on with the board?"

I looked down at it. Seeping out of its seams, almost like an oozing wound, was a thick black goo, chalky and opaque.

"What is that?" Kasey asked. She started to reach her hand toward it, but I grabbed her arm.

"I don't know," I said. "But don't touch it."

As the black stuff reached the edge of the planchette, the little wooden piece gave a startled jolt and tried to move away. It struggled to get across the board, but with a sizzling sound, the substance bubbled up and covered it completely. It was like one of those nature shows where the crocodile grabs a zebra at the watering hole. Kasey and I watched breathlessly as all of the blackness on the board converged on the big blob in the center. It pulsed lightly, like it was breathing, and then made another furious bubbling sound and evaporated, revealing the undamaged pointer.

Kasey reached down and touched it timidly. "Elspeth?"

She tried a few more times, but Elspeth was gone.

"What was that?" Kasey asked.

"I don't know," I said. But there *was* something familiar about it. The way it absorbed light absolutely, without any luminance of its own. The creature in Lakewood had been that same kind of shadowy black. I almost said something, but Kasey spoke first.

"I hope she's okay." Kasey stared down at the lifeless planchette. "That kind of looked like it hurt."

I was relieved when she began to box up the Ouija board.

Elspeth wasn't helpful, anyway—another gut feeling.

"I'm not sure if it's worth it, to be honest," I said. "She was just joking around! She even said so. And we don't want to know what happens if more of that black stuff shows up."

Kasey shook her head slowly. "No," she said. "I guess not." She carried the box to her closet and buried it under a pile of clutter.

My childish anger had melted away, leaving me feeling slightly guilty. "Anything else you want to try?"

She shook her head and looked up from behind her hair. "I think I'm done for the day."

My heart began to flutter in my chest. "That's too bad," I said.

But it was a lie.

Because something inside of me was glad.

13

THE NEXT MORNING, I sat down next to Carter. Was it just me, or did he seem distant? Distracted?

"Carter," I said, just wanting his attention. When he looked straight at me, I regretted it, imagining how grotesque I must look—my wide, shiny face washed out in the sunlight, revealing my yellow teeth with every word I spoke.

"Did you floss this morning?" he asked.

I reared away—was he trying to hint at something?

"I'll be right back," I said, hurrying toward the girls' restroom.

I leaned in to inspect my teeth in the hazy mirror. They were the color of old mayonnaise, and thanks to my wisdom teeth starting to grow, the bottom ones were crowding in toward one another like a mob of miscreants—but there was nothing actually stuck between them.

Then I recalled my fictional dentist appointment.

I sighed, blotted my skin with a paper towel, and went back outside.

Carter was talking to a girl.

As I got closer, I recognized Zoe. At the party I'd found her dull, but now she struck me as beguilingly wholesome. Her pale blond hair reached almost all the way down her back, glowing in the sunlight like corn silk. Her skin was peachy and fresh, and her features were elfin. I felt like an elephant trundling across the court-yard toward them.

Carter held his hand out to me when I got close. But I didn't take it. Instead, I stuck my hands in the pockets of my skirt to hide my ragged fingernails and sat down.

"You guys haven't officially met, have you?" Carter asked. "Alexis, this is Zoe . . . Zoe, my girlfriend . . . Alexis."

"Hi, Alexis," Zoe said, smiling like a skin-cream model.

Zoe, my girlfriend was all I heard. Why would you ever want *Alexis, my girlfriend* if you could have this beaming, healthy young thing?

I felt something rise in my chest as humiliated tears pricked at my tear ducts. I wiped them away and stared at the sky, trying not to hear the happy lilt of Carter and Zoe's conversation.

"I have to go," I said, standing abruptly. In answer to

Carter's questioning look, I added, "—talk to my sister."

"Okay," Zoe said. "Nice to meet you!"

Even her voice was sweet and springlike. I wanted to knock her down.

"Hey, Lex, you've got a spot," Carter said, grabbing my shirt to hold me still. I looked down to find a dark gray smear on the side of my jeans.

"Oh, no! You should probably try to wash that off," Zoe said, clucking with fake concern.

"It won't come off," I said, pulling my shirt out of Carter's reach. "See you later."

Now I had a giant sloppy stain on my pants, which was reason enough to flee. But more than that, I wanted to get away, hide my hideous self from Carter before he had the chance to realize the enormous mistake he'd made when he decided to be my boyfriend.

I got up early the next morning and spent an extra twenty minutes picking out a cute skirt and white shirt, wrestling with my hair, and slathering on makeup. I pictured Carter's face lighting up when I found him, enchanted, enthralled, captivated—all the Disney princess words.

But he hardly even looked up from his book.

"No cavities?" Carter asked.

This time, I remembered the lie. "Nope," I said, sitting down, trying to spread my skirt out beneath my legs so the grit of the wall didn't touch my skin.

"Are you all right?" he asked. "You seem . . ."

"I'm fine," I said, sucking in my stomach.

"Looking forward to dinner tonight?" he asked.

"Oh," I said. "Yeah." Another chance to gain a pound or two. Just what I needed.

"Hey, do you mind if I pick you up at seven instead of eight?" he asked. "I kind of need to get home early so I can finish my speech."

Right. Student government speeches were tomorrow. That meant an assembly in the auditorium, bright lights, me in the front row. Everybody looking at me.

I shook my head. "Not at all," I said.

Finally, he lowered the book and turned to me. "Lex, what's wrong? All week you've been kind of out of it. Is your sister doing all right?"

I told myself to focus and gave him as much of a smile as I could muster. "Kasey's good. I'm good too."

"Okay," he said. "I've just been worried."

Worried how? I wanted to ask. Worried that when the school sees the drab chubster you're dating, it will make them question your judgment and cost you the election?

Miss Nagesh noticed my efforts, at least. She gave me the once-over and said, "Ooh la la! Check out Miss Fancypants!"

She was cataloguing a new shipment of audiovisual equipment, and I was starting the 400s—Languages. Eager to do something that would take my mind off Carter, I lost myself in the work.

"We're going to have to clean off some shelves in the equipment room," Miss Nagesh said, interrupting me.

I glanced up to see her holding an ancient film canister.

"I hate to lose these cheesy old filmstrips, but they take up so much room," she said. "Oh, well. How are you?"

"I'm up to . . ." I looked down and blinked.

"What?" she said.

"The five-forties," I said.

She gave me a confused smile. "No, you just started the four hundreds."

"I know," I said. "But I . . ."

She knelt and looked at the shelves. "Wow," she said at last. "Okay, well. Great."

I stared at the hundreds of books I'd reshelved.

"Maybe you should wear your fancypants more often," Miss Nagesh said, carrying the film can away.

When she was gone, I started back at the beginning of the section and skimmed every single number on every single book.

They were perfect.

* * *

The Sunshine Club called a special meeting that day. I tried to tuck myself into a far corner so no one would notice me. I was hyperaware of how much less polished I looked than the other girls, and a sense of certainty grew inside me that someone was going to know I was a fraud and call me on it. No way could a real member be so awkward and ugly.

Part of me was convinced that the whole reason for the meeting was to expose my lies.

What would they do to me when the truth came out?

I held my breath during Betterment, petrified that someone would bring up my lack of sunniness. My hands went cold when Lydia stood up and her eyes brushed over mine.

"Being part of this club involves a commitment," she said. "Not just to come to the meetings and try hard to be your best, but to accept the gifts that Aralt wants to give you."

Like *they* needed gifts. Every time I looked at another Sunshine Club member, I was reminded again. They all seemed to get prettier every day, while I felt uglier and more like a reject. It was completely unfair that Aralt would keep showering them with beauty and poise while I was left out.

And all because I'd gamed the system by swearing with the wrong hand.

We were up to twelve girls, and I would have sworn there were twenty-two eyes on me as Lydia spoke. I waited to hear my name. To hear an accusation that I was a faker, an imposter.

But then Lydia smiled. "I just wanted to remind everyone. Remember, Aralt loves you—not just for who you are, but for who you *can* be."

And that was it. That was the whole meeting. No one outed me, no one even seemed suspicious.

They still don't know, I thought.

I ducked away as quickly as possible. I was outside waiting by Megan's car when she and Kasey came out.

"What's wrong, Alexis?" Megan asked.

"I have to get home," I said. My voice was brittle. "I have dinner with Carter tonight."

At home I locked my bedroom door and threw my closet open, searching for something that might look okay. I found a simple black dress and put it on, then slipped on a pair of black shoes and went to the bathroom to do my hair. I brushed my hair back into a high ponytail and put on red lipstick and mascara.

Then I inspected myself.

Wrong. Wrong, wrong, wrong. On so many levels I couldn't even explain it. The boxy shoes made my legs

181

look stumpy. The sleeves of the dress stopped on the fattest point of my arms, and the high neckline made me look about eighty. Plus my severe pink hair and red lips made me look like a decommissioned Russian spy robot from the 1980s.

I stared at the mirror, wondering what Carter would say if he saw me. . . .

What the Sunshine Club would say.

He deserves better than this.

And I thought of the way everyone else managed to look like they were right out of the pages of one of the fashion magazines that were passed around the lunch table every day.

The clock said it was five. Two hours—was that enough time?

What difference did it make? I had no choice. Worst-case scenario was staring at me in the mirror.

I called Lydia.

Forty-five minutes later, I sat on the edge of the tub while she massaged dye into my scalp. While it processed, she read a magazine, and I tried to focus on the book I was supposed to be reading for English.

Finally, the timer dinged and Lydia rinsed the dye out. I looked at myself in the mirror. My face was still shiny and puffy, my eyes were too close together, and I saw with alarming clarity the bushiness of my eyebrows.

But my hair, which just an hour earlier had looked like a Brillo pad on a bad day, was a relief. It was soaking wet, but it was dark and healthy looking. Pink hair had been part of my identity for years, but already I knew I wasn't going to miss it.

"Ready for a cut?" Lydia asked, smiling. She wore a crisp black apron over her white button-down shirt and pleated red skirt. With her hair turned under, she looked like a retro housewife. In a million years, I'd never try to handle hair dye in a white shirt, but she didn't get so much as a droplet on herself. She picked up a pair of wicked-looking scissors. "I was thinking longish layers that end around your shoulders."

"Do whatever you want," I said.

"I intend to," she said, using her left hand to fluff my hair. "I'm so happy that you changed your mind, Alexis."

I had no choice but to look almost straight up at her. "Me too."

"I meant what I said at the meeting, you know. Aralt gives us so much," she said, "and asks for so little."

I was sure that was true for her and the rest of them. But so far, all I'd gotten out of the Sunshine Club was a healthy dose of paranoia.

Her hands—and the shears—were outside of my peripheral vision.

And I realized how very, very exposed my throat was. I could feel the delicate curve of it, stretched out like an apple on a cutting board.

I snapped my head down.

Lydia laughed. "Oh, Alexis. What are you thinking?"

"Nothing," I said, trying not to be obvious as I tucked my chin down protectively over my neck.

"I'm sure that's true," she said, and her smile was like a poem in a different language.

She went to work, combing and parting and cutting. Big chunks fell to the floor. After the cut, she attacked me with a blow-dryer, cans of hairspray, tweezers, and a whole palette of makeup.

"Ready?" she asked.

I wasn't sure.

"Too bad! Turn around!" Lydia said, like an inventor unveiling a miraculous machine.

Then I saw myself, and I understood why.

"Who is that?" I asked. Because it wasn't *me* staring out of the mirror.

I didn't have hair that hung in smooth waves of chocolate-colored silk. And I didn't have eyebrows that arched like a 1940s movie star's. Or eyelashes so thick and long that they made little picture frames for my blue eyes. Which, by the way, were not usually that blue.

And my lips didn't look like that.

So it couldn't be me.

I took a deep breath. But it *was* me. This was the new Alexis, like it or not.

Like it, came a little voice from inside me.

And something, some sensation, came bubbling through my body, starting at my feet and ending in a shiver at the crown of my head. It wasn't like *I* was happy. It was like that feeling you get watching someone open a gift you gave them, when you know *they're* going to love it.

This is what he deserves.

I felt my chest tighten. Because the "he" that popped into my head wasn't Carter.

It was Aralt.

Lydia leaned in close to my ear. "Can you feel it?" she whispered. "He's pleased."

I watched the reflection of the dazzling stranger shake her head. "But Lydia, you don't understand. I'm not the same as the rest of you. There's something I . . ."

"What, your left-handed stunt?"

I waited for a blast of anger. But she gave my hair an affectionate ruffle.

"It doesn't mean anything, Alexis. The hand on the book—Adrienne made that up because she thinks it looks cool."

Inside my head, my thoughts reeled. I *had* taken the oath. I *was* connected to Aralt. And everything I was feeling was tied to the Sunshine Club.

"You poor thing," Lydia said, her voice as sweet as honey. "All this time, you've been feeling so alone. But you were one of us all along."

One of us all along.

I should have been scared, right? Or worried? Angry?

But I just couldn't make myself feel those things.

"All he wants," Lydia whispered, "is for you to be the best you can be."

The thought came to me again: *This is what he deserves.*

And then a sparkling happiness burst and made my whole body feel radiant and beautiful, brilliant and clean. After a week of being filthy and hideous, it was enough to make me go limp with relief.

Lydia rested her chin on my shoulder. In the mirror, I could see her delighted smile. *"Aralt thinks you're lovely."*

Mom started to turn toward us. "Did you offer Lydia anything to drink?"

Her mouth formed into an O, and she set her wooden spoon down on the counter.

"Hi," I said.

"Well, honey," she said. Her eyes went wide and then narrow, like she couldn't focus.

True, it was more dramatic than Kasey's gradual transformation had been, but I wouldn't have thought it was enough to strike a person dumb.

Apparently I was wrong.

"Thank you, Mrs. Warren, but I can't stay," Lydia said, daintily popping a single grape into her mouth. "And I know Alexis has dinner plans."

Mom nodded, still staring at me.

"I'm going to go say good-bye to Kasey," Lydia said, walking away. I listened to her shoes *click click click* on the tile floor.

Still, Mom didn't say a word.

I was sort of afraid she was having a neurological episode or something. "Do you like it?"

"Alexis, I . . . You look beautiful, but . . ."

But? There was a but? Throughout my entire high school career, Mom's fondest wish was that I would somehow find my way back to the social norm—to mall-bought clothes, shiny hair, tasteful makeup.

I'd expected . . . I don't know. Squealing. Clapping. Hugs.

Not a *but*.

"I do. I like it. You're stunning, but . . ."

But again. I took the offensive. "I thought it was

time for a change. You know, I'm going to start thinking about college soon and all that. And the photography contest."

"It's just so . . . different," Mom said. "How long is it going to take you to do that to your hair every day?"

I shrugged. "It's just a blow-dry."

She gave me a long appraisal. "You certainly *look* grown up."

The glow inside me faded. "I thought you'd be excited."

"Oh, honey." Mom came closer and hugged me. "I really am. It's a bit of a shock, that's all. And you know there was nothing wrong with you before."

I pulled away stiffly. "But why not improve? If you can?"

She didn't have an answer for that. She sighed, then tried to cover it by raising her hands in surrender. "Maybe I just don't like the idea of my two little girls growing up."

The polite thing to do was to smile as though she'd made me feel better, so that was what I did—even though she hadn't. I walked away, feeling self-conscious. It was a relief to turn the corner into the hallway, where I found Lydia and Kasey standing outside the bathroom, talking.

Kasey didn't look surprised to see me.

"Isn't she miraculous?" Lydia asked.

"She was fine before," Kasey said. "But . . . you do look nice, Lexi."

I trailed Lydia to the front door, where I could see she'd parked her dad's red car right in the street, in front of the sidewalk.

"I hope you didn't get a ticket," I said.

"A ticket?" She gave me a bemused smile, like she'd never even heard of the word. "You have a lot to learn, Alexis."

A lot to learn? About Aralt? I fought the urge to ask her what it was that I didn't know about him. Because now that I knew I was stuck, I found myself intensely curious. It wasn't, I told myself, that I wasn't aware of how dangerous it was to get involved with ghosts. Or that I wasn't committed to ending this whole thing as soon as possible. It was just . . .

That feeling—that bursting-with-brilliance feeling—I wanted more of it.

"Stay sunny!" Lydia said, hopping into her car.

Inside, Mom was on the phone. "Oh, here she is," she said, handing me the receiver. "It's Carter."

"Hello?" I glanced at the clock. It was three minutes to seven.

"Hey, Lex."

"What's wrong?"

"Listen, I'm really sorry, but I have to cancel tonight.

I started making some adjustments to my speech and it kind of unraveled. I can't stop working now or I'll be up all night."

"Oh," I said, going into my bedroom and closing the door behind me. The shoes Lydia had helped me pick out were sitting on the bed. I swiped them off and sat down. "Do you want another set of ears? I could come over. I can bring dinner."

"That's sweet," he said. "But Mom made me a sandwich. And I don't want to bore you."

"You wouldn't bore me," I said. "It sounds like you need help."

"No, listen, I'll be fine," he said. "I'm working some of the new ideas in, and I think they're going to really, ah . . . really make an impression."

"I'm looking forward to it," I said.

"Okay, good," he said. "So I'm pretty busy. I can try to call you later, if you want."

"If you have time." What the perfect girlfriend would say. "Otherwise, no worries."

"All right," he said.

"So, yeah," I said. "Bye."

As I went to hang up the phone, a voice in the background asked, "What did she say?"

It was like the bottom fell out, except it was the sides, the top, and everything else, too. Everything inside me shattered into a thousand pieces.

Because I knew that voice.

It was Zoe's.

I sat on the bed and let stunned tears spill from my eyes. Then I got up, kicked off my shoes, and went across the hall to the bathroom to take off my makeup.

Streaking down my cheeks like ink spilling from a bottle were the lines of coal-colored tears.

After staring at myself and watching fresh, inky-black teardrops bubble out of my eyes, I grabbed a handful of tissues and daubed at them before they could drip onto my shirt. When I pulled the tissues away, they were covered in gray splotches like the ones on Megan's shirt and my jeans. The occasional thicker patches of color were the same endless black as the goo that had covered the Ouija board.

Instead of leaving the tissues in the trash bin where Kasey might find them, I flushed them down the toilet, then scrubbed at my cheeks until they were clean. When I was done, the washcloth was basically ruined.

If I'd needed a reminder that I was different now, that something else was at work inside of me—inside of all of us—here it was.

Stay sunny, we said to each other.

Because if you don't, the whole world will know you're a monster.

14

I COULD HARDLY SLEEP THAT NIGHT. When my alarm went off thirty minutes earlier than usual, I practically rolled off the side of the bed and trudged to the bathroom. I needed the extra time to do my hair and iron my clothes—but considering how tired I was, it seemed likely that I'd run late anyway.

Surprisingly, the process of getting myself all prettied up was as invigorating as a strong cup of coffee. I finished dressing with plenty of time to spare and slipped on a pair of black flats. Then I thought of what Lydia had said about trust, and put on Mrs. Wiley's pumps, even though they were two inches higher than the dress code allowed.

Megan pulled up out front at 7:40. She gave me an up-and-down glance. "Alexis! Look at you!"

"I know," I said.

"Carter's going to lose his mind," she said.

"We'll see."

When we got to school, Megan looked at me. "Ready

192

to show Surrey High the new and improved Alexis?"

I wasn't sure what she meant. I'd changed my hair and plucked my eyebrows, and I was wearing my interview outfit from the other night, all the way down to Mom's earrings. But under it all, I still felt like me.

There was the Aralt factor, but I wondered if I'd misunderstood what Lydia had been trying to say.

Having Aralt in my life (in my body, I guess) hadn't helped me sleep. It hadn't prevented my boyfriend from hanging out with ninth-grade nature-baby tarts.

I guess I could see Carter being sort of surprised, but "new and improved" seemed to be overstating the case.

But as Kasey, Megan, and I sailed down the hallway, it was like all conversation, everywhere, stopped.

"Holy . . ." I heard one girl say as we passed by. *"Alexis?"*

As we walked, I felt my stride smooth out beneath me, my shoulders press down and back, and my chin rise. By the time we made it out the other side to the courtyard, I was kind of enjoying myself. No matter how much attention my pink hair had ever attracted, it wasn't *this* kind of attention. Was it so wrong to bask a little? Considering what I'd been through?

Carter was in his usual spot, standing next to a campaign poster on an easel, talking to some kids.

As soon as I saw him, I froze. I felt like I couldn't

make myself move another step. It was like stepping out onto a stage on opening night—sure, the rehearsals were okay, but this was real. And there was no going back. What if he hated it?

Don't be stupid, I told myself. How could he hate it? Who wouldn't want their girlfriend to change from dumpy and rough around the edges to sleek and beautiful? Who would take an ugly duckling over a swan?

Megan squeezed my arm. "Good luck," she said, and headed toward the picnic tables.

Carter was so absorbed in his conversation that he didn't notice me, even when I stopped a couple of feet away.

I waited for him to finish up, and then I tapped him on the shoulder. "If I vote for you, will you put Pepsi in the water fountains?"

He turned around, blankly courteous, like he was looking at a stranger.

Then he blinked and drew back. *"Oh my God,"* he said.

I'd learned, from my mother's reaction, not to expect applause and adoration. But I expected, at the very least, polite acceptance. Especially from Carter—my boyfriend, who was supposed to care about me.

"What have you *done* to yourself, Lex?"

"Done to myself?" I took a step away. One of my

heels wedged in a crack in the sidewalk, and I caught myself just shy of twisting my ankle. "You don't like it?"

"You look . . ." He put his hand to his face, over his eyes, and pushed it back through his hair. "You look like a Barbie doll. It's like a costume."

The air settled between us.

"Oh, okay," I said. "So I wasn't right before, and now I'm all wrong again."

"There was nothing wrong with you before!" he cried.

"That's such a lie," I said. If there hadn't been, why would he have Zoe come to his house at night? "Why do people keep saying that when it's so obviously a lie?"

Suddenly he was gripping both of my arms. "Lex, does this have something to do with your sister? That club?"

"Please take your hands off me," I said, letting each word have its own space. "That's ridiculous. I just wanted a change."

His expression softened, and I thought, desperately, fleetingly, that he would apologize. Tell me that he was wrong. That I looked beautiful, better than ever.

"I don't know who this person is," he said, gesturing from my feet to my head. "I don't know . . . where Alexis went."

My heart seemed to crumple, like it was a hollow

ball of aluminum foil. For a moment, I almost gave in, let myself hurt, let myself cry.

Then I remembered the black tears.

And something hardened inside me. "Well, if anyone asks," I said, "Alexis went to find some people who don't make her feel like a freak or call her a Barbie doll. *Or* tell her to stay home while inviting Zoe over to help with their speeches."

His eyes widened at the mention of her name. "Zoe stopped by for five minutes to drop off a book of political quotations. If you got some other idea, you should have said something."

"No, Carter," I said, my voice venomous. "It doesn't work like that. I shouldn't have to follow you all over town, asking if every girl you sneak around with is going to be the one you dump me for."

I turned and walked to the picnic tables, where a space was quickly cleared for me. For a good ten minutes, I didn't even try to catch a glimpse of Carter.

But when I finally did look up, he was involved in a conversation. With Zoe.

Mimi followed my gaze. "Who *is* that girl?" she asked. "Why does she keep talking to your boyfriend?"

"Her name is Zoe," I said, smoothing my skirt over my legs. "And she has problems with boundaries."

"She's trying to steal Carter from you?" Emily asked.

196

"She doesn't know who she's messing with," Mimi said. "That's all."

But I knew. As I looked around, I saw nothing but suspicious faces and pitiless eyes.

All aimed at Zoe.

And it almost made me feel bad for her, to be honest.

Almost.

The elections assembly was held sixth period. I sat in the front row, feeling everyone watching me as Carter delivered his speech. I could tell they all admired my new look. And if the rest of the school felt that way, Carter would come around soon. He had to.

When the final bell rang, he disappeared backstage, so I went to my locker, then out to the parking lot, and headed for Megan's car.

"Lex!" Carter's voice.

I turned around to see him rushing toward me like he had on so many other days. I reached out as he approached.

"Alexis," he said, ignoring my outstretched hands. "How could you?"

"Pardon me?" I asked.

He grabbed me by the elbow and came closer. There was fire in his eyes. "Zoe's just a stupid kid. She was so upset, she had to go to the clinic!"

"I'm not sure what you mean," I said. "But if she's so stupid, why do you spend so much time together?"

His nostrils flared angrily. "You know there's nothing going on between me and her!"

I raised my eyebrow and angled my body away from him. "Do I, Carter?"

"Of course you do," he growled. "*I'm* not the one telling half-truths lately, Lex."

I blushed. "I don't know what you're so mad about."

"Zoe found *this* in her locker," he said, handing me a piece of folded paper.

only disgusting bottom-feeders eat leftover carcasses.

leave carter blume alone.

A bitter taste came into my mouth. I handed it back gingerly, as if it might bite me. "I didn't write that."

"I know that," he said. "But one of your *friends*—and I use that term loosely—did."

"Why would you assume that?" I asked, even though he had to be right.

"You want to go ask them?"

"No," I said. "I'll take care of it."

"Look at those girls. I don't get why you're mixed up with them."

I looked up at the Sunshine Club, clumped together in the dappled shade of an oak tree like a flock of songbirds.

Carter balled the note up in his hand. "They're like a pack of wolves."

I took it from him and stuffed it in my bag. "I'll take care of it," I said. "Meanwhile, tell Zoe to grow up. Nobody likes a crybaby."

He took a half step back. "What is *wrong* with you?"

"Oh," I said. "So now there *is* something wrong with me?"

His jaw dropped.

"Tell you what," I said. "When you figure out exactly what my defects are, why don't you call me up and let me know? I'm on a real self-improvement kick these days."

He stood there, open-mouthed, as I spun on my heel and sauntered toward the Sunshine Club. He was upset, but I'd deal with it later. At the moment, I had somewhere to be.

I passed by a car and glanced down to catch a glimpse of my reflection in the windows. The words floated into my head:

Hello, beautiful.

By the time we got home after the Sunshine Club meeting, I was sliding headlong into a bad mood.

Mom was standing in the kitchen next to the answering machine.

"Alexis!" she said. "Listen to this!"

She hit the PLAY button. "Friday, two p.m.," the machine said. *"Hello, this is Farrin McAllister, representing the Young Visionaries program. I'm pleased to let you know that Alexis has made the final five and is invited to the mocktail reception Saturday night."*

Mom stopped the playback. "One step closer!" she said. "You're going to win this. I can feel it."

"Great," I said. I knew I should try to be more chipper, but my heart wasn't in it. I was tired and confused and felt weirdly left out. Aralt was there for everyone except me, it seemed—even when I'd put my relationship on the line to look good for him.

A nagging, worrisome thought had been born in my head during the meeting—what if Aralt didn't want me and Carter to be together? What if he felt my having a boyfriend was too much of a distraction?

Mom came closer and pulled me into a hug. "Maybe this change *is* the right thing for you. You're going to knock their socks off when you walk in there."

"You think so?" I asked. I felt vaguely disappointed. I almost wished Mom hadn't come around so easily. I wanted Carter to fall all over himself, but there was a degree of comfort in having your mother insist you're perfect the way you were.

* * *

All through the celebratory dinner my parents insisted on, I had to hide how non-celebratory I felt.

When we got home, I decided enough was enough. It was time to take action. I waited until Kasey went into the bathroom for her shower, then I sneaked into her bedroom and dug around under the piles of dirty clothes in her closet, pulling out the small, flat box with the Ouija board inside it.

My pulse throbbing through my body, I locked my bedroom door and set up the board on the bed. I turned my stereo up loud and then took a few deep, trembling breaths, looking down at the array of letters and numbers in front of me. I didn't really know where to start.

"Hello?" I asked. "Elspeth?"

No movement. Had the black goo scared her away for good?

Then, just as I was heaving a hopeless sigh, the planchette jerked and began to move. Unlike the last time, when it tottered around the board, this time it practically skidded from letter to letter.

It got as far as D-O-N-O-T-T-R when the board started to emit a sizzling noise. I tried to keep an eye on the black ooze that was bubbling up like tar from the seams, while trying not to miss what Elspeth had to say.

U-S-T

"Who?" I asked, urging her on. "Do not trust who?"

The whole board was now covered in a thin layer of streaky blackness, like the first layer of black paint on a white wall. The little wooden triangle rocked and wobbled as it moved across the uneven surface to the M.

Then it hobbled left to the E.

Just teasing. Do not trust me.

I was beginning to detect a theme.

Again, the black substance converged on the pointer, stopping it in its tracks. This time, though, it didn't converge and disappear. It grew up around the planchette like a second skin.

Then it began to move again, more smoothly than before. The letters were still barely visible.

A-L-E-X

It was spelling my name.

It knows my name.

Before I could stop myself, I slammed my hands down on top of the pointer, blackness and all.

A massive charge of energy moved through my body like a shock wave. It was like when you see a dog thrash a toy by shaking its head—I was like the toy in that equation, even though my body hadn't actually moved.

Under my fingers, the pointer continued on its way.

I-S-I-A-M-H-E-R-E-F-O-R-Y-O-U

And then it stopped.

"Who are you?" I asked, my voice as thin as a strand of thread.

Even though I knew.

A-R-A-L-T

I should have knocked it off the bed. I should have snatched my hands away.

I shouldn't have let it spell that word. And I definitely shouldn't have let it spell more words.

But I did.

I-W-I-L-L-H-E-L-P-Y-O-U-B-U-T-Y-O-U-M-U-S-T

"Stop!" I didn't mean to say it. And I didn't expect Aralt to do it.

But he did. He stopped. Just like that, because I asked, the pointer stopped moving.

I studied it, thinking that maybe . . .

Maybe Aralt *did* care what I wanted.

I mean, he *listened*. How many evil ghosts are good listeners?

"Aralt . . . ?" I lowered my voice and let my fingertips brush against the surface of the board. "What? What do you want me to do?"

L-E-T-G-O

Megan and I spent the better part of Saturday at the mall, where everything I wanted miraculously came up on sale. We struggled through the town house under the weight of the bags, and Megan helped me get dressed for the party. I put on one of my new dresses, cornflower blue and flowing from a gathered neckline. At the waist was a simple band of black velvet. I put on a pair of three-inch velvety black heels while Megan looked on, like an artist studying a painting.

"Smoky eyes," she said. "Pale lips. Hair up—but deconstructed."

"Um . . . I don't know what that means," I said.

"Don't worry," she said. "I'll handle it."

Somehow she got my hair up, hiding about a hundred bobby pins in the process. I covered my face and she doused me with hairspray from all 360 degrees.

"See?" she said, like a sales pitch. "Looks natural, feels secure."

"Feels like chicken wire," I said. But it did *look* totally natural. "It's impressive. I just can't let anyone touch it."

She laughed, and then went quiet. "You look gorgeous."

"Thanks."

"I'm so proud of you," she said. "You're really going to do great things. Isn't it exciting to think you're going to have this amazing career?"

I looked up at her. "What do you mean?"

"With Aralt," she said, sorting through the box of

jewelry she'd brought with her. "You can do whatever you want."

"Why do you say that?" I asked.

She laughed. "Because Aralt cares. He looks out for us."

"I know he does," I said. "It's just . . . I don't mean to sound disrespectful, but . . . do you ever wonder what he gets out of it?"

Megan had found one earring, a big black pearl, and was looking for the match. "What do you get out of taking pictures?"

I thought about it. "I'm creating something."

She looked at me, an expression of utter peace and trust in her eyes. "Maybe that's what Aralt's doing."

"But he's just making us pretty."

She cocked her head. "What are you talking about, Lex? It's so much more than that. Haven't you noticed?"

More than that? I thought back over the week.

I'd aced the Young Visionaries interview. I'd gotten nothing less than a hundred percent on every quiz I took, including a chemistry quiz with material I wasn't really familiar with. I'd quadrupled my speed in the library.

And the dress code thing. And Lydia's lack of concern for parking rules.

Not to mention that when I got on the scale that morning, I found I'd actually lost three pounds.

"But he wouldn't give something for nothing. You said so yourself," I said. "That's not supposed to be how it works."

"But I was wrong, Alexis." She leaned down and took my hands in hers. "I know you're unsure. But you have to trust. You have to let him help you."

"I'm trying!" I said.

"You're not, though," she said. "You may not even know you're fighting it, but you are. I know you, Lex. I can see that you're holding on to something. To fear."

Then, without looking, she reached into the mess of earrings and pulled out the perfect match. She dropped it into my open palm and her deep brown eyes gleamed.

"*Let go,* Lex. All you have to do is let go."

The mocktail reception was held in the main lobby of Farrin's building. I walked in, with Mom at my heels, and stopped short.

Dominating the far wall was a giant print of my self-portrait-with-new-camera.

"Oh, Alexis!" Mom breathed. "Wow!"

I was slightly embarrassed but also pleased. Mom and Dad were always saying they liked my photos, but this was real—her gut reaction.

"Alexis!" I turned to see Farrin, in a drapey black dress. She leaned in and gave me an air-kiss on each cheek, like we were a couple of Europeans embracing at a fancy art gallery. "Let me look at you . . . how classic. Almost Grecian. I'm so glad you came."

She shook hands with Mom.

"It's down to five now," Farrin said. "Would you like to meet your competition?"

Was "no" an acceptable answer? "I guess," I said. "Mom, will you be all right . . . ?"

"Of course," Mom said. "I'll go look around."

In the middle of the room was a small clump of people. They opened up to make room for Farrin and me, and I recognized some of my competitors from interview day: the boy with the Mohawk; the boy who'd been wearing the purple suit; the ultra-preppy girl, in a blue-and-white sailor dress; and a girl with dark blue hair wearing a dress made out of a pair of overalls with a giant skirt made from the legs of other pants.

Clueless, I thought, and then I realized with a start that, but for Lydia and my sister, that could have been me.

"Everyone, this is Alexis Warren. Alexis, this is . . ."

She went through all the names: Jonah. Bailey. Breana. My eyes stopped on purple-suit boy: *Jared*. Tonight he wore green.

He caught me looking at his suit and frowned.

"I'm going to go say hello to your lovely parents. I

207

recommend that you all try to mingle a bit. Don't forget, this is a party." Farrin glided away into the crowd.

The five of us just stood there. *Mingling* wasn't high on my skill set, but I knew enough to know we weren't doing it.

I heard my voice before I knew I was planning to talk. "I guess I'll go look at the pictures," I said. "Excuse me."

"I'll come with you," Sailor Girl—Bailey—said, cutting through the center of the circle.

Mohawk Boy followed us, and out of the corner of my eye, I saw Jared and Blue-Hair Girl turn away from each other.

We started on the far left side of the lobby, looking at a blown-up photo of a rock formation.

I stood back and studied it, trying to quiet the endless whir of thoughts in my brain. That was the only way I could really appreciate photographs. To let go of everything else in the room and lose myself in the stillness of the moment.

Let go, Alexis.

As I let down my guard, I felt a jolt—almost like something inside me woke up. Something I hadn't known was asleep.

I closed my eyes, and suddenly, when I opened them, it was like seeing the world in color after growing up in black and white. I looked around the room and thought, I can do this. I know how to do this.

Next to me, Sailor Girl turned her head to the side. "This is . . . nice."

The rock formation in the photo was striking, but the picture itself was off-balance somehow—the proportions were wrong.

A suitable reply popped into my head. "The way the cool and warm tones contrast is unsettling."

"Is it one of yours?" Mohawk Boy asked.

We shook our heads.

"In that case," he said, "it's boring."

"Okay, I'm not the only one!" Bailey laughed, and I found myself joining in, even though on a typical day, I wouldn't find anything funny about a mediocre photo. "Let's go before we get the uncontrollable urge to buy khaki pants." As we drifted toward the next picture, she came closer to me. "*Love* your dress."

"Thanks," I said. "I like yours too."

"It's vintage," she said. "From San Francisco."

"Fabulous buttons," I said.

Fabulous buttons? Did those words really just leave my mouth?

Bailey gave me a friendly grin, which I returned. I could feel a connection between us—a spark of something that wasn't quite friendship. It was more like she was taking notice of me—deciding that I was a person *worth* noticing.

It was so easy, I thought. I just had to take the way I looked at photographs and look at the rest of the world that way—climb into the passenger seat and let my instincts drive.

I turned to look for my mother. Instead of Mom, I saw Breana—Blue-Hair Girl—standing alone in the same spot where we'd left her. Her eyes jumped to the rock photo and then to the floor.

She couldn't have heard us, I told myself. The lobby was like an echo chamber—it was hard enough to hear someone standing right next to you. But she'd been watching.

I felt a tiny tightening at the back of my throat, and I knew that if I stopped to think about it, I'd feel guilty.

So I didn't stop to think. We moved on. Bailey stood up extra straight, and I knew the next one must be hers.

It was an extreme close-up of a brick.

I looked at it for ten solid seconds, trying to find something that made it more than just a picture of a brick.

Nope. Fortunately, my subconscious was prepared.

"It's so static that it's totally *dynamic*," I lied.

"I know, right?" Bailey squealed. "It's mine!"

Mohawk Boy kept walking.

The next photo was mine, the close-up of the grille of the car.

"Cool," Mohawk Boy said, leaning in.

"I'm not into cars," Bailey said, stifling a yawn. "I'm going to get some food."

Mohawk Boy followed her away.

Happy to be left alone, I moved on to the fifth photo, which had to be Jared's.

As soon as I raised my eyes to look at it, I felt like I'd been punched in the stomach—hot and cold all at once, and slightly dizzy.

"That bad?" came a voice from behind me.

It was phenomenal. Better than phenomenal, actually. It was one of the most haunting photographs I'd ever seen.

It was a little girl in a hospital bed. She was hooked up to about fifteen monitors, with tubes and hoses and electrodes snaking off every visible part of her body. The background was flatly lit by fluorescents, green and dull. But the little girl was lit with a spotlight that made her look like she was onstage. And she wore a superhero cape and mask.

"Where is this?" I asked.

"I did some work with a children's hospital," he said. "A fund-raising thing. This is Raelynn. She has—uh, *had*—stage four leukemia."

Even before he told me, I felt the entirety of the little girl's struggle. You could see it in the shallow exhaustion of her eyes.

I was afraid that nothing I could say would convey how I felt. So I looked at Jared and nodded.

He looked at the floor, trying not to smile. "Thanks."

We walked on, wordlessly examining the pictures. When we got to my self-portrait, he turned to me. "That's you."

"Yep."

He stared up at it, and then at me.

Feeling self-conscious, I opted for some lame photography humor. "Take a picture," I joked. "It'll last longer."

"No, I'm . . . comparing. You, and that person."

"It's not 'that person,'" I said. "It's me."

"I know," Jared said. "That's what intrigues me."

I guess that was better than being called a Barbie doll. "I know it's really different, but—"

He squinted. "You don't owe anyone an explanation. People change."

I looked at his face, sharp angles and dark brown eyes behind a hipster pair of tortoiseshell glasses.

People change.

They do, don't they?

Maybe I was *allowed* to change. And maybe it wasn't

the end of the world, even though Carter seemed to think it was.

Jared stuck his hands in his pockets, still looking at the picture, like he was trying to decipher it. Then he turned and looked at me the same way. "Want to go out some time?"

"Excuse me?" I asked.

"Would you like to . . . have coffee, or . . . bowl, or something?"

"Um," I said. Wow. I'd never actually been asked out by any boy besides Carter. It was strangely unnerving, and yet, part of me was curious to know what it would be like to have coffee with someone who took such incredible photos.

"You have a boyfriend."

"Yes," I said, relieved that I didn't have to say it. "Kind of."

"Let me guess: big man on campus. Captain of the football team? Student Council president? Eagle Scout?"

I shot him an irritated look, but he just laughed.

"Well, if *kind of* ever turns into *kind of not*, let me know," he said. He looked around. "I'd better go make sure my father isn't telling the story about me riding my tricycle naked to the grocery store."

"Aren't you a little old to be doing that?" I asked.

Jared smirked. "Funny girl," he said as he walked away.

"Dad," someone said. "She's right here."

Bailey was dragging a man over to me. I recognized his face, but couldn't place it.

"He likes your car picture," she said. "He wants me to take pictures like that of our cars. But that's not really my style."

"Do you work on commission?" The man stuck his hand out, and I shook it. "Stuart Templeton. Nice to meet you."

And I realized how it was Bailey could afford a dress with such fabulous buttons. Her dad was a gazillionaire software mogul.

Which also explained how a close-up of a brick could make it to the final five.

Don't mess this up, I told myself. Say something. And then the words were just there.

"I'd definitely be open to an arrangement," I said. "Depending on the size of the finished prints and how many you wanted."

He nodded and passed me his business card with a friendly smile. "E-mail my office."

"We should hang out," Bailey said to me, fishing the cherry out of her mocktail and sticking it in her mouth. "I'm so bored with the losers at my school."

But I'm just like the losers at your school, I wanted to protest.

But—people change. Maybe that wasn't the case anymore.

Bailey and her father wandered away and I was left standing alone, wondering how all of a sudden it had come to pass that I, Alexis Warren, was one of the pretty people.

Well, I thought. Might as well go work the party.

15

FARRIN STOPPED MOM and me on the way out. At her side was a tall woman in a pantsuit. "Alexis, I've been trying to catch you between conversations for an hour! I'd like you to meet a friend of mine—Barbara Draeger."

The name sounded familiar. "Nice to meet you," I said.

Mom's eyes widened, and she brushed nonexistent dust off her blazer. "Senator Draeger!"

Oh, right. *That* Barbara Draeger.

Mom shook the woman's hand like it was a water pump. She feels about female senators the way some pre-teen girls feel about boy bands. "What an honor!"

"Alexis, I really enjoyed looking at your pictures," the senator said. "You're very talented."

"Thank you."

"Did you know that the top-ranked university photography curriculum in America is in California?"

"No," I said. "I didn't."

"The Skalaski School of Photography at Weatherly College," Farrin said.

The senator gave Farrin a sparkling smile. "Our alma mater!"

"Alexis would be a great fit for Weatherly," Farrin said. "She's just the type."

Senator Draeger was beaming at me so intensely that I couldn't look away.

"Can you spare your daughter for one last thing?" Farrin asked. Mom's enthusiastic nod made her look like a bobble-head doll.

When we were standing off by ourselves, Farrin smiled warmly at me. "It's such a pleasure to have you in the competition."

Shiny Happy Party Alexis was fading fast, but I dredged up an appropriate "Thank you."

"When I said you were welcome to use my darkroom, I really meant it."

"I appreciate that," I said. "I'm not sure if it's a realistic option for me, but it's such a generous offer."

She frowned. "Not realistic?"

"I don't have a car," I said. "And I live twenty miles away."

"Oh. Can't you borrow your mother's car?"

"After she's home from work. But . . . that would have to be at night."

That didn't faze her in the least. "I can be here at night, if necessary."

"Wow," I said. "That's so generous, but . . . no, I really couldn't ask you to do that."

"Alexis," she said, her hands on my shoulders. "Anything for one of Aralt's girls."

It took every single bit of control I had not to stumble backward.

That's when I saw, on the fourth finger of her right hand, a thin gold ring, covered in a lacy patina of scratches.

She squeezed my hands. "Go on. Your mother's waiting."

I nodded and turned around, running directly into Senator Draeger, who gave me a vigorous farewell handshake. I glanced at her right hand.

Another gold ring.

The night of the interview, Farrin wasn't looking at my bone structure. She was looking at my ring.

I hardly noticed the walk to the car. I don't even remember opening the door or sitting down or fastening my seat belt. I only snapped out of it when Mom started rejoicing over the night's events.

"What a night!" she said, pulling the car out onto the road.

"Um, yeah," I said.

"A Pulitzer prize–winning photographer?" Mom

said. "A United States senator? And all you can say is '*Um, yeah*'?"

I decided not to mention Stuart Templeton. She might actually lose control of the car.

"That woman, Farrin McAllister, said you're *talented*." She sighed happily. "And Senator Draeger said Weatherly is very generous with merit-based scholarships! If she wrote you a recommendation letter—just *think* . . ."

Merit-based—or gold-ring-based?

"Weatherly is a small school, but it's *very* highly regarded. It's practically Ivy League. Honey, this could be huge for you. Are you worried that you can't get in? Because—"

"No, I'm really not worried," I said. My sparkling facade had melted like a chocolate off a peanut in a hot car. I didn't want to talk about Farrin or Senator Draeger or Weatherly College. I wanted a ham sandwich, my pajamas, and my bed, in that order. "I'm exhausted. Can we talk about it later?"

She nodded, not taking her eyes off the road. I leaned my forehead against the cool glass and stared at the lights flashing by. My body was tired, but my brain was going a mile a minute.

If Farrin and Senator Draeger knew Aralt, that meant . . . the oath didn't kill you. Not for a couple of decades, at least. They were both at least fifty, and neither of them seemed to be worried about dropping dead.

And not only did taking the oath not kill you, but there was a really, really good chance that it made your life totally wonderful.

I might book a photography job from one of the richest men in the world. If he liked the pictures I took of his cars, who's to say he wouldn't let me shoot an ad campaign for his company? In his company's TV commercials he claimed to be big on innovation and young talent. If I said precisely the right thing and dropped precisely the right hints, I could turn this into something huge.

And then I'd go to Weatherly College, on full scholarship, and study photography with real teachers, people who knew what they were talking about. I'd be surrounded by other people—maybe like Jared—who really understood taking pictures.

After graduation, who knew? I could travel the world. See every continent. Photograph famous people and places. Meet my photography idols. Win awards. Have shows in New York galleries.

I could do it. I could do anything.

I felt a core of strength forming inside me and knew that tapping into it would mean achieving whatever I wanted.

All thanks to Aralt.

So . . . *why* were we trying to stop him?

* * *

Dad and Kasey were watching TV when we got home. Dad paused it and turned to me expectantly.

Mom took over. "How does it feel to be related to the most fabulous sixteen-year-old in Surrey?" she asked. Then, realizing she should tone it down in the interest of sibling equality, she lowered her voice. "Alexis did very well."

"Wonderful, honey!" Dad said, beaming. "Come tell us about it."

As I rounded the sofa, Kasey jumped up. "I have some homework to do."

Mom watched her go, then turned to me with an apologetic frown. "I guess this might be a little hard for her."

"Yeah," I said, staring disapprovingly down the hall. It was totally un-sunshiny to be jealous and petty.

I tried to perk up and give my parents a good rundown of the night. When I was done, I stifled a huge yawn and excused myself.

Kasey was in the bathroom brushing her teeth. I waited until she'd rinsed her toothbrush before giving her a nudge.

"Want to hear about the party?"

She shrugged.

The gesture stung more than I would have thought. As she passed me on the way to her bedroom, I spoke to her back—keeping my voice low so our parents wouldn't hear.

"Aren't you happy for me?"

"Sure, Lexi. Why not," said Kasey.

I couldn't believe what I was hearing.

She came closer. "But how much of this is really you, and how much of it is Aralt?"

"Why does that matter?" I asked. "I still made the effort."

She gave me a flat frown.

"You know what? Fine. Don't be happy for me. But if you don't mind my saying so, you could stand to be a little sunnier."

She rolled her eyes. "And you could stand to be a little *less* sunny, Lexi."

I felt a swell of emotion so powerful that it made me turn away. It was like the moment a thundercloud opens up and soaks anything unlucky enough to be caught under it—only this storm was a hurricane of rage. I stared at the family portrait that hung across from Kasey's bedroom door, trying to will myself not to turn around.

Then I surged toward my own room and slammed the door behind me, locking it.

I believed with all my heart that if I even *looked* at my sister, I might break her neck.

16

"ALEXIS? MEGAN'S ON THE PHONE." Mom opened my door a crack and peered around. "Goodness, I think this is the messiest your room's ever been."

I scowled. It was Sunday, and I hadn't so much as tidied up since Monday. The bed was unmade, and a week's worth of clothing changes were draped on various surfaces, from the desk to the edge of the trash can. Shoes were scattered like abandoned cars after the zombie apocalypse.

"I've been busy," I said. I grabbed the phone and waved her out.

"What's up?" Megan asked. "We're hanging out at Monika's today."

"Who?"

"Everybody," she said. "Can you be ready in ten minutes?"

"Sure." After my week, a day of doing nothing sounded wonderful.

"We'll park," she said. "Come out when you're done."

I took a quick shower, braided my wet hair, slapped on some makeup, and slipped on a summery skirt with a sleeveless top and a pair of sandals. I had a vague recollection that Monika had a pool, so I emptied a tote bag on the foot of my bed and stuffed a bathing suit and a towel inside it. At the last second, I grabbed my camera.

I was about to leave when a splash of color caught my eye.

I walked to the window and peered through the slats of the wooden blinds.

Megan's car was parked across the street, and she and the girls she'd brought with her—Mimi and Emily— were leaning against it, faces to the sky, absorbing the sunshine.

There was something about them—some unquestioned sense of entitlement, the right to sun oneself wherever one chose. They were like a pack of lions lounging on the Serengeti Plain. These were the girls who would grow up to be senators, or movie stars, or best-selling novelists. They were beautiful and effortlessly powerful.

And I was one of them.

When I came outside, Megan tilted her sunglasses down her nose to look at me. "Ready?"

"Yeah," I said.

"Where's Kasey?" Emily asked.

"I'm not sure," I said. "Studying?"

"Studying?" Emily repeated. "Why? Doesn't she trust Aralt?"

"Of course she does," I said, but even as I said it, I began to wonder if it was true.

Monika lived in the older section of town—mostly rambling ranch houses on half-acre lots. In the tree-shaded backyard, a pool surrounded by lounge chairs reflected the aqua sky.

Everyone else scattered to change into their swimsuits, but I stood and let my toes dig into the grass. A shadow fell on the ground beside me.

"What's wrong?" Megan asked.

"I miss having a yard," I said.

"You can always come use mine," Megan said. "You haven't been over lately."

"I know," I said. "I'm sorry."

"Don't apologize. We're all busy." She sighed. "How's Carter?"

"I'm not sure. I haven't talked to him since Friday."

"You need to be careful." She turned to me. "Lex, if he's not willing to accept you the way you are, he doesn't deserve you in the first place."

For some reason, that made me think of Jared, who

found the idea of Old Alexis and New Alexis interesting, not aggravating.

"I know he doesn't like the Sunshine Club," Megan said quietly. "He doesn't talk about us with respect."

I looked up, surprised at the undercurrent of heat in her voice, like a small, slow-burning flame. "It's not that," I said. "I think he's really stressed out about the election."

Her voice was cold. "If he thinks it's going to be less stressful after he wins, he's deluded."

"Look," I said. "I'll deal with it."

"This sisterhood isn't a joke," she said. "And you shouldn't let Carter treat us like one."

I was frustrated by the onslaught, when she knew I hadn't even seen him since Friday. "I don't want to talk about it, okay?"

Megan looked at me in surprise. She scowled, kicked her shoes off, and plopped to the ground at the edge of the pool, dunking her legs in the water like a debutante who'd wandered away from a fancy party to pout. Schlumpy but regal.

"Hang on," I said, reaching into my camera bag.

"Oh, come on, Lex," she said. "I'm *so* not in the mood."

"Please?" I said. "I need four new pictures by next week. Can you take off your sunglasses?"

"Whatever," she muttered, slipping them off and tossing her hair over her shoulder.

I clicked off a couple of shots.

"Chin down a little," I said.

Megan shot me a dirty look through the camera.

"Don't be mad at me," I said, and then, almost as a joke: "Aralt wouldn't want that."

Instantly, her expression changed.

Her eyes went from petulant to misty—her lips relaxed, her cheekbones lifted.

These pictures were going to be pretty—really pretty. Never mind that I had no idea what to do with a pretty picture. "You look gorgeous," I said.

"I know." Her voice was dreamy.

We lay around all afternoon like a bunch of Roman empresses, trading magazines and compliments.

"Alexis, I saw your picture in the newspaper," Lydia said. "Maybe you should invite Bailey Templeton to a meeting."

"She doesn't need Aralt," I said. "She has a billion-dollar trust fund."

It was like I'd pressed the "awkward silence" button. Scandalized looks greeted me from every angle.

Aralt was about more than money. I knew that. "If I see her again, I'll invite her."

Later, we went inside to bask in the air-conditioning.

Tashi sat on the floor, painting her nails on a giant Oriental rug, not using a paper towel or anything.

"You think Carter's going to win tomorrow?" she asked, glancing up at me.

I shrugged.

"That would be cool," Emily said, her eyes dreamy. "It would be great for getting new members."

"Does *he* think he's going to win?" Mimi asked.

"I don't know," I said. "He's kind of doing his own thing this weekend. We haven't really talked."

"Do you think he's been with Zoe?" Paige asked, sitting up.

"No," I said. "He told me there was nothing going on."

"And you believe him?" Lydia asked.

"Yes!" I said, a little too snappily. "A hundred percent."

"Then he needs you!" Emily said, her voice soft. "I mean, you're in love. I'm sure he wants you there."

"In love?" Megan repeated. "You've never actually said the words, have you?"

In fact, we hadn't. And I can't say I was thrilled with her for announcing it in public like it was some juicy piece of gossip, instead of one of the most intimate and private details of my existence.

But everyone was watching me, rapt.

"No," I said. "Now can we please change the subject?"

Thankfully, they all got the message and found something else to talk about.

"Is something wrong with you guys?" Tashi asked.

She'd spoken so quietly that I was the only one who heard her. She wasn't even looking at me. She was bent over, blowing on her toenails, which were a perfect sparkly pink.

From anyone else, I might have resented the question, but there was something about Tashi that was so nonchalant. The way she asked, it was like she didn't really care if I answered or not.

"Something," I said. "I just don't know what."

"People do grow apart, you know." She gazed out the window. "My boyfriend can be distant sometimes."

"I don't think that's what's happening," I said. "This is more sudden than growing apart. He's really mad at me, but he won't listen to my side of the story."

She stuck the cap loosely onto the bottle and turned to look at me. "Do you *want* to save your relationship?"

"Yeah, of course," I said. "But . . . I don't know. What if Aralt doesn't want us to have boyfriends?"

Tashi squinted. "No offense, Alexis, but that's absurd. Love is a gift . . . when you find the right person. Aralt wouldn't deprive anyone of that."

"All right," I said. "Then I guess Carter just hates the way I look now."

"Maybe he doesn't know what to think," Tashi said.

"I guess he's going to have to figure it out."

"Have you ever thought of *telling* him what to think?" She tipped her head to one side and absently played with the ruffled hem of her dress. I looked at her ring: it was prettier than mine, more like an heirloom or antique, with a softer sheen and a carved braid encircling it.

Oh, sure, because Carter's the type who'll blindly go along with whatever anyone says to him. Even Aralt couldn't pull that off.

"Sometimes you have to change people's minds for them." Tashi gave me a little smile as she turned back and pulled the brush out of the bottle, and then it happened:

The bottle tipped over.

One instant, I saw a giant drip of sparkly pink spreading into the carpet fibers, and the next instant, Tashi had reached her hand over it and closed her fingers.

When she opened them again, the bottle was in her hand, the cap neatly screwed on. There was no nail polish on the carpet, or her fingers, or anywhere except exactly where it was supposed to be.

MEET ME IN THE COURTYARD? I texted.

VERY BUSY TODAY, was Carter's reply. A second later: BUT OKAY.

The election was that morning. He was staring at his watch when I got there, as if to remind me that he was taking time away from crucial Student Council activities to humor me.

"Still campaigning?" I asked.

"Yeah. By the bus loop." He fidgeted with his cuffs, checked his watch. "What is it, Lex? This isn't a great time."

A word came into my head like it was written on a script: *Listen.*

I reached out and grabbed his arm. "Listen."

Like magic, he stopped fidgeting and stood perfectly still.

I know this is a big change. "I know this is a big change." *But it's not what you think.* "But it's not what you think." *I never saw the Sunshine Club as a long-term thing.*

I repeated that, too, and saw his face muscles twitch.

"I joined for Kasey," I said. "And I'm going to stick with it, for Kasey. Because she's my sister, and she needs to know I'm there for her. I can't just quit. But it's not the kind of thing I'm going to be doing forever."

Come on, Carter. "Come on, Carter."

Do you really think some silly group of girls is more important to me than you are? More important than us?

Staring deeply into his eyes, I said it all, every last word. When I stopped speaking, he didn't seem to know what to say.

I need you, said the voice. "I need you," I said, "to support me while I'm supporting Kasey, and then this will all be behind us, and we'll be back to the way we were. Most of all, I need you . . ." —*to forgive me.*

Inside, everything came screeching to a halt.

Forgive me? Why? What was I guilty of?

Carter was waiting, holding his breath. This was it, the moment that determined how things would be with us.

It's not like you've done a brilliant job of maintaining this relationship on your own, said the voice inside me.

Only I knew better than to repeat *that.*

"I need you . . . to forgive me," I said, looking at the ground.

"Lex," Carter whispered, taking my hand and pressing it to his chest. "I'm so sorry. I've been a jerk. You're trying to help Kasey, and I'm acting like a spoiled little kid."

I felt washed clean, utterly renewed and reassured.

It was everything I'd wanted to hear him say.

"We're okay?" I asked.

"We're better than okay," he said into my ear. He closed his eyes and kissed me.

We pulled apart and I gave him a tiny smile, my sudden happiness only momentarily shadowed by the fact that it felt like I was kissing a stranger.

17

"LET'S HEAR IT FOR ALEXIS!" Adrienne said. "Girlfriend of the Student Council President!"

Everyone golf-clapped as if Carter's win weren't his achievement, but mine, somehow—and therefore the property of the whole club.

It was our Wednesday meeting, and I was antsy.

I was driving over to Farrin's office that night, to use her darkroom for the first time.

But before that, I had something important to do.

"Now," Adrienne said. "Betterment?"

A couple of girls got called out for minor offenses—chewing gum, swearing, switching from heels to flip-flops after school.

Finally, collecting all of my courage into a ball inside my chest, I stood up.

"I think we're all doing really well, actually," I said. "I look around and everyone looks just as Aralt would hope."

Complacent smiles and murmurs crossed the room.

"But . . ." I said. "Looks aren't everything."

I turned to my sister.

"Kasey, listen," I said. "Yes, academics are important, but if you don't *act* the part, you're not being a good representative of this organization."

Kasey stared up at me, drawing shaky breaths. On the surface, she was every inch a Sunshine Club girl—a pretty linen skirt, a soft blue shirt, tasteful makeup, and neat hair. It was hard to pinpoint what was missing. But there was definitely a difference between her and us.

Next to me, Lydia shot to her feet. "What do people see when they look at us?" she asked. "They don't see smart girls."

Kasey flushed to a fiery shade of pink.

"They see charisma," Lydia said. "Charisma and physical beauty. Now, every kind of beauty is important to Aralt, but why would someone even bother getting to know you if you aren't pretty enough to approach? If they admire you for *this*," she paused and gestured to her whole body, "then they'll stick around enough to see what's in your head. But it doesn't work the other way."

"I know," Kasey said, nearly a whisper. "I'm sorry."

"The thing is," Lydia said, her voice breaking oddly, "I've tried to talk to you about this before. And you make excuse after excuse. So do you *really* know? Are you *really* sorry?" She inhaled and then let her hardest hit fly: "Are you truly committed to Aralt?"

"Of course I am!" Kasey cried. She shot me a helpless look, but I averted my eyes.

"Then you need to make the effort," Lydia said shortly. "Because to some of us, it doesn't seem like you care at all."

This set the whole room buzzing.

"I'm sorry!" Kasey said, not to anyone in particular. "I—I didn't mean to let anybody down."

She was petted and cooed over like an injured kitten for the rest of the meeting. In the car on the way home, she kept her head tucked down, staring at her folded hands. She didn't even give me an angry look.

I was annoyed with myself for feeling a stab of sympathy. *She* was the one choosing to ignore Aralt. So she had to live with the consequences.

Nobody liked to be ganged up on, but sometimes you have to break something down so you can build it up stronger.

And if Aralt thought Kasey needed breaking, who was I to question him?

I ate an early dinner and borrowed Mom's car so I could be at Farrin's studio by seven. All the doors had been left unlocked for me. I looked around the workroom for

Farrin, but there was no sign of her. Next to the conference room was another door, marked PRIVATE OFFICE. It was closed—but not locked.

Parking tickets, dress code, spilled nail polish—these things ran through my brain like a flip book labeled "Things We Get Away With." I pushed the door open and added *barging into people's private offices* to the list.

The office was a perfect reflection of its owner—graceful, spotless, and decorated in clean, modern lines. There were so few objects lying around that I was able to make a quick visual sweep of the room. Perfectly normal, no creepy talismans or other dark supernatural things.

The only thing that didn't seem to fit was a framed photograph on top of the bookshelves. It was old—from the seventies, judging by how faded the colors were—and it was a posed group picture of about twelve or thirteen girls who looked a little older than me—college, maybe? There was a unity to them that resonated deep inside me.

Aralt's girls.

I leaned closer and found Farrin—young and intense-looking. Next to her, with a square jaw and ruler-straight posture, was a girl who had to be Barbara Draeger.

Before I could look at the rest of the girls, I heard a click behind me and turned around, ready to apologize.

"Alexis," Farrin said. "It's a real pleasure to have you here. Did you bring something to work on?"

Not a word about snooping around her private office.

"Yes, film," I said. "But I can just develop . . . I don't need to print tonight. I don't want to keep you too late."

She smiled. "I can stay as late as you need. I don't require much sleep."

That didn't surprise me.

"Come along," she said, leading me through the workroom.

We stepped into a black cylinder about three feet in diameter with a two-foot-wide door cut into it. Farrin grabbed a handle inside the cylinder and rotated the whole thing so the opening was on the other side, releasing us into the darkroom.

"Everything you need is in here," she said, indicating a giant wall of shelves. The dim red light was bright enough for me to see package after package of different types of paper, filters, and tools. An entire section of shelves was dedicated to immaculately labeled bottles of chemicals. Across the room were the enlargers. There were five of them, in different sizes.

"Changing bags and processing canisters are over here," she said. "And there are timers all over the place." She scooped one off the counter and handed it to me. "Smocks and aprons by the door, but I think you'll find that we don't tend to spill."

We.

"Go ahead and get started." In the dark, her eyes looked black. "Call if you need me."

The cylinder closed around her, and I was alone.

The darkroom was so airy and clean that I felt like I was on some sort of spaceship.

As the film processed, I set the timer and wandered around, enjoying the way the rubber mats absorbed the sound of my footsteps, and wondering if I could ever stand the crowded, dirty community college darkroom again after working in this faultless place.

When the film was dry, I cut the negatives into rows of five and made a contact sheet.

Farrin came in without making a sound, picked it up, and motioned for me to follow her back to the workroom.

She set the contact sheet on the light box. Then she took a loupe—a small handheld magnifying glass—and began studying the pictures of Megan by the pool.

"Which of these would you print?" she asked, handing me the loupe.

I studied them, trying to get past the fact that I was basically getting a private photography class with Farrin McAllister.

Megan pouting. Megan glaring. Megan looking like a little girl who's mad she didn't get the last piece of cake.

"This one," I said, pointing to the sulkiest photo.

"Why?"

"Because . . . it's edgy, I guess." And *edgy* was my kind of picture.

She stood back. "Any others?"

I'd missed something. I leaned forward and looked again, more carefully. On the first pass, I'd disregarded the ones where Megan was smiling. I looked over them again. . . .

"Here," I said, putting my finger over one near the end of the roll.

"Why?"

I bent down again. Megan's dark hair, carefully set in large, loose waves, whipped wildly out to the side where the wind had caught it. The rippling water in the foreground seemed to echo the pattern. Her skirt hung in smooth, graceful folds, the wet edges sticking to the tiled side of the pool. On her mouth was the tiniest touch of a smile, and her posture was relaxed, and her eyes . . .

"She looks like she has a secret."

Farrin smiled.

"Can I grab something?" I asked.

She made a gracious gesture, and I went past her to my backpack, where I kept a binder of all of my negatives, neatly filed in plastic sleeves. Behind each sleeve was its contact sheet. I flipped through them to find that first roll of self-portraits.

The disgruntled photo of me with my new camera, the one that had been blown up for the party, was the tenth one on the roll. But I kept scanning, past that one, past a dozen or so more. All the way to the final exposure.

I remembered that picture. I'd finally gotten a sense of the new camera, but I thought I was out of film. I'd been sitting there and accidentally squeezed the bulb.

My head was turned so you could see the full, scalded-off, jagged side of my hair. There was a haughty half-smile on my face. In a way, it was an edgier picture than the other one could ever hope to be, because who sits in front of a camera with burned hair and a broken collarbone and wrist—and *smiles?*

I stood up and found I'd been holding my breath. I took a gulp of air, like I'd been underwater.

"That one," I said, and Farrin took the loupe from my hand.

A moment later, she stood up. Some strange light seemed to flicker behind her eyes as she turned her body squarely to me. "Brilliant," she said.

For a moment, I saw stars.

"Let's blow these two up," she said, and I looked to find her tapping the photo of Megan.

She stood over my shoulder, mostly watching but occasionally offering a bit of advice, like recommending a high-contrast filter. We processed the print of Megan and hung it to dry. Even in the dim red light, I could tell it was extraordinary.

Then we printed the picture of me. Blown up, the image looked old-fashioned, gothic. Like something that would be hung in a haunted house—and when you walked past it, it would turn into something horrifying.

And all because I was smiling.

When we were finished, Farrin pointed to the corner of one of the shelves. "You can just set the timer right up there."

When I reached up, something stabbed my finger, and I yelped and jerked away.

"Oh, dear. What happened?" Farrin asked. "Are you bleeding?"

In the low red light, my finger looked like it was dripping chocolate sauce. "I guess so," I said. "There was something sharp."

I blinked furiously to suppress the tears that came snapping up behind my eyes. Finally, the sting went away, and the danger had passed.

"How strange," Farrin said, leading me to a sink, where I washed the wound, a deceptively deep little scrape. "I take a lot of care to make sure the broken bulbs get thrown away safely, but sometimes the assistants get careless."

"Do you think it needs stitches?" I asked.

"No," she said, handing me a piece of gauze to press against it. "I'm sure it doesn't."

While she taped the gauze to my finger, I watched her face, lit richly red. Her eyes were black dots rimmed by thick black lashes. Her lips were washed out, almost skin color.

But there was no reason for there to be a broken lightbulb on that shelf. And—what was more—I'd never said that was what had cut me.

It was almost like Farrin had known there was something up there. Something dangerous.

Was this a test? To see if I'd cry?

I jerked my eyes away just as she looked up at me. According to the clock, it was almost ten.

"I should go," I said. "Thank you so much."

"I'll walk you out," she said.

"No, that's fine," I said. "Thanks again. Tonight was an honor. Once-in-a-lifetime."

"Well, that's silly. It doesn't have to be. I'm at your disposal," she said, nodding in a way that was almost a bow. "You'll call me in the morning and let me know how your finger is, won't you?"

Good morning, Farrin. My finger is slightly less bloody today.

I knew I wouldn't call her, but I tried to smile, and said I would.

* * *

When I awoke the next day, my promise to Farrin was the first thing that popped into my head. Still groggy from sleep, I unpeeled the bandage from my finger.

Nothing. Not a cut, not a scratch, not a mark.

I sat up, checking my other fingers, thinking that maybe Farrin had somehow wrapped up the wrong finger.

But there was nothing wrong with my fingers—any of them.

I called Farrin.

"You see?" she said, sounding pleased with herself. "We are a very healthy bunch."

We.

I hung up and stared at my now-uninjured finger for a long time.

All that week, Carter was chivalry personified; he even sat with me at lunch. He seemed a little zoned out—but then, who wouldn't be, in the middle of sixteen chattering girls?

He's trying to save our relationship, I told myself. It certainly had nothing to do with the lines dictated to me in my head, whole conversations that I got through by parroting that sweet, cajoling voice.

Tashi told me to give myself credit for Carter's change of heart. She compared it to pouring water on a neglected plant so it can bloom and thrive.

There was certainly no denying that he'd undergone a transformation. Gone were the pointed remarks about the Sunshine Club; gone were any hints of sarcasm or cynicism.

Totally and completely gone was Zoe.

After school Tuesday, he drove Kasey, Lydia, and me to our house. My sister and Lydia went inside, and I stayed in the car.

"Call me later?" he said.

I tilted my head. "I might not have time."

"Then I'll call you," he said.

"Okay," I said, taken aback. "If you want to."

As I reached for the door handle, he leaned over and took my hand.

"You are so beautiful," he said, gazing into my eyes. "Have I told you that yet today?"

"Yes," I said, pulling gently on my hand. "Three times."

But he didn't let go right away. He got in a little more gazing first.

I looked away. There was something about the adoring stare that made me uneasy. I mean, yes, I wanted things to work out with Carter and me. Yes, he was being the ideal boyfriend.

But to be completely honest—I could see it getting a little dull.

"I really have to go," I said, snaking my hand away and hopping out of the car. "Thanks for the ride. Talk to you later, maybe."

For a second, he looked confused, and then that dreamy, veiled look overtook his face again. "I'll miss you."

I went inside without waving good-bye.

Lydia and Kasey were in the kitchen, their voices echoing in a start-and-stop conversation. No denying that Kasey was making a real effort to show her devotion to Aralt. But it was obvious to me that where everyone else was cheerful and confident, she was stressed and anxious. She tried too hard, and the things she tried to add to our conversations rang just a little off to my ear.

As I walked by, Lydia looked up. "You guys are so cute together," she said. "I should get a boyfriend."

"Go for it," I said.

"There's nobody I really like," she said. "But Nicholas Freeman is cute."

"I think he's dating someone," I said.

"So?" She gave me an amused look, her pink lips smiling mischievously against her creamy skin.

"Good point," I said. If she decided to pull them apart, the other girl stood zero chance. Lydia was as tiny and perfect as a little porcelain doll.

And possibly just as dangerous.

Wednesday afternoon, Megan had cheerleading practice before the Sunshine Club meeting. I waited for her on the bleachers, browsing the fashion magazines we traded at lunch.

Carter was really amping up the chivalry—trying to carry my bag, meeting me outside my classes, even when they were nowhere near his own. He came to my locker after school and offered to drive me home, but I didn't mind watching Megan at cheer practice. It was like being allowed into a secret world that had been forbidden to me for the first sixteen years of my life.

Kasey walked home and said she'd walk to the meeting. No one questioned her—they just assumed she had homework. She was carving out an identity as our little academic poster child. And she'd bought another few days of approval with her revamped hair.

But everyone knew there was something off about a Sunshine Club girl who didn't want to spend as much time as possible with her sisters. Secretly I suspected that, even with her new hair, she still wasn't truly committed to Aralt. Not that I was worried. At some point she would need to rearrange her priorities, that was all. Or have them rearranged for her.

As the practice should have been winding down, I heard a cry of pain.

Megan hurried across the gym toward a clump of cheerleaders all gathered around someone on the floor. After a few seconds, a girl got to her feet and hopped away, leaning on the shoulders of the coach and a spotter.

Megan walked over to me, eyes clouded with worry. "We're going to run long tonight. I might have to miss the meeting. Sydney just ate it on a basket toss, and we have to rework the whole routine." She looked around helplessly. "I don't know what we're going to do. She and Jessica are the only ones who can do the halftime tumbling sequence."

I watched her searching the other girls, trying to figure out who could fill in for Sydney. She was biting her lip, and I knew she was remembering that it used to be *her* tumbling sequence.

I glanced down at my finger. At the flawless skin where there used to be a gash.

"Megan," I said, "how's your knee feeling?"

She stared at me for a second, trying to digest what I was suggesting. "No way." She spoke in a hushed voice. "Lex, after that fall at your house—I can't afford to take any chances."

"But that didn't actually *hurt* you, did it?" I said. "You haven't been limping. Have you had any pain at all?"

If I was wrong, I could be costing my best friend the ability to walk.

But I knew I wasn't wrong. "Start small," I suggested. "Do a cartwheel."

Megan gave me a wary look and handed me her notebook. Then she tucked her T-shirt into the front of her shorts and turned an effortless cartwheel. "But that doesn't mean anything."

"Are you sure?"

"Lex, it's *hard*, and it's been a year since I did anything remotely like that." Without thinking, she reached back and redid her ponytail. When she could see I didn't believe her, she said, "Hey, Jess!"

One of the cheerleaders bounced up to us. "Yeah?"

Staring right at me, Megan said, "Could you please demonstrate the tumbling run from the top of the half-time routine?"

Jessica nodded, walked a few feet away, and took a springy running start. Then she went through a series of flips and handsprings and landed perfectly, her hands clasped in front of her.

"Thank you," Megan said sweetly. "That's all." She gave me an expectant look.

"You can do it," I said, though her set jaw told me she wasn't convinced. "Adrienne doesn't even use her cane anymore."

"That's different," she said. "Walking can't break your knees."

"Or maybe . . ." I said, "Adrienne just has more trust?"

Her face fell. "That isn't fair, Lex."

"I'm just saying," I said. "You're the one who told me to let go. Do you have faith in Aralt or not?"

She pursed her lips and glared into the corner of the gym—because glaring at your sisters was a total no-no. Without saying a word, she walked away, got a running start, and did the whole thing flawlessly. She even added an extra handspring at the end.

The cheerleaders let out a collective squeal and converged on us. "I didn't know you could cheer again!" Jessica crowed. They enveloped her in a huge hug.

After a minute, Megan came back to me. There was something in her eyes—wonder. Shock.

"I guess we won't run late," Megan said. "I have plenty of time to run through the routine before Friday."

"How does your knee feel?" I asked.

"It's . . . fine," she said, a bewildered smile blooming on her lips. "It's great."

"Sorry for the drama," I said. "I just thought you needed a reminder."

"No," she said, her eyes shimmering. "You were right. I did need it."

We grabbed our bags and started for the door. I paused in front of Coach Neidorf, who kept stealing glances at Megan.

Mrs. Wiley really doesn't need to know about this. It's just a one-time thing, and it's for the good of the whole squad.

"Mrs. Wiley really doesn't need to know about this," I said, and the coach's eyes jerked to meet mine. "It's just a one-time thing, and it's for the good of the whole squad, don't you think?"

She looked from me to Megan and then down at her notebook like she couldn't remember what we were talking about.

"No," she said. "No, of course not."

Megan gave her a radiant smile. "Thanks, Coach. You're the best!"

The meeting was great. We had two new girls. And best of all?

Kasey called someone out in Betterment. And then she contributed as much as anyone else, coming up with recruiting ideas and taking the affirmative in our debate against ever wearing athletic shoes at a non-athletic event.

Thursday and Friday at school, she was bubbly, happy. She practically glowed.

She was finally, finally committing to Aralt.

I was so proud I could hardly stop smiling.

* * *

Friday afternoon, we all went home to change before the game. As I was getting ready to do my makeup, my phone rang with a number I didn't recognize.

"Hello?"

"Hello, Alexis?"

"Yes, who's calling?"

"Jared Elkins. We met at the, uh, party the other night."

"Oh, right," I said, wedging the phone between my cheek and shoulder and starting to work on my eye shadow. "Tricycle Boy."

"The one and only. Listen, I have a huge favor to ask you. The final two interviews were scheduled for next Thursday, but I'm going to be out of town. They said they'd move them if you could make it Wednesday instead."

"Final interviews?" I asked. "What do you mean?"

"Oh, man," he said. "Spoiler alert. I suck. We're the final two. Didn't they call you?"

I laughed. "I haven't checked my voicemail for a couple of days."

"Listen, if you can't do it, that's okay."

"Wednesday's fine," I said. "It's great. Congratulations."

"You too," he said. "I don't think I would have been satisfied with anyone else as my opponent."

That made me smile at myself in the mirror.

"In fact, I've been wanting to ask you," he said. "Do you remember what film you used for the car picture? I love the grain."

"Oh, yeah," I said. "It's just T-Max. That's pretty much all I use."

"Really?" he said.

"It was probably four hundred ISO. . . ."

We went on talking for a few minutes, and then said our good-byes and hung up. A pleasant enough conversation, but I didn't give Jared another thought the whole night.

18

COMBINE A THOUSAND keyed-up teenagers, a couple hundred over-involved parents, a bunch of teachers bitter about having to work on Friday night, and the smell of churros. What do you get?

A Surrey Eagles football game.

Friday night was the first home game of the season, and the Sunshine Club planned to sit together, unified, showing off our school spirit. I noticed that, as a rule, we put more effort into *showing* how much we cared about football than actually caring about the outcome of the game.

We met outside of the gym before the game. Everyone was wearing Surrey High colors—red and white—and there was a dazzling energy in the air that I had never noticed before. The sun was setting behind the gymnasium, and I stood and listened to the happy buzz of the sounds around me, the idyllic way the kids pulled into the parking lot and poured out of their cars, coming together in excited groups.

Every blessing I could ask for was laid at my feet. I was young and beautiful, and I had loyal friends and a boyfriend and a happy sister and parents who loved me and a future that was as bright as I dared to let it be. The breeze wove gently through our hair and set our skirts undulating around us like flags from some precious, golden memory.

Megan, in her cheer uniform, came over to say hi and folded herself into the group, and I could hardly breathe for the sharp, intense beauty of the moment. It was like I was nostalgic for my own youth, while I was still living it. If I hadn't gotten so good at not letting myself cry, I might have felt tears well up. But I held it in—stayed sunny.

Then the ticket-takers got in place and the gates opened. The kids around us went inside. But we stayed out until the last second, because we weren't done saying our hellos, and we knew we would find the best seats vacant no matter how long we waited.

Then we were moving together—not quite in formation, but in a well-defined group, an army of the prettiest, brightest, best girls—and we came around the side of the bleachers like a school of sharks: glamorous and dangerous and sleek, stepping in time to a beat only we could hear.

The beating of Aralt's heart, I thought.

The hum in the stands dipped slightly as people noticed us, admired us, wished they could be like us.

I soaked it in. My hair was perfect, my clothes were perfect, my best friend and my sister walked perfectly at my side.

Everything was perfect, and I was right in the center of it all.

The thought was in my head before I could stop it: *I would rather die than give this up.*

With our dresses and skirts, sweaters and full makeup, it was like a little time machine had perched itself on the edge of the bleachers and the class of 1965 had popped in for the night.

Someone passed out little flags, which we flapped along with the crowd. A wave came through; we stood and sat with it. It came back, and we stood again and sat again.

"Try to look like you're enjoying yourself," I said to Kasey.

"It's kind of fun . . . I guess," Kasey said.

I laughed. "You look completely miserable."

"Do I?" She waved her flag in my face.

It was so easy to get along with her now that she was making an effort. Overcome by a rush of affection, I pulled her into a sideways hug.

A few minutes later, the loudspeaker blared, welcoming the opposing team. Across the field, their ragged group of fans filled only a couple rows of the bleachers.

Then it was time for the cheerleaders' entrance.

I didn't *plan* to get excited, but it was easy to get caught up in the crowd's whooping and clapping as the girls came running out. Megan was in the middle of them, looking like the queen again—her ponytail held back by a white ribbon, pom-poms hoisted high in the air.

Then the football team came barreling out, ripping through their big paper sign, and the game started. Kasey and I watched the field in utter confusion, cheering when the people around us cheered but otherwise having no idea what was happening.

"Lex?" I looked up to see Carter standing over me, smiling.

Kasey and I shifted over, and he squeezed himself onto the bench next to me.

"Are you excited about your speech?" I asked him.

He nodded and showed us a small stack of note cards. "I've been practicing for hours."

Something exciting happened on the field, and the people around us began hooting and stomping their feet. Carter grabbed my hand and held it.

Like a wave pulling back to sea, the crowd went quiet.

"Do you want to hang out tomorrow?" he asked.

"And do what?" I asked.

"Whatever you want." He was wriggly and giddy, like a piglet.

I didn't respond. Carter and I had never been *I don't know, what do you want to do?* people. We had interests. Hobbies.

"I don't know," I said. "I kind of need to go shopping. At the mall."

Carter and the mall went together like a bucket of nails and a bucket of water balloons. If absolutely forced to go, he spent the whole time whining and checking his watch.

"Sounds great!" he replied. "What time should I pick you up?"

My heart sank a little. I let my eyes drift back to the game, hoping I looked wrapped up in what was going on.

Carter touched my arm and pulled me close, his mouth next to my ear. "I have something to tell you tonight."

I heard people shouting *"Touchdown!"* and everyone around us leaped to their feet. I jumped up, away from Carter, and cheered along with the crowd. The band played a few jubilant notes, the cheerleaders started chanting, and everything slid together to form a discordant roar.

When everyone else sat down, I had no choice but to rejoin Carter on the bench.

"Aren't you curious?" Carter asked, his words almost lost in the noise around us. He said something else, but the crowd let out a giant shout, and I missed it.

"What?" I yelled back.

Then the crowd was quiet again, finished with their celebration, finding their seats.

Carter leaned toward me, holding me in a tight embrace.

"I said," he went on, the words gauzy in my ear, "you're a really incredible girl, and I have something important to say."

I sat up, dazed, staring at him. Our hands were in a death grip between us.

He was going to tell me he loved me.

Of all the times I'd imagined we'd say those words— of all the places, all the situations . . .

"No," I said, almost pleading, twisting my body to get free of his arms. "Not here, Carter."

"What do you mean?"

My heart seemed well on its way to pounding right through my skin. Saliva filled the back of my throat. I needed to stop him. At least stall him.

Carter's eyes searched my face, like a lost kid looking for someone in a crowd. "Lex, you don't even know what I'm going to say!" he protested. "I just wanted you to know that I—"

You know you're really special to me.

"You know you're really special to me," I said.

Maybe later tonight we can have a really serious talk.

"Maybe later tonight . . . we can have a really serious talk?"

He smiled, a little confused, and dropped my hand. But as quickly as the hurt reached his eyes, it was wiped away, replaced by blankness.

"Yes, of course. Later," he said.

Like a counterweight to our emotions, the crowd was up on their feet again, shrieking with glee. Carter looked like he'd been dropped out of the sky into a strange, crowded place.

"I should go get ready," he said, standing up and excusing himself down the aisle.

Kasey sat down, waving her flag. "I think I'm starting to get it," she said. "Their guy dropped the ball, and we picked it up and that's called a—where's Carter going?"

"To read his speech," I said.

She gave me a weird look and went back to watching the game.

Just sitting there was starting to feel like suffocating. "I think I might go take some pictures," I said, reaching for my camera. "Watch my bag?"

I roamed the edge of the field while the football players scrambled around as meaninglessly as a bunch of field mice. I got some good shots—I'd never tried action shots before, due to my stinginess with film and darkroom time. But now, I knew, if I needed more film, I could get it from Farrin. If I needed darkroom time, all I had to do was breathe half of a hint, and she'd offer it up.

When halftime came, the cheerleaders' music came piping through the loudspeakers, and then Megan and Jessica bounced across the field, landing in flawless unison.

I zoomed in and took as many photos as I could. Their intense expressions, their sweaty, muscular limbs, the vibrant red and white of their uniforms, all stood out against the black night sky and the vivid green of the field.

Megan's face lit up as they went through the routine. She kicked, jumped, got tossed into the air, and balanced on somebody's shoulder. As they finished, I lowered my camera and applauded, feeling almost as breathless as the cheerleaders were. Monday morning, I'd ask if I could attend some of the practices, shoot some more. The motion and energy were addictive.

"And now," the announcer boomed, "please give a

warm welcome to our newly elected student body president, Carter Blume!"

School politics didn't merit quite the same level of cheering as football, but Carter got a decent amount of applause. He took his place on a little makeshift stage, his golden hair glinting under the stadium lights. In his slim gray pants and white button-down shirt, he looked tall, powerful, and charismatic, like some 1940s movie heartthrob.

There was something different about him, though.

I raised my camera and took a few shots.

Just before he started speaking, he caught sight of me and gave me a quick smile.

That's when I realized what was different.

In the stands, he'd been wearing a long-sleeved black sweater over his shirt. Now he'd taken it off.

And rolled his sleeves up, almost to his elbows.

Since the day we'd met, he'd never let anyone but his parents and me see the scars on his bare wrists. Now they were exposed for the whole school to see.

My eyes wandered up to meet his, to see his face, his confident master-of-the-universe grin.

For a split second, I was paralyzed.

I couldn't see any trace of Carter behind that smile.

Just emptiness. A reaction where there had once been action.

Oh my God.

This can't be happening.

I totally stole my boyfriend's soul.

"People say," he began, his voice strong, "that high school is the best four years of your life. And tonight is"—his voice was all clanging metallic sounds; did anyone else hear it?—"the culmination of that for me."

I looked around for an escape, but I was basically *on* the field. Standing still, I didn't attract attention, but to move would have been like shining a spotlight on myself. Carter went on, talking about how great his years at Surrey had been and how excited he was to have a chance to give back to the school that had given him so much.

"Not only steadfast friends," he said, "and top-notch academic opportunities. But a well-developed extracurricular program, the best technological resources in the county, and a caring staff and faculty."

A polite smattering of applause.

"So I'd like to dedicate this year to all of you, and to all of the students who came before me and will come after me," he said. "But most of all—"

He was staring right at me.

I raised my camera, not wanting to look him in the eye, not knowing what else to do.

"I want to dedicate this win to the most incredible

girl I've ever met and probably will ever meet in my life—"

My finger kept hitting the shutter button, like I could pretend I was just an observer, not even there.

"My girlfriend, Alexis Warren."

The crowd said, *"Awww."*

"Lex," Carter said, laughing. "Put the camera down."

I had no choice.

He looked straight at me. And then he said:

"Alexis . . . *I love you.*"

The words rushed at me over the painted stripes of the field. They hit the school building in the distance and echoed back.

I was surrounded. Helpless.

It was the kind of public horror show that you'd see in some awful romantic comedy, not on the football field of Surrey High. The crowd went crazy, whooping and whistling and catcalling. I stood there, staring at his big, bright, oblivious grin.

And then I ran.

The throngs of people around me blurred together as I fought my way through, pushing to the sidelines, trying to escape into the night. People talked to me, laughed at me, exclaimed in surprise as I shoved them out of my way, past the front of the bleachers, toward the exit.

"Alexis? Are you okay?" Miss Nagesh called out as I ran by, but I didn't stop.

"Lexi!" Ahead of me, my sister clambered down the stairs, carrying my bag. "Lexi!"

Our paths intersected. Kasey grabbed my hand and ran, pulling me around the back of the bleachers, where the speakers could only throw muffled sound instead of bladelike words.

In the sudden darkness, I ran smack into someone.

Mrs. Wiley. "Alexis," she said, her voice sharp. "Have you seen Megan?"

I think I would rather have run into an angry grizzly bear.

"I'm sorry," I said. "I don't have time to talk!"

Mrs. Wiley watched in shock as we took off.

I held my camera with one hand and held on to Kase with the other. All I knew was that we had to get out of there. We had to go.

We were almost to the exit. *Almost free.*

"Alexis?"

Tashi sidestepped into my path. I stopped inches short of colliding with her.

"What are you doing?" she asked. "Where are you going?"

"Home," I gasped. "I'm not feeling well."

I was so used to Tashi's serene smile—I'd never seen

her look harsh before. Her eyes flashed, and her lips came together in a pout.

"You need to collect yourself," she said, "and get back in there. You're going to embarrass Carter and the whole Sunshine Club."

"Carter embarrassed *himself*!" I said. "I didn't ask him to get up in front of the whole school and say . . . say he . . ." I couldn't even say the words. It was too terrible. I felt like I'd been punched in the stomach.

Tashi stepped closer. Involuntarily, Kasey stepped back. "You mean to tell me," Tashi said, "that *nothing* you said or did inspired his little confession?"

My head ached. I mean—yes. Of *course* things I said and did inspired it. But that didn't make it my fault! Carter and I had gone five months without saying "I love you." It was supposed to be precious, private. Now it was ruined.

"How much worse will it be for *Carter* if you don't go back?" Tashi asked.

I pictured him—standing out there on the stage, mic in hand. Having to walk down the steps. Face everybody. Alone.

A scream of feedback came through the sound system.

My heart cringed for him.

"You have no right to do this, Alexis," Tashi said

quietly. "You can't run away. This isn't all about you. You need to get in there and be the girl Aralt wants you to be."

Kasey, still panting, gave me a look that begged me to leave.

Be the girl Aralt wants you to be.

I literally didn't have a choice.

"I have to go back," I said to my sister. *For Aralt.* "For Carter."

Kasey stared down at the ground.

Tashi focused on my sister for the first time. "You should be there too," she said. "Your sister needs you. We all need you."

But Tashi's serious face didn't scare Kasey. She just cocked her head to the side and said, "Alexis can stay if she wants. But I'm going home."

I expected some offended reply from Tashi—something about our duty to the sisterhood, or the bond we shared, or whatever. But Tashi just stared at Kasey like she was trying to memorize her face.

Then she turned and started walking back toward the football field.

"I'm leaving, Lexi," Kasey said. "I feel sick."

"Come on, Kasey," I said. "Please. Stay. You can handle it. You're strong. You can—"

"You're wrong, I'm not," she said. "Not strong

266

enough to stand here and watch you do this."

"But you have a duty to Aralt," I said. "At least think about *that*."

She shook her head. "No, I don't," she said, breathless. "I don't have a duty to anyone."

Then she started to cry—big fat tears of crystal-clear salt water.

And before she said another word, I knew.

"I never took the oath," she said.

I felt myself rock backward, away from her.

"There. Now you know. I'm a terrible sister." She looked toward the field, her eyes almost wild. "I got you into this, and I can't get you out."

She reached up and pulled the ponytail holder out of her hair.

"The worst part is," she said, "you don't even *want* out anymore."

There were no words. Literally not a single word I could think of to say in reply. So I took a step backward, toward Carter and Tashi and the Sunshine Club.

"I have to go," I said, walking away.

My escape had felt like fast-motion, but now everything slowed to half-speed. Carter was just coming off the field as I emerged from behind the bleachers, and a lane cleared between us. He held out his arms to me, and I went straight into them. The sounds blended together into one loud hum, and my eyes swam with spots from the stadium lights. Carter smushed his lips against my forehead.

"Hey," he said. "Where'd you run off to?"

I swallowed hard and stared into his eyes.

Show me Carter, I thought. Show me one glimpse of my Carter. Then I can do this. Then I can get through it.

His eyes were blue and wide, and they sparkled in the night, reflecting back everything around us. But there was no Carter.

I started to take a step back.

"Alexis?" he asked, a hint of hurt in his voice. He was still waiting for my explanation.

I had a wardrobe malfunction.

Behind Carter, Tashi stood with her arms folded in front of her, waiting.

I put my hand behind his head and pulled his ear down to my mouth.

And I whispered that I'd had a wardrobe malfunction.

But I was sorry I'd run away.

I wouldn't be running anymore.

I closed my eyes against his chest, inhaling his smell—laundry detergent and sweat. I loved his smell. He didn't act like Carter. He didn't talk like Carter, and his eyes weren't Carter's eyes. But he still smelled like himself. Somewhere under it all, he still *was* Carter . . . right?

I could be happy. I really could.

If I was just willing to lie to myself about everything that mattered . . .

I could be happy.

Carter dropped me off at home after we made appearances at three postgame parties in three hours. When I got inside, I was so tired that I practically swayed on my feet.

But halfway down the hall to my room, I was stopped by my mother's silhouette in the near blackness.

"Alexis?" she asked. Her voice was strained. "Do you have a second?"

"Sure," I said, turning on my bedroom light and sitting on my bed. For a second I was afraid that she'd noticed something was up with Carter. Had somebody called her? A nosy teacher? A meddlesome parent?

"It's about Kasey," Mom said, sitting in my desk chair. She took a deep breath. "She was using my computer earlier, and she left, and I—I guess I'll admit it, I was snooping. I checked the Internet history."

The breath went out of my lungs. "What did you find?"

"Oh, Alexis." Mom closed her eyes and shook her

head. "Weird stuff. Spells, charms, books about dead people . . . Something called a *creature*? A *creatura*? I don't know. Everything she was supposed to be staying away from."

"Wow," I said.

Deep inside me, something perked up.

Something dark.

"I don't know what to do. I have that phone number, but I'm afraid to get her in trouble without at least talking it over. But then I think about last year—talking wouldn't have helped then."

This was it. The perfect chance to get Kasey—and her traitorous hidden agenda—out of the way.

"You spend time with her. Did you know about any of this?"

No, Mom. Wow, it sounds dangerous. I hope she's not planning anything violent.

I stared at my mother. The voice in my head tried again, louder this time.

No, Mom. Wow, it sounds dangerous—

I closed my eyes, inwardly focusing every bit of strength I had left inside me.

"Um . . . you know what?" I said. "She mentioned it to me, actually—it's a project she's doing for school. She's taking European history, and I think they're on the medieval unit. You know, Merlin, Camelot . . ."

Mom sat back while a fresh pulse of pain worked its way up my arms.

"She hasn't been acting weird at all," I said, and the words physically hurt to say, like I had a mouthful of tiny shards of glass. "Trust me. I'm on the lookout."

It was like Mom had been holding a breath inside herself for three hours. She sighed—a big, quivering openmouthed sigh that could just as easily have ended in a sob. "Oh, thank God."

"I'll let you know if anything changes, though," I said.

"Thank you so much, Alexis," Mom whispered. She got up, took my face in her hands, and kissed me on the cheek.

As soon as she was gone, the headache began, way back at the base of my skull. It grew stronger and stronger until I couldn't think about anything but the throbbing pain in my head, like a baby dragon trying to break out of its egg.

I didn't brush my teeth or wash my face or change out of my dress. I just pulled the pillow over my eyes and braced myself for a very long night.

But a minute later, my door opened.

"Lexi?"

I wasn't asleep. I didn't even pretend to be. I flipped over and looked at Kasey. Being distracted soothed the aching in my head, so I sat up and turned on my light.

She didn't come into my room. She leaned against the doorjamb, examining me from a distance, like I was an animal in a zoo.

"What do you want?" I asked.

"You lied to Mom," she said.

"So?"

"Why? You could have turned me in. Then I'd be out of your way."

But part of me didn't want to turn Kasey in. She was still my sister.

Because everyone deserves a second chance, said the voice. *And it's not too late for you. If you just take the oath, you won't be a liar anymore. And I'd be so proud of you.*

If I said all the right things, there was a really good chance I could use a combination of guilt, threats, and charm to coax her into taking the oath, joining us for real.

But for some reason, I didn't want to do *that*, either.

I just wanted to go to sleep.

Not that I was any less furious with Kasey.

"I felt like it, okay?" I said. "Now leave me alone before I change my mind."

19

FARRIN AGREED TO MEET me at eleven. When I pulled into the parking lot, she was waiting for me outside the main door, reading a magazine in a very Sunshine Club–like manner. The difference was that this magazine cover was a picture *she'd* taken.

She stopped in front of suite six and unlocked it. "What did you bring to work on today?"

"Actually," I said, "I was hoping we could talk."

"Is everything all right?"

I followed her to her office but didn't answer.

She sat down and gave me a concerned smile.

"How much do you know about Aralt?" I asked.

"Ah," she said. She was silent for such a long time that I was afraid I'd offended her. Then she turned to me. "How much do *you* know?"

I shook my head. "Not enough."

She pursed her lips and stared at me. "Things are happening that you don't understand."

"To put it mildly."

"Have you ever heard the term 'a charmed life'?"

"Of course."

"And you know what it means."

"That things go well for you," I said. "It's like being lucky."

"The phrase is tossed around these days, but once upon a time, it actually meant something. To lead a charmed life was to lead a life that was . . . touched. By a supernatural force. A spell, or an incantation—"

"Or an oath."

"Precisely. Now, when you have this force acting inside you, it's a form of energy. And the laws of the universe state that energy is neither created nor destroyed. It's only transferred."

"And how does that happen?"

"All of the wonderful changes in your life," she said. "How you look and feel. How your mind works. The energy is burned off through all of those things. You sublimate it into your regular life—it becomes your edge."

"But not every change is wonderful," I said, thinking of the odd, blank look in Carter's eyes, my moment of feeling like I could kill my sister.

"Aralt cares for us, Alexis. He wants the best for us. It's all he wants. So if you are experiencing problems, you have to question your own precepts."

I wasn't quite sure what a precept was, but I got the distinct feeling I was being told it was all in my head. "But what does he get out of it?"

"When you're at your best, he's at his best," Farrin said. "It's as simple as that."

She considered it simple? That a supernatural being was feeding off of us?

"Have you cried lately?" I asked.

"I have nothing to cry about." She folded her hands and looked directly into my eyes. "And neither do you."

I slumped lower in my chair.

"I care about you, too, Alexis," she said. "I don't like to see you struggling needlessly. You could make this very easy for yourself."

Just swallow the blue pill, right?

Farrin was staring right at me. "This could be the best thing that ever happened to you," she said softly.

"But I—" I stopped mid-sentence.

Suddenly I couldn't remember what I was going to say.

All I could think was, *This could be the best thing that ever happened to me.*

"This is a lot to process, Alexis. Why don't we look at your photos? I don't believe that you didn't bring anything," she said.

"Well, I did, but . . ."

"Let's get some work done," she said gently. "You shot color, didn't you? I'm excited to see the pictures. You can think about the rest of it later."

I can think about the rest of it later. She had a point. I could think at home. I couldn't process color negatives at home.

The office phone rang. "Excuse me, please," she said, grabbing the portable handset from her desk. "Hello? . . . Oh, yes, I'll be home by five . . . No, don't. I'll order in."

Her tone was silky, hypnotic. I drifted to the bookshelves and looked at the picture of Aralt's girls again. This time, my eyes had leisure to wander across each of the faces, ending up on the angelic face of a pretty, tanned girl. Behind her headband, her hair was a thick mane of curls.

She could have been sixteen or twenty-five—it was so hard to tell in old pictures.

But I knew the face.

It was Tashi.

"Are you ready?" Farrin asked, hanging up the phone.

"Actually," I said, "I . . ."

She came over to me and, in a gesture that felt almost maternal, tucked my hair behind my ear. "Of course you're ready, Alexis."

I felt myself smiling. "Yes," I said. Of course I was ready.

20

WE WENT THROUGH my film from the football game and printed two pictures for the final interview. I wondered what Jared would say if he knew I had Farrin's help.

But then, Farrin was really the least of my advantages, wasn't she?

Carter called a few times. I let the calls go to voicemail. When I got home, I found that he'd left two messages at the house, but they were lighthearted "call if you get a chance" messages, so I wasn't worried.

I lay in bed that night, staring at the clock for a while before drifting into a light sleep. I'd always been a solid-eight-hours kind of girl, but that wasn't the case anymore. Now I basically had to force myself to stay in bed if I'd gotten more than five. In the beginning, I'd suspected that Kasey was sneaking sleeping pills or something. Now I knew the truth.

I awoke suddenly at the sound of a light *click*. My feet hit the floor, and my eyes hit the numbers on the clock—2:17—and I was on my way to the hall when I ran into something:

A box.

It was the size of a shoe box, but taller, wrapped in silver paper with a silky pink ribbon tied around it.

I froze and looked around my room—suddenly realizing how many pockets of darkness were hidden amid the furniture.

"Hello?" I whispered.

No one answered.

Lightly pushing the box out of the way with my foot, I reached for my bedroom door and pulled it open.

My breath felt as shallow as a bird's as I walked down the hall. From the end of the hallway, the main room seemed vast and empty. I switched on the lights and looked around.

Finally, I went back toward my room, stepping inside and reaching down to move the box.

It was gone.

I straightened up. And someone grabbed my shoulder.

A yelp almost escaped my mouth when I heard a familiar voice in my ear.

"Don't be frightened . . . it's just me."

"Carter?" I whispered, spinning around and shutting the door so my parents wouldn't hear us. I flipped on the lamp to see him standing right behind me. "What are you *doing* here?"

"I came to drop this off," he said, passing the gift to me. His wide blue eyes seemed to track even my tiniest movements. "I didn't think you'd wake up."

"How did you get inside?" I asked, plunking the package gracelessly on the bed.

"I have a spare key, remember?" he asked.

"That's for emergencies!"

"This is an emergency," he said, giving me a mischievous smile that didn't reach his eyes. "A happy emergency."

I couldn't think of anything to say.

"Aren't you going to unwrap it?" he asked.

My mouth open in disbelief, I sank onto the bed and helplessly reached for the box. I knew what it was as soon as I peeled the paper off: a digital camera. A really nice one. More megapixels even than Daffodil/Delilah's.

For about thirty seconds I couldn't speak. All I could do was stare.

"What is this?" I asked.

"It's a blender," he said. "What does it look like?"

"No, but I mean . . . where did you get it?" Based on the miniscule research I'd done when I signed up for photography class, I estimated this camera's cost in the twelve- to fifteen-hundred-dollar range.

"Jeff's Cameras, out on Langford Street," he said. His expression was alert but oddly unchanging, like a mask or a mannequin. Or a Ken doll.

His straightforward answers set sirens wailing in my head. "Carter," I said. "Why did you bring this here?"

Finally I'd stumped him. "Because . . . it's . . . for you."

"You bought this?" I asked. He nodded. "With what money?"

"I have a savings account," he said. "Don't worry. I still have plenty of money. I can buy you whatever you want, Lex."

Oh my God.

Oh my God oh my God oh my God.

"I can't accept this," I said, shoving the box into his hands. "This is *not* okay. You have to take it back. And you have to leave right now, before my parents wake up."

He took the box and gave me a quirky smile. "I watched you sleep for a couple of minutes. You're really pretty when you sleep."

The air between us seemed to waver.

"You can't do this," I said, my voice hardly more than a breath. "Please. You have to go. You can't come here. You can't"—I could hardly say it—"*watch me sleep*."

For the first time, he seemed bothered by what I was saying. His forehead wrinkled.

"I brought you a very nice gift," he said, an impatient, childish edge creeping into his voice. "And you didn't even say thank you."

"Thank you," I said. "Now you have to go."

His lip curled in annoyance. "Not like that, Lex. Not just a throwaway *thank you*. I mean, I went to all the trouble to go out there and get it and buy the wrapping paper and—"

"Thank you," I said, to stem the rising volume of his voice. "Thank you, Carter, it was very sweet."

It worked well enough—barely. He was still agitated as I steered him down the hallway and opened the front door.

"You have to go," I said. "Please take the camera with you."

He gazed down at it, expressionless.

"And you have to give me the key back, Carter," I said. "You can't do stuff like this."

His face fell, but he reached into his pocket and pulled out his key chain. He unhooked the key from it and handed it to me.

"Never again," I said. "I mean it."

"Do you want a ride to school in the morning?" he asked. "I can drive you."

"Megan takes me to school," I said. "You know that."

"But I'm your boyfriend," he said. "You always see Megan. And you're too busy for me."

"Fine," I said. "Whatever. I don't care."

He smiled, finally happy again. Then he held out the box. "But this is for you."

"No," I said. "*I don't want it.* Take it back. Please."

"Fine," he said, heading toward his car, which he'd parked in the driveway. But he didn't stop at the driver's door. He went around the back and set the box on the ground behind one of the tires.

"What are you doing?" I followed him down the driveway.

"I don't need a camera," he said, climbing into the car and turning it on. "And now you won't have to worry about it."

He was going to *destroy* it?

"Come on, don't," I said, looking through his open window. "This is crazy!"

He shifted into reverse.

"Stop it, Carter!" I cried.

He paused, then spoke to me as if I were a kid who needed to be taught a lesson. "Then go pick it up, Lex. I told you—it doesn't make a difference to me."

I hesitated, then ran to the back of the car and

swiped the box to safety. I held it, panting, as Carter backed smoothly out onto the road.

He watched me walk to the front door, then blew me a kiss and drove away.

I lay in bed, fully dressed, staring at the ceiling. I'd tucked the camera between the bed and the wall and tried to go back to sleep, but my ability to do so had apparently left the building with Carter. Not that I was tired.

Except for all the obvious reasons why I knew I shouldn't feel fine, I felt fine.

Dad came to the door. "Are you all right?"

"Fine," I said.

"Do you have a meeting this morning or something?"

"No," I said. "Why?"

"Because Carter's parked out front, and I thought you might have forgotten. You know how he's too polite to honk."

I glanced at the clock.

It was 7:20. Twenty minutes earlier than when we usually left.

I knocked on the bathroom door, and Kasey stuck her head out.

"I have to go to school early," I said. "Tell Megan, okay?"

She nodded, curious but wordless.

I couldn't find my cell phone, but I didn't have time to look for it. I grabbed my book bag and walked slowly across the street to Carter's silent car. He hurried to open the door for me, then gave me a kiss on the cheek. He made happy small talk the whole ride to school, but I could hardly hear it over the commotion of my own thoughts.

When we pulled into the parking lot, I reached for my door and unlocked it.

He reached down and hit the lock button again.

I didn't want to make too big of a deal out of it, so I looked out the windshield at the school building.

"I'm just curious," he said. "Who's Jared Elkins?"

"What?"

"Jared Elkins?" he said, taking my cell phone out of his pocket. "You talked to him Friday night for ten minutes. Which is weird, because . . . you wouldn't answer when *I* called."

"You *took* my phone?"

"Who is he, Lex?"

Every muscle, every cell in my body was on high alert. "He's from the photography contest," I said. "He's nobody."

"Nobody," Carter said, pressing his lips together.

We stared at each other for a few seconds, then Carter relaxed.

"I believe you," he said, smiling and unlocking the door.

I grabbed my phone, half expecting him to close his hand over it. But he didn't. He let it go easily.

"Carter . . . what's going on with you? Are you okay?"

"I'm fantastic, because I'm here with you." I flinched as he reached his hand up to caress my cheek, smiling his relaxed smile. "It's no big deal, Lex. I just wondered."

"Wow." Megan had listened with wide, sympathetic eyes. Then she took a bite of her salad and gave me a half-cringing smile. "Well, Lex . . . you *did* kind of talk to that guy after blowing Carter off."

I sat back.

"Think about it. He spends all that money to buy you this super-expensive gift. And you won't answer the phone when he calls?" She stared at the veneer of the cafeteria table. "I think you might actually owe him an apology."

"That's"—I tried to think of a word that was strong enough yet still within the boundaries of politeness—"nuts."

"Is it?" she asked, her voice cooling. She sat back and patted her hair. "Why don't you think about it this way? What would Aralt want you to do?"

What would Aralt want? "He would want me to not be totally freaked out by my boyfriend."

"Yes," Megan said. "And how do you do that?"

I stared at her. I had no idea—aside from breaking up with Carter. Talking hadn't worked, although he had, at my request, sat with his guy friends at lunch that day.

"Easy, Lex." She poked the air with the tines of her fork. "You focus on making yourself a better girlfriend."

I blew a puff of air out of my nose.

"Don't be like that," she said. "You don't even know how lucky you are. He adores you. He's, like, totally obsessed with you. Just look at him."

I swung my head around in the direction of Carter's table.

He was sitting in the very middle of the group. But all he was doing was staring directly at me.

21

AT THE MONDAY afternoon meeting, I avoided eye contact with Tashi. I felt Kasey's presence in the corner of the room like a splinter; suddenly I wondered how I'd never noticed how foreign she was, how different.

As I expected, I got called out in Betterment for Friday night's wardrobe malfunction. Megan got called out too, for speaking disrespectfully to her grandmother in public.

As soon as we got home, I closed myself off in my bedroom while Kasey went to study—since she had to, obviously. I dodged a couple of phone calls from Carter and ate silently enough to attract my parents' concerned attention. I mumbled an excuse about cramps, and hid out in my room afterward while they watched some lame reality show.

I couldn't get that thirty-year-old picture of Tashi out of my mind.

Just as the stars were beginning to appear, I slipped

on a pair of shoes and headed for the front door.

My mother asked if it was safe to walk alone at night. *I'll be fine,* said the voice. "I'll be fine," I said. And then no one tried to stop me. I headed down the front steps and farther into the white maw of Silver Sage Acres.

A Sunshine Club girl would never hurt another Sunshine Club girl.

I repeated that to myself, almost like a mantra, all the way to Tashi's house.

But as I walked up to the door of #133, my whole body thrummed with adrenaline.

My heart sank in my chest. All the lights were off.

I rang the doorbell anyway, just to be sure.

After giving it another minute, I turned to go.

Then I stopped. Tashi said her house had the same layout as mine.

Which meant hers also had that one window in the back where you could knock the latch open by hip-checking it just right. We had it. The Munyons had it. In fact, Mrs. Munyon was the one who taught me how to do it, the time I locked myself out.

I started for the side gate.

My heart slammed against my rib cage, but I told myself, over and over: We don't get caught. We don't get caught. We don't get caught. Fortunately, to give some semblance of privacy, the fences were tall and solid, so none of the neighbors would see me sneaking around.

I gave the window a healthy bump, and the latch came unfastened. I opened it and hesitated.

If there was an alarm system, I could end up in jail. And if Tashi really was some kind of supernatural being and found out I knew her secrets . . . it might mean something worse than jail. Sunshine Club rules or no.

I swung my leg inside. But as soon as I got through the window, I felt the magnitude of my mistake.

The house was empty.

I mean, someone clearly lived there, but not in the conventional sense. Even the most basic situation would involve some type of furniture—a ratty La-Z-Boy, a mouse-infested couch. . . . But where my family had a couch and loveseat and entertainment center and coffee table and a couple of potted plants, here there was only a small piano against the far wall.

Other than that . . . nothing.

One of the kitchen lights was on, casting a dim glow on the counter. Sitting on the tile was Tashi's red and white flag from the football game.

Forget the lies about her mother holding dinner for her. Was she even paying to live here, or had she crawled in the back window and set up shop?

I went farther into the room, flinching as my footsteps echoed off the bare walls. A quick trip around the kitchen revealed more of the same barrenness, which had a distinct air of transience—no garbage can, just a plastic grocery bag hooked over a drawer handle. No kitchen towels—just a roll of paper towels lying on the counter.

I opened the fridge and recoiled. It was packed full of protein shakes, giant blocks of cheese, and meat— every imaginable kind of meat. Whole chickens, steaks, slabs of ribs, tubes of ground beef, a dozen bulk packages of hot dogs, half-full deli containers of tuna salad, all wedged in like Tetris blocks.

More food than my family could eat in a month.

I shut the door and wandered out of the kitchen toward the darkness of the hall.

The first bedroom was empty. The second bedroom was empty.

The master bedroom door was closed.

I cranked the knob and pushed the door open.

In a horror movie, this room would have been draped in black velvet and lit by a thousand dripping, flickering candles. There would be an altar in the center of the room and shelves full of potions and evil talismans.

But I was just looking at another empty room. In the far corner was a rumpled sleeping bag. No sheets. Not even a pillow.

The bathroom counter held the bare essentials of a makeup kit. The shower door was open, revealing a bottle of shampoo, a disposable razor, and a bar of soap. A single towel was slung over the bar. There were no rugs or bath mats.

The closet was open. Except for a neat row of still-price-tagged clothes, a pile of dirty laundry, and a tidy line of shoes, it was empty. I peeked around at the shelves that I knew were behind the door.

On the third one from the bottom, just lying there in its blue wrapper, was the book.

Before I could lose my nerve, I tucked it under my arm and stepped out of the closet. I carried it to the kitchen counter, where I unwrapped it.

I cursed myself for not bringing my camera. Instead, I pulled out my cell phone and flipped the book open, using the edges of the blue velvet to touch the pages. They had an unsettling habit of falling open and staying that way, like they were weighted.

I started taking pictures with my phone. They'd be blurry and low-res, but it was better than nothing.

The end of the book was actually two pages that had been blank once, but were now covered in names—women's names, handwritten in as many types of ink and styles of print and script as there were names.

Almost like a sign-up sheet.

I raised my phone and took a picture.

One of the names, written in a flowery script, caught my eye: *Suzette Skalaski*.

I set down my phone and stared at it for a moment, trying to remember why it sounded familiar.

Suddenly, I heard a noise outside and saw the taillights of a car through the frosted glass of the foyer window. The high, happy sound of voices exchanging good-byes hit my ears.

I slammed the book shut, threw the wrap around it, and ran for the hallway, smashing my shoulder into the wall as I went. I dashed into the master bedroom closet, shoved the book back on the shelf and looked around.

Which lights had been on when I got here and which ones had I turned on? I hadn't even thought to pay attention. The closet—on. The bathroom—on or off?

Finally, I flipped the switch off and raced back out, hoping I could make it through the living room before Tashi came inside. But the key was already turning in the lock.

I dashed back into the closet and shut the light off just as the front door opened with a squeak. I stood helplessly in the dark, trying to plot my next move. Could I sneak out while she took a shower or after she went to sleep? Could I slip into the garage, open the door, and run for cover before she made it outside?

There was a noise from the main room—a sudden, short, high-pitched, tumbling sound. My whole body went ice-cold, but seconds later, I heard a waterfall of notes.

She was playing the piano. She ran through the scales twice and then a few jaunty bars of a march.

I should chance it. I should make a break for it. I could probably even fit out the bedroom window. Any sane person would leave. And I almost did—

But then I heard the song.

It started with a series of high notes, twinkling apart from each other like stars on a cold night. Then they all rushed together and exploded, and the song rose and rose, growing louder and louder. It was like hearing a battle being fought from the other side of a wall, and I couldn't tear myself away.

The melody came climbing up through the middle, surrounded by violent, dancing, pestering notes, buzzing birds trying to throw it off track. But it pushed through and came out free on the other side, strong and confident, like a soldier marching off of a smoking battlefield.

Then from the shadows came a winding approach, thin and sinister, like a murderous woman hiding in the darkness—and suddenly there was a mighty struggle, and when the chaos cleared, all that was left was a plaintive voice—she killed him but she's sorry, she just realized she always loved him, and she's spinning, spinning, driven mad by her loss, wishing she could bring him back . . . spinning, spinning . . . but she can't undo what she's done.

The notes spun out of existence.

The piano went silent.

I wasn't even aware that I was standing in a dark closet—I wasn't aware of anything but the music. I wanted to hear more. Another song, the same song—anything.

She didn't play anything else. And I'd missed my chance to run.

I stood there for a moment, shivering, then slowly pushed the door open and looked to my left, at the window. I'd have to pop the screen out, but I could fit—

"Sort of a strange place to find you," said Tashi. She was in the bedroom doorway, leaning against the wall with her arms crossed in front of her.

"Yes, definitely," I said. "So . . . I should go, I guess."

"No hurry," she said. "You can stay for a little while."

At that point, my courage failed me entirely. "I'm really sorry," I said. "If you let me go, I won't tell anyone anything about anything that you do—or have, or—don't have—"

"Alexis, calm down," she said. "You're making me antsy."

Antsy was never good. Especially in carnivorous supernatural beings.

"Come on out here," she said, starting down the hall. "Are you hungry?"

As I followed, I thought of the fridge full of raw meat and my stomach turned. "I don't think so."

"Sorry there's nowhere to sit," she said. "But then, you knew that, didn't you?"

I nodded quickly and without a trace of dignity. "Yes," I said. "Sorry again."

"Relax," she said, starting to come around the counter. I slid to the floor and shrank back, until I noticed she wasn't headed for me. She sat down on the piano bench and casually ran through a few scales.

"I heard you play," I said, half out of a desire to butter her up, and half because I couldn't help myself. "It was incredible."

She smiled. "*Serenada Schizophrana*, first movement. Elfman. I have it almost where I want it." She moved her hands over the keys. It was almost like the notes followed her fingers, charmed like a snake out of a basket.

I dared to speak. "How long have you been playing?"

"A hundred and sixty-seven years," she said.

"Oh," I said, like that was a totally normal answer.

Her fingers meandered through the beginning of a song.

"So . . . do you know Farrin?" I asked.

"Of course."

Something occurred to me. "Was it a coincidence that I ended up entering the contest and meeting her?"

For that, Tashi gave me an approving smile. "Not exactly," she said. "I sent the flyer to your principal and suggested she give it to you."

"Suggested how?" As soon as I asked it, I knew the answer. The same way we suggested anything to anyone. "But . . . that was before we even met."

Tashi gave me a veiled smile. "I'd heard about you."

"Who . . . ? I don't understand."

She looked at me again, and her fingers paused on the piano keys. Her eyes weren't smiling anymore. "I'm glad you came, Alexis. I need to talk to you."

As she spoke, she touched the keys absently, playing scraps of different songs and melodies, adding chords every once in a while for emphasis.

"I've never done this before," she said. "But I feel I can trust you."

I had no idea what I'd done to earn her trust, but I kept silent.

"I'm not like the rest of you, obviously. I came with the book. With Aralt."

I stared at her. "Are you the gypsy? The one who was with him when he died?"

The one who took his heart?

Her lip quirked up. "You can call me that, if you like."

"And you . . . made the book?"

"Yes," she said. "I was seventeen and in love, so I formed the book and joined my energy with Aralt's. I thought it was a way we could be together forever."

"I guess you were right," I said.

She shot me a look out of the corner of her eye.

"What's next?" I asked. "What does Aralt want from us? How long does this go on?"

"Not much longer," she said. "Usually he stays a month, six weeks. Then we have the graduation ceremony, and he moves on. I go with him."

"Usually?" I asked. "Not this time?"

"Not this time," she said. "Something has changed."

"What is it?"

"I don't know. But I . . . feel it." She segued into a sweet, sad song. "I love Aralt, as much as I always have. But he tires of me. He grows restless. I can feel it. He is impatient."

"For what?"

"I don't know," she said. "Do you remember the night at Adrienne's, with the dog? Aralt slipped out of my grasp for a few minutes. He's never done that before."

So that thing in the woods *was* Aralt. Which meant our golden hero, our ideal man, our benefactor—was a hideous monster?

"Can't you stop it, though?"

"I'm his, Alexis. I want what he wants. Good or bad. If he wills it, it becomes my will too." She glanced at me. "As with all of the girls in the Sunshine Club. All but one."

All but one? All but me.

Because by the time I'd fully committed to Aralt, I'd already screwed things up too badly to have any time to enjoy it. The thought left me feeling dejected.

"I don't have much time, you see," she said.

What did that mean?

"Are you dying?"

Her expression was sad. "Not yet."

I was leaning back, relieved, when the doorbell rang. We both shot to our feet, and Tashi held the flat of her hand out to me.

"Stay," she said. I heard her at the front door, calling out a greeting to someone and saying she'd be right there. Then she hurried back to me.

With surprising speed and strength, she grabbed my arm and pulled me down the hall toward the garage door.

"What's going on?" I asked.

"I'm sorry, Alexis," she said. "There's less time than I thought."

"Time for what?"

She shoved me against the wall and glanced back at the front door. "Forgive me," she said. She grew more agitated by the moment, shaking her head like she was trying to shake an image out of her mind. "Forgive me. I would never do this, except—"

I would have screamed, but her hand was over my mouth. Her face contorted as if she was in physical pain, and then she looked up at me.

Her cheeks were covered in the black tracks of tears, all melted together like someone had colored her face gray.

"To abandon—try again," she whispered. "I need to show you."

"Try what? Wait—!"

She opened the garage door and shoved me down the single stair. The door closed behind me, and the dead bolt clicked with finality.

22

I STUMBLED BUT managed not to fall. Then I charged at the wall and flipped on the light switch, preparing to start banging my fists on the door and screaming my head off.

But in the moment that the fluorescent lights flickered on, I forgot about all that.

Because everything I'd expected to see when I went into the master bedroom—the symbols, the candles, the movie set?

I was standing in it.

The plain concrete floor had been drawn on with a dark, thick marker, or some kind of black paint—a web of symbols that radiated from the center outward, stars and moons and other stuff I didn't understand. Instinctively, I raised my feet, trying to get clear of it the way you'd try to get clear of quicksand. But it was sticky. It pulled on the soles of my shoes.

Forced to be still, I finally took a long, slow look around me.

Then, like when you're standing in the ocean and a giant wave hits you out of nowhere, I was knocked over. I fell to the floor and curled into a ball, my hands over my ears.

But what struck me wasn't a *physical* force.

It was emotion. Raw, surging, torrents of emotion—ranging from tattered tendrils of fear and pain to huge pulses of anger, jealousy, paranoia—

They formed into a roar that filled my head, my soul, my entire being.

Suspicion, disgust, torment—

I was like a helpless bird caught in a thunderstorm, buffeted from every side by a venomous black wall of hatred, selfishness, hunger—most of all, hunger—and if it continued, it would wear me down like a layer of paint under a sandblaster. Already I was losing pieces of myself, my thoughts—I couldn't recall who I was or where I was or why I was there.

With my mind wiped clean, the hatred began to take root, filling my head with a pulling, tar-like need to destroy, devour, hurt—and I expanded to meet the force, began to feel its desires as if they were my own.

How I wanted to hurt someone. How I wanted someone to cower before me, begging for mercy, so I could crush them between my fingers. The world swirled dark and terrible, and I was dark and terrible too. The shrieks of pain on the edge of my consciousness were delicious to me; they soothed me and gave me an outlet for my most horrible awarenesses—

That I was imprisoned. Trapped. I contained so much force, and yet I was being held inside this place, rendered powerless. My fury flared up like flames and burned everything inside me.

I wanted to raise my arms and watch the oceans rise with them. I wanted to beat down everything in my path like a meteor shower of death and annihilation. It was a feeling of tremendous power and tremendous frustration, and at the edges of it all was a hunger to escape and be cruel, sadistic, merciless. I wanted to explode. I wanted *out*.

And then it stopped.

I don't know how long it took me to uncurl myself. To let my own thoughts trickle back into my consciousness. To separate myself from the black, all-consuming hatred that had filled me.

But when I opened my eyes, I saw that the room around me was blank. All of the symbols were gone. The burning candles were dead hunks of wax. The talismans had been swept to the floor and turned to dust.

Numbly, I went to the wall and hit the glowing button, then watched the garage door open with a quiet rumble. I stared out into the night, still feeling like I was walking six feet behind my own body.

He's evil.

He manipulated us. Controlled us. And we spent every minute of every day trying to please him. But he was a monster who only wanted to feel blood on his hands and taste fear on his tongue.

I made it about halfway home before my legs began to swim underneath me. I sat down on the curb outside of #65 and wrapped my arms around myself. My body shook, rattling the breath in my lungs.

He was evil, and there was nothing we could do about it.

He was evil, and he was inside us. So deep inside us that I didn't know where Alexis ended and Aralt began.

He was so evil that even the girl who had loved him for almost two hundred years was terrified of him.

I ambled home, waved a senseless hand at my parents, and lurched down the hallway to the first door, which I knocked on, quietly, slowly, steadily, until my sister pulled it open.

She took one look at me and her face turned as gray as death.

"I need your help," I said, my parched throat crackling behind the words. "I just met Aralt."

23

WE WAITED UNTIL our parents went to sleep and then sat on the sofa, wrapped in blankets we'd pulled off our beds. I was in my pajamas, a robe, thick socks, and slippers, and I made a cocoon for myself with my comforter. If I could have settled between the couch cushions, I would have. The rawness of Aralt's emotions left me feeling vulnerable, exposed. My shoulders still quaked under all my layers.

"Try again," Kasey said, for the eightieth time. We'd been sitting there trying to figure out what Tashi had meant. "It's what Elspeth said, too."

"I don't get it," I said. My voice still had the dusty rasp of a lifelong smoker. "Why apologize and then push me into that place?"

"She said she was dying?"

"No, not yet. But she said there was less time than she thought. And that Aralt was impatient. And she chose me because I was different from the other girls."

Kasey wrinkled her nose. "I always knew your rebellious streak would come in handy someday."

"But handy for what? What does she want me to do?"

Kasey shrugged and ran her finger along the length of her braid. "She wants you to try again."

I sighed. "We could always . . . go ask her." Even though my body went cold all over at the thought of being back in that house.

Kasey shook her head. "Not tonight."

I settled back against the cushions, relieved. "One thing I don't get."

She looked up at me.

"Before Megan and I joined the club . . . why didn't you just *say* you weren't in danger?"

Not the question she was expecting. "I was trying to keep you from being too interested," she said, pushing on her forehead with the side of her hand. "I really thought I could explain to them why we needed to stop."

"But that wouldn't have worked."

"I don't know," she said. "I still wonder—if I'd been able to really talk to them . . . to Tashi . . ."

"And then what?" I asked. "How would you have stopped it?"

"I don't know." She buried her face in her hands. "I'm sorry, Lexi. I'm so sorry."

"No," I said. "It's not all your fault. I should have been there for you."

"But I was being stubborn," she said. "They were *my* friends. I knew you'd help me if I asked, but I wanted to show you I could do it alone."

"We're just a pair of idiots," I said.

The moon shone its flat blue light on the wall bordering the backyard, making the view even more depressing.

"So what now?" I asked. "Do you trust me to help you?"

"I don't know," Kasey said. "Do you trust yourself?"

I thought about it. *Should* I trust myself?

There were aspects of Aralt I'd begun to count on—always knowing the right thing to say. Believing in myself, in my future.

Yes, Aralt was a being of unspeakable evil. But was I really strong enough to forsake him, or would I wake up the next day and immediately sell my sister out?

"Maybe there's a way around that," I said. "If we can come up with some sort of—not blackmail, but . . . an insurance plan? So if I get tempted, you have something to hang over my head?"

I thought it was pretty inspired, actually.

But Kasey shook her head. "No," she said. "I'm tired of lies. I'm tired of bullying. I don't want to have something hanging over your head. If you don't want to help me, that's your choice."

"But I could get you in huge trouble, Kase," I said.

"Yeah," she said, leaning back and staring up at the ceiling fan. "I guess so."

"I wasn't strong enough before," I said.

"That's not true," Kasey said. "You just didn't know what you wanted. Do you know what you want now?"

"I know what I *don't* want," I said. *But . . .*

It's so much to give up. It would be like sacrificing a part of myself.

"Shut up," I said out loud. "Shut up, shut up, shut up."

Kasey watched me. She knew I wasn't talking to her.

"Yes," I said. "I'm sure. I know what I want."

I pulled the gold ring off my finger, walked to the sliding door, and threw it over the wall into the hills. It was just an outward symbol, not part of the supernatural connection. I was still connected to Aralt, like you'd still be connected to your spouse if you threw your wedding band into the ocean. But it was a start.

I wanted my life back.

When I woke up the next morning, there was a dark circle around my finger where my ring had been, like a bruise. I pulled a random ring from my jewelry box and put it on to cover the black.

Before I left my bedroom, I sat and tested my thoughts. I thought about Kasey. And Carter. And Aralt. And the Sunshine Club.

There was a pull—a craving, almost like a constant low-grade headache behind my ears. But Kasey was right. I was strong enough to see through all of it.

As I headed for the kitchen to get some breakfast, my sister waved me into her room. I closed the door.

"How are you?" she asked.

"Good."

"No, I mean . . . how *are* you?"

I made my mouth an O. *"Gooooood."*

She tossed a pillow at me, but I could tell she was relieved. "So about getting started. I've officially reached the end of the Internet," she said. "I was thinking about going to the library later. Can you come?"

"There's no use," I said. "All of the paranormal books at the city library are locked up."

Her face fell.

"And so are the ones at school," I said. "Although . . ."

Miss Nagesh seemed surprised when I asked her to keep the library open late for us. But she agreed right away. "I'm just revising my novel," she said. "I can work at the school as well as I can at home."

At lunch, Carter came up behind me and touched

the curve of my back. "Can we eat by ourselves today?"

I turned to him in surprise. "Sorry," I said. "You know I can't."

"Come on," he urged. He stared at me, unblinking. I felt his fingers move lightly across my shirt. From around the table, eye beams bored into us like lasers.

Sit here. I miss you. "Sit here," I recited, too tired to resist. "I miss you."

"Ah . . . it's okay." He let his hand fall from my back. "I'll sit with the guys."

"Oh," I said. "All right."

All through lunch, I stole glances in his direction. But he wasn't looking at me.

Ever. Not once.

Miss Nagesh fumbled with a giant ring of keys, looking for the one that would unlock the metal cabinet in her office. "I never even thought about opening this thing. What kind of librarian keeps books in a locked closet?"

I shrugged. The kind who gets fired, apparently.

"It's ridiculous. Your first job this week is to put these back into circulation," she said. "If we ever get them out."

"What's your book about?" Kasey asked.

Miss Nagesh glanced up, her eyes shining. "The next big thing in teen fiction," she said proudly. *"Harpies."*

"Wow," Kasey said.

"Obviously not with feathered bodies or anything," she said. "I'm taking some liberties."

"Can't wait to read it," Kasey said.

"I have to finish it first," Miss Nagesh said. "Wait . . . wait . . . *got it!*"

The cabinet door swung open, revealing shelves piled high with books.

"Go for it," she said, backing away. "I'll be at the main desk if you need me."

We spent the next few hours poring over the books, looking for anything that might help.

"Listen to this," Kasey said. " 'One aspect constant to every *libris exanimus* is its attendant *creatura*. The *creatura* functions as bodyguard and servant to its *libris*. It will always be found nearby; if you come across a *libris exanimus*, you can be sure a *creatura* is close at hand, and vice versa. Be wary, for a *creatura* will take any means necessary to protect and serve its master.' "

And that would be Tashi. "But is it a human or a spirit or something else?"

"I don't know," she sighed. "That's all it says. This is a book of cheat codes for a video game called *Spirit Killaz 2*."

"Oh," I said.

Kasey heard the doubt in my voice. "But it talks

about power centers, too. I think the people who made the game actually did their homework."

My phone buzzed. I glanced at it, expecting to see Carter's name on the caller ID. But it was Megan's. "Hello?"

"Where are you?" she asked.

I hesitated. Luckily, the question had been rhetorical.

"Because I can tell you where *I* am," she said. "Sitting on my bed studying my French vocab."

Studying?

"There was a pop quiz today!" she said. "And I totally bombed it."

"Wow, that sucks," I said.

She made a disgusted noise. "I know, I'm so mad."

My ears pricked up. Mad at Aralt?

"I keep thinking, what did I do that Aralt would want to teach me a lesson? Am I taking him for granted? Was I ugly today?" She sniffed. "I'm never wearing that skirt again . . . Did you notice anything?"

"No," I said. "I thought the skirt was cute."

She sighed. "All right, well, I thought I'd ask. . . . I'll talk to you later. Or tomorrow, maybe. *Je dois étudier.*"

"*Bonjour*," I replied.

She laughed. "All right, Lex. Stay sunny."

"Stay sunny," I said. And hung up.

Kasey was watching me.

"Megan said—"

"I heard."

"Something's going on," I said.

Kasey let the book rest in her lap. "I hate to say it, Lexi, but . . ."

I knew what she was going to say before she said it. We needed to go talk to Tashi.

24

THE GARAGE DOOR GAPED OPEN.

A bright pink envelope was wedged between the front door and the frame.

As Kasey and I stood in the driveway and stared, a car pulled up in the road behind us.

"Excuse me, girls," the driver said through the passenger window. "Is this your house?"

We shook our heads.

He leaned across the seat and held something out. Another bright pink envelope. The words HOMEOWNERS' ASSOCIATION CITATION were printed across it in bold red letters. "Would you mind slipping this next to the other one?"

Kasey took it, nodding.

The guy glanced at the open door and shook his head, his eyes narrow with contempt. "Some people have no respect, you know?"

"It's a shame," I said automatically.

"Absolutely," he said, raising his hand in an affable way. "See you later."

I wondered if he would have been so nice to me with my pink hair.

"So she's not home," Kasey said.

"I guess not." I knew the door leading from the garage to the hall was locked from inside. "Come on."

Kasey came tripping behind me through the side yard and stopped short when she saw me unlatch the window. "This is illegal!"

Amazing how low on my priority list legality had sunk. I hoisted myself inside and extended a hand to my sister, who gazed around the empty house with a look of dread on her face.

First, I hit the button on the wall to close the garage door. Then I got the pink notices from the doorway and set them on the piano bench.

It was obvious that no one was home. We started looking around, checking every room, every closet.

I was in the master bedroom when my sister yelled out for me. I raced through the house to find her standing by the kitchen counter.

"What is that?" she asked, angling her head to look at something. "Is it blood?"

I leaned down to look at puddles of congealed dark liquid.

"Yeah," I said. "It is."

I turned to get a paper towel and noticed that there was a small pile of trash on the floor—Tashi's crumpled football game ticket, a used-up matchbook, and the wrapper from a package of ground beef.

"Why would there be blood on the counter?" Kasey asked, on the verge of freaking out. "Did someone hurt Tashi?"

And why would there be trash on the floor?

Someone had dumped it out and taken the bag. But what would they need the bag for?

"Excuse me," I said, weaving around her.

I opened the fridge.

One of the shelves was completely bare, except for a few puddles of dried blood. Whoever it was—Tashi?—must have stacked packages of meat on the counter and then put them in the plastic bag and taken them away.

At least it wasn't Tashi's blood.

But she'd been scared. Scared enough to run? To take herself, the book, Aralt, and enough meat to last a few days? But where would she go?

My heart began to thump against my chest as I made my way back down the hall and into the master bedroom, where my suspicions were confirmed.

The closet was noticeably emptier. Half the shoes and most of the clothes on hangers were gone, although the dirty laundry was still piled up in the corner.

The book was gone, too.

Then I went into the bathroom, where my eye was drawn to the cup on the counter.

What I saw there stopped me short.

Because if Tashi had really gone away . . .

Why hadn't she taken her toothbrush?

25

WEDNESDAY MORNING, you could tell something was different. Even though the Club converged in the courtyard as always, it didn't feel like a normal day.

We were scattered where we'd been a unit, distracted where we'd been focused, jumpy where we'd been as tranquil as a herd of cows. There was a spark in the air, as if lightning had struck too close.

It lasted through lunch. Paige spilled yogurt all over herself, and our usual conversation was replaced by a miniature study group. It turns out Megan wasn't the only one bombing quizzes.

After the bell rang, a group of us went to the bathroom together to touch up our lipstick. Emily and Mimi were next to me.

"What's wrong with your hair, Em?" Mimi asked. "The back's all . . . flattish."

Emily reached up to touch her hair and then twisted to look at it. "Really?"

"Yeah, it's . . . weird." Mimi gave it a futile fluff and then shrugged. "You should fix it."

Gradually, everyone else trickled out, and it was just me and Emily. She was still swinging from side to side, trying to see what Mimi saw.

"Stop worrying. You look great," I said.

She inspected herself from a few more angles, looking like she might burst into tears at any moment. "You're so nice, Alexis. But I can't go to class like this," she said. "Can you help me? Do you have a curling iron?"

Um. "A curling iron . . . ? At school? No, sorry."

Emily glanced around frantically, like one was going to *poof* into midair.

"Maybe in the drama club supply room?" I suggested. "Or with the cheerleading stuff?"

Her eyes popped open wide. "The cheerleaders! Of course!"

"But the bell's going to ring in, like, two minutes. We have to get to Math."

She came up to me and pressed her hands together, like she was praying. "Can you just make up an excuse for me?"

I sighed. "I don't know, Em . . ."

"Please! It's an emergency. I'll be there as soon as I can. Just stall him."

I finally agreed. But only because it was Emily.

All I had to say to Mr. Demarco was that Emily was dealing with "feminine issues," and he shooed me away.

The rule at Surrey High was that phones had to be on silent or vibrate during class, and they could only be used between class periods. So when my phone lit up against the lining of my purse, I almost ignored it. But then I flipped it on its side and read the screen. It was a text from Emily.

NEED U GRLS BTHRM

I rolled my eyes. Calling me out of class to help fix her flat hair? But when I thought about ignoring it, I felt the tiniest pressure in my temple. It didn't let up until I got up and went to Mr. Demarco's desk.

"Emily needs me," I said.

"Go, just go," he said. "No details."

When I got into the bathroom, the first thing I did was instinctively check the mirror.

Still good.

Then I saw Emily.

She was crouching in the corner, her legs tucked under her, a curling iron in her hand.

Half her hair was burned off. There was a bright pink, shiny, painful-looking patch of skin just above her forehead. Onyx-colored tears streamed down her face, spreading onto her shirt in dark clouds.

She raised the curling iron again.

"Why isn't it working, Alexis?" she snuffled, reaching up and wrapping a thin strand of hair around it, then bringing the whole thing down against her scalp. "I don't understand."

"Oh my God, stop!" I cried, rushing over to her.

"It's not working!" she said. "It's flat! You have to help me. I'm not good enough!"

I tried to get the curling iron out of her hands, but she yanked it away, ripping a whole section of hair out of her head. I pulled the cord from the outlet.

"Hey!" she protested.

Up close, her head was a mess of dark red welts. She gave off the sick, rancid smell of burning hair. My stomach shifted dangerously.

Her face crumpled. "I'm ugly," she sobbed, holding the curling iron up against her cheek.

"Quit it!" I shrieked, snatching it from her hand and throwing it across the room. "Come on, you need to get to the hospital."

"No!" she said, swinging her arms at me. "No, I can't go out like this. I look terrible. Everyone will see."

I couldn't drag her. And I couldn't leave her alone.

I thought about calling for help, but what would I say? How could I explain?

I pulled out my cell phone and dialed Megan's number. "Please pick up," I mumbled. "Please."

She did. "Lex, you know I'm in class, right?"

"I need you. In the four-hundred wing bathroom."

She hesitated.

"Just get here," I said. "No questions."

While I was on the phone, Emily had started crawling across the floor, going after the curling iron again. I raced her to it and grabbed the metal end with my left hand just as she was grabbing the handle.

It took my brain a moment to feel the heat, and by then, my fingers had instinctively released it, splaying out like a spider having a seizure.

"Why did you do that?" Emily asked, cradling the curling iron and turning away from me. "I *need* this. I need to be beautiful. I'm not good enough."

For a few long seconds, we stared at each other. She wouldn't give it up without a fight. And I didn't particularly feel like wrenching it out of her hands and getting burned again.

"Alexis? What are you doing?" Megan appeared in the doorway. She looked past me and saw Emily on the floor.

Megan switched into student-coach mode without missing a beat. She turned on one of the faucets. "Help me get her over here."

As long as we didn't try to take her precious curling iron, Emily didn't mind being moved. She let us herd her to the sink, where we started scooping handfuls of cool water over the iron and her scalp.

"We need to get her out to my car," Megan said. "I can drop her off at home."

"At *home*?" I asked. "She needs to go to the hospital!"

"That's not realistic, and we both know it," Megan said. "Besides, Aralt will help her."

As I was scooping, I rammed my injured hand into the faucet and gasped in pain.

Emily looked up at me. "Oh, no, Alexis . . . you burned your hand," she said, her voice sorrowful. "That's really going to hurt."

Then she slowly lifted her eyes from the curling iron to her own reflection in the mirror.

And reached a hand up to her raw, burned scalp.

And screamed—

And screamed, and screamed.

This wasn't the full-throated screeching of horror-movie victims; it was an endless wail of agony, thin and panicked, broken into shrieking yips like the cries of a wounded animal. It made your chest hurt all the way through to your spine just to listen to it.

Emily let the curling iron drop to the floor and went into a fit, running away from us, trying to climb up the walls, her hands clawing the smooth tiles.

I went closer, to calm her down, but she lashed out at me.

"Emily," Megan ordered, "*sit still!* And don't touch my clothes—you're filthy!"

Finally Emily's wailing tapered off into a long whimper. Megan made a few phone calls, and within two minutes, Lydia, Kendra, and Paige had joined us.

"We need to get her out to Megan's car," Lydia said. "How can we do that without attracting attention?"

Emily, clearly in shock, sat perfectly still on the floor, like she was a polite stranger we'd brought in from the street, watching all of this happen to somebody else.

"Pull up as close to the exit as you can," Paige said. "I'll put my sweater on her head."

I winced at the thought of anything touching that raw scalp. But everyone else was all for it. So a minute later, we were walking through the hallway, guiding Emily, who had a sweater wrapped around her in a vague imitation of a head scarf.

When Megan pulled up, we stuck Emily in the front seat. I reached across her and fastened her seat belt. "Are you sure you won't take her to the hospital, Megan?" I asked.

Megan gave me a disapproving look. "*Chill*, Lex. We know she'll heal."

I backed away and closed the door, wishing I'd just

yelled for help and let the teachers deal with it. But then the Sunshine Club girls would have known something was wrong—maybe even suspected that I wasn't fully committed anymore.

Because we took care of our own business. That was just the way it worked.

After Megan had pulled away, Paige came up next to me. "You should go back to class. I brought your stuff." She held out my purse but grabbed it back before I could take it. "Oh, you're hurt!"

As soon as she pointed it out, the skin on my palm began to ache in a painful, torn-up way, like when you accidentally scratch a sunburn.

"I guess so," I said. It hardly seemed like anything compared to Emily's burns.

"Oh, well," Paige said, hooking the bag over the upturned palm, "it'll heal."

As I walked back to my classroom, the security guard stopped me. "Did you hear any strange noises around here a few minutes ago?" he asked. "Would you duck into the ladies' room and tell me if everything's okay?"

I popped my head in and then forced my brightest smile. "It's fine. Everything is perfectly fine."

It was a short and relatively subdued Sunshine Club meeting that day; nobody stood up for Betterment.

When Adrienne brought out the book, I looked around for Tashi, but she didn't show. No one but her, Kasey, and me knew that the book was actually kept at Tashi's house; so how had Adrienne gotten hold of it?

I held my tongue, wanting to give things a chance to play out before attracting attention to myself.

Nobody asked how Emily was doing, but everybody knew she'd had to leave school. Nobody let on that anything was wrong. But we all knew something was.

In spite of the weirdness, Adrienne was eager, excited as she made the opening announcements.

"You guys, I have wonderful news!" she said. "As of today, we'll have twenty-two members . . . which means . . . we can graduate!"

Then the door opened and Paige escorted in the new member, presenting her to me like a 1950s housewife bringing out the Thanksgiving turkey:

Zoe.

As she took the oath, she was so eager, so guileless, I wondered how I could have ever been threatened by her. Everything about her shouted *Love me love me love me!*

"Anyone have anything to say before we wrap up?" Adrienne asked.

"Um," Monika said, her hand half raised. "Where's Tashi?"

Adrienne and Lydia exchanged a troubled glance,

and I felt the breath catch in my lungs.

"All right," Lydia said. "Here's the thing. Tashi was starting to feel like the club was too much for her."

There was a room-wide intake of air, the first half of a gasp.

"So . . . she quit."

The silence was peppered with offended whispers; I distinctly heard Kendra say, "But Aralt *gives* us strength!"

"Listen," Lydia said. "It's not a big deal. It's a shame, but it's her choice. It doesn't affect our graduation. And of course we wish her the best . . . right?"

A reluctant chorus of agreement rumbled up in answer.

"All right, everyone," Adrienne said, her usually chipper mood downcast. "Stay sunny."

Afterward, I went home and got ready for my final Young Visionaries interview. My hand was no less tender, so I put some aloe on it, to help Aralt along. When Mom asked what happened, I told her I'd burned it doing my hair.

"Ah, vanity," she said. "It can be a dangerous thing."

Yeah, whatever.

The judges stood when I came into the room.

I handed over an envelope containing my four new photos—the prints of me and Megan and two from the football game—Pepper Laird in midleap, all vivid color against the black night sky. You could see shards of wet grass flying off her shoes, a bead of sweat about to drip from her knee. And Carter, looking like a cross between a movie star and a preacher at a revival meeting, golden and tall and surrounded by a halo of light.

The judges murmured over the photos.

"Very nice," the bow-tie man said. "I've been consistently impressed by your work."

"Thank you," I said.

"There's a degree of . . . maturity," said one of the women, Mrs. Liu. "Your choices are quite unexpected, from a person your age."

"The only thing . . ." The other man's brow furrowed as he held up the photo of Carter. "The eyes bother me in this picture. They're almost . . . empty."

I sat back.

Farrin held up the Pepper picture. "You could do sports photography," she said. "The more I look at this, the more I like it."

"Are you thinking about exploring digital?" Mrs. Liu asked.

Even though I wasn't fully committed to Aralt, there was still that thread of trust inside me, that I could come up with the right answer. I waited for him to feed me my lines.

But nothing came. Like a trapeze artist who looks down and sees that they forgot to put up the net, the words flashed in my head: *You're on your own.*

"Alexis?" Farrin prompted.

I couldn't stall any longer. "Yes. Digital is good," I said. "Actually, I just got one. A digital camera. I've played with it a little."

Four pairs of squinting eyes watched me.

Think, Alexis. Think. Hold it together.

"Digital is more like . . . um, instant gratification," I said. "But it's definitely fun. I'm glad I learned on film, but . . . I can see why people like digital."

"Why are you glad you learned on film?"

"Um," I said. "Well, because . . ."

And then I totally blanked. I couldn't remember the question, or the answer, or what I wanted to say, or what I'd already said.

"Alexis?" Farrin asked.

"Digital," I said. "Um. When you shoot film, you have to, like, budget. And you learn to . . . choose."

"To edit?" Farrin prompted.

"Yes," I said. "As you go. Like, be disciplined."

There was a long, horrible pause.

"Well, it's been a pleasure," Mrs. Liu said, not beaming quite as brightly as she had at the beginning of the interview.

The others said their good-byes, mostly without eye contact.

"Alexis," Farrin said, "on your way out, would you mind sending Jared Elkins back?"

"Okay," I said. "Thank you all."

"You're welcome," Farrin said. And then she coughed.

Our eyes met. Hers were wide and shocked, and I imagine mine were the same.

Aralt's girls didn't get sick.

They didn't completely space out during important interviews, either.

I hurried back to the lobby. Jared waited on the bench, studying one of his new prints. I paused to look over his shoulder.

It showed a young girl on a swing, her hair streaming behind her and her feet pointed forward in the perfect expression of action and innocence. But behind her lay a wasteland—some kind of junkyard. The whole image was colored in the muted, hopeless tones of waste and destruction.

"Like it?" he asked.

I nodded without looking up. The joy and freedom of the little girl starkly contrasted with the horror behind her. In a single moment, the picture made you happy and afraid and desolately lonely. It kind of blew my mind a little.

"How'd it go?" he asked.

"Fine." Then I remembered myself. "They asked me to send you back."

"Okay, thanks," he said, sliding the book out from under my gaze.

I swallowed hard. "Good luck."

"Thanks." He reached a hand out and shook mine decisively. "May the best man or woman win."

"Yes," I said, my breath catching in my throat.

He gave me a slight wave as he disappeared down the hall. When he was gone, the lobby seemed thick with an almost dead stillness.

Would the best man or woman win?

How would I live with myself if the answer was no?

The next morning, I avoided the Sunshine Club altogether and went to the library, where I got a head start on the day's shelving. But I couldn't hide out at lunch. I set my lunch box down at the very end of the table.

I thought about saving a chair for Carter, but he was nowhere in sight. Whatever was going on with us—with Aralt—was loosening my hold on Carter, too. Which was partially fine—but I didn't want us getting so loose that we fell apart.

Megan slammed her tray down and took the chair to my right. She bent over her food like she wanted to be ignored, but the way she was breathing—through her nose, as fast and hard as if she'd just run a marathon, made that impossible.

"Um . . . are you okay?" I asked.

She didn't look up, just kept slurping soup off her spoon. *"Fine."*

All right, then.

Kasey ended up in the seat next to mine. A low buzz came from the other end of the table, and I looked down to see Adrienne glaring in our direction.

I elbowed Kasey. "Is Adrienne looking at us?"

"It's me," Megan said, dropping her spoon. "She's looking at me."

Adrienne started to get up, but the girls around her pulled her back to her seat.

Kasey leaned closer to me and whispered so quietly I could barely hear her. *"Swttzz."*

What? Sweaters? Megan was wearing a pale yellow, scoop-necked sweater with three-quarter sleeves cuffed by a delicate ruffle of sheer ivory ribbon.

And so was Adrienne.

Megan's tractor-trailer breath hadn't gotten any softer.

"Whoa, take it easy," I said, like she was a horse. "There's nothing to be upset about."

Megan's eyes shot daggers at me. "I told her *last*

night I was going to wear this today."

Adrienne escaped her handlers and stalked to our end of the table, carrying a small carton of skim milk. "And *I* said, no, that's what I'm going to wear, you should find something else!"

"I said it first!" Megan said.

"Well, I *planned* it first," Adrienne growled.

Before I could stop her, Megan drew back her bowl and doused Adrienne with soup. Then Adrienne pounded her skim milk into Megan's shoulder.

The carton imploded. Milk went everywhere.

In a split second, they were all over each other.

"Girl fight!" someone called, and in no time a gleeful crowd had encircled us.

But this was no stereotypical slapping-and-squealing catfight.

Megan landed a hard punch on Adrienne's left cheek. Adrienne grabbed Megan's hair and whipped her face down, missing the rigid edge of a chair by about a centimeter. With a free hand, Adrienne grabbed a lunch tray and smacked Megan with it in the back of the head, hard enough that Megan reeled. Adrienne pinned her arm behind her back and began to twist it.

Then I saw Megan's hand dart out and grab a metal knife from a nearby table.

They were literally trying to kill each other.

"Stop!" I said. "Megan!"

"Get her!" Kasey said, and we dove into the fray. Another group of girls went in after Adrienne.

"I'm trying!" I dodged kicks and clawing fingernails to wrap my fingers around the hem of Megan's sweater. I took a stiletto heel to the shin and limped backward, hauling her with me.

The school security guard converged on us. "Break it up, girls! Break it up!" he yelled, trying to push between them, tweeting his eardrum-piercing whistle as hard as he could.

Megan tore a path through the crowd, dragging me behind her out the side door of the cafeteria.

A couple of teachers held on to Adrienne, who spat and sputtered like an angry alley cat.

Outside, Megan pulled away from me and sprinted toward the staff parking lot, half of which was taken up by portable classrooms.

I walked the line of portables until I heard muffled coughing coming from a set of back stairs. I found Megan on the steps, head bent between her legs. When she heard me, she jumped to her feet. For a moment, it seemed like she was going to charge me, but then she backed down. "Oh, Lex," she said. "It's just you."

She was drenched in milk, and her face wore four fingernails'-worth of fresh red gashes. Her sweater was ripped and stained, and her nose was bloody. When she spat, a splotch of pink liquid stained the sidewalk.

She tried to wipe the dark tearstains off her skin with the sides of her hands. "I'm not being unsunny, I swear," she said. "I'm just kind of in pain."

I let out a shaky breath. "Are you okay?"

"Uh-huh," she said, lowering herself back to the stairs. She lifted a hand to her abdomen. "She got in a few serious kicks, though. Might have broken a rib. No big deal, though."

"It's a huge deal! You just got in a *fight*," I said. "Over a *sweater*. You could be in major trouble. Not to mention that you could have really gotten hurt."

She gave me a *so what* look. "I'm not turning myself in," she said matter-of-factly. "I can't go to the office looking like this."

I heard footsteps approaching. We both tensed, but it was just Kasey, clutching a handful of napkins for Megan.

"I don't even know what happened," Megan said, blotting her cheek. "I got so mad all of a sudden. I mean, I *did* tell her I was going to wear this sweater today . . . Whatever. I guess I should go home."

"You have to go back in," Kasey said. "They know it was you."

"Never mind that," I said. "She needs to get out

of here. And it's probably best to keep her away from Adrienne for a while."

I hoped Aralt was still looking out for us enough that this incident would be overlooked.

"I guess," Megan said, looking skeptical. "I'm not even mad anymore. It's just a sweater, you know?"

Yeah, I knew. We all knew. And that was what worried me. Even the most fashion-obsessed Sunshine Club member would know that making that kind of scene in public was way worse than wearing the same sweater as somebody else.

We weren't supposed to fight. Just like we weren't supposed to cough. Or flip out and burn ourselves. Or completely lose it in the middle of an important interview.

Kasey went back for our bags while I herded Megan in the direction of her car, keeping an eye out—mostly for Adrienne, but also for faculty members.

Someone stepped into our path about thirty feet ahead, and I made an abrupt left. But the sounds of running footsteps followed us, and I turned, prepared to be busted.

It was Carter. "Lex? What are you doing?"

He hurried to catch up with us.

"I heard something about a fight—was that you? Are you hurt?"

"No, I'm fine—it was Megan and Adrienne."

For the first time, he turned to Megan, who looked like she'd been through a cage match. Her face was stained black, like she'd smudged a gallon of mascara on her cheeks. She gave him a red-toothed smile.

He grabbed me by the sleeve and half-pulled me across the hall, out of her earshot.

"We have to talk about this," he said, casting a freaked-out glance at Megan. "About a lot of things. Seriously. Like, a real talk. Can I come to your house after school?"

"No," I said. "I'll meet you at the park."

"Lex," Megan called, "can you hurry? I'm getting blood in my eye."

Carter backed away, a horrified look on his face, and I kept walking with Megan out to the parking lot.

The campus police officer watched us drive away without batting an eye.

I sat in the grass, watching for Carter, and got to my feet when I saw him coming down the path, watching as he headed for the footbridge that crossed the murky drainage ditch.

"Hi," he said, enfolding me in a half-hug. Every impulse in my body longed to turn the half-hug into a kiss, but Carter held back, so I did, too.

We ended up sitting about two feet apart, facing the brook, not each other.

"How'd your interview go last night?" he asked.

"Great," I lied.

"Now, *please* tell me what's going on."

I shook my head. "It's compli—"

"Yeah, I get that it's complicated, Lex. But some people consider me highly capable of complex thought." He leaned closer. "I want to help you."

"It's nothing like that," I said, picking up a pine needle and twisting it. "I don't need help."

Carter leaned away again. Birds sang and insects buzzed, and the wind bullied its way through the leaves. In the past, sitting in silence like this would have been completely comfortable. Now it felt like something was missing.

"Megan's okay?" he asked, the tiniest bite to his voice.

"Yes. Fine," I said. The pine needle, nearly shredded, fell from my fingers.

Carter picked it up. "I saw Zoe at your lunch table. I didn't know you guys converted her."

"We didn't *convert* her," I said. "That's not how it works."

"Lex, I really don't care. If Zoe wants to be a Sunshine Girl, that's her decision." He paused. "I just think . . . if there's something else going on . . . I mean, people are getting hurt—the fight today—and there are these weird rumors about Emily . . . The whole thing is either dangerous or insanely stupid. Or both."

It wasn't that I totally disagreed with him. In fact, we were pretty much in complete agreement.

But when he calls the Sunshine Club stupid, he's calling me stupid.

The thought pissed me off. "Okay," I said. "Whatever you say."

He grabbed my hand. "Lex, look at me."

I looked at him.

"Is it drugs?"

That made me snort. "Drugs? Oh, please."

"This isn't funny," he said. "I have no idea why you're laughing."

"Because," I said. "It's a *club*. If you think it's dumb, then fine. Think that. But you can't just insult me and expect me to dump my sister and all of my friends because you said so."

"No," he said. "Not because I said so. Because something is happening. Under normal circumstances, you wouldn't go within ten feet of those girls." He drove his fist lightly into the grass. "I know you don't see it that way—but maybe that's because you *can't*."

But I could see. I could and I did, and all I had to do

was tell him, and he'd stop thinking I was brainwashed, and I could stop pretending everything was great. But then what would happen? He'd insist that we go to the authorities. Call Agent Hasan. Get Kasey shipped off to who knows where.

"You know, that girl Tashi—she doesn't go to All Saints. I asked my friend Dave, and he said—"

"Are you kidding?" I asked. "I can't believe you're checking up on my friends."

This wasn't going right. We were supposed to reconcile, forgive each other, admit we belonged together—not fight.

Joining the Sunshine Club was a huge mistake.

The words came into my head like a line in a script—Aralt's irresistible whisper, back when I needed it most.

No. No. No. I couldn't.

But—it wasn't like I would embrace the whole thing. Only the parts I needed. Just enough to keep Carter from freaking out.

"I don't even know why I bothered trying." Carter shook his head and started brushing off his pants. He was mad. He was going to leave me there.

This one time, and then I'd stop. I'd never do it again.

I turned to him, putting my hand flat against his chest to keep him from standing up. "Joining the

Sunshine Club was a huge mistake."

He looked down at my hand and squinted, like he was trying to remember something.

Whispered words flooded my head. *But it means so much to Kasey and Megan that I have to see it through.*

Carter watched me warily as I repeated everything the voice told me.

It's a short-term thing. It'll be over soon.

For a moment he glanced away, but then his expression turned hazy.

And I hope that, when it's over, you can forgive me.

"And I hope that—" I stopped.

Those words would draw Carter back to me like a cat to a bowl of cream, have him fawning over me and following me around and carrying my bag and hanging on my every word, the perfect devoted boyfriend. All I had to do was open my mouth and speak them.

—when it's over, you can forgive me.

"What do you hope?" Carter asked, tracing my cheekbone with his finger.

Sure, I could get Carter back. If I swallowed my pride and recited a bunch of wimpy, lying apologies.

Was the Sunshine Club stupid? Yes. Dangerous? Yes. Was it a huge mistake? Yes. Yes to everything. Except the part where had to I play sick mind games to earn Carter's love.

I jumped to my feet. "I have to go."

"No, Lex, wait!" He scrambled to his feet behind me, but he headed for the bridge. I just hiked up my skirt and ran for the ditch, taking a huge leap, utterly confident that I would land neatly on the other side.

My purse made it.

But I didn't. Halfway across, my confidence abandoned me like an octopus letting go of a fish, and I hit the edge of the far bank and splashed backward into the water, landing hard on my backside.

"Lex!" Carter called, running over.

I hauled myself onto the grass, refusing to take his hand or look up at him.

"What were you thinking?" he asked. "That's a seven-foot jump!"

My whole body shook with anger and humiliation. I pushed my wet hair away from my eyes and realized with horror that I was crying.

He hovered over me, a helpless onlooker. "Are you all right? Are you hurt?"

And then the voice filled my head again.

I'm sorry I've been acting so strangely. I know I'm not being the girlfriend you deserve, but—

"No!" I said, turning my face and trying to rub the tearstains away. "Stop it!"

Stunned, Carter backed away.

If you just give me a chance, I'll show you that I can be worthy of your love—

Forgetting to care about my own appearance, I stared in horror at Carter's. And he stared back, his expression teetering on the edge of utter devastation.

There was no way to separate him from the voice. No way to be around him and turn off Aralt's constant coaxing in my head.

The only way to keep Aralt from controlling my thoughts and feelings was to leave Carter behind.

"Please don't," I said. "I don't need your pity."

My words cut him to the quick. "Lex, I just want to help you." He looked around helplessly. "We're supposed to be a team."

"No," I said, backing away. "We're not. We can't—there's no more team. There's no 'us.' Stay away from me . . . please, just stay away from me."

I turned around and walked away, putting one foot in front of the other, thanking God I felt too numb to feel sad or scared—to feel anything at all.

26

MEGAN CAME TO THE PARK and picked me up. She was so distracted that she didn't even ask if I was okay. Instead I asked her if *she* was okay.

She checked her mirrors, like there might be someone tailing us. "No," she said. "I talked to Mimi. She rear-ended some guy on the way home, and it took three girls to drag her away so she wouldn't kill him. And Monika and Paige were standing in the hall and being super mean to all the freshman girls—calling them horrible names. Lydia tripped one girl and threatened to beat her up if she told anybody. And Tashi *quit*. You can't just quit!"

"Tell me about it," I said. It was all I had the energy to say. Then I noticed that she'd hung a left instead of a right. "Where are you going?"

"My house. We're having an emergency meeting."

Oh, for the love of God. I'd just broken up with my boyfriend. The very last thing on a list of fifty things I didn't feel like doing would be going to a Sunshine Club meeting.

"Everyone's going out of their minds," Megan said. "I don't get it. Did Tashi leave because she knew this was going to happen? Why isn't Aralt helping us?"

She was right, of course. Everything was spiraling out of control. Somehow Aralt had packed up and left us flailing.

It had to stop soon, or someone could get seriously hurt.

Betterment was a zoo. At one point it turned into a shouting match.

I got called out eight times. Not the least of my offenses was thoughtlessly falling in a ditch before an unplanned Sunshine Club meeting. There was also my unwillingness to trust Aralt in the matter of Emily, which came from Emily herself, with her head covered in a short blond wig; the way I'd skipped Monika's house over the weekend; the way I'd been absent from the courtyard before school; and so on . . . I nodded, nodded, nodded, and apologized too many times to count. We all did. We were all guilty of something.

Finally we moved on to the matter of Tashi.

Lydia got up and calmly recounted her conversation with Tashi, in which Tashi had decided that the

Sunshine Club wasn't right for her and she was going to leave town.

Could it be true? Could Tashi just decide to leave Aralt behind? Was that why she'd been scared, because he didn't want her to go? And maybe that was what caused Aralt to start freaking out.

Part of me figured, well, if somebody wants out, the sunny thing to do would be to let them go, right?

But I was apparently alone in that line of thinking.

"She can't quit!" Mimi said. "It's so completely disrespectful! Just take Aralt's gifts and leave? No wonder he's angry. You can't blame him!"

"It's like she knows all of our secrets," Monika said. "She's exploiting us. She might even be telling other people our private business!"

Even Lydia hadn't expected such a violent response. I could tell by the way she backed out of the discussion and stood silently, looking from person to person.

Emily straightened her wig and stood up, a concerned look on her face. "I think we need to contact Tashi, reason with her. Say we want her to come back."

Inwardly, I sighed with relief. Finally, someone was being sensible.

"And if she doesn't want to?" Megan asked.

"What do you mean?" Emily's soft eyes hardened. "She doesn't have a choice."

"Listen," Adrienne said. "We know she's out there. So Aralt can help us find her. And then we'll . . . bring her back. And help her see the error of her ways. Her disloyalty."

"We'll better her," Paige said. "We'll better her so much she'll never run away again."

Emily's mouth curled into an ugly smirk. "She'll learn that you can't leave Aralt."

I raised my hand. "Why do we have to worry about Tashi?" I asked. "Why can't we just graduate?"

Adrienne went all deer-in-the-headlights, and Lydia took over.

"We can," she said. "Soon. But we're just ironing out one little wrinkle."

Everyone groaned, and Adrienne looked around anxiously. "If anyone knows of any prospective new members . . ."

"Are you kidding? No one wants to join *now*," Mimi said. "Not after all the weird stuff."

"I thought we had enough people!" Paige protested.

Lydia's smile superglued itself to her face. "So did we," she said.

And then it hit me:

They were counting Kasey. If we really needed twenty-two people to graduate, my sister was the wrench in the machine.

My eyes cut sharply over to meet my sister's. Then I looked around.

From her spot on the bed, Megan was watching us both.

"So if we got Tashi back," Monika said, "that would work?"

"I guess," Lydia said. "But in the meantime, everyone focus on recruiting."

"And let this be a reminder to us all," Adrienne said. "In case anyone is ever tempted. This situation proves that you can't just desert Aralt."

"And if you try," Emily said, "you can *die*, for all we care."

"This is ridiculous," Kasey said, following so close she was practically on top of me. "You can't just leave me behind! I'm not a helpless little kid."

"You don't need to be spending any extra time around Sunshine Club members," I said. "The last thing we need is for people to figure out that you're a filthy traitor."

Kasey's mouth fell open.

"Joking," I said.

"*Not* funny."

"I'll think of something funnier on the road," I said, grabbing Mom's car keys from the hook, "and tell it to you when I get home."

* * *

I pounded on the door. Adrienne opened it, fully made-up and dressed to the nines.

"Alexis? What's wrong?"

"Are you going somewhere?"

"What do you mean?"

And then I realized that this was just how she dressed now. How we all dressed now.

"Never mind. I was hoping we could talk," I said. "About Aralt."

Every Sunshine Club girl's favorite topic. Her eyes lit up, and she led me over to the dinner table.

"Where did you get the book?" I asked.

The lights turned off. The glow faded. She mashed her lips together and looked away.

"Adrienne?"

She fixed her eyes on the ceiling. "Here's the thing, Alexis. I'm really not supposed to say."

For all I knew, she really wasn't. Maybe that was one of Aralt's rules.

"Can I see it?"

She shook her head furiously. "No," she said. "I'm sorry. You can't."

"I won't touch it," I said. "I just think it's so pretty."

She gave me an apologetic frown. "I know," she said. "It totally is. Except . . . it's not here."

"Where is it?"

For a moment there was a flash of distrust across her features. But then she folded her hands and looked directly at me. "It's at Lydia's house."

"But why?"

"Lydia thought it would be safer there."

"Safer from what?" I asked.

Adrienne shrugged. "I don't know. But it's her book, so she can decide."

"I'm sorry, wait," I said. "Did you say it's *Lydia's* book? Kasey told me it was yours."

Her eyes went wide and she clapped both hands over her mouth.

"No, it's fine," I said. "I won't tell her you said anything."

"But I promised!" Adrienne said, drooping. "She'd just be so embarrassed if she knew I told anyone."

"What's there to be embarrassed about?"

"I don't know. I think because it's about, like, being popular and pretty, and Lydia never wanted people to think she cared about those things. But we wouldn't judge her. . . ." She gave me a questioning glance.

That was my cue. "No, never!"

"I tried to tell her that, but she *seriously* didn't want people to know it was her book. She asked me to say it was mine. And what did I care, you know? I knew I was a loser. Everybody knew."

"So she brought it to your house and asked you to lie?" I asked.

"No, not to lie," Adrienne said, reluctant to be disloyal. "Just . . . not to tell the truth."

"But she didn't think it would be safe here?" I took a chance. "Didn't Tashi have it for a while? And she was a total stranger."

"Tashi wasn't a stranger to Lydia," Adrienne said. She gave me a worried look. "Tashi was Lydia's friend. They met at . . ." The worry in her eye sharpened to mild suspicion. "Why do you want to know any of this?"

"I want to know as much about Aralt as possible," I said. "I don't care how Lydia and Tashi met. I care about making sure the book is safe."

"Of course," Adrienne said. "I understand."

I dialed it back and spent a few more minutes making polite small talk. But my body practically quivered with impatience to leave. Adrienne was no longer any use to me.

I had bigger fish to fry.

The Smalls' house wasn't just a little house in a shabby neighborhood. It was sloppy. There was something distasteful about the little signs of neglect—junk mail scattered on the porch. A trash bag leaning against the steps, waiting for who-knows-how-long to be taken all the way out.

I rang the doorbell, and a man answered it—Mr. Small. He wore a pair of jeans and a wrinkled plaid button-down shirt that looked like it had been caught in a dust storm.

"Hello," he said, polite but baffled.

"Is Lydia home?" I asked.

He turned and stared at the empty room behind him. "She ran out. . . . Was she expecting you?"

"No," I said. "I guess not."

"Well, come on in. She just went to the store. She should be back soon." He glanced at the clock. "I told her I'd need the car at nine thirty, so it shouldn't be more than fifteen minutes."

He pointed me toward the tiny living room, where a huge, modern sofa was stuffed awkwardly against the wall. I recognized it from back when Lydia and I would watch TV and talk about how much we hated everyone. It was totally out of place in the new house.

"Can I get you a glass of water?" Mr. Small asked.

"No, thank you." Noticing the way he kept glancing at the stairs, I said, "Don't let me keep you. I'll be fine waiting here."

He hovered in the doorway. "Oh, well . . . if you don't mind . . ."

"Please," I said.

He smiled and went around a corner, and I heard thumping footfalls on the staircase.

All of a sudden, the silence was broken by a shock of loud music—a weird smooth jazzy sound, mixed with awkward melodic riffs—coming from a keyboard, by the sound of it.

The song went on and on. I couldn't help but compare it to Tashi's playing, so heartfelt, so passionate, with so much subtlety and emotion behind it. Mr. Small seemed to be banging the keys randomly with boxing gloves.

A few minutes later, the front door opened with a creak, and a disheveled Lydia came in, arms loaded up with bulging grocery bags. She stopped just inside the door and looked up at the ceiling, taking in the music.

"Oh, *come on*," she muttered.

Then she noticed me.

Her face turned bright pink, like I'd been digging through her underwear drawer. She dropped her bags and raced out of the room. The keyboard playing stopped abruptly, and the sound of Lydia's outraged voice blasted down from upstairs.

A minute later, she returned, trying incredibly hard to stay in control.

"So sorry about that. . . . Give me one sec to put this stuff away." The whites of her eyes showed over the tops of her irises, making her look completely rabid-chipmunk insane. She half-carried, half-dragged the bags out of sight, and after a fair amount of clanking and thumping, she came back and sat, her hands folded in her lap. "Now. How can I help you?"

I noticed a thick layer of concealer under her eyes. And her lipstick leached away from her mouth in tiny red rivers. She was tired.

"Something's going on, Lyd," I said. "This whole Tashi thing is messed up."

"What are we supposed to do about it?" she asked. "Honestly, Alexis. Face reality. I don't like it either, but she's gone."

"Yes, but where did she go? Didn't she say anything to you?"

"When would she have done that?"

"When she told you she was leaving. When she gave you the book."

She looked at me blankly.

"I know it's here, okay?"

She sighed and leaned back. "Tashi wasn't who she claimed to be. She was totally using us. She walked up to me at the mall one day, all talky-talky-let's-be-friends. We were hanging out, and she mentioned this book she had. She acted like it was something she'd picked up at a garage sale. She was lying, obviously."

"But *you* brought her to the party," I said. "*You* gave the book to Adrienne. And you took the oath."

"I told you before," she said, glaring, "I did it as a joke, okay? I was going to make fun of them for being naive. How was I supposed to know Aralt was so amazing?"

"Why did you tell Adrienne to pretend it wasn't yours?"

"I never said that," she said, shaking her head. "I asked her to say it was hers, not that it *wasn't* mine. It's not mine. It never was. It's Tashi's."

"But now she's gone, and she just left it here?"

There were footsteps on the stairs, and Mr. Small appeared. Over his clothes, he wore a black apron with SCHNELKER'S HARDWARE embroidered on the front.

"Going out tonight, Lyddie?" he asked, rubbing his hands on his jeans. "I'm working stock. Home before sunrise."

She shrugged, staring at the wall over my head like she couldn't bear to look at him.

"Well, leave a note if you do." With a nod, he scooped the car keys off the table next to the door and started out. He paused at the last second. "Love you."

Lydia gritted her teeth. *"You're embarrassing me,"* she hissed.

He went out the door without another word.

Lydia shrugged, a contemptuous look in her eyes. "Tashi was having trouble dealing with things. She was really . . . sensitive. And kind of paranoid. You know, the prissy, artistic type? No offense."

I let that go. "She never hinted that she was going to leave? She just showed up one night, handed you the book, and said she was heading out of town?"

"Basically," Lydia said. "Look, she was nice, but we weren't exactly BFFs. And I can't say I'm thrilled that she dumped the book and ran—as much as I love Aralt. I mean, it *is* kind of her job."

"Right," I said. Never mind that the girl was essentially Aralt's slave for two hundred years. God forbid she not do her job.

"Was there anything else you needed?" Lydia asked, standing up.

"Can I look at the book?" I asked, following her.

"Honestly, Alexis," she said, stopping on the tile in front of the door. "I don't mean to sound inhospitable, but I haven't had dinner yet and—"

"You heard what everyone said tonight," I said. "Things are falling apart. We need to figure out how to stop this before it gets even more out of control."

"Oh *that's* what you care about?" Lydia raised her eyebrows. "And here I thought you were actually worried about Tashi."

"Well, I am, but—"

"I *know* how to stop it, Alexis." She shook her head. "Why didn't you just ask? You come in here all *CSI*, like you're trying to track down a missing person, and what you really want is to know how to fix your own problems?"

When she put it that way, it made me sound like a jerk. "I'm worried about Tashi *and* the rest of it," I said.

"Well, let me ease your mind," she said. "Tashi gave me the name of the graduation spell before she left."

"Seriously?"

"Yeah," she said. "Why, like it's a secret? I have it written down upstairs."

"Can you go get it?"

Lydia was teetering dangerously on the edge of Sunshine Club behavior, and every new request I made threatened to dump her back into Doom Squad territory. But she gave me a pained smile, said, "Wait here," and headed up the stairs.

I looked around the room and at the dirty floors, imagining what I could do to this place with a few hours and a bucket of bleach. I took a step back and realized that there was something wet and sticky on the tile, right where Lydia had set her grocery bags. I knelt down.

Blood.

Glancing at the stairs, I wondered if I had enough time to get to the kitchen. I took a tentative step but heard Lydia starting her descent. So instead, I tiptoed to the small side table where she'd set her purse and grabbed the piece of paper sticking out of it—what I hoped was her grocery store receipt.

Going against every fiber of my being, I swiped the sole of my shoe across the blood on the floor until it was spread so thinly that you'd never know it was there.

"What are you doing?" Lydia asked, coming around the corner. "Tap dancing?"

"I'm just trying to keep moving," I said, faking a tense little jig. "I'm nervous. We all are. Or hadn't you noticed?"

"You know, Alexis, if you aren't careful, you're going to wake up one day and realize that you're no fun to be around." She pursed her lips. "I can't find the spell. My room's kind of a mess. But believe me, I'll find it. I'm as eager to get this over with as you are. What do you think about having the meeting on Saturday?"

"I guess that's fine," I said.

"Now, not to be rude, but could you go? I'm starving."

I left, but I waited until I was stopped at a traffic

light a block away before opening the paper I'd grabbed.

Then I stared at it so long that the cars behind me started honking.

It was a grocery store receipt. The total was $139.24.

And all she'd bought was meat.

"So Lydia's the new *creatura*?" Kasey asked, scanning the receipt.

"I guess so. That might explain why she's been so ragged these days."

Kasey shot me a wary look. "She looks fine."

"I'm not being sunshiny. I'm just saying. Protecting the book is a big job. Even Tashi couldn't handle it."

"Well, Lydia won't have to do it for long," Kasey said.

Lydia had suggested we have the meeting Saturday, assuming someone came through with a new member. Whatever the graduation ceremony involved, we'd get through it. Then Kasey and I would find some excuse to get the book and destroy it.

It was such a simple plan that it kind of made me uneasy, to be honest.

Because nothing with Aralt was ever as simple it seemed.

27

MY CELL PHONE RANG at 6:30 the next morning. I turned over and answered it without checking to see who was calling.

The voice hit me like a freight train. "Alexis. Where is Tashiana?"

I sat up. "Farrin?"

"She's not responding to my calls. Have you seen her?"

"No," I said, rubbing my eyes. "Not this week."

"Not this *week?* What do you mean?"

"She left."

"*She left,*" Farrin repeated. Something in her voice took me from sleepy to vividly awake.

"Yeah, but it's okay," I said. "We still have the book."

"That's impossible. Tashiana would never allow the book to be unattended."

"But . . ." I didn't know how to sugarcoat it. "She did."

"*Never,*" Farrin said. "She is physically unable to be

away from the book for more than a few hours. Do you understand what I'm saying?"

For a moment, I *didn't* understand. Then, in a flash, I did.

Tashi was dead. She had to be, if she couldn't survive apart from the book.

Because it had been at Lydia's house all week.

But that didn't seem to be the part that concerned Farrin. "The book is unprotected," she said. What scared me the most was how quiet her voice became. "The energy is untended. My God, Alexis. What have you girls done?"

"But it's not untended. It's . . . tended," I said. "There's a new *creatura*."

"Excuse me?"

It felt like every word I said was one more spoonful of dirt out of a giant hole I was digging for myself. But I didn't know what was wrong with what I was saying, so I didn't know what not to say.

"There's a new *creatura*," I said. "She'll look after the book."

Farrin's voice dripped acid. "Do you even know what that word means?"

Well—I *thought* I did. But maybe not. "It's the creature," I said. "She takes care of Aralt?"

"*Creator*, you dumb child!" Farrin snapped. "It's Latin. Not creature! *Creator*."

360

Creator?

"You can't have a *new* creator! She was joined to the book—she was the only one who could properly direct Aralt's energy. And now you foolish little girls are running around with the potential to completely destroy yourselves." Then her voice went eerily calm. "Maybe more than just yourselves."

I was reeling. I couldn't speak.

We were all doomed.

"I'll call you back in five minutes. Answer the phone!" Farrin slammed her receiver down so hard it hurt my ear.

Two minutes later the phone rang.

"Here is what you must do," she said. "There is a spell in the book that you'll find and read. Every one of you. Write this down. The spell is called *Tugann Sibh*. Look for those words. Everyone reads it. And one of you must read it twice."

I went to my desk and wrote it down, fumbling the pen between my clumsy fingers. "*Tugann Sibh*? What does it mean?"

"Never mind that," Farrin said. "Just do it."

"When?"

"As soon as you can," she said. "Today. And when you are done, bring the book directly to me."

"I don't know if I can—I mean, we'll try. But we

don't have the right number of people yet."

"There's no such thing as a right number," she said. "You've got to stop being stubborn and do as I say. Without Tashiana, you and your friends are like a speeding car without a driver. She spent *hours* each day ensuring that Aralt's energy flowed properly. Things are bad already—but they could easily get worse."

All of that power, nothing to guide it. I thought of the force that had battered me in Tashi's garage, and a chill went up my spine.

"Have you noticed any fluctuations?" she asked. "Besides your disastrous interview and my illness?"

Where would I even start? "Um . . . maybe one or two," I said.

"Be careful. You may behave erratically; try to make sure no one gets hurt."

Oh, sure. Easier said than done.

"This is such an enormous catastrophe," she said. "I wonder if any of us will be able to recover from it."

I was too frightened to reply.

"By the way," she said. "You won the contest. This should have been a great day for you." She hung up.

No such thing as the right number of people? Then why were we obsessed with getting a new member? Would Adrienne and Lydia really hold the whole process up for another "put your hand on the book" trick?

I sighed and looked down at the words I'd written: *Tugann Sibh.*

I dodged Kasey long enough to borrow Mom's laptop and find the translation on a Gaelic web site: *We give.*

Give—like a sacrifice?

There was a line in the oath—something about a gift, a treasure. . . . So what were we giving? Farrin had said one girl had to read the spell twice.

I sat back from the computer in confusion.

Then I remembered the last page of the book—the one covered in signatures. I scrolled through the photos on my phone until I found it. The picture was so blurry I could only make out a few of the names.

But there it was: *Suzette Skalaski.*

Skalaski. *Where* had I heard that name before?

In my head, I could hear it spoken in Farrin's satiny voice . . . at the mocktail party.

Weatherly College. I turned back to the computer and searched for *Suzette Skalaski + Weatherly College.*

There was a whole section of the college's website devoted to the Skalaski School of Photography. At the top was a link labeled OVERVIEW.

The Skalaski School of Photography at Weatherly College was founded in 1988 in honor of Suzette Skalaski, a member of the class of 1974 who passed away before graduation. The state-of-the-art facilities were dedicated at a ceremony attended by California governor George Deukmejian, officiated by Skalaski's classmate Barbara Draeger, the first female (and youngest) mayor of Las Riveras, California. Another classmate, noted fashion photographer Farrin McAllister, served as a consultant on the building and equipping of the college, and spoke at the dedication. "Suzi was passionate about two things: education and helping others, and to know that this program is made possible in her honor would be among her proudest achievements."

I found several more references to buildings, scholarships, even a residential street named after Suzette. Finally I found a biography, on her private high school's "Notable Alumnae" page that gave details about her death: 1973, an aneurysm.

I went back to my phone to look for another name. Even zoomed in all the way, the resolution was so low that it was hard to make them out. The one at the very bottom of the list—the most recent?—looked like "Narelle Simmons."

I typed it in and hit ENTER. The first result was a hit: Narelle Simmons, White Pine, Wisconsin.

A blog. The graphic at the top read:

❤ ❤ ❤ *NARELLE'S WORLD* ❤ ❤ ❤

Her picture came up in the sidebar. She was a pretty black girl, with short, curly hair and a toothy smile.

Beneath it were three lines of bolded type:

REST IN PEACE

NARELLE DANIQUE SIMMONS

FOREVER IN OUR HEARTS

And then a paragraph telling how the bright, ambitious Narelle had passed away of a brain aneurysm.

I stared breathlessly at the screen.

One more. The next name I could make out was "Marnie Peterson."

There were too many results, so I went back and made it *Marnie Peterson + dead teenager.*

I clicked on an article from the *Palm Beach Post,* dated five years earlier.

Area teens and parents are distraught over the sudden death of Guacata High School junior Marnie Peterson. Principal Helen Fritsch said that Peterson had begun her high school career as a problem student but had recently turned her life around and begun committing to both her studies and her future. Grief counselors will be available at the school. Peterson's cause of death was reported as . . .

An aneurysm.

Farrin stood over a tray of chemicals, tongs in hand, watching a print.

"How can I help you, Alexis?" she said.

"So you sort of left out a minor detail," I said, trying to keep my voice level.

"What's that?"

"Oh, you know. Just that somebody *dies*."

There was a cold, mocking edge to her voice. "I wouldn't have thought you'd have a problem with it. Tashiana's death didn't seem to disturb you."

That wasn't true—or fair. I was horrified by Tashi's death. I just knew I didn't have time to let the horror of it get to me.

"The way you said it—I could have just picked someone at random—and they would have *died*. Because of me." I tried to suppress the anger I felt when I thought that I might have asked Megan—or Emily—or—

"Well, it won't be random now. Is that a comfort?"

"No!" I said. "I don't see why someone else should have to *die*. And why didn't you tell me last night?"

"You didn't ask."

"I can't do it," I said, bringing my fist down on the counter. "I won't. How can you say being popular or getting out of a few parking tickets is worth a human being dying?"

She hadn't moved. "You're still not getting it, Alexis," she said gently.

"But don't you feel *bad*?" I asked. "Suzette

Skalaski died for you. And you get to drive a Mercedes. Congratulations."

She actually laughed—a harsh, short laugh. "I can assure you that Suzette did *not* die so I could drive a luxury car."

"Then *why?*"

Farrin turned away from her print. "Listen to me. Listen very carefully."

Oh, I was listening, all right.

"Suzette sacrificed herself *because she wanted to.*"

The phrase hit me like a physical blow.

"Alexis, for thousands of years, men have been throwing themselves in front of cannons and arrows so that some king could own another few million acres and grow richer off the taxes."

"That still doesn't make it *right.*"

"When Suzette gave her life for us, she was giving to a cause greater than herself. Suzette's friends have gone on to be senators, to win Oscars—"

"And Pulitzers?" I interjected.

She nodded. "Yes. And to make incredible medical discoveries, to create timeless sculptures. Every day we're alive, with everything we do, we all pay tribute to her sacrifice."

"Yeah, but what did she get out of it?" I asked.

"Have you ever sacrificed for someone you cared

about?" she asked. "Have you ever traded one important thing so another important thing could thrive?"

"I don't know," I said.

All of my problems seemed to have started because I *wasn't* willing to do that.

"Beauty. Popularity. Winning the contest. Getting a full scholarship to Weatherly College," she said, her eyebrow arched. "Those are only external things. But Alexis, what about your injured finger? What about the way you think and react when you trust in Aralt?"

All of those good grades, charmed teachers. The cut that had disappeared from my hand. Even the burns from the curling iron were healing quickly—though the healing seemed to start and stop at random intervals.

"It would be selfish to keep such blessings to one small group of people. So when the time comes, one of your friends—or it could even be you—will volunteer, make a gift of her own life force so Aralt can keep going, keep helping others. It replenishes his strength."

I closed my eyes. "That's so wrong."

"Why?" she asked. "If Suzette was happy to do it, why should we not accept her painless, happy death as the generous and precious gift it was?"

"That's horrible," I said. "It's not worth a life."

"Easy for you to say," she said, rearing her head back. "You're a confident, talented, healthy young

368

woman. But what about the others?"

Healthy—that made me think of Adrienne. How she was next in line for her mother's disease and wheelchair-bound existence.

"All I'm saying," Farrin said quietly, "is that maybe it doesn't seem like a very significant thing to you. But there are others for whom it is quite a big deal."

Would Adrienne really let someone die so she could stay out of a wheelchair?

"Dr. Jeanette Garzon discovered a treatment for a genetic disorder that has saved the lives of thousands of children," Farrin said. "Jeanette was a freshman at Weatherly when Suzi, Barbara, and I were juniors. She was dirt-poor and in danger of losing her scholarship."

I stared at the floor.

"Ask the parents of the children Jeanette has saved," Farrin said. "Ask the children themselves. If it's worth the death of one willing person so that they all might be alive today."

"But maybe if she hadn't gotten into medical school, someone else would have, and maybe they would have discovered the cure to a totally *different* disease."

Farrin lifted her chin. "You can't live according to theoretical models, Alexis. You can only make the most of the opportunities you've been given."

I sat back and sighed. "But if Tashi's really—

gone, then who's going to manage the energy?"

Farrin turned away. "That does complicate things. But we have no reason to believe that we can't keep the book in a safe place and continue to benefit from Aralt's generosity."

"Not send it to a new group of girls?" I asked. "Then . . . no one else would die."

"I suppose not," Farrin said. "We couldn't risk sending the book out without Tashiana. Does that make it easier for you?"

"No," I said, trying to sound more sure than I was.

"Anyway, the simple fact is, you have no options other than *Tugann Sibh*. You're incredibly lucky that such a simple solution exists. You would be wise not to question it."

"If I weren't one of Aralt's girls," I said, "would I still have won the contest?"

She didn't look up from her work. "But you *are* one of Aralt's girls."

"But if I *weren't*."

She finished clipping the print over the air vent and turned to me. "Alexis, with your camera, you can change the world. You can affect the way people think. You can fight wars and end them. You can make heroes and destroy them. You can shine a light on injustice. It's not just doctors who make a difference."

I thought about that—finding something I cared about and bringing out passion in other people. For a treacherous moment, I was filled with a lustrous feeling of power.

"But I don't—I mean, I *do* want to achieve things. But not because of some magical ring. Not because someone died for it."

"Aralt isn't a genie in a bottle. I've worked hard, very hard, to get where I am. And you will have to work hard too. But when you do the work, you will see the results. That's all."

I was starting to get a headache.

She came toward me and grabbed my hands. "This is your destiny, Alexis. *Embrace it.*"

"No." I backed away. "I can't. I'm sorry."

"*I'm sorry* is not an option." Her fingers were still wrapped around my own. "You don't have a choice."

"I do," I said. "We could just not do anything. Or we could get rid of the book."

In the dark, with the red light behind her, her eye sockets were shadows. Her hair was a mass of blackness outlined by a red halo. "Now don't go doing anything foolish."

I swallowed hard, fighting the urge to back away. "No, I mean, give it back to you."

She relaxed. "You're so *smart*," she said, twisting the

word derisively. "Why don't you go home and research the South McBride River incident?"

She followed me out through the workroom, though in a way it felt like I was being chased out. As she held the door open, she looked down her nose at me.

"You have a responsibility, Alexis. Remember that."

I ran out to the parking lot, huffing and puffing painfully by the time I got to Mom's car.

Stuck beneath the windshield wiper, flapping in the wind, was a parking ticket.

I drove straight to the library.

In the summer of 1987, a group of sixteen high school girls in the town of South McBride River, Virginia, were all struck with a debilitating mental illness. The most accepted theory was that the girls had somehow stirred up some toxic sludge from the bottom of a local lake, exposing them to a previously unknown bacterium. The infection shut down their brain functions and left them all comatose. One by one, they died.

There were entire websites devoted to it, most of them set up by conspiracy theorists, who pinned it on everything from aliens to a deliberate government effort. One man had somehow gotten hold of the girls' school records, showing that every one of them, even the most mediocre students, had finished the school year with straight A's. He went on to say that, in the depths of their madness, several of them carved the word ARALT into their bodies. This, he claimed, was an acronym for the U.S. government's top-secret "Advanced Research in Atomic and Laser Technology" department.

So the door to Aralt, once opened, must be closed again or you'll be driven insane, and then your brain will turn to useless mush.

I sat back against the hard wood of the library chair, feeling this new information like a twenty-pound weight on my chest.

We had to read that spell. One of us had to die . . . or we'd all die anyway.

28

I WENT STRAIGHT HOME, got in bed, and stared at the ceiling. I didn't answer my phone. I lied to my parents about feeling sick, and I ignored Kasey when she tried to talk to me. Finally, teary-eyed with hurt, she got the idea and left me alone.

Tashi was dead.

We were all bound to an incredibly selfish and angry spirit.

And the only way to fix it was for someone else to die.

I kept feeling this weird urge to just act normal, to pull the covers up to my chin and try to get some sleep. Wake up and have everything be fine. Just an ordinary day.

That is never going to happen, I told myself. *You are never going to have another normal day. Unless you find some way to stop this, you will never be normal again.*

* * *

The orange glow of the sodium halide streetlights mixed with the shadows of tree branches on my wall.

I ran through everything I could remember about the book, about Aralt, about Tashi. Especially Tashi. That night I'd been there, she'd been afraid. Why? Had it been Lydia at the door? Why had she pushed me into the garage?

I need to show you, she'd said.

Show me that Aralt was evil?

Because she'd known someone was going to die? But women had been dying for more than a century for Aralt. There had to be a hundred and fifty signatures on those pages. What was different now? What had changed?

And I kept repeating her last words to me: *Try again.*

Elspeth had said so too. Try again.

But try *what* again?

The Ouija board?

I got up and reached under my bed, where I'd hidden it. I sat on the floor and set the board up in a patch of bright orange light.

"Tashi?" I whispered. "Can you hear me? I'm sorry you died. I need your help. . . . I don't understand what it was that you wanted me to try."

No response.

"Elspeth?" I whispered. Then, helplessly, "Anyone?"

The pointer gave a quick jerk, startling me. I pulled

my hands off and watched it move. It seemed to swing, more than wobble—great sweeping motions, full of purpose, like a pendulum.

I-A-M-H-E-R-E

"Elspeth?" I asked.

But I knew it wasn't Elspeth.

Slowly, I reached down, intending to upturn the board, breaking the connection, and fold it up before any more words came out.

But as my hands got closer, the planchette stood perfectly still.

Was he gone?

I *slooooowly* lowered my fingers toward the pointer.

Just before I touched it, it bubbled up with inky black goo.

I tried to grab my hand away, but I was too late—

In a fraction of a second, it exploded into a sheet of black that stretched to cover my whole body like a cocoon. I opened my mouth to scream, and it poured in through my lips, silencing me. It was as sticky and impenetrable as a giant spiderweb. I tried to pound against it with my fists, but with every move I made, it squeezed and constricted me more. As it thickened over my eyes and my ears, I lost my balance and fell sideways onto the carpet.

Within a minute, my whole world was contained in

a shrinking womb of black webbing. I could breathe, but I couldn't hear my own breath. I couldn't see or move.

I lost track of how long I lay there, driven into a frenzy of fear but bound as tightly as a straitjacketed mental patient. I knew I was sobbing, and I could feel the vibrations of moaning in my throat, but all sound was silenced by the impassible shroud.

There was no such thing as time, or light, or movement.

Only darkness as endless as death.

Finally, mercifully, I lost consciousness.

I awoke—how much later?—on the floor. My whole body shook as the memory pounced on me. Had I dreamed it? The Ouija board was on the carpet by the window. My fingernails had dug bright red half-moons in my palms. The wounds stung in the open air.

And I was thirsty. God, I'd never been so thirsty.

There was a cup of water on my nightstand. I downed it in one long swig. That did nothing to soothe my parched throat, so I went to the kitchen and filled and emptied the cup twice more.

I was unsteady on my feet, like I'd had too much cold medicine. I had to lean against the counter to keep my balance.

Then I went to the bathroom and washed my hands,

noting how filthy my fingernails were. I found the nail-brush under the sink and scrubbed until the tips of my fingers were pink and almost raw. At first, dark red liquid—my own blood, from my torn-up palms—ran from them. But then the water ran clear, and there were *still* black crescents under my nails. They wouldn't come clean.

I flipped on the light and studied myself. Aside from my palms and my fingernails, there was no evidence that I'd just been attacked.

I leaned toward the mirror and opened my mouth.

The sight made me stagger backward into the wall behind me.

The whole inside of my mouth was charcoal black, as dark as the inside of the cocoon. My teeth, my tongue, my gums . . . as far down my throat as I could see—black.

Collecting myself, I leaned in closer and noticed a gray overlay covering the whites and irises of my eyes, as thin as a pair of sheer black panty hose. I blinked a few times, but couldn't feel it—thank God.

I wasn't in pain. Actually, considering everything I'd just been through, I felt pretty okay.

I turned off the bathroom light and went back to the kitchen, filling my cup again. I left it on the counter so I could come back and get it. The energy seemed to be draining out of me. The thought of climbing back into my bed filled me with a sense of almost giddy anticipation.

To stretch out and feel the smooth, soft sheets against my arms, the coolness of the pillowcase against my face—to sink into a sweet, sumptuous sleep—

But not yet. There would be time for that later.

First, I had to kill my sleeping family.

29

I PULLED A CARVING KNIFE out of the block and grabbed the hand towel from the refrigerator door. I thought with regret that the bloodstains would probably ruin the little white towel.

I'll buy a new one, I thought. With my own money.

Aralt's approval coursed through me like a cool breeze.

Parents first. My dizziness intensified as I made my way down the hall. I knocked into the wall on one side, then wobbled too far in the other direction and hit the other side, too.

But I made it. I put my hand on my parents' doorknob and turned it so slowly, so quietly.

Kasey had tried to kill our mother this way last year, but only got as far as the hallway.

Amateur.

My parents were snuggled together in the center of the bed. The light from the window fell across them in a triangle of blue. They looked so peaceful, so content. It was nice that they'd been able to pull together when the family needed it most. Some couples would fall apart, but they just got stronger. It had really made things easier for me and Kasey.

Dad slept closer to the door. Better to start with him. Then Mom would be trapped.

Kasey I'd save for last, because let's face it—she wasn't going to be a problem.

As I looked for an angle that would let me make a quick, deadly impact into my father's throat, I thought, I hope Kasey appreciates everything they've done for us.

I lifted the knife in the air and hesitated.

Where was the towel? I must have dropped it in the hallway.

Without it, I wouldn't be able to wipe the knife clean when I was through. I would have to carry a bloody, dripping knife to Kasey's room and then all the way back to the kitchen, ruining the carpet in the bedrooms and maybe even the grout between the tiles in the hall.

I found the towel on the ground just under the family portrait.

As I went to stand up, I felt a tiny point of pressure on my back.

"Don't move," Kasey whispered.

I stayed bent over.

"Drop the knife," she said.

"*Excuse* me, I'm using it," I said.

She swallowed hard. "For what?"

"Mom and Dad. You."

The pressure on my back increased. "*Drop it*, Alexis."

Drop it? Like I was a bad dog running around with a sock in my mouth.

"How long will this take?" I asked, setting the knife on the floor. "I'm in the middle of something."

"Get in the bathroom," she said.

The faster I indulged her, the faster it would be over with. So I walked into the bathroom. She followed, kicking the knife toward the end of the hallway and flipping on the bathroom light.

"What's this all about, Kasey?" I asked, turning around. At the sight of my face, she gasped, and the point of the fireplace poker she was holding wavered in her hands. I realized a second too late that I'd missed a chance to grab it and smash it into the side of her head.

"What's happening to you?" she whispered.

I glanced in the mirror. The darkness had begun to spread from my mouth and eyes. It leached out inky puddles with thin tendrils of black snaking out in delicate feathery patterns.

What's happening to me? What was she talking about?

"So you have a pointy stick," I said. "Big deal. Get out of my way."

She shook her head.

The poker had a sharp point at the very tip and another piece of hooked metal that curled out to the side and ended in another point.

"What are you going to do?" I sneered. When I spoke, I could taste the sourness of the black coating in my mouth. "Poke me?"

"I'll hit you, Lexi." Her face was stony. "As hard I have to."

Whatever. I was really not in the mood.

"Can't we talk about this in the morning?" I asked. *After I kill you?*

"No." Her eyes hardened. "Get your toothbrush."

"What?"

"Pick up your toothbrush," she said, careful not to let the poker dip a second time, "and stick it down your throat."

"Kasey—" I said, and suddenly the sharp tip of the poker was touching the soft part of my stomach.

"Do it," she said.

"Ugh, fine," I said, picking up the toothbrush. "You're sick, you know that?"

"Get in the tub," she said.

Cocking one eyebrow, I lifted one foot and then

the other and stood in the tub. "Happy?"

She waited.

I stuck the toothbrush into my throat. Instantly, I gagged and doubled over.

"Do it again," she said.

"God, Kasey," I cried. What was the point of this? Stabbing people was one thing. But making them barf—that was just disturbing.

But I did it again, and suddenly I was overcome by a tsunami of nausea, dropping to my knees in the bathtub, vomiting up mouthful after mouthful of bitter black liquid.

It got in my nose and stuck in my throat and made me feel like I was choking.

But the less of it that was inside me, the more I wanted to keep throwing up—forever, if necessary. I was crying and gasping and retching, my arms covered in the remnants of the black goo, and then it hit me—how close I'd come to killing my family.

That and the memory of being trapped inside the black cocoon crashed through my body and left me a shaking, sobbing wreck.

After watching me for a minute, Kasey set her poker on the counter and came to the edge of the tub.

"Lexi?" she whispered.

I retched again, overcome by another wave of nausea,

and rested my head on the filthy surface of the bathtub.

I couldn't speak. I could hardly breathe. My nose stung, and my throat felt like it was wallpapered in fire.

"Shh," she said, gently rubbing my back. "It's okay."

"Did I . . ." I paused to gag and spit out another mouthful of black fluid. "Did I hurt anyone?"

"No," she said. "We're fine."

When the nausea subsided, I started shaking.

"Come on, Lexi," she said. "Let's get you cleaned up."

I couldn't believe how calm she was. She raised me to my feet and helped me undress. She ran a hot shower and sat on the lid of the toilet seat while I rinsed off. When I got out, she was waiting with a towel and a fresh pair of pajamas.

I brushed my teeth for what felt like ten minutes. When I was done, the toothbrush was black. Kasey dropped it in the trash can.

Then we stood looking at each other.

"I guess we're even," I said.

She frowned. "I haven't been keeping score."

So this was it. This was the train off the rails. I shuddered to think of what might be happening in the houses of Sunshine Club girls across Surrey. I consoled myself with the idea that the goo and I went way back; that our relationship was somehow a step ahead of everyone else's.

But Farrin was right. We had no choice. This had to end.

I reached a shaky hand down and opened the drawer, pulling out a tinted lip gloss and rolling it over my raisin-dry lips.

Kasey passed a comb through my hair, dabbing the ends with a towel to keep the water from soaking through my pajama top.

"You need some rest," she said, separating my hair into three sections and weaving them into a simple braid.

"You have to lock me up," I said. "In a closet or something. Someplace I can't get to anyone. Someplace safe."

"You'll be safe," she said, but in the mirror I saw her chest shudder with an intake of breath.

"Where?" I whispered. The world was huge and dangerous, full of people I could hurt without a second thought.

She wiped the wet comb on a towel and stuck it back in the drawer, then put her hands on my shoulders and met my eyes in the mirror. "With me."

I looked at the dimples in her cheeks from the determined clench of her jaw.

If I could get the fireplace poker, I thought, I could make those dimples a lot deeper.

Oh, God. I ran past her to my bedroom, where I

pulled on a pair of jeans and zipped my jacket over my pajama top.

Kasey knocked lightly and pushed the door open a few inches. "What are you doing?"

"I'm sorry," I said. "I have to go."

Her mournful eyes looked up at me, and she hugged herself tightly. "Where?"

"I don't know," I said. "I'll try to send you a message."

"What do I tell Mom and Dad?"

"Make something up," I said. I was afraid to stay an instant longer than I had to.

Kasey followed me to the foyer and locked the dead-bolt behind me, as I'd told her to.

I crossed the street and climbed to the top of the jungle gym, where I took out my phone and called Megan.

Her tires crunched on the cheap asphalt as she parked. This road would be dust in five years. She pushed open the passenger door for me and watched me fasten my seat belt.

"So what happened?" she asked.

I didn't want to say it out loud.

"That bad, huh?" She headed back to the main road.

"Please help me," I said. "I need to go somewhere safe."

Suddenly everything caught up with me and I started to cry. It was a full-on ugly cry—dark, stinging tears pouring down my cheeks, my mouth open in a wide, hiccupping wail, snot welling up in my nose.

Megan dug through her purse, pulled out a packet of tissues, and drove.

Through all of it—all of the meetings, the glamour, the stuff with Carter, Tashi's death—what I'd really needed was someone to talk to. A best friend. *My* best friend.

"Megan," I said, "everything is falling apart."

"Shh," she said, patting me on the shoulder.

"No, you don't understand," I said. And then I told her everything—thinking I'd had Aralt fooled, finding myself caught anyway. Tashi's weird disappearance. Farrin's threats. *Tugann Sibh.* Winning the contest, even though I didn't deserve it.

Everything but Kasey.

I was so busy talking that she pulled into Lydia's driveway before I noticed which direction we were headed.

"What are we doing here?" I asked.

"You'll be safe here," Megan said. "Lydia's parents aren't home."

She saw me looking warily up at the foil-covered window, with light leaking around its edges.

"It's not like I could take you to my house, Lex," she said. "Grandma would have us both committed."

True.

Lydia let us in, speaking in soft, soothing tones, and even brought me a cup of tea. We sat on the couch for a minute until my nerves got the better of me and I had to stand up and walk around. I could feel their eyes on me like I was a loaded gun. And, after all, wasn't I?

The walls of the living room were hung with random family photos. It looked like they'd just put whatever picture was handy on whatever nail happened to be in the wall. The scale was off, the frames didn't match.

I leaned in closer to see a picture of eighth-grade Lydia—pre-goth—grinning and leaning against an older woman. It was some kind of church social or something—they both wore goofy straw hats and name tags.

HI, MY NAME IS: LYDIA!

HI, MY NAME IS: ELSPETH!

I stared at the photo for what felt like a very, very long time, until my vision seemed to swim.

"Lex?" Megan asked. "Are you feeling any better?"

"Why don't you come sit down?" Lydia asked, gliding to my side. She took my teacup and led me back to the couch.

Don't trust me, Elspeth had said.

"Who is that?" I asked, and my tongue was fuzzy. My words came out dull.

Lydia glanced up at the picture. In my head, the image echoed:

HEAD TURN/GLANCE, HEAD TURN/GLANCE, HEAD TURN/GLANCE

"That's my grandmother," she said, her voice vibrating in my head like she was talking into a fan. "She died in May."

GRANDMOTHER/DIED IN MAY, GRAND-MOTHER/DIED IN MAY

Megan appeared above me, her hand under my chin.

"Hello in there?" she asked. Then she turned away. "Yeah, she's gone. How long will it last?"

DON'T TRUST ME/DON'T TRUST ME/DON'T TRUST ME

No.

The world went dark like the curtain being lowered on a stage.

DON'T TRUST MEGAN.

30

DRIPPING WATER, INSULATED; a pipe leaking inside a wall somewhere.

The distant, dim orange glow of a night-light.

A headache like a pod of dolphins slamming up against the inside of my skull.

And I was tied to a chair.

Nope, wasn't shaping up to be a great day.

I let my chin drop and noticed that I was wearing an unfamiliar dress. Then my thoughts came into focus and I realized that I did recognize it. It was one of Megan's. And on my feet were a pair of Mrs. Wiley's best shoes— not hand-me-downs, but a pair plucked fresh from her closet. I couldn't see my fingernails, but I had a feeling they were immaculately painted. I could smell powder and lipstick—presumably on my face—and determined that part of the facial tightness I was attributing to my headache was due to the pull of one of Megan's hairstyles.

I was dressed for a party. A really important party. But I was still woozy enough to take it in stride. I guess we found lucky number twenty-two, I thought.

That sobered me up.

Because if we were having a party, that meant someone was going to die.

And what about Kasey? Would she come looking for me? What would they do to her?

I was in a small, windowless room. I didn't bother screaming for help—I didn't want to attract Megan and Lydia's attention any sooner than I needed to. Anyway, I figured, they would never have risked putting me in a room within shouting distance of the neighbors.

Behind me, a door creaked open. I tried to let my head fall limply against my chest, but whoever it was had seen the movement.

"Well, good afternoon, Miss Sunshine!" It was Megan.

I didn't answer.

"Are you ready to celebrate?" she asked. "It's going to be so much fun."

I flexed my wrists and felt the pull of tape against my skin.

"How can we graduate if we don't have enough people?" I asked.

"Who says we don't?" Megan said, her voice frosting

over. "Cheer up, Lex. I brought you a friend."

I heard the sound of someone being shoved. The door slammed shut, and there was a faint, offended "Ow."

I knew that *Ow*.

"Kasey?" I cried, straining to look over my shoulder.

"Lexi?!?" She came barreling across the room and hugged me from behind, chair and all. "Oh my God, are you okay? What happened?"

"I'm all right," I said. "Can you undo my hands?"

"Yes," she said, going to work. "But tell me what happened! Is Megan...?"

"Evil? Yeah, basically." I craned my neck to watch her fingers fumble with the tape. "Why are you here, Kase? Are you okay?"

"I'm fine," she said, eyes wide. "I called Megan to see if she knew where you were, and she said to come to Lydia's. So I came, and then they told me you were in the basement, and I was like, *why*, and Megan was like, *see for yourself*, and then she pushed me in here and told me to talk some sense into you."

I closed my eyes. At least they hadn't hurt her.

"Lexi, what's happening? Megan said there's a Sunshine Club meeting. The last one. What's going on?"

"It's graduation day," I said. "Listen to me, Kasey. You have to play along, do whatever it takes to get away from here before the meeting. It's not safe for you here."

"No way. I'm not leaving you," she said. "Every time you do something alone, disaster. So no. Forget it."

"You don't understand," I said. "If they learn the truth, they'll kill you."

"But they don't know, do they?" she asked. "And how would they find out?"

She had a point. They would never have let her in to see me if they suspected she was less than perfectly devoted to Aralt.

I shifted my focus to my hands. "Are you done yet?" I asked. "Maybe there's something lying around that you could use to cut the tape."

"Lexi, please. I know there's something you don't want me to know about. But whatever they want you to do, just do it. It's not a big deal. If you got hurt, what would I tell Mom?"

"It *is* a big deal, though," I said. "Someone's going to get killed, Kasey."

"Well . . . so what?" she said. "It's not you or me."

So what? "What do you mean, it's not me or you? How would you know?"

"I mean—it doesn't *have* to be you or me. It could be anybody."

I gave my hands a tug.

They were no closer to being free than when she'd come in.

"Kasey," I said, "come here."

A pause, and a rustling behind me. "We don't have time for all this, Lexi."

"Just come around," I said. "I want to look at you."

"What do you mean?"

"I just want to see something."

Her voice turned petulant. "There's nothing to see—"

"Kasey!"

She snapped like a rubber band. "Stop bossing me around, Lexi! I'm trying to save you! Save all of us!"

"Come here."

She came around and knelt in front of me. "Why won't you let me help you?" she asked. "I've been through this once, remember? This is different. You can't just smash up a doll and be a hero this time."

"We can't let a person die, Kase," I said. And even if we could—it wouldn't set us free from Aralt. We'd still be his—his to control, his to feed from, for the rest of our lives.

Kasey's face fell. "I can't lose you," she said, lowering her face and crying softly. "You're the best big sister in the world. Please just do what they say."

For a moment, I was touched. Beyond touched. I looked at the shining hair on top of my sister's head and watched her raise her eyes to me.

Her blackened eyes. Her gray-streaked face.

"You took the oath," I said.

"So what if I did?" she exploded, springing to her feet.

The room fell silent.

She drew in a deep breath and let it out evenly. "It's not my fault," she said. "They figured it out."

"How?" I asked. "Without you coming out and *telling* them, how would they figure it out?"

Slowly, she turned around and lifted her hair, revealing her neck. Drawn across it was a long, dark slash, like a sinister smile.

She turned back, her eyes crinkled with something like an apology. "I panicked," she said. "I knew I wouldn't heal, so I confessed before they did anything . . . serious."

I closed my eyes.

A dark ball of anger was born inside me. Megan and Lydia had invited my baby sister over and ambushed her, held her down and tortured her. And then bullied her into swearing allegiance to Aralt.

I'll kill them. I let the thought fill my head for a dark, satisfying moment, and then I pulled myself back.

"But it's okay! It's fine. I'm so much happier now. Look, Lexi," she said. "I'm all for taking a stand—in general—but what choice do you have?"

My chest felt heavy. In the stuffiness of the closed-off room, it hurt to breathe.

No choice.

I had no choice.

"And when you think about it . . ." she said, "isn't it almost a little exciting?"

In the dim light, her expectant smile was as sweet as antifreeze.

She reached her hands out, rested them on my knees. I gazed down at the ring on her finger, expecting another one of our shiny gold bands. But what I saw instead was something older—much older.

Around the circle of it snaked a carved gold braid, and its surface was a haze of soft scratches.

A hundred and sixty-seven years' worth of scratches.

"Where did you get that?" I asked.

Kasey glanced at it. "Lydia had it lying around. She said it belonged to a friend of the family who died."

I closed my eyes tightly.

"For God's sake, don't cry," Kasey said. "You'll wreck your makeup."

"Get out," I whispered.

She drew back. "What?"

"Leave me alone."

"Rude, Lexi!" She sniffed. "Do you know how much easier this is going to make our lives? Do you think it would have been easy for me to get into college with attempted murder on my record?"

"Go," I said.

"*Fine*. But if you think I'm untying you now, you're crazy!" she said, storming out and slamming the door behind her. From the other room, I heard her voice rise. "She's being *totally* unreasonable!"

A second later, the door opened and Megan stuck her head in.

"I just want you to know," she said, "that the meeting's going to start in a half hour."

"So?" I asked.

"Come on, Lex," she said, coming inside. To my surprise, she came up behind me and began cutting the tape from my hands. "Think about it. You should be thanking Lydia and me. We took care of the Kasey problem for you. Now you can go through with it and ensure this unbelievable life for you *and* your sister."

I flexed my hands in front of me, trying to get the feeling back in my fingers.

"I know how much you care about her," she said quietly. "If you want to know the truth, Lex, I've been kind of jealous. I'll never have that bond."

I focused on rubbing my wrists.

"Maybe that's why you weren't as devoted to Aralt as I was," she said.

My head jerked up. "I was plenty devoted to Aralt," I said. "I just decided that free will is more important to me than getting everything I want."

Hostility didn't faze Megan. She just gave me a puzzled smile. "Aralt is all about free will," she said. "You make your own choices. That thing with Carter was all you. You wanted the perfect boyfriend. So Aralt delivered him to you."

My definition of the perfect boyfriend didn't include stalking, but I didn't say so. There was too much truth in what she'd said. Carter had been fine until I started manipulating him.

"One way or another, you're going to read the spell," Megan said. "One way or another, you'll realize how important Aralt is. The mature thing would be to stop whining and start being thankful for all of the things he's doing for you, even if you don't deserve it."

"I'm not doing it," I said.

She sighed. "So ungrateful."

"Tashi's dead," I said. "And Lydia killed her. I can't let anyone else die."

Megan shook her head. "Well, then, the solution should be perfectly clear to you."

I looked up at her.

"*You* read the spell twice," she said. "Sacrifice yourself."

"That's *suicide*."

"Suicide, murder," she said, shrugging. "Until you

learn to look at this from a more enlightened point of view, nothing's going to sound good. I can't help you there."

She walked to the door, and I leaned down and began untying the ropes from my ankles.

"Besides," she said over her shoulder, "we have a volunteer. Good news, Lex—it's just Zoe."

The door clicked shut behind her.

I tried not to think of what she'd said, but the thing is, she and Kasey were right. We had to resolve this, one way or another, and as far as I knew, obeying Farrin— reading *Tugann Sibh* and letting one girl die, letting *Zoe* die—was the only way to do it that didn't involve all of us going insane and dying in a mental ward.

But it could be me. It was such a simple solution. It would save Zoe, my sister, my friends . . . and I wouldn't have to live with someone else's death on my conscience.

The only thing was . . .

I was scared.

I could no more imagine volunteering to take Zoe's place as the sacrifice than I could imagine climbing to the edge of a smoking volcano and jumping in.

Coward, I scolded myself. Selfish coward.

Did I really care if someone else died? Or did I just care about making sure it wasn't my fault? I wanted it all: I wanted the easy way out, and I wanted to be guilt-free.

At least my sister and Megan were willing to acknowledge that someone would be dying for them.

Selfish, scared, useless coward.

My breath turned shaky and I felt my shoulders quiver. I held my hands over my eyes, expecting tears, welcoming them, not caring about my dress or my face.

But they didn't come. I couldn't cry.

Because you're afraid to ruin your makeup, snapped the angry voice inside me.

And I was. I was so afraid.

And so exhausted from the effort of holding Aralt at arm's length, being an outsider, feeling like I'd failed everyone.

It will feel so good, said the voice in my head. *It will make you so much stronger.*

Just for a second, and then I can keep fighting, I told myself, and then, like a trickle of water under a door at the start of a flood, I let go of just a tiny bit of control.

Immediately, my pounding headache was smoothed into the soft, golden feeling that you get when pain ends suddenly. A sudden shock of well-being.

Tentatively, I let go of one more thread—the guilt I felt over Kasey taking the oath.

She's so happy, I thought. She finally gets to know Aralt. To feel his presence.

Then, like the thin fibers of a rope snapping one

at a time, my resistance began to fall away.

Nothing seemed as bad as it had just a few seconds earlier.

Of course you're afraid, the voice purred. *Of course you don't want to die. Who could blame you?*

A bright future began to take shape in my mind. I would get Carter back, but things would be different. This time I wouldn't manipulate him. I would go to work at the internship and do important things. I'd get a car of my own. My parents would be so proud.

It was like falling backward onto a feather bed after spending a day doing hard labor.

And like some vile parasite, the traitorous thought writhed in my head: *It's just Zoe.*

By the time I got my feet untied and stood up, I was like a new girl.

I was Aralt's girl.

31

LYDIA WAS DRESSED like a movie star from the 1940s, in a slim-fitting red dress with a deep V-neck and a floppy red bow on her hip. Her hair was pulled back tightly, and she had a small red feathered barrette pinned near the top of her head.

She looked beautiful. The dress caught the light and held it; it hadn't been cheap. I thought I recalled seeing it in one of the magazines we'd passed around at lunch.

I didn't think about her giving Tashi's ring to my sister. That didn't automatically mean Lydia had killed Tashi, anyway—maybe Tashi gave it to her.

Yes, of course, said the voice inside me. *What a smart girl you are to figure that out. What a sweet, good girl.*

"We protect your dwelling with our blood and our lives," Lydia said. And every voice in the room repeated: *"We protect your dwelling with our blood and our lives."*

"As you all know," Lydia said, "for the past several weeks, we've had the privilege of being part of the

Sunshine Club. With Aralt's blessing, we were all able to improve ourselves and become more beautiful, popular, successful, and smart. We've taken what he offered and made the most of it, and now it's time to make a real change. To dedicate our lives to a cause bigger than our little group."

Like curing diseases. Negotiating peace treaties. Creating art.

"Tonight . . . we graduate."

Applause.

I sat back in my chair and looked around while Lydia continued her speech.

We all looked overdressed in the Smalls' dank, dingy basement. The room was about twenty by thirty feet. The poured concrete floor had crumbled with age, and the ceiling was so low that it seemed to push down on us, stifling the air in the room. The stairs that led down from the creaking hallway were hardly more than a glorified ladder.

One side of the room was completely filled with piles of boxes, leaving the rest open. A long snack table was set up under a wide, low window, but no one had touched a bite of food.

It was for afterward, for the celebration.

The Sunshine Club occupied a circle of folding chairs. Every girl was perfectly coiffed and made-up, every dress perfectly pressed.

In the center was a makeshift podium.

Kasey had sat down a few chairs away from me. Like everyone else, she was brimming with excitement. Why shouldn't we be? After tonight, we would begin leading the kind of lives most people can only dream of. Money. Success. Fame. Anything we wanted, basically.

Zoe, for her part, had never looked as radiant as she did sitting there, practically overflowing with her secret. Her eyes glowed with affection as she glanced around the room. There was also a tinge of self-satisfaction. Almost smugness.

She really was happy to do it, just like Farrin had said someone would be.

Lydia reached down and opened the book.

"And now," she said, "we begin. Alexis, would you do the honor?"

This distinction—letting me be the one to lead the spell—was Lydia's idea. She'd been so thrilled by my renewed devotion that she suggested it immediately.

I walked over to the book and gazed around the room at the happy faces looking back at me.

Forget Elspeth. If someone was holding out a lottery ticket to you, you'd take it, wouldn't you? Not taking it would make you a fool, wouldn't it?

This could be the best thing that ever happened to me.

The best thing that ever happened to me.

Where had I heard that before?

It was what Farrin had said to me.

And I believed it.

But not because I'd thought about it—only because she'd made me believe it. She'd manipulated me the way I manipulated everyone around me. She probably did it without thinking. Like reading lines out of a play.

Was she ever real? Did she ever get to choose for herself? Or was it always about the right thing according to Aralt? The right thing to further the aims of her friends? Was she free?

Or was she only as free as Aralt let her be?

I looked back down at the spell and opened my mouth. Then I closed the book.

Disappointed sighs rose around the room like bubbles in a fish tank. Lydia was on the verge of leaping out of her chair.

"I . . . just wanted to tell you," I said, "how much I care about you all. And how great it's been . . . being your sister."

Everyone muttered polite replies. You could tell they all hoped I'd just get on with it.

But I couldn't get on with it. I'd made up my mind—my *own* mind, for once. The other girls might tear me to pieces and go on without me. But as far as my part in it was concerned, I knew I could never bow down to Aralt.

I'd once thought I'd choose death over a life without Aralt.

But now a life *with* him felt like death anyway.

I opened the book again. Lydia sat up straight. "I marked the page," she said.

I expected to see TUGANN SIBH at the top of the page. But the one Lydia had marked was different. It said TOGHRAIONN SIBH.

The names were similar, and the book was full of spells. It would be easy to mix them up.

I glanced at Lydia. "Are you sure this is the one?"

"Yes," she said. "I triple-checked it."

If *Tugann* meant "we give," what did *Toghraionn* mean?

Either Farrin was wrong or Lydia was wrong.

All of this flashed through my head in the space of about two seconds.

I glanced up at Lydia. At her red dress.

No.

At Tashi's red dress—the dress Lydia had taken from her closet after she'd killed her and taken the book and slid the ring off her dead finger.

After she murdered her.

My eyes brushed across the room, and then I looked down at the book.

407

TOGHRAIONN SIBH was on the right page.

There was another spell on the left.

TRÉIGANN SIBH.

The words were underlined with a violent slash of dark gray, obviously made by someone in a rush.

Someone like Tashi.

What Tashi had said to me, whispered frantically when she knew some great danger was approaching: *To abandon . . . try again.*

And what Elspeth had spelled out on the Ouija board: *try again.*

Not "try again."

Tréigann.

The abandoning spell.

It was the spell we needed—and if Tashi had to entrust it to someone who could resist Aralt, that meant that Aralt wouldn't be happy about the results. Aralt wanted the giving spell, because he wanted someone's life energy.

So maybe the abandoning spell would rid us of Aralt—without anyone dying.

The only question was . . . what on earth was *Lydia* trying to get us to do?

32

Tréigann Sibh. *We abandon.*

At the moment, I trusted the advice of two dead women more than I trusted anyone else. Including myself.

So I read the abandoning spell, line by line. And the girls in the room recited it after me.

Halfway through, I felt a sharp pain in my side, like a stomach cramp. But I kept reading. And if anyone else felt anything, they ignored it too. There was no reason to suspect that a few small jabs of pain were something that shouldn't be expected, endured. Anything could be endured for Aralt.

None of them knew the truth—that with every word, they were pushing him out of themselves, back into his book.

When I was finished, I closed the book and heaved a shaky sigh. My legs began to ache as if I'd just run a marathon. Around the room, I could tell that other girls were feeling it too. They rubbed their foreheads and stretched their necks from side to side.

Lydia, on the other hand, looked fine.

And that's when it hit me: she hadn't followed along when I read the spell. She'd sat silently, unmoving.

She didn't know I'd read the wrong spell. She would have reacted.

So what was she doing?

"Now . . . we have one more task ahead of us," I said, and my voice caught in my throat. I coughed convulsively a couple of times before forcing myself to stand up straight.

Everyone tried to smile, but they were feeling pretty bad. Zoe smoothed her skirt. But before she could take a step toward the center of the circle, Kasey was on her feet next to me.

"I want to do it," Kasey said. "I want to be the gift for Aralt. Please. Let me."

Zoe looked exactly how I felt—like she'd been body-slammed.

I stared down at my sister's unblinking blue eyes, the pupils as big around as pencil erasers.

"Kasey," I said. It was just shock. But she thought I was arguing with her.

"Please, Lexi," she said. "Let me be the gift."

Lydia watched us, uneasy curiosity on her face.

So, because it had to look like things were going as planned, I numbly pointed to *Tréigann*. And Kasey read it again.

I prayed that I'd made the right choice, that reading this spell twice didn't do something horrible to you. Maybe trusting Tashi and Elspeth had been foolish.

When she finished, the room was silent. "Okay," I said, my fingers scrabbling with the pages. I hadn't really thought past this part of the plan. I guess I'd been hoping there would be a big epiphany moment, everyone rubbing their eyes and saying, "What was *that* all about?"

Nope.

"I have to sign, right?" Kasey asked.

"Yes," I said. "We should go . . . be alone."

No one said anything, because everyone thought she was dying. They'd just sit there in their folding chairs with their manicured hands in their laps and wait while my sister died. Or would they get started on the snack table? Was Kasey supposed to go somewhere else and lie down and expire peacefully and not ruin our party?

Lydia's voice cut through the room like a hot knife through butter. "There's a little room around the corner."

She meant the dark room they'd held me in earlier. I gave her a hard look. "Kasey deserves to be comfortable."

My sister's nerves started to fail her. "I think I'd

rather go upstairs," she said, her voice trembling. "I think I want to be in private."

"Fine," Lydia said. "We'll go upstairs."

"No, just me and Lexi," Kasey whispered.

A few feet away, Mimi started fanning herself.

"I feel sick," Kendra complained.

"Don't worry," Lydia said. She got up and looked around the room, searching the dark spaces, as if she was waiting for something. When she spoke, she sounded distracted. "It'll only be for a minute."

Kasey dragged herself up the steps, and I came behind her, holding the book.

She looked paler, thinner, somehow. "Should I lie down?" she whispered.

I knew she hadn't read the giving spell, but my skin broke out in goosebumps. She'd meant to. She'd wanted to. She'd tried to sacrifice herself.

"Sit on the couch in the front room," I said. The closer to the exit, the better. "I'll get a pen."

She shuffled away while I eased back toward the basement door. There was an old, loose doorknob that shifted around under your hand when you touched it, and a small metal hook that fit into a loop on the frame. I gently pressed the button lock on the knob; as I'd guessed, it jiggled uselessly. Then I slid the hook in the loop and slowly shifted one of the kitchen chairs under the knob.

I went back to the living room, where Kasey was laid out like a fainting victim.

"I don't feel good," she whispered.

Neither did I. "Come on, Kase, get up."

She sat up. "Where's the pen?"

"There is no pen," I said. "We're leaving."

Her jaw dropped. "But I—"

"You're not dying. That was a different spell. I think Aralt is back in the book, and now I need to destroy it. You have to come with me, because they'll think you were in on it."

"Oh, Lexi!" she said, her face falling. "How *could* you?"

The only thing worse than the sheer absurdity of the question was the fact that she really was disappointed that she wasn't going to die.

"We have to get out of here," I said. "I'm going to go see if there are any car keys sitting around. You wait here."

She slumped over, utterly forlorn.

I went back to the kitchen and looked for stray purses. Aha! Megan's was nestled in the corner of the counter. I dug through it, but couldn't find the keys.

From behind me came a jingling sound. "Looking for these?"

I turned to see Megan standing in the doorway.

"I believed you, Lex. I stood up for you." She shook her head. "Even when you excluded me, abandoned me for your boyfriend or your sister . . . I was always ready to be there for you. And this is how you repay me?"

Then she drew her hand from behind her back to reveal a kitchen knife. Not some dollar-store apple peeler, but a big, fat one from the days when the Smalls had a fully stocked gourmet kitchen.

"Seriously," she said. "I'm *so* disappointed."

She lunged at me, but the separation from Aralt was slowing her down, dulling her reflexes. I dodged out of the way, and the knife just barely nicked my arm. I forced myself to ignore the sting and ran around the other side of the table.

"It's too late," I said. "It's over. If you stop to think about it—"

"I don't want to stop to think!" she said. "I want to teach you what it means to be loyal to Aralt. And the price you pay for betraying him. Betraying *me*, Alexis."

From the living room came my sister's timid voice. "Lexi? What's going on?"

Megan froze. "Or maybe your sister can be the gift after all."

Knife raised, she spun around and headed toward Kasey.

From the end of the hallway, the doorknob rattled. "Hey!" Lydia yelled. "What are you doing up there?"

I grabbed the first thing I could find, a heavy metal kitchen stool, and ran after Megan. She was waiting for me, a few feet from my sister.

"Oh, you found a chair!" Megan said, her voice mocking. "I'm so scared. What are you going to do, sit on me? Or are you going to kill me? I mean, you couldn't kill your family, but I'm just your best friend. I hardly even count."

She lunged toward Kasey, who tried to dash away—but Megan's knife grazed her leg.

My sister yelped in pain and limped backward as Megan steadied herself for another charge.

I didn't stop to think. I swung the chair low, like a croquet mallet. It hit Megan's left knee with a sickening crunch. She screamed and fell sideways, grabbing her leg as she hit the ground and curled into a ball.

Kasey, snapped out of her self-pity spiral by the sight of someone coming at her with a knife, was on her feet, halfway to the front door.

There was banging from the basement, then a more concentrated rattle. They were trying to get out—and it probably wouldn't take them long.

I scooped up the book and followed Kasey to the front yard. It was dark out; I'd been unconscious in the basement for almost an entire day. My sister could hardly even walk on her injured leg.

"Go on without me," she said. "I can hide in the bushes."

"If they find you, they'll kill you," I said.

"They won't find me," she said. "Now run!"

I was about to protest, to try to figure out something safer, but then I looked at the shrubs. Kasey was right. They were so wild and untended that nobody would ever see her. She was already hobbling toward them.

I took a split second to look around, kicked off Mrs. Wiley's shoes, and ran.

Like my life depended on it.

Which it did.

33

THE ROUGH PAVEMENT tore at my bare feet as I sprinted away from the house.

From behind me, I heard my name: *"Alexis!"*

I wasted a fraction of a second looking over my shoulder.

Lydia was chasing me. She was out of breath, but she was moving fast, catching up. She hadn't read the spell with us; she could still draw speed and strength from Aralt's energy. Meanwhile, thanks to the abandoning spell, I was growing weaker by the moment.

"Come back!" she screeched.

Two blocks later, I felt like I might pass out, but I forced myself to keep going. Lydia was so close I could hear her footsteps slapping the sidewalk. I turned onto a side road and ended up running toward the back of a mini-mall, through a parking lot that was littered with broken bottles glinting in the moonlight. The glass gouged the soles of my feet as I crossed it.

I leaped over a deep pothole; a second later, Lydia screamed, and I looked back to see her on the ground, holding her ankle. She climbed to her feet and ran toward me with a dragging, unbalanced stride.

One of the doors to a store had glass windowpanes; I scooped up a chunk of asphalt and busted it through the glass, clearing enough room to slip my hand through and unlock the door.

I was closing it behind me when Lydia hurled herself at it, knocking me backward into the room. The book went flying from my hands. Lydia tumbled inside right after me.

While she flailed, I picked up the book and ran for the front of the store.

But the front door was bolted. And outside of that was a locked metal gate.

I was trapped.

I glanced around the place I'd chosen to escape to: a beauty parlor. In the front window was a neon sign—the name of the salon. Glancing at one of the mirrors, I read: JUST TEASING.

No Just Teasing, Elspeth had said.

For a moment, the air got heavy around me.

Something horrible was going to happen here. Elspeth had done her best to warn us, but we'd totally ignored her.

Lydia was having trouble getting to her feet—her ankle seemed to be causing her a lot of pain. She hauled herself off the floor and limped toward me. "Aw, what's the matter?" she asked. "Did you forget you're in the ghetto, Alexis? We have bars on our windows here."

I needed something to start a fire with. I saw the open bathroom door at the back of the long room and sprinted past Lydia, who pawed madly at me and lost her balance again, falling onto one of the swivel chairs.

There were matches on the counter, next to an incense burner with a stick of incense in it.

Now all I needed was fuel.

Just outside the bathroom was a supply cabinet. I threw open the doors, looking for flammable hair products, aware that Lydia was dragging her way toward me, grunting and howling like Frankenstein's monster.

I emptied a bottle of hairspray over the book. The fluid spilled out, soaking the leather cover. I flipped through the pages, trying to cover as much of the surface as I could.

I pulled a match from the box.

"Leave it alone," Lydia said, her voice low and gravelly and dead serious. "Or you won't leave this place alive."

I turned around, holding the book in my arms.

"You lied," I said. "That wasn't the right spell. What were you trying to do, Lydia?"

She made a disgusted noise and sneered at me. "*You* lied," she said. "That was the summoning spell. If you'd just read it like you were supposed to, Aralt would be gathering all of your energy, storing it, preparing for his triumphant return to life."

Gathering our energy . . .

"You were going to kill us all?"

"For a good cause!" she snarled.

"Your own grandmother tried to warn you."

"Warn me? Grandma's the one who told me stories about Aralt. *He makes you beautiful, he makes you popular.* . . . then she dies and gets all holier-than-thou." She sniffed. "If Grandma *really* cared, she would have left us some of her money, instead of donating it all to some stupid charity. You know what she left me? Cookbooks!"

The matches were pressed between my sweaty hand and the edge of the book.

"You know plenty about lying, don't you, Alexis?" she asked. "This whole thing was just a game to you. You never cared about Aralt."

I had, but never in a way that would satisfy her. "But you did?" I asked. "You cared?"

Her face crumpled. "I love him," she sniffled. "More than anything. And he loves me."

"But you killed Tashi. You took her away from him."

"He didn't need her anymore," she said. "He didn't want her. He has me now. I can be the new *creatura*. I can control his energy. I'm learning."

"Seriously," I said. "If this week was what you call controlling his energy . . ."

She rolled her eyes. "I'll get better. I'll stay with him. He promised me we could be together."

"But why would you want to be with a ghost?"

"That's why I have to summon him. He'll come out of the book. And he'll take care of me," she whispered. Her voice hardened. "You have *no idea*, Alexis. No idea how horrible my life is. My dad lost his job, and now he works part-time at a hardware store. He's living in a fantasy world—he thinks he's going to be some big rock star. The whole thing is *pathetic*. It makes me sick."

"I'm sorry," I said.

"And we had to move into that filthy little house, and my mom goes out and drinks every night. I haven't seen her in two days. All they think about is themselves. It's like I don't even exist anymore."

"I'm really sorry, Lydia. I didn't know." I thought of all the times I'd been snide to Lydia, because I was in the habit of doing it, and all the while her whole life had been collapsing around her.

"Do you know how I got my lunch money?" she asked. "Before Aralt? I mowed lawns, Alexis. I went around the neighborhood on Saturdays and begged lazy slobs in muumuus to let me spend the whole afternoon in the sun, pushing a freaking lawn mower, getting ant bites all over my feet. Do you know how many lawns I had to mow to buy Aralt's book? To convince Tashi to come to Surrey? And you got it for free! No wonder you never appreciated it."

She seemed to be growing kind of wired—all jittery and twitchy. If she hadn't separated herself from Aralt, then she was the only person still connected to him. That was a lot of energy to feed into one person.

"Lydia, listen to me. You don't want Aralt taking care of you. He's not what you think. I met him, and—"

Her expression, suddenly rigid with jealousy, told me it was the wrong thing to say.

"He's *evil*. Just read the abandoning spell and live your life. Things will be different."

"Oh, you're going to make me your charity case?" she asked. "No thanks, Alexis. At least Aralt loves me for me. Not out of pity."

"He doesn't love anyone, Lydia."

She stared at me through glazed eyes. Tashi's dress, which would have cost about thirty mowed lawns, was torn and smeared with dirt and blood. "Give me the book. I'll walk out that door, and you'll never see me again. You have until the count of five. And then I break your neck."

"Okay," I said. "Fine."

"Set it on the counter."

I turned my body halfway and set the book down. Then I raised my arms, holdup style, and took a step back.

As Lydia rushed toward the book, I threw myself at her. We fell to the floor. She reached up, grabbed a container full of sanitizer from the counter, and swung it at my head. It didn't shatter, but the impact stunned me, and a wave of liquid splashed my face.

For a few seconds I felt like I was in a dream, watching this happen to someone else.

Then I stumbled backward and fell to the ground.

I closed my eyes and curled into a fetal position, waiting for the furious pain in my skull to subside. After a minute, I pushed myself to my hands and knees.

I opened my burning eyes.

My vision was hazy and gray-tinted. I held on to a chair and stared at the ceiling like a shipwreck victim staring at the distant lights of a rescue ship.

"What's wrong? Is it your precious eyes?" Lydia said, her voice syrupy with fake concern. "That stuff is *nasty*. Mom always wore goggles just to dilute it."

My eyes began to tear, but the tears felt different, somehow—thicker, sticky, like they were trying to hold my eyelids shut.

A whole-body terror gripped me—

"O-M-G—what if you go *blind*?" Lydia asked. "Can hotshot photographers be blind?"

Her taunts were nothing to me, nothing at all, compared to the panic expanding in my chest. I tried to crawl toward the shampoo stations, but Lydia blocked my path.

"I don't know, Lexi," she said. "Adding water might make it worse. Are you willing to take that chance?"

She was bluffing. She had to be.

"I think I know something that could help," Lydia said. I swung my head toward the sound of her voice, and she laughed bitterly. "You look like a drunk sea lion."

I can't be blind.

I'd ruined everything else in my life. The only thing I had left was photography.

"Seriously? What is it?" I said. "Help me! Lydia, please!"

My eyes were starting to feel hot and dehydrated. They weren't tearing anymore—even blinking was hard.

"You know what it is, Alexis." Her voice was suddenly dry, humorless. "It's Aralt."

But I couldn't. It was out of the question.

Just for a couple of minutes—just until I'm healed, I told myself. And then I'll read *Tréigann* again. It won't even matter.

But *no*—I *couldn't*.

"Tick-tock," Lydia said. "Those darling corneas are blistering as we speak."

Blind. Never to see the so-blue-it-hurts sky on a late summer day; never to look through the viewfinder of a camera or watch a print fade to life in the darkroom; never to see Carter—even from afar.

"Fine! I'll do it!" I said, my voice breaking into a sob. I didn't have the strength to pretend to be dignified. "Hurry, Lydia, *please*."

"Are you sure?" she asked. "It's not a very Alexis thing to do, you know. Don't you want some time to think it over?"

It was starting to feel like the walls were closing in on me, panic compressing my body.

"No," I said. "I don't want to think about it."

She seemed to go as slowly as possible, but she led me through the oath, phrase by phrase.

I repeated every word.

As soon as I spoke the final sentence, energy surged through my body, like ice water poured on a man who's been crawling through the desert. My eyes no longer stung; my limbs no longer ached; I felt forgiven. I felt alive again. I lay down on the linoleum and stared at the ceiling, watching the tiles slowly come back into focus, tasting relief like honey in my mouth.

From the back of the room I could hear muttering,

but I was too overwhelmed to even wonder about Lydia. After a minute, I sat up and twisted my body to look at her. She was bent over the book on the counter. Her lips were moving.

I came up behind her in time to see the word at the top of the page: TOGHRAIONN.

"Lydia!" I gasped. "What are you doing?!?"

"I summoned him," she said, arms crossed triumphantly. "Aralt. He's coming for me."

"Why would you—you *can't*," I said. "He's not what you think he is."

"You're forgetting, Alexis. He loves me. He would never hurt me. You wouldn't understand that kind of trust." She shrugged. "And you know what? None of this would have happened if you'd minded your own business. I tried to summon him the very first night. But the stupid dog had to get out. . . . Aralt came looking for me, but Tashi got him back in the book before he could find me."

She had no idea. She didn't know what he really was. She was expecting some Prince Charming to come carry her off on his white horse.

The room, which a minute earlier had seemed so full of noise and chaos, now seemed like the inside of a chapel. The only sounds were our breathing and a strange sizzling sound in the air.

"Lydia," I said. "Please. Read the other spell."

"We're going to be together forever," she whispered. "I'm so happy."

She set the book into one of the sinks and smirked at me. "And no one else is going to try to take Aralt away from me. Stay sunny, Alexis."

She lit a match.

"Lydia, no!"

And she dropped it on the book.

Her eyes were starry, enthralled. Her lips formed a sweet smile. Her gaze fixed on a spot over my shoulder. "I'm so happ—"

Her eyes went wide. From behind me came a scraping sound.

"What is that?" she cried.

I turned just in time to see a hulking, formless black shadow slither past me.

Lydia tried to run, but the shadow was on top of her in an instant. It knocked her to the ground and wrapped itself around her like it was melting, a thin black membrane spreading across her whole body. When she tried to scream, it filled her mouth.

She struggled, but her flailing arms were enveloped by the black web.

My head was filled with sound, a watered-down version of what I'd experienced in Tashi's garage.

Aralt didn't love Lydia. He didn't love anything. He was greedy, ravenous, selfish. And the chorus of smaller voices, fearful and sad, that I'd heard underneath it all—

The women who gifted themselves didn't die painlessly.

They didn't become a soft, glowing halo around the edges of their friends' lives—

Their spirits existed, imprisoned by Aralt's hunger, in a state of torment. Lonely and terrified.

"No!" I shouted, pulling at the layer that covered Lydia's mouth. My fingers sank into its flesh, leaving oozing holes, but the thing didn't seem to notice me.

All it cared about was Lydia.

When it had her in a tight cocoon, it began to pulse, like a beating heart.

Like it was feeding.

I kept bashing at it, but nothing I did made any difference.

"GET OFF!" I screamed, but I could barely hear my own voice above the cacophony in my mind. "GET OFF!"

Then, suddenly, the shadow was gone. The mix of voices, Aralt's vicious roar with the cries of his prisoners . . . it all faded away.

I looked down at Lydia. Her body, pale and bent, lay on the floor like a broken mannequin. Her eyes were wide with terror, her mouth frozen midshriek.

I pressed my fingers to her neck, just under her ear.

No pulse. I shifted her body so she was flat on her back, then started chest compressions.

Count, press, wait, feel for a pulse. Count, press, wait, feel.

Then I was being pulled away.

"I have to save her!" I said, flailing. "Let me go! I have to save her!"

"You can't save her, Lexi," Kasey said, holding me tightly. "Look at her. She's dead."

She was right, of course. There wasn't a whisper of life left in Lydia's body. She was a shell. A corpse.

"Come on," said Kasey. "Let's get out of here."

"No, wait," I said, remembering the book.

"It doesn't matter," Kasey said. "The book is basically ashes."

But . . . if the book was destroyed, where did that leave me?

Insane and dying, like the South McBride River girls?

I turned to Kasey in horror.

"I called Carter," Kasey said. "I know you guys broke up, but . . ."

Outside, a pair of headlights swung into the parking lot. Carter vaulted out of the car and ran through the door of the salon. He glanced at Lydia, then grabbed my hand.

"Lex, what happened?"

"We can figure that out later," Kasey said. "We have to get out of here." She steered me toward the door. I stepped onto the asphalt, and the pain in my half-healed feet made my knees buckle.

Carter bent down and picked up my foot, looking at it like a blacksmith inspecting a horseshoe. The sole was a reddish-black mess of dirt, blood, and patches of sensitive pink skin.

"Put your arms around my neck," he said.

"No, I'm too heavy."

"Alexis," he said. "Come on. For once, I'm asking you to trust me."

I hesitated.

"That's the whole problem, isn't it?" He turned his face toward the night sky and let out a horrible laugh, like a gasp of pain. "Why are you the only person who's allowed to be strong?"

I put my arms around his neck.

As if I weighed nothing at all, he lifted me off the ground and carried me away.

34

"WE'VE HANDLED THE police department, the coroner, the hospital, the EMTs, the fire department, the superintendent, the principal, and the relevant teachers." Agent Hasan checked her notebook. "The students will have to figure out their own explanation. They always do, and it's usually better than our story anyway."

I nodded.

My parents stared at the kitchen counter.

"We've done quite a patch-up job on this, and I wouldn't be surprised if some of the paint peels and a few of the nails pop out," Agent Hasan said. "But I think it'll blow over."

She looked at Mom and Dad. "May I speak to the girls alone for a minute?"

They slowly got up from their seats and walked out to the front porch.

Agent Hasan glanced from me to Kasey and back again.

"Normally, I'd have a lot of questions for you girls," she said, "but seeing as how I've been 'asked' by my superior, who was 'asked' by *his* superior, who was 'asked' by the Senate subcommittee that handles our budget—not to ask you anything, I get to go home early today."

She leaned toward us conspiratorially.

"Listen. I like you guys. I'm glad you have mysterious friends in high places who can get you out of this. But the fact is, you got lucky. Luckier than you can fathom. That book was responsible for the deaths of more than a hundred and fifty innocent women, and I'm happy it's gone. Personally, I think you did the right thing. But listen to me."

Her eyes bored into mine. "To the people I work for, doing the right thing means *nothing*. You follow orders, or you vanish. I don't know *why* you got messed up in this stuff for a second time. Once you were in it, you took care of your business. I respect that." She narrowed her eyes. "But I'm telling you—*there are no third chances*. Keep your noses clean."

Kasey looked confused.

"It's an expression," Agent Hasan said, stacking her untouched paperwork and sliding it back in her briefcase. "Stay out of trouble."

She walked herself to the door. We stayed seated;

I'd been advised to avoid putting unnecessary weight on my bandaged feet, and Kasey had to protect her injured leg.

I wanted to stop her, to ask her what was next for me—what would the side effects be, of taking the oath to the book just as it was destroyed. I kept waiting to feel my mind start to loosen at the seams, but so far, I didn't feel any less sane than a person would reasonably feel after what we'd been through. But I was afraid to ask, because—unlike Kasey—I didn't think I was brave enough to go to a place like Harmony Valley for a year.

"Take care, girls." And with a curt nod, she left.

Mom and Dad came back inside, not looking at each other or at us.

"I guess I'll go finish up my homework," Kasey said, easing herself out of the chair.

"Me too," I said.

She disappeared down the hall while I was still hoisting my way to a standing position.

This put me in the distinctly unfortunate position of being alone with my parents.

It seemed like there was something I should say. I took a breath.

"Alexis," Dad said, his voice heavy with hurt and disappointment, "please. Just go to your room."

* * *

The office was in disarray.

I wandered through the workroom, looking for Farrin, finally passing through the cylinder into the darkroom.

The lights were on, and Farrin was on the floor in the corner, labeling a box. She didn't look up. "I wondered when you would come."

I tried to hide my surprise when she looked at me. I'd never seen her look so bedraggled. Actually, I'd never seen her look less than perfect.

She looked at me as though she knew what I was thinking. "Well, what did you think was going to happen?" she asked. "Turns out I'm bankrupt. The people I thought I could count on have disappeared, and suddenly I find that I'm an old woman."

"But you still have your talent," I said. "They can't take that away from you."

She shrugged. "I've spent my whole life watching people with talent be overlooked in favor of people who had better connections, more money, the right friends. People like *me*."

"I'm sorry," I said, and I was. Not sorry that the book was gone. But that Farrin's life was collapsing around her like a house of cards. "Will you tell Senator Draeger I said thank you?"

"I'll try," Farrin said. "She's very busy these days.

Her campaign finances are being audited. Things aren't going terribly well for any of us. And I'm sorry about the contest. You know the magazine is folding."

"I understand," I said.

"You're fortunate, Alexis," she said, her voice a little wistful. "You're young enough to start over."

I nodded.

"Very tragic about your friend," she said. "You were there . . . when it happened?"

I nodded again. She was watching me, her eyes burning.

Then I realized that her question was about more than whether I'd been there. There was something else she wanted to know.

I looked at her and saw that she was just a broken woman, alone and afraid.

She'd lost everything. I couldn't let her lose Suzette too. Maybe I should have—but I couldn't.

"It was . . . painless," I said. "Very peaceful."

She managed a quivering smile and then looked away, and I knew my lie hadn't totally convinced her. "Go on, then. I have a whole life to put into boxes."

35

THE DAY OF THE funeral, it was ninety degrees in the shade. Mourners showed up in black tank tops and miniskirts.

Kasey and I stood alone under a tree, at the back of the crowd.

Mr. and Mrs. Small clutched each other at the edge of the grave site. Mrs. Small kept leaning like she was going to fall on top of the coffin. She'd probably been drinking, not that you could blame her.

Megan wasn't there. She hadn't even come back to school. She was grounded from talking on the phone, e-mail, texting, or any other form of human contact. She'd been enrolled at Sacred Heart Academy by Tuesday morning. Her grandmother had been threatening it for years.

There was no cheerleading squad at Sacred Heart, which was just as well, because I'd destroyed what was left of Megan's knee. Mrs. Wiley told me so just before she hung up on me.

I watched Carter approach from the road, wearing a short-sleeved gray shirt and black pants.

We hadn't seen each other at all since the night Lydia died. I was amazed that so much time had passed. There had just been other things to take care of.

He nodded to Kasey, who nodded back.

"Um . . . I'm going to go say hi to Adrienne," Kasey said, limping away. Adrienne, cane in hand, stood by her mother's wheelchair on the paved road at the edge of the lawn.

When she was gone, I turned to Carter. "How are you?"

"I'm all right. You?"

"Fine."

We looked over the throngs of students. In death, Lydia was popular. Apparently a lot of people found her funny. Who knew? I'd never thought about it that way.

"It's so weird," I said. "Like half the people here, she was trying to kill."

He shook his head. "She didn't mean it," he said. "The real Lydia."

"Ha," I said.

"Underneath all her attitude, she was just sad, Lex." He gazed at the yellow-rose-covered casket.

I detected the dig and turned to him. "How can you defend her?"

Carter turned to me. "It wasn't all her fault."

"What do you mean?" I asked. "She set up the whole thing. She planned all of it. She pretended that she didn't mean to kill Tashi, but she knew all along that was what she was going to do. How is that not her fault?"

"Never mind." He shrugged. "This is tough for you. I don't want to make it worse."

"Tell me," I said. "I can take it."

Carter stuck his hands in his pockets. "You knew better than to let something like this happen again."

"*Let?*" I asked. "Are you kidding me?"

"Yes, let," he said. "Why didn't you ask for help as soon as you found out what was really happening?"

"And tell me," I said, "who would I have asked?"

He stared. "Uh, *me*, maybe?"

"Oh, *right*."

"See? You wouldn't even consider it."

"Because it's a ridiculous idea!" I stared up at him. "If something happened to you—if you got hurt—"

"Or not me, I don't care. Your parents? Anyone, Lex."

"That's not even fair."

"It would never occur to you *not* to shut everyone out. You never for one second trusted me. Do you even know *how* to trust?"

I couldn't tell if his words made me angry or sad, but tears tried to spring to my eyes. I forced them back and stared into the distance, willing myself to stay in control.

"I could have done something," he said. "But you had to do it all alone."

I lowered my voice. "I'm sorry, Carter. . . . I was trying to protect you."

Carter's hand came haltingly toward my face. His fingers ran up my cheek and touched the edge of my lips.

"Don't you get it?" he asked. "Every time you try to protect me, you end up breaking my heart."

I looked up at him, and before I knew what was happening, we were kissing again, urgently, terribly, like a pair of war-torn lovers about to leave for opposing armies.

"Carter . . ." I whispered.

"I need some time, Lex," he said, taking a half step away. "I haven't been feeling like myself lately, and . . . I have to figure some stuff out."

I broke away and shaded my eyes. When I looked up again, he was gone.

A few leaves fluttered to the ground where he'd been standing.

Kasey came back to me, her face dewy with sweat. She linked her arm through mine. "Are you okay?"

My boyfriend needed "time." My best friend was locked away from me. My parents would never trust me again. For all I knew, Aralt was still inside me somehow, still infecting me.

And Lydia was *dead*.

I didn't even know what "okay" meant anymore.

At least I had my sister.

I rested my head on her shoulder, and we watched the service for a few minutes. The casket was painstakingly lowered into the ground, and a slow procession formed as people walked past the grave and dropped roses down on top of the coffin. Kasey and I ended up in line, and then suddenly we were looking down into the hole, at the earthen walls covered by a thin green cloth. A smell like a rainy summer day wafted up toward us.

Kasey tossed her rose, and then I went to let go of mine.

Something hit the back of my knee, making it buckle underneath me. If Kasey hadn't been holding on to my arm, I would have fallen into the grave.

The people around me gasped, and Mrs. Small let out a fresh burst of choking sobs.

I practically hurled my rose into the hole, managing to pierce my thumb on the nub of a single thorn that the florist hadn't lopped off.

"Come on," Kasey whispered, tugging at my arm.

But before I moved, I glanced past Mrs. Small, off into the distance, where the older gravestones, gray with moss and mildew, dotted the hill.

And I stopped.

And stared.

At Lydia.

She stood under a tree, her body almost solid but somehow hazy, like a distant road on a hot day. She was probably a hundred feet away, but I could feel her eyes burning into mine across the distance, feel her anger like a thunderstorm gathering on the horizon.

"She needs to move on," someone behind me in line said, and I looked at them bewilderedly until I realized that they meant *me*, that *I* needed to move on so the rest of the line could pay their tributes and then get into their air-conditioned cars and go home.

I ignored the murmurs and stared up the hill for a long minute.

Suddenly Lydia's figure shook, and then she was rushing down the hill, toward the crowd of mourners, toward all of us. She disappeared among the people around me, and I cried out like a car was hurtling at me.

But she never emerged.

Then Kasey's grip on my arm got firmer, and I looked down into her eyes, to see if there was a flash of recognition.

Nothing.

I was the only one who'd seen anything.

"Let's go, Lexi," Kasey said.

My body limp, I let her lead me back toward the car.

Mom was there waiting for us, wiping her eyes with her fingers and staring into the cloudless sky. Kasey climbed into the backseat, and I went around to open my door.

On the pavement in my path was a single yellow rose. I bent down and picked it up, once again stabbing my thumb on the nub of a single thorn.

"Those poor parents. This is so awful," Mom said, sniffling back tears. "Thank God it's over."

As we drove out of the cemetery, I searched the hillside where Lydia had been standing.

She was gone.

But it wasn't over.